CITY of GLORY

Set against the dramatic backdrop of America's second war for independence, Beverly Swerling's gripping sequel to the acclaimed *City of Dreams* plunges deep into the crowded streets of old New York. They are all here—the butchers and shipwrights, the doctors and scriveners, the slum dwellers of Five Points, and the money men of the infant stock exchange—conspiring by day and carousing by night, while the women hide their loyalties and ambitions, their very wills, behind pretty sighs and silken skirts. Allegiances are more changeable than the tides, love and lust often indistinguishable, the bonds of country weak compared to the temptation of fabulous riches from the East, and only a few farseeing patriots recognize the need not just to protect the city from the redcoats but to preserve the fragile Constitutional union forged in 1787.

Joyful Patrick Turner, brilliant surgeon and dashing war hero, loses his hand to a British shell, retreats to private life, and hopes to make his fortune in the China trade. To succeed he must find a ship and a captain that can run the British blockade; if he fails, he will lose not only a livelihood, but the beautiful Manon, daughter of a Huguenot jeweler who will not accept a pauper as a son-in-law. When stories of a lost treasure and a mysterious diamond draw him into a treacherous maze of deceit and double-cross and the British set Washington ablaze, Joyful realizes that more than his personal future is at stake. His adversary, Gornt Blakeman, has a lust for power that will not be sated until he claims Joyful's fiancée as his wife and half a nation as his personal fiefdom. Like the Turners before him, Joyful must choose: his dreams or his country.

"The author brings the <u>time</u> alive with true characters . . . This book has all the qualities of a good winter's read: conflict, tension, romance . . . and a satisfying finale. Highly recommended." – *Historical Novels Review*

"Enthralling . . . Swerling's swashbuckling tale brings old Manhattan vividly to life, throbbing with restless energy and populated with a diverse and intriguing cast of characters both real . . . and richly imagined . . . [An] evocative and entertaining saga." – *Publishers Weekly*

BEVERLY SWERLING is a writer, a consultant, and an avid amateur historian. She lives in New York City with her husband.

Author photograph by Sigrid Estrada

City of Glory

A Novel of

War and Desire

in Old Manhattan

BEVERLY SWERLING

SIMON & SCHUSTER PAPERBACKS

New York   London   Toronto   Sydney

SIMON & SCHUSTER PAPERBACKS
A Division of Simon & Schuster, Inc.
1230 Avenue of the Americas
New York, NY 10020

SIMON & SCHUSTER PAPERBACKS and colophon are registered trademarks of
Simon & Schuster, Inc.

For information regarding special discounts for bulk purchases,
please contact Simon & Schuster Special Sales:
1-800-456-6798 or business@simonandschuster.com.

Designed by Jaime Putorti

Manufactured in the United States of America

10   9   8   7   6   5   4   3   2   1

The Library of Congress has cataloged the hardcover edition as follows:
Swerling, Beverly.
   City of glory : a novel of war and desire in Old Manhattan / Beverly Swerling.
   p. cm.
   Sequel to: City of dreams.
   1. New York (N.Y.)—History—1775–1865—Fiction. 2. Manhattan (New York,
N.Y.)—Fiction. I. Title.

PS3619.W47C59 2007
813'.6—dc22

ISBN-13: 978-0-7432-6920-9
ISBN-10:   0-7432-6920-9
ISBN-13: 978-0-7432-6921-6 (pbk)
ISBN-10:   0-7432-6921-7 (pbk)

For Bill, as always, and for Michael, who would, I think,
have loved all the swash and buckle.

Author's Note

THE GEOGRAPHY OF New York City is as accurate for the time as research has allowed. In some cases changed street names will confuse those who know the modern city. There were many incarnations of George Street. The one where this story opens is now Rose Street at the southern edge of Tribeca. Little Dock Street became Water Street. Chatham Street is now Park Row. Mill Street is Stone Street. French Church Street is Pine Street. North Street, the city limits at the period of the story, is present-day Houston Street. In the neighborhood known as Five Points (today occupied by the city's courts and a large swath of Chinatown), Anthony is now Worth Street, Cross is now Mosco Street, and Orange Street is now Baxter. Amos Street, location of the infamous Newgate Prison in what was then known as the Village of Greenwich, is now West Tenth Street. And one further point: in the matter of the Battle of Bladensburg, what is now called the Anacostia River was known at the time as the Eastern Branch of the Potomac.

And the rockets' red glare, the bombs bursting in air,
Gave proof thro' the night that our flag was still there.

—Francis Scott Key at the battle of Fort McHenry,
Baltimore, September 14, 1814

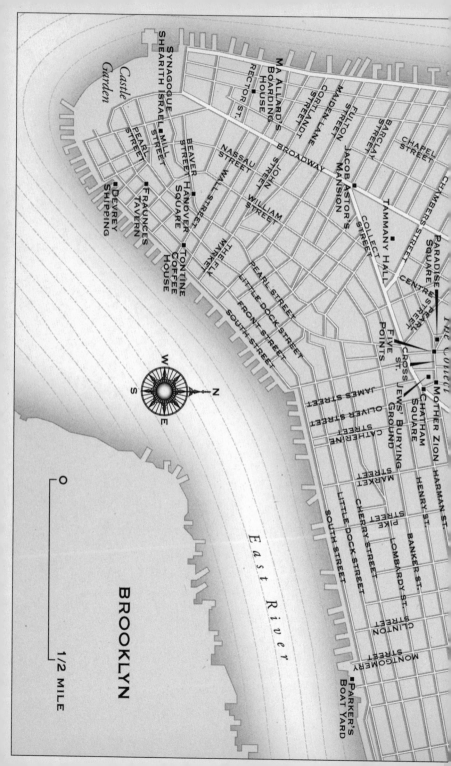

Hudson River

WEST STREET
WASHINGTON STREET
GREENWICH STREET
HUDSON STREET

McDERMOTT'S OYSTER HOUSE

HUDSON SQUARE

ANTHONY STREET
CHURCH STREET
CANAL STREET
GRAND STREET
BROOME ST.
SPRING ST.
PRINCE ST.
HOUSTON STREET
BLEECKER STREET

SULLIVAN STREET
LAURENS STREET

ELM STREET
STREET

ORANGE ST.
MULBERRY ST.
MOTT ST.

BULL'S HEAD TAVERN AND ABBATOIR

MULBERRY STREET
MOTT STREET

CHATHAM ST.

WALKER ST.
HESTER STREET
GRAND STREET

CHRYSTIE STREET
FORSYTH STREET
ELDRIDGE STREET
ALLEN STREET
ORANGE STREET
LUDOW STREET
ESSEX ST.
NORFOLK ST.
SUFFOLK ST.
CLINTON
ATTORNEY
RIDGE
BROOME STREET
DELANCY STREET

THE DANCING KNAVE

STANTON STREET
RIVINGTON ST.

PITT ST.

DIVISION STREET

COLUMBIA ST.

AVENUE C
AVENUE B
AVENUE A

NORTH STREET
1ST STREET
5TH STREET
1ST AVENUE
2ND AVENUE
10TH STREET

BROADWAY
BOWERY

NEW YORK

Manhattan Woods

A Time Line

HERE IS A BRIEF HISTORY of the run-up to the events in this book, and a few details about life in the infant United States before the opening of the tale. It is intended for those who find context important. There are no penalties for skipping straight to the story.

Most of the action here takes place in New York City during ten days in the early period of the great experiment that is the United States. Because it aspires to be a good book, it is about love and hate and greed and passion, and sometimes selfless heroism, in this case told against the backdrop of the War of 1812. That last confrontation with Great Britain is often called the final act of the American Revolution, but it is the nation's most obscure conflict.

1792 to 1796: George Washington's second term. Two strong political parties emerge in his cabinet, the Democratic-Republicans led by Thomas Jefferson, and the Federalists led by Alexander Hamilton, who is nothing if not a man of New York City.

At that moment Hamilton's town has some 90,000 residents and is poised to overtake Philadelphia as the nation's most populous center, as well as the undisputed queen of commerce. No longer the capital city (the federal government moved to Philadelphia in 1790, awaiting the completion of a ten-mile-square Federal District on the Potomac River) New York has become the city of capital, the nation's economic center. Hamilton and the Federalists believe America's future lies with great industrial cities that will be merchant barons to the world. A strong central government is vital to that vision, and an enlightened autocracy the only way they see to manage it. Jefferson's ideas are demonstrated in the rural idyll he has labored to create at Monticello in Virginia. His America must remain what ninety percent of it is at the time, a nation of great landholders and yeoman farmers. He believes passionately in states' rights, and only slightly less passionately in the rights of the common man. (Despite being a slaveholder himself, he is honestly conflicted over slavery, and wrote an antislavery clause into his original draft of the Declaration of Independence, only to see it struck out by others among the signers.)

In Europe, France and Britain have been at war since shortly after the 1789 French Revolution. America has struggled to remain officially neutral, but on the street—particularly in New York—everyone takes sides. The city's artisans and craftsmen, a class known collectively as mechanics, along with the unskilled laborers, declare themselves republicans and are hugely pro-French. At home, despite relying on the city for their living, the working people support the rural dreams of Jefferson and the Democratic-Republicans, and hunger for the equality promised by both the American and French revolutions. The merchants and professionals, on the other hand, are appalled at the heads rolling off the French guillotine. They become more and more pro-British, and more than ever convinced that giving the masses control of the government is madness. Federalism, with its promise of strong central control, is firmly established as the philosophy of the ruling class of New York and New England.

1796 to 1800: John Adams, a Federalist, is the nation's second president and Thomas Jefferson (elected separately in the manner of the time) is his vice president. Adams is the first president to live in the

District of Columbia in what is termed the President's Palace or the Executive Mansion, though it is from the first painted white.

1800: Adams runs for a second term. Jefferson opposes him. On the ballot are two vice presidential candidates, Aaron Burr of New York and Thomas Pinckney of South Carolina. By December of 1800 everyone in the bitterly divided country knows that the Democratic-Republicans Jefferson and Burr have been elected, but to what? Each has the same number of Electoral College votes, and since by law the electors do not say which man they are choosing for which office, the election for president is declared to be a tie. Following the procedure laid down in the Constitution adopted fourteen years earlier, responsibility for the decision is given not to the senators, who are appointed by the legislatures of the fifteen states (Vermont and Kentucky have joined the original thirteen), but to the House of Representatives, whose members are voted into office by the people. In February of 1801, after six days of balloting, Jefferson is declared the nation's third president and Burr his vice president.

Jefferson slashes the federal budget, lowers taxes, reduces the national debt, and in 1803 buys Louisiana from the French. This vast territory of 828,000 square miles (today's state of Louisiana is 48,523 square miles) stretches from the Mississippi River to the Rockies and from the Canadian border to the Gulf of Mexico. The Louisiana Purchase almost doubles the size of the country, but much of it is unexplored.

1804: In May, Jefferson dispatches Meriwether Lewis and William Clark to explore the new territory and report back to Americans exactly what their country now looks like. The expedition will take two years. Meanwhile, in July of that year, Burr kills Hamilton in an illegal duel. Warrants are issued for Burr's arrest and he flees to Philadelphia, where he plots to make himself emperor of a new country to be formed from Mexico and the American West. In the autumn Jefferson is elected to a second term.

At this point Canada is a nation of 500,000, while the American population is about to top 6 million—not including nearly 2 million black slaves—but the Canadians are feared and demonized because it's believed they encourage their fierce Indian allies to threaten U.S. settlements on the frontier.

1806: In Europe Napoleon Bonaparte has helped subdue France's Reign of Terror and led her army to a series of triumphs, but he cannot defeat the British navy and instead declares war on commerce. No ship that has called at a British port may afterward enter any continental European port. As a counter move, Great Britain declares it illegal for the ships of a neutral nation to visit a port from which the British are excluded, unless those ships first call at a British port and take on British goods. Direct trade between the United States and Europe is thus made an act of war. At the same time, Britain continues to claim the right to board any American vessel and look for those she says are deserters. Many naturalized Americans, particularly those who still have British accents (pronunciation has been diverging on both sides of the ocean for nearly two centuries) are impressed into the Royal Navy, a fearsome organization ruled by the lash and offering only the dubious satisfactions of rum and buggery.

1811: James Madison is America's fourth president, a Democratic-Republican handpicked by Jefferson as his successor. (Madison's wife, Dolley Payne Todd Madison, is the first first lady to capture the popular imagination, and the first to preside over an inaugural ball.) The Twelfth Congress is in session. It includes a number of young and exuberant members from what is then the West—Kentucky, Ohio, and Tennessee—who are anxious to again take on Great Britain. They say they wish to fight for free trade and sailors' rights. Their real purpose is to annex Canada, Florida, and Texas. They are called the War Hawks and they are to have their day.

1812: On Thursday, June 18, the United States under President James Madison declares war on Great Britain. In the first year three attempts to take Canada fail, but the tiny American navy distinguishes itself, in part because much of the huge British fleet is occupied elsewhere. Madison is reelected. Nonetheless, the country seethes with debate led by Federalists such as Josiah Quincy of Massachusetts, whom the Democratic-Republicans accuse of "secretly advocating, and insidiously trying to effect, a disunion of the United States."

1813: The focus moves to actions on the Great Lakes of Ontario and Erie, and there are a series of military thrusts at Canada. York (present-day Toronto) is twice invaded and burned, but never held. On the southern Tennessee frontier there are battles with the Creek Indians, who are urged on by the Spanish in Florida. Pensacola on the Gulf Coast is eventually occupied and will prove to be the only territory America permanently acquires in this war. At sea, however, the British begin to exploit their superiority of numbers and their patrols make coastal trading perilous. Americans are forced to use their terrible roads to conduct vital interstate business. As a result, there are shortages everywhere, along with price gouging and wild speculation, while overseas trade has come to a virtual standstill.

1814: In January the British offer to negotiate and a peace commission is established, but progress is slow. Federalists continue to protest the war, particularly the Canadian strategy, and continue to be called disloyal by the Democratic-Republicans. Meanwhile, except for those gone privateering—given government permission to prey on enemy shipping—the oceangoing merchant vessels of the great shipping companies lie rotting in harbor, escaped slaves help British troops harass and plunder the Chesapeake area, and the British make plans to invade what is now Maine.

In the face of all this the American government is virtually bankrupt. A failed earlier financial experiment means there is no national bank to bail them out, and in a time of no reliable paper currency, curtailment of trade has led to there not being enough coin money in circulation.

One other vital development has taken place before the story opens, though few realize how crucial it is to be to the future of the new nation. The moneymen—traders in various types of risks and commodities—long accustomed to holding wild and rowdy auctions under a buttonwood tree (a sycamore) on Wall Street, realized they were responsible for rampant speculation and the resultant bubble bursting and financial panic, all bad for business. In 1792 the twenty-four most powerful such traders drew up what they called the Button-wood Agreement, which laid the foundation for a structured market in securities (known as scrip). Early in 1793 these pioneers of what would be the New York Stock Exchange built the elegant new Tontine* Coffee House on the corner of Wall and Water streets, and moved their trading activities into an upstairs room. They continued to meet and do business there during the anxious days of the war.

The stage is now well and truly set for pirates and lovers, thieves and heroes, men—and indeed women—with ambitions big enough for young America's city of dreams.

---

*A tontine is a financial arrangement whereby a fixed group takes shares in an invest-ment—in this case the coffeehouse—paying out pro rata as each dies or drops out; the last one standing gets the whole shebang.

Characters

THE DOCTORS

Joyful Patrick Turner: Son of Morgan Turner, one-time privateer and later hero of the Revolution. Joyful was raised in the Chinese trading colony of Canton until age sixteen, when he was sent home to New York to become a physician. One of the early graduates of the Medical Department at Columbia College (known as King's College before the Revolution), he is thirty when the story opens and has been a ship's doctor for six years.

Andrew Turner: A hero of the Revolution, a doctor and a surgeon. At seventy-five he is a member of the Common (city) Council, and a respected voice in New York's affairs. Andrew is Joyful's cousin, and was his patron when he first came to New York from China.

THE CANTON TRADERS

Gornt Blakeman: A man in his prime at forty-some, and owner of the most important stagecoach company in the nation. A trader with a countinghouse on Hanover Street, Blakeman is a man who would be king.

Lansing "Bastard" Devrey: Cousin to Joyful and Andrew, and the illegitimate son of the deceased Sam Devrey, who was a doctor and hero of the Revolution as well as a lifelong bachelor. Lansing, called Bastard by one and all, was not acknowledged until he was twenty-eight and Sam was on his deathbed. When the story opens, Bastard is thirty-seven and head of Devrey Shipping. Once enormously wealthy and still owner of the elaborate house on Wall Street built by Will Devrey in 1706, Bastard has squandered much of his fortune and put the rest in thrall to the speculators of Wall Street. Nonetheless, he believes himself a prince among men.

John Jacob Astor: Known by all as Jacob Astor. German by birth, Astor arrived in New York via London in early 1783 when he was just twenty, and soon began trading in furs. In a short time he had a warehouse in Montreal, capital of the fur trade, as well as a countinghouse on Little Dock Street in New York City. Dabbling in the China trade quickly led to a fleet of ships and subsequently a worldwide mercantile empire. Early on he became a speculator in Manhattan property. At the time of the story he is the young nation's first tycoon, the richest man in America, and has recently built himself a palace in the rural reaches of Broadway between Vesey and Barclay streets. Could he not then become an emperor?

THE WOMEN

Manon Vionne: Daughter of one of the many Protestant Huguenot families who came to America to escape persecution in Catholic

France, Manon is lovely, but she is also smarter than most men and unable to hide it. Some think that's why she is unmarried and unpromised at twenty-two.

Eugenie LaMont Fischer: A twenty-four-year-old widow. Beautiful as well as clever, she has been forced by circumstances to live by her wits. Eugenie is struggling to maintain a fine household on Chatham Street, while she searches for a husband who can take over her debts and support her in style.

Delight Higgins: A stunning woman of mixed race; in the accepted term of the time, a mulatto. This subjects her to the laws governing blacks, but Delight claims to have been born free in Nova Scotia. (She admits to twenty-nine, though she may be older.) Delight runs a gambling club and discreet parlor house—i.e., a bordello—known as the Dancing Knave on semirural Rivington Street. It is an area that speculators hope to make fashionable after the war.

Holy Hannah: An ageless creature living in a shack in the no-man's-land between the city and the heavily wooded Manhattan wilderness to the north. Hannah is given to quoting Old Testament scripture, but only a few know her precise history. Though she has never married, Holy Hannah is known to care for a brood of children.

THE JEWEL MERCHANTS

Maurice Vionne: Father of Manon—whom he fears to be condemned by her intelligence to spinsterhood—and the most respected of the cluster of mostly Huguenot gold- and silversmiths and jewel traders to be found in the vicinity of Maiden Lane.

Mordecai Frank: A goldsmith, Frank is a member of the tiny but well established Jewish community who have been in the city since it was Peter Stuyvesant's Nieuw Amsterdam. Like Vionne, Frank deals in precious gems when they come his way. He is an elder of Shearith Israel on Mill Street, the first, and at the time the only, synagogue in New York.

THE OPIUM DEALERS

Jonathan Devrey: Molly, his twin sister, vanished sixteen years before—a never-explained mystery—leaving Jonathan the sole heir to the elegant apothecary shop in Hanover Square, where perfumes and handmade soaps are sold along with herbal simples and curatives. Jonathan inherited as well the recipe for a secret elixir, which many in the city are convinced they cannot do without. Small wonder. It is almost pure laudanum, an opium derivative made from the seeds of ripe poppies.

Thumbless Wu: A Cantonese and among the first Chinese to come to New York.

Ah Wong: Jacob Astor's butler, and head of the Chinese family Astor has brought over to be servants in his fabulous Broadway mansion.

THE PEOPLE OF NEW YORK CITY—
INCLUDING MEMBERS OF THE PROFESSIONS,
POLITICIANS, MECHANICS, WAGE EARNERS, AND SEAFARERS

Will Farrell: A twelve-year-old boy employed as a lookout for Devrey Shipping.

Peggety Jack: A one-legged former tar in charge of Devrey Shipping's dockworkers.

Captain Finbar O'Toole: An Irishman who came to America at the age of ten. Four years later he joined Washington's army and served under Morgan Turner. After the war he became a merchant sea captain and made frequent trips to Canton.

Barnaby Carter: A member of the craftsman-small-business-owner class known as mechanics, he owns a workshop that produces stagecoach bodies.

Lucretia Hingham Carter: Wife of Barnaby and one of the town's numerous abortionists.

Henry Astor: A butcher, cattle trader, and Jacob's elder brother. Henry arrived in New York during the Revolution with a British commission to provision the Hessian mercenaries. At the time of the story he remains important in the meat trade, much of which is centered on his Bull's Head Tavern and the adjoining abattoir and stockyards located on the Bowery just above Chatham Square.

Francis Xavier Gallagher: Another butcher, but one who has as well a different trade: organizing (and exploiting) newly arrived Irishmen who think because the man known as F.X. also happens to be Irish, he can be trusted.

Tintin: A shadowy figure recently arrived in the city and rumored to be one of Jean Laffite's pirate captains. Laffite is head of a renegade colony based in the secluded islands of Barataria Bay, south of New Orleans. The Baratarians prey on Spanish commerce and dispose of their plunder—which often includes slaves—through merchant connections on the mainland.

Jesse Edwards: An eleven-year-old powder monkey on the brig *Lawrence* during the 1813 Battle of Lake Erie. He later lives in New York.

Tammy Tompkins: A tar who served on the *Lawrence* in 1813.

Samson Simson: The first Jewish member of the bar, he studied law at Columbia under Aaron Burr. An elder of the Mill Street Synagogue, Shearith Israel.

Reverend Zachary Fish, Absalom, Joshua et al.: Members of the African Methodist Episcopal Zion Church—called by all Mother Zion—located in the already notorious Five Points section of the city.

Patrick Aloysius Burney: An Irish laborer who lives in Five Points.

Slyly Silas Danforth: A scrivener, and perhaps the most clever forger in New York City.

Adele Tremont: A Huguenot widow who works as a mantua-maker and dresses the most fashionable women of the city.

Vinegar Clifford: A chucker-out—a bouncer—who retired as the city's public whipper shortly before the story opens, when New York abolished flogging as an official criminal punishment.

City of Glory

Prologue

New York City
Friday, June 19, 1812, 12:30 A.M.

It was a fine, quiet night, the balmy warmth of early summer a comfort, not the fiery curse it would become in a few weeks. There were no streetlamps in Canvastown—hard by Hudson's River, the area got its name when it burned down at the start of the Revolution and the locals took to living in tents—but bright stars and a full moon. That plus the pair of coaching lamps swinging either side of the small black shay provided light enough for the single horse, an aging piebald, to make its way.

The two men in the rig had been playing billiards at McDermott's Oyster House. On their way home now, cue sticks wedged either side of the shay's single seat, they were reliving the game by talking about it. "Ah, but if that last carom had succeeded, I'd have won again, making it six games to five, so you needn't—" The speaker, who held the reins, broke off. A knot of men stood some twenty yards ahead, a short distance from the intersection of Greenwich Street and George, where the shay had to make the turn to head back to the better neighbor-hood downtown.

There were five of them, dressed in the leather breeches and home-spun shirts that marked them as laborers, and they were ominously quiet. The men stood in a tight circle, focused on something or some-one in their midst.

The shay's passenger and owner was Barnaby Carter, a coach maker by trade. "Just put on a bit of speed and shoot past them," he said. "Old Rufus won't let us down." The piebald, hearing its name, snorted and tossed its head.

The driver was Joyful Patrick Turner, doctor and ship's surgeon, due to go back to sea the following day. He heard his friend's sugges-tion and later told himself it was exactly what he'd intended to do. Just shoot past the men ahead. Neither he nor Barnaby was spoiling for a fight. As for the woman standing in the men's midst, whores—called hot-pockets in Canvastown—were one of the area's prime at-tractions; this woman, though, held a small valise, the sort people packed for a journey, and a whore was unlikely to troll the streets for custom carrying a change of clothing. All of that aside, Joyful reined in because of what he heard—"All right then, who's going to be first?" spoken in a tone full of menace.

He stood up, keeping the reins taut in one hand. "Leave her be."

"Couple o' gents," one of the toughs muttered to his companions, looking at their cutaway coats and stovepipe hats. "Your kind comes to Canvastown looking for pleasure," he said "No harm in us having ours."

"There's plenty of hot pockets available. I don't think this lady chooses to be bothered."

"Ain't no lady," the man closest to the shay offered with a nearly toothless smile. "This here's a mongrel bitch as you might find in any kennel got broken into when the master wasn't looking. A runaway most likely. When we're done, we'll be takin' her to a magistrate. See if there's a reward. So you gents best be minding your own concerns and driving yourselves straight on by."

"I don't think we shall do exactly that." Joyful pitched his voice at the woman, hoping she would take his meaning, prepare herself. She stared straight at him. He returned her gaze for a second, then a movement at the edge of the circle caught his eye.

Barnaby had seen it as well. "One of them's got a knife," the coach maker murmured.

"Probably more than one," Joyful said. "Hang on." He cracked the reins over the horse's rump. The piebald plunged forward. For a sickening moment the shay tilted dangerously to one side, then righted itself and surged ahead. The ruffians fell back, intent on avoiding the horse's hooves; the woman stood her ground. Joyful stretched out his hand, but instead of taking it she remained motionless.

Joyful yanked on the reins, forcing the horse to pull up slightly, then leaned down and swept the woman into the shay, at which point some of the would-be rapists threw themselves at the rig. Joyful planted his boot firmly on the knuckles of one. He was conscious of Barnaby using his cue stick to fend off another. Joyful loosed the reins slightly. The horse sensed he was being given his head and charged straight ahead. Joyful kept his left arm around the woman's waist. In seconds they had to make the turn onto Greenwich Street or drive straight into a stone fence backed by a thick stand of trees. "Hang on!" he shouted again, tightening his grip on the woman while using his other hand to tug the horse's head to the right. The animal neighed loudly and half reared, confused and frightened. Joyful pulled harder. The horse gave in to the demands of the bit and changed direction, hauling the shay behind him in a sharp turn. This time the sickening lurch seemed to last forever, until finally the small carriage righted itself and they were hurtling down Greenwich Street, Joyful and Barnaby both laughing aloud in triumph.

When he finally reined in enough to slow them some and allow for getting the woman settled safely between him and Barnaby, the thing Joyful found most remarkable was not her beauty—though she was unquestionably beautiful—but that she was still staring at him. And he had the distinct impression she'd not stopped doing so since the first moment she saw him.

Late the following afternoon word reached the city that in the Federal District of Washington, on Thursday, the eighteenth of June, 1812, Congress had declared war on Great Britain. Dr. Joyful Patrick Turner gave up his berth on a merchant ship, and offered his services as surgeon to the navy of the United States.

September—November 1813

Chapter One

INSTEAD OF INHALING THE DEEP breath of fresh air Joyful Turner longed for when he came topside, he had to pull his neckerchief over his nose and mouth to keep from choking. The fight had been going on for two hours—six British ships against nine American, but the British far superior in tonnage and arms—and the air was black with the smoke of gunpowder and thick with the stench of death.

"Dr. Turner, over here, sir!"

Joyful made his way toward Commodore Perry's voice. It was slow going, impossible to see much of anything, the decks of the *Lawrence* slick with blood and the brig listing dangerously to port. He had to hang onto the gunwale to keep his footing. Perry's flagship was too close to the British lines for the enemy's superiority in the larger long guns to be useful, but their gunners had found the range with smaller weapons. A shell from a short cannon known as a carronade landed close behind Joyful. A great gust of sparks flared for a moment, then died. The deck shivered beneath his feet and the list to port worsened. The blast had been close enough to make his ears ring. He shook his head to clear it, heard nothing at first, then, as if from a far distance, Perry's second shout: "Dr. Turner, I want you!"

"I'm here, Commodore."

"Yes, so you are. Good Christ, man, you look a sight."

Thirty-two years old, Joyful was tall and lean, with blue eyes and red hair, now flattened with sweat. The long oilskin apron he wore during surgery was spattered with blobs of gore and splinters of bone. Joyful looked down at himself, then squinted up into the rigging. The sails were in tatters, and most of the lines and braces had been shot away. "We're none of us at our best at the moment, sir."

Perry managed a wry smile. There was another blast from the British. "The flag, man! Get the flag!"

The man who rushed to follow Perry's command was an ordinary tar; the commodore was the only officer not flat on his back below decks in Joyful's crammed hospital quarters. Joyful's gut tightened as he watched the sailor head for the foremast. "Are we striking our colors, sir?" Surrendering to the British might make sense, but the thought sickened him.

"Indeed we are not, Dr. Turner. It's my battle flag I want. *Lawrence* has become impossible to control, as you can see. I'm taking over *Niagara*." Perry nodded toward the row of American ships stretched beside them, half shrouded in the fog of the engagement. "You're to come with me, Doctor, and bring any crew who are able to come topside. I don't care if they must crawl."

"I have sixty-three severely wounded patients below—"

"And twenty-one corpses. I'm aware of the numbers, Doctor."

Both men knew that fewer than a hundred of the brig's hundred-thirty-man complement had started the action fit for duty. The single rowboat being lowered over the brig's side would easily accommodate the survivors of this experiment in close-quarters fighting on which Perry had staked his chance to defeat an enemy that, while a smaller squadron, both outgunned and outmanned him.

The man who had been sent to get the battle flag returned. Perry took the blue banner and quickly folded it. Joyful couldn't see the words embroidered in large white letters, but he knew what they said. DON'T GIVE UP THE SHIP. "Any man who can crawl, Doctor," Perry repeated. "If he can haul a line, I want him. Even if it's to be his last move. And yourself."

"I will inform the men of your orders, Commodore. But few of the wounded will be able to comply, however much they want to." God alone knew how many legs he'd amputated in the last couple of hours. Joyful had stopped counting when the number went above two dozen. "As for me, I can't leave my patients."

As ship's surgeon, he was in the employ of the navy, not a member of its armed forces; Perry could not command him. "As you wish, Dr. Turner. I pray you Godspeed for the rest of the engagement and beyond."

"And I you, Commodore."

"Do not fear for me or our country this day, Doctor. We shall prevail, I promise you." Perry swung one leg over the side, then paused and reached for his pocket watch. "I shall wait five minutes for any of the wounded as are able to join us, then we're away."

"May I ask for ten minutes, sir? Even the sick or wounded who can come topside won't be able to move quickly."

"Ten minutes then," Perry agreed.

The two-masted brigantine *Niagara* had been moving to the head of the line while they spoke, all the while keeping the American ships between herself and the enemy. Now she was athwart *Lawrence*. Perry and three sailors began clambering down to the waiting rowboat. Joyful turned and headed back to the hold. The list of the vessel was definitely worse, and the smoke thicker. One of the British ships—the *Queen Charlotte*, Joyful thought—was still firing. *Lawrence* had eighteen carronades to *Charlotte*'s two, but no one to man them. And for the last half hour there had been no powder monkeys to bring them shot.

Joyful found the hatch by feel and instinct. He was about to start down the ladderway when Jesse Edwards's small blond head poked above it. "What's happening, Dr. Turner, sir?"

Wonderful! There had been three powder monkeys when the action began. All boys under twelve, they did what was arguably the most dangerous job in any battle—running the ammunition to the guns—and two were in the pile of corpses below. He'd figured the third to be lying dead somewhere else. "There you are, Jesse. I was just wondering about you."

The lad didn't meet his gaze, speaking instead to some point over Joyful's shoulder. "I was down in the powder magazine, sir. Getting the charges the way I'm s'posed to, and—"

Cowering in the stores most likely, God help him. "It's all right, lad. No need to worry about that now. The Commodore and what's left of the crew are about to row over to *Niagara*. They're waiting for any others as are able to join them. Get on with you. Over there on the port side. Hurry."

The boy started to go, then turned back. "What about you, Dr. Turner?"

"Nothing about me. Go on, Jesse. Look lively. That's a good—" The blast landed between them, knocking Joyful back against the bulkhead. At first he felt nothing, only smelled burned flesh, but he knew this time it was his own. He waited, half expecting to collapse, sensing his legs. No, they were fine. But there was pain now, and dizziness. Christ Jesus, don't faint, you stupid bastard. You're a dead man if you do. His heart thumped violently in his chest. "Jesse! Where are you?"

He tried to take a step forward and staggered. "Jesse!" Still nothing. Can't hang about here. Have to tell the men below they can . . . The weakness almost overwhelmed him, but Joyful fought it off. Something not right about his left arm. He reached across his body: The upper arm was whole. So was the elbow and the forearm. No broken bones, so . . . Oh, Christ Jesus. He had no hand.

The wound was pouring blood. Joyful, trembling, felt his gorge rise. Shock. Ignore it. Must stop the hemorrhage. Finished otherwise.

It seemed to take forever, but eventually he managed to untie his neck-erchief.

Behind him the guns were still booming, but *Lawrence,* listing, and with no firepower, was no longer the target. He managed to get the neckerchief tied around his shattered wrist, but it had to be tighter if it was going to keep him from bleeding to death. He kept short wooden dowels in the pocket of his apron so his patients could bite something other than their own tongues when he cut. Damn! The fingers of his right hand were slippery with blood. He finally got a grip on one dowel, forced it into the knot of the makeshift bandage, and began to twist. Not the best tourniquet he'd ever fastened, but it would do the job. "Jesse! Are you there, lad?"

Still no answer, and he had no idea how much of Perry's allotted ten minutes remained. The men below had a right to take the offer if they could.

He staggered over to the hatch and started down the ladderway. His left foot reached for the quarterdeck and made contact with Jesse's body. The boy had been hurled backward by the blast.

Joyful was weak and dizzy, but he made himself crouch beside the crumpled figure. "Jesse? Can you hear me?" One quarterdeck lantern remained lit; still, it was nearly impossible to see in the gloom. "Jesse. C'mon boy, answer me." The powder monkey didn't move. Joyful pressed his ear to the boy's chest. Thready and very rapid, but the heart was beating. His eyes finally adjusted to the half light, and he saw that the boy's right arm had been shot off virtually at the shoulder. "Got us both, the poxed English bastards," he muttered. Jesse didn't move.

The blood coming from the boy's shoulder was oozing, not pump-ing. A blessing. There was no way to make a tourniquet effective in such a position. The powder monkey's kersey shirt had been shredded by the shot. Joyful was able to grip a piece of the fabric with his single hand and rip it free. He wadded the kersey into the wound, then got his one good arm underneath Jesse. He couldn't heave him up the first time he tried, but he succeeded the second. Joyful slung the youngster over his right shoulder and staggered down to the hospital quarters deep in the hold.

There had been three lanterns lit when he left the sick bay, strung on a pulley stretched abaft the long, narrow cabin. Now there was only one. "Grubbers! Where in hell are you? How come you let the damned lights go out?"

"Right here, Dr. Turner. I was just goin' to trim those wicks and get some—"

Useless, like most of the surgeon's mates he'd been assigned over the eight years he'd been at sea. "Forget it. Clear the way for another operation. No, wait. I'll do it. You go above. The commodore's waiting for any as can leave the ship with him." Joyful leaned forward and let Jesse's body drop onto the operating table, ignoring the pulpy remains of the previous surgery that still dotted the canvas covering. The effort jarred his own wound and a wave of pain caught him unawares. Joyful sucked air into his lungs and waited for it to pass, then held his bandaged wrist up to the light. No fresh blood. The tourniquet was holding.

"You're wounded, Doctor. You want me to—"

"I don't want you to do anything." He'd never had much patience with Grubbers's whining. "Just go topside so you can get away."

"We're surrendering, sir?"

"No, Commodore Perry and any of the crew as can join him are transferring to *Niagara.*" He raised his voice. "Do you lot hear me? If you can drag yourselves topside, you can get off this floating charnel house. But you'd best be quick."

There, he'd done his duty. Joyful didn't bother to see if any of the men were managing to turn themselves out of their hammocks, or rise off the pallets spread side by side on the floor. He bent over the operating table and carefully removed the wadding of shredded kersey he'd stuffed into Jesse's wound.

Grubbers looked down at the unconscious boy. "Shot up real bad, ain't he, sir?"

"Yes, he is. I'll deal with it. You get above while you can."

Grubbers hesitated another moment, then dashed for the ladder-way. Joyful was vaguely conscious of one other seaman following behind him. The rest were too ill to move. Probably too ill to have heard him, come to that.

He put his good hand on Jesse Edwards's forehead. Cool and clammy. The boy was in shock, but his breathing was steadier than it might have been. And when Joyful moved his hand to the lad's chest, he still felt that regular if too-rapid beat. "All right, Jesse. We're going to do this, you and I. And if I can operate with one hand, you can bloody well live to tell the tale. You hear me, Jesse Edwards?" He knew the boy was unconscious, but no matter. It made him feel better. "You are going to survive this operation and this day, my reluctant young powder monkey, because you are a tough little Yankee bastard from Boston, despite creaming your britches in every battle. And I . . . well, I am the best goddamned surgeon in the goddamned United States Navy. Hell, no. I'm better than that. I'm the best goddamned surgeon in the world."

Actually, his cousin Andrew Turner back in New York was. But he'd once done just this sort of surgery with Andrew. Joyful was studying medicine at Columbia in those days, and living in Andrew's house. A woman had been run over by a horse and carriage and brought to his cousin's Ann Street surgery. The wheel had ripped her arm off practically at the shoulder, same as the bloody English guns had done to Jesse Edwards. Joyful had to act as his cousin's assistant, and he remembered every step of the operation. He could hear Andrew's voice as clearly as if the older man stood beside him in *Lawrence*'s fetid hospital quarters.

The wound requires amputation just below the scapula. Thing is, Joyful, there are many surgeons afraid of the procedure. Terrific danger of hemorrhage, of course. But she's going to die if we don't operate. And if we are very careful, very skilled, and a little bit lucky, she may survive.

Andrew had picked up the longest of his knives. Joyful turned to the instrument case on the table beside him and did the same. The scalpel he chose had a bone handle and a flexible blade six inches long and an inch wide. It was one of his favorites and stained with the blood of the many surgeries of this day. His was not a profession for the overly fastidious, he reminded himself, and clamped the instrument between his teeth while he reached overhead and pulled the single working lantern into position above the operating table.

Now, Joyful, hold what's left of that arm horizontal.

Given the quality of tars assigned as surgeon's mates, Joyful had long since installed a wall-mounted heavy hook fitted with a leather strap that he called the Assistant-as-Doesn't-Talk-Back. He moved the lad's inert body as close to the table's edge as he dared and fixed what was left of the shot-off arm in position with his contraption. Clumsy work done one-handed, and getting the boy's body strapped to the table was almost as difficult, but eventually it was done.

We make an incision like this, through the adipose membrane, from the upper part of the shoulder across the pectoral muscle down to the armpit.

That first swift cut brought the powder monkey around, and his scream reverberated off the cabin's walls. There was a spate of murmured protests as the few wounded men still conscious registered the boy's agony. "Quiet, all of you! Squealed like stuck pigs yourselves when it was your turn. But the only reason some of you are still breathing is me and my knife." There were a few whispered assents, even a blessing or two, but Joyful ignored them. All his attention remained with the patient on the table.

The lad's shout was actually a cause for celebration. A faint deep enough not to be ended by surgery might indicate a coma that would never give way. Joyful set down the scalpel, fetched another of the dowels from his apron pocket, and placed it in the boy's mouth. Jesse's eyes were wide open now, and staring into his. "Bite down, as hard as you can, lad. You are going to get through this. So am I. Because if we don't, you're dead." He pinned the youngster with his gaze. "Do you understand me, young Edwards? This time there's nowhere to hide. You muster every scrap of courage you have and withstand this, or you die. Now make a choice—do I go ahead?"

Tears rolled down Jesse's cheeks, but he nodded. "Good," Joyful said. "Bite as hard as you can on that stick. I'll be as quick as I can."

Now, we turn the knife with its edge upwards and divide the muscle.

Joyful concentrated on the muffled boom of the guns and ignored the strangled screams of the boy under the knife as well as the moans of the sick and the dying that surrounded him. Pray God they were American guns. What would the British do with the wounded if they boarded *Lawrence*? Probably return those who could live through the transfer to the Americans. As for him—most likely they'd impress him into the godrotting Royal Navy. Be a real pleasure to get some of those English bastards under his knife.

He put down the scalpel and turned to get ligatures to tie off the large artery. Oh, Christ Jesus. How was he going to thread the needles with one hand? Maybe that useless bastard Grubbers had prepared some in advance. He pawed through the things on the instrument table searching for a threaded needle. Nothing. He hadn't really thought there would be.

Joyful found a largish needle and put the pointed end between his teeth, then teased out a length of catgut from the tangle Grubbers had left behind. He craned his head back, stretching his neck as far as he could, trying to get as much light as possible on the task. Bloody impossible to make the catgut go where he wanted it to. Might as well try to sprout wings and fly. But if that bit of arm were left attached, Jesse Edwards was guaranteed a slow and agonizing death from blood poisoning. God damn him to hell if he let a boy die because he couldn't thread a—

"Here, Doc. Let me do that." A pair of hands reached up and took the needle and the length of catgut.

Joyful peered into the gloom beyond the pool of light cast by the single lantern. "Tompkins, isn't it?"

"Tammy Tompkins. That's right, Doc."

The tar had been one of those in the sick bay before the battle began. "Your fever's broken."

"Looks like it, don't it? Still some shaky on my pins, but I can do this. No harder than a bit of scrimshaw, this is."

Tompkins was one of the most adept whalebone carvers among the sailors. "You'll make a fine surgeon's mate, Tammy. You've got the hands for it."

"Not the stomach though, Doc. In the ordinary way o' things, I can't stand the sight o' blood."

"Well, control yourself. And prepare three more of those needles."

Joyful took up the scalpel and turned for one quick glance at his patient. The boy was staring at the knife. "Bite down, Jesse. This is the worst of it, but it will soon be over. I was raised in Canton, that's in China, and the Chinese would say it's not your joss to die this day. Not your fate. Otherwise you'd be dead already."

This time the steady stream of talk was for the boy's sake, not his own. Joyful made a swift, sure cut through the deltoid muscle; the artery began pumping blood. He dropped the scalpel and took hold of the artery, pinching it tight, issuing orders without turning his head. "Put your fingers where mine are, Tompkins. Grab this tubelike thing I'm holding and squeeze. C'mon, damn it, do it! The boy's a corpse otherwise." A tentative hand stretched above the bloody mess that was Jesse Edwards's shoulder. Finally, Tompkins's fingers were in position next to his own and Joyful could let go. He grabbed the threaded needle and tied off first the large artery, then the veins. Not as hard to do one-handed as he'd have expected.

The scalpel again. And Andrew's voice calm and clear in his head: *We pursue the incision through the joint, and carefully divide the vessels, then stop them with ligatures as we did the others.*

Thank God Tompkins had done as he was told. The additional needles were ready. Joyful bent over his task, taking another quick look at his patient. Passed out again. He scooped the dowel out of the boy's mouth for fear he'd swallow it, then retrieved his scalpel. He was in total control now: each step of the process as clear to him as if it were written out and held before his eyes, transported to that special place where he and the scalpel were one perfect instrument.

Minutes later the shredded stump of arm fell free. Still attached to the strap on the wall, it hung above the pile of severed limbs Joyful had been kicking below the table throughout this long day. "Tompkins, watch what I'm doing. Damn it, man, I need you. Stop retching and pay attention." He carefully rolled down over the wound the skin he'd painstakingly preserved.

In any amputation the amount of skin you're able to save is a gauge of your success, Joyful. Without enough you'll leave an ugly lumpy scar that will fester and suppurate at worst, or be a constant irritation to the patient at best.

"Hold the skin together while I stitch, Tompkins. Yes, like that. Good, you're doing fine."

So was he. The wound was closed. Done and well done. Andrew might have given him a word of praise if he'd been there.

"Jesse's going to be all right, ain't he, Doc?"

"Yes, Tompkins, he is. At least I think it's likely. And without your help, it wouldn't have happened."

Joyful put his hand on the powder monkey's forehead. Not even a hint of fever, by Almighty God. You've good joss, Jesse Edwards. As for me, I'm a bloody genius, I am.

"What about that, then?" The sailor nodded toward the tourniquet still tied around Joyful's left wrist.

"Ah, yes. This." A bloody one-handed genius. "I think you'd best thread me another few needles, Tammy Tompkins. Time I cleaned this up as well. You'll have to— Listen." What he'd heard was silence.

"No more guns, Doc."

"Exactly. Not ours and not theirs."

"What do you think, Dr. Turner? Have we surrendered or have they?"

"I'm afraid I've no idea. But, if we're going to be boarded, I'd prefer to get this done first. Let's have a tune, Mr. Tompkins." Tammy Tompkins was the ship's champion whistler as well as a master of scrimshaw. "Not 'Old Zip Coon' as usual. Something different. Something to put heart into us."

Tompkins pursed his lips and complied, doing a little in-place jig to help things along. Joyful meanwhile bit down on one of his own dowels, then used his right hand to cut the jagged bits of bone and flesh from his shattered left wrist and stitch the remaining skin in place. All to the tune of "Yankee Doodle Dandy."

At 4 P.M. on that September Friday, the British fleet on Lake Erie—two ships, two brigs, one schooner, and one sloop—struck their colors. Commodore Oliver Perry, USN, now flying his blue and white battle flag aboard the *Niagara,* accepted the Royal Navy's surrender and scribbled on the back of a letter a hasty message for General William Henry Harrison: "We have met the enemy and he is ours."

Chapter Two

.

THE SNOW FELL in large flakes that lasted a moment then melted to nothingness, but the air was cold and getting colder. Early for it, but there was a real storm brewing. Joyful smelled the tang of it on the afternoon air.

The smells of good cooking as well. Most folks had their dinner about now, not at three the way it was in the old days. An extra sixty minutes to work. That was always the way of things in New York. Do more, do it faster, get richer. But even here a man had to quit at some point to fill his belly. Ann Street—a jumble of shops and residences like most thoroughfares in the oldest parts of the city—was closed up tight, so silent Joyful could hear the ring of his boots on the cobbles.

The house he was headed for was at the end of the road, built of wood like most of its neighbors, and like them it was four windows wide and three stories tall, with a dormered roof and two chimneys. There was a sign beside the front door: ANDREW TURNER, M.D., PHYSI-

CIAN. Below, in smaller letters, SURGERY ALSO PERFORMED. Joyful hesitated a moment, then lifted the knocker.

The servant who opened the door was the same woman who had let him in sixteen years before, when he was barely seventeen and newly sent home to New York from China. She had been an indenture back then, but ten years was the usual span to work off a passage; she must be earning a wage by now. "Afternoon, Bridey. How are you?"

"All the better for seeing you, Dr. Turner."

Like most servants, Bridey knew everything. She was bound to have heard the fierce argument Joyful had with Andrew the month before when he returned from Lake Erie to the hero's welcome New York gave the veterans of the September battle, but neither of them acknowledged it. "I'm glad to see you as well, Bridey. Is he in?"

"Indeed, and expecting you." She held out her hands and Joyful slipped out of his greatcoat and handed it to her, along with his stovepipe hat and his right glove. Bridey waited. "Will you not be after leaving the other glove as well, Dr. Turner?"

"No, Bridey." Joyful held up his left arm. The week before he'd had a blacksmith make him a shoulder harness attached to a black leather glove stuffed with sand. Stupid vanity. He should simply let the stump hang out and be damned.

Bridey flushed. "I forgot, Dr. Turner. It's that sorry I am."

"Not to worry, sometimes I forget as well." Maybe if he said it often enough, it would be true.

The maid knocked lightly on the door to her right and opened it immediately. "Dr. Joyful Turner, Dr. Turner."

Joyful stepped inside. "Cousin Andrew," he said formally.

"Cousin Joyful." The men nodded warily at each other. "I appreciate your coming on such short notice," Andrew said. "Had your dinner?"

He hadn't, but he'd eat later. Just now he was too curious to be hungry. The note that summoned him to this visit had arrived at his lodgings on Greenwich Street an hour earlier. It spoke of a matter of urgency. "I'm well enough fed, sir, thank you."

"Good. Leave us then, Bridey. We won't need anything for a time."

The room they were in served as both Andrew's study and his consulting chamber. Sometimes—spread with oiled cloths to protect the furnishings from spurting blood—it was where he performed his surgeries. Square, paneled in oak that had mellowed gold over the years, it had one wall lined with cupboards and drawers that held the medicaments, bandages, and instruments for blistering, bleeding, and cupping that were the arsenal of a physician, as well as the flutes and probes and straight and curved knives and big and small saws of the cutting trade. Andrew Turner was the only medical practitioner in the city to also advertise a surgeon's skills, much less sometimes encourage his patients to submit to the knife. Joyful had never believed there was room for two such hybrids in the city. That's why he went to sea.

Andrew had not quarreled with that choice. It was Joyful's recent decision to stop doctoring altogether—*God's truth, Joyful, what will you live on?*—and take a room in a boardinghouse on Greenwich Street rather than continue to lodge with his cousin as he had in the past, that caused the trouble between them.

Andrew seemed to want to pretend the argument had not happened. "Perishing cold out there." He thrust a poker into the mix of logs and coals in the fireplace. A funnel of sparks rose up the chimney.

"A storm coming, I think," Joyful said.

Andrew grunted. "My joints say the same."

His cousin had still seemed young and vigorous when Joyful first met him. Now, seventy-three, with his hair gone entirely white, Andrew looked fragile and gaunt with age.

He gestured to a decanter of brandy on a small table between the windows. "Pour us each a tot, Joyful. Then come over here and warm your bones."

Joyful covered the bottom of two bulbous snifters with spirit, but carrying two glasses at the same time was beyond him these days. He brought one to his cousin, then went back to claim the second before returning to the leaping flames and offering a toast. "Your health, sir."

"And yours."

Joyful took a long swallow, enjoying the flash of warmth that went from his throat to deep in his belly, then set the drink on the mantel. He had to consciously resist the urge to extend his hands over the coals. Instead he put a foot on the brass fender surrounding the hearth.

"Let me see that." Andrew reached out and lifted the arm that ended in the black leather glove. "Wound giving you any trouble?"

"None. It's well healed."

"I'd expect as much. Managed to leave plenty of skin for the final closure, eh?"

"Exactly as I was taught."

"The glove's clever." Andrew ran his hand along the sleeve of Joyful's black cutaway coat. "Got straps keeping it on, have you?"

"Yes. I had the rig made by a blacksmith a couple of weeks ago. Taking a while to get used to the weight of the thing, but all in all, it seems to work quite well."

"Considered a hook? It would let you do some things. Not as good as a hand, but useful."

"No hook," Joyful said. "Make me feel like a pirate."

He expected Andrew to smile at the weak joke. Instead the older man frowned. "Your father was a pirate for a time."

"A privateer," Joyful said. "That's not exactly the same."

"Perhaps," Andrew said with a shrug. "Are you still determined to give up the practice of medicine?"

"Yes. As I've already said, I don't believe I have much choice."

"There's a great deal of doctoring can be done with one hand."

"But not," Joyful said, "a great deal of surgery."

"You took off that boy's arm with one hand, didn't you? And from what you tell me, that was the most difficult sort of amputation."

"Yes, I did, and yes, it was. But Jesse Edwards was a captive patient. He had no choice in the matter. Convincing the gentlefolk of New York to go under the knife of a one-handed cutter is a much more daunting prospect. Particularly when they can find the best surgeon in Christendom right here on Ann Street."

"You flatter me."

"No," Joyful said. "I do not."

This time Andrew did smile. "Very well, you do not. But I shan't be the best much longer, lad. I'm getting old."

"Hold out your hands," Joyful said.

"There's no need—"

"Next to mine," Joyful extended his good right hand. After a moment Andrew stretched out both his beside it. Joyful let a number of seconds go by. "Not a tremor," he said after almost a full minute. "Rock steady as you've always been. And if we stayed this way for a while longer, I daresay mine would be the hand to start trembling first. I know my place in the hierarchy, Cousin Andrew. In New York, with two hands, I was the next best after you. In the service, far and away the best. Now . . ." He shrugged and allowed his arm to drop to his side.

"I still wish you'd reconsider, lad."

"I know you do, Cousin Andrew. But I won't."

"And you won't come home? This is your home, you know."

"I know that it was my home, and I am forever grateful for that. But I can't live off your charity—" He held up his good hand to forestall Andrew's protest. "I know you're going to say it isn't charity. And I know you mean it. But I have to make my own way."

"And that's the end of it?"

"That's the end of it."

"I assumed as much, but I felt I had to make a last try. I take it then that you're still decided on becoming a Canton trader."

"I am. I was raised in the Canton trade. It's the one thing other than medicine I know."

"Have you talked to your Devrey cousin about the fact that you mean to go into competition with him? I fancy he won't like it much."

Joyful tossed back the last of his brandy, and shook his head when Andrew motioned toward the decanter. "No thanks, not just now. And word is that Bastard Devrey has too many problems of his own to be worried about me."

"Yes, I've heard that too. But this China trade business—there's nothing you can do until after the war is over, is there?"

"Nothing much," Joyful agreed.

"And as I recall, you supported this misbegotten military adventure."

"I thought it imperative that we not let Britain continue to treat us like a colony."

"So you did. Talked about it at the time, didn't we?"

"We did, sir." Joyful was well aware of Andrew's strong Federalist leanings and that his cousin considered President Madison and the Democratic-Republicans a pack of radicals.

"Thing is," Andrew's voice was milder than his meaning, "you shouldn't start a war with incompetent officers, and an army of mostly militia who refuse to carry the fight beyond our borders."

Joyful shrugged. "I'd have thought that would please you. I remember you telling me once that a standing army that answered to the president and Congress rather than the states would be a threat to civilian government."

"Did I? Well, I've said a lot of damn fool things in my day. What's one more?" Andrew stood up and went to the window. The short winter day was ending, the dusk deepening. "Come over here, Joyful." His tone had changed. "Look out and tell me what you see."

"Houses, Cousin Andrew." The view held no surprises and he answered before he actually reached the other man's side, though once at the window he obediently peered into the street. "The homes of upstanding Americans like yourself. But I warrant a good many of them are republicans, as they call themselves. Rabblerousers, as you would call them."

"And I warrant you are correct. But beyond Ann Street what do you see? Not just with your eyes, with your mind and heart."

Ah, perhaps that was what this was about. "The Manhattan forests and streams and hills you and your damnable Common Council mean to destroy with a grid of streets and avenues," Joyful said. "Fit for a population as great as China's."

Andrew chuckled. "Not quite that many, but nearly."

"You don't sound upset by the prospect."

"I'm not. And given your present state of mind, neither should you be. More people means more business. That's what you'll need for this new venture of yours, isn't it?" Andrew reached up and took hold of the curtains but didn't pull them shut. "Light that oil lamp over there, lad. And the one by the fireplace." He waited until Joyful had thrust a taper into the fireplace and did as he was bid, then the older man continued, "I risked my skin for the Revolution, Joyful. "Now . . ." Andrew's voice trailed away as he pulled the curtains closed and turned to face the younger man.

"Now what, Cousin Andrew? Your note said a matter of urgency. I admit I'm curious."

"Yes, I expect you are. But you'll have to be patient a few moments more. Let's sit down." And when they were both in the chairs beside the fireplace: "Tell me what you know of the *Fanciful Maiden*."

"Only that she was a fine sloop, and a very fortunate privateer back in the 1750s. And that my father captained her."

"Nothing specific about the voyage of 1759?"

Joyful thought for a moment. "Nothing specific, no."

Andrew sighed. "I rather hoped Morgan had told you. It would have made this easier." He reached inside his breast pocket, withdrew a small, much folded piece of paper, and put it on the low table between them. Dark now, the room full of shaded corners where the ghosts of the past could lurk, but enough light from the lamps for Joyful to see that a faint red stain indicated that once there had been a wax seal.

"This is for you," Andrew said. "It's your legacy."

"From you?" Joyful was surprised. "I'd have thought Cousin Christopher . . ." Andrew had one surviving child, a son a dozen years Joyful's senior, also a physician. Christopher lived in Providence, and father and son were not particularly close, but he'd never thought they were estranged.

"My son will have what's justly his. This belongs to you. It's from your father."

"I don't understand. I had my father's legacy some years past." A trunk of personal effects and a pouch containing coins worth two thousand pounds, put into his hands in 1809, seven months after Morgan Turner died, by a merchant captain called Finbar O'Toole. *Fourteen years old I was when I fought in the Revolution, and if it weren't for your da looking after me I'd o' been dead in a month. Told him I'd bring you this. He gave it me night afore he died and t'ain't a gram lighter now than it were then.*

"This bit made a detour," Andrew said. "Go on, take it. It's yours."

Joyful leaned forward and used his right hand to unfold the paper while it still lay on the table—he'd learned many such tricks over the past two months—then picked it up. The creases and the ink faded to the color of rust made it difficult to read, but there was no doubt it was written in his father's hand.

"Indulge me, Joyful," Andrew said softly. "Read it aloud."

"Seventy-four degrees . . . thirty minutes west of Greenwich, just south of . . . twenty-two, no, twenty-four degrees north. Twice around thrice back." He stared at the paper a moment or two longer, then looked up. "The first part's navigation coordinates, but leading to where? As for the last, it's gibberish."

"I've never been entirely sure where the coordinates lead, except that they're in the Caribbean. But they're clear enough for a clever sea-man to find his way. As for the rest, if I were a younger man, I'd go after it and assume the words would make sense once I got to wher-ever it is."

"After what?"

"The treasure."

"You're saying . . . this note is a sort of treasure map?"

"That's what I think, yes. I can't be certain, mind, but I believe your father wrote these directions with the intention of going back and get-ting what he'd buried, and that he never did."

"How can you be sure?"

"I said I wasn't sure. But the *Maiden* was in the Caribbean in '59, and she never again sailed there. Then there was the Revolution, and

Morgan was a British prisoner for almost three years. That's how he lost an eye."

"I know." Also that Morgan Turner had been a fighting man, and that all through the war Andrew allowed everyone to believe him a Tory, while he spied for Washington in the heart of the British stronghold that was New York. "My mother said my father was not the same after his time as a prisoner. He couldn't concentrate; he forgot things."

"There was a good deal worth forgetting. You've wanted stories since I've known you, Joyful. The family history, what we did when we had to choose, your father and me. Most of the tales are too black for telling. It wasn't pretty getting to independency. You have to have lived through it to understand."

"I've seen battle, Cousin Andrew. I know it's never pretty."

Andrew swirled the remaining brandy in his glass, then finished it in a single swallow. "Not pretty isn't the half of it. In 1759 we were at war with the French up in Canada and their bloodthirsty Indians. The *Maiden* was the most successful privateer afloat, but after that strange voyage she came back with only Morgan, his first mate, and a crew of three. And the hold dead empty. Morgan said they hadn't taken a single prize. Since the *Maiden* had made most of the men who invested in her a good deal richer than they'd been before, his investors accepted that this time fortune hadn't smiled. Except for the few who said Morgan lied. There were rumors that because one of the investors in that voyage was Squaw DaSilva's—" Andrew broke off. "You know about my aunt, your grandmother?"

"Jennet Turner DaSilva. Whoremistress to the city and my father's mother. I know."

"Jennet was many things, not all of them what they seemed, but undoubtedly the best hater I've ever known. Forgiveness wasn't in her vocabulary. She detested Caleb Devrey with a rare passion, and he was indeed one of the investors in that voyage. He thought she didn't know that, but it appears she did. And so did Morgan. It's not difficult to believe he would rather bury the profits of that cruise than see Cousin Caleb reap any gain from it."

"My father would have been taking an incredible risk."

"Indeed. If they could have proved anything, they'd have strung him up from the nearest tree, and cut him down before he was dead so they could hang him a second time. But that wouldn't have stopped Morgan. Not in those days. Especially not if the thing could cause Cousin Caleb harm."

"In God's name," Joyful whispered, "how could you all have hated each other so much?"

"I didn't hate Caleb. I'd no reason to. If your father wanted to tell you his reasons, he'd have done so while he was alive. Just accept that they were sworn enemies." Andrew leaned forward and tapped the note lying on the table. "That's why I believe this is the answer to the puzzle of the voyage of '59."

"Did my father give it to you?"

"He did not. I took it from Caleb Devrey's—"

"But if Caleb had it, if he knew what had been done and where the profits were, why didn't he go after them?"

"You didn't let me finish. I took it from Cousin Caleb's dead hand. My assumption is that by the time he got this—however he got it—it was too late for him to do anything with it. And if you're wondering, he died of natural causes. A malign tumor in his belly, I suspect, though he was never my patient."

"I see. Cousin Andrew, forgive me, but I have to ask. Did my father know you had that paper?"

Andrew didn't avoid Joyful's gaze. "No, he never did."

For a time the two men sat in silence, the enormity of all the old hatreds and betrayals heavy between them. Finally, Joyful said, "This treasure . . . If it exists, you could have gone after it any number of times over the years. Why didn't you?"

"I had many excuses. No opportunity, no knowledge of seafaring, no captain I'd trust . . . The plain truth is, I always knew it wasn't mine to claim."

Joyful stood up, the tension making his chest tight and every muscle quiver. "But it is mine. The blood legacy belongs to me." His heart was pounding and he could feel the sweat running down his back.

"That's what I'm saying."

"Why now? I lived three years under your roof. Until a month past, I've been a constant visitor in this house any time I've been in the city. In good Christ's name, Cousin Andrew, why now?"

Andrew took a deep breath. "Because," he said, "I believe the Union, everything your father and I and so many others fought for, to be in peril."

It took a few moments for Joyful to take this in. "Are you speaking of the United States?" he asked finally.

Andrew nodded.

"But we've bested the British in a number of battles this year, and even if they do invade New York, we—"

"I'm not talking about the redcoats, Joyful. I'm talking about a far worse danger. The kind that comes from within."

"I don't understand."

"You must have heard the talk. New England and New York to secede, become a separate country."

"Well—yes, I suppose I have. A word here and there. But surely it's not serious. War has always been a fountain of rumors."

"Indeed. And ninety-nine times out of a hundred it's talk and nothing more."

Joyful started to say something, but Andrew held up his hand. "Let me finish. Those few men promulgating this notion of disunion are the men with the most to gain. Men of business. Traders. Federalists with the most power."

"I always thought you counted yourself a member of that party."

"A Federalist, perhaps. When the war ended in '84, I saw what so-called ordinary folk can do if you give them enough power. Right here in New York the very people we'd struggled and died to make free appointed themselves judge and jury and dispensed what they called justice on the Common in front of screaming crowds, no less. Women hamstrung so they'd never walk again, men tarred and feathered so they skinned themselves alive when they tried to clean up . . . The rabble disgusted me then and they still do. I believe in a strong central government, Joyful, led by educated and thoughtful men. I do not believe in money being the arbiter of all. Business and profit are fine in their place. They cannot be the ultimate goal of a nation."

"It's not my intention to profit at the expense of my country, Cousin Andrew." The words sounded pretentious enough to make Joyful feel slightly foolish. Nonetheless, they were true.

"I know that, lad. That's why I have decided to stake your venture into trade. I believe you will be an honest businessman, a leaven among the thieves, if you will. I'm not wealthy, and what I could offer you from my own resources would be hardly enough to make a difference." He nodded toward the paper that still lay on the table in front of the fire, squinting at the faded words that might or might not lead to treasure. "That's my contribution. Take it, Joyful, and take them on. Beat the bastards back. Don't let them destroy what we gave so much blood and innocence to gain."

Thursday, August 18, 1814

Chapter Three

the South Street Docks, 11 A.M.

WILL FARRELL was twelve years old. The last three of those years he'd spent most daylight hours one hundred sixty feet above the earth, atop the Devrey tower overlooking the recently built South Street docks.

Will's vantage point allowed him to see the activity on the docksides, across the great sweep of masts in the harbor, and past the harbor islands to the Narrows. If he made a half turn to his left, he could see Long Island, the farms and houses of Brooklyn Village at the foot of the Old Ferry Road, and out to the open sea beyond Gravesend. When Bastard Devrey added the South Street docks to the dozen he owned on the East River side of Manhattan and built his tower, he'd reckoned a sharp-eyed lookout with a decent spyglass could see twenty miles. Will had repeatedly proved himself sharp-eyed—and clever with it.

Will spotted the arriving vessel when she was only a speck of white on the horizon, but he didn't immediately descend from the tower to raise the alarm. The day he started the job, old Peggety Jack, who ran the porters and suchlike on the Devrey docks, told him what was expected. "Don't matter so much knowin' first, boy. It's knowin' more what puts brass in Devrey pockets. And your own, come to that." Peggety had only one tooth, which hung over his lip like a fang. Folks said he was maybe the oldest man in all New York, but anyone who worked for Devrey's and wanted to get ahead could do a lot worse than listen to Peggety Jack. "Don't go off half-cocked, boy. Keep your powder dry till you're sure."

The ship was different from anything Will had seen since he'd been doin' the job, but that didn't mean it was the Devrey East Indiaman, *China Princess,* trapped in Canton near on to three years since the start o' the war. A few months back there was talk of how she'd decided to make a run for home. Bastard said if she had, and if she managed to slip past the British warships and the French privateers, it'd be the greatest thing as ever happened in this city. Didn't say it to Will Farrell, of course. The likes o' Bastard Devrey didn't talk to lookout boys. But Bastard sometimes appeared at his South Street warehouse soon after dawn, when Will was drinking a last cup of ale and hot milk before climbing up to his post. And Will's ears were as sharp as his eyes, for all that wasn't why Bastard paid him twenty coppers a week.

Holy Lord Almighty, he'd never seen a ship come that fast. One by one her sails rose above the horizon. The royals appeared first, then the topgallants, and beneath them, taut and bellied with wind, the topsails and mainsails of her three masts. Will lowered the spyglass, blinked rapidly to clear his vision, then raised the glass again. If it was *China Princess* she would— No, it couldn't be. This ship didn't move like an East Indiaman. Her bow didn't lift and plunge with the ocean swells. Instead her sleek black hull seemed to glide on top of the water. A merchantman, but for speed and grace such a one as he'd never seen. "Ship ahoy!" he screamed. "Ship ahoy! Ahoy! Ahoy!" Stupid to yell now when no one could hear him except the clouds, but he did it anyway, dancing up and down and shouting until he was hoarse. "Ship ahoy!" Soon he could see tiny men clambering up into the rigging, beginning to reef sail as the ship made for the harbor.

For a moment or two he was distracted by a pilot sloop setting out from the Narrows to guide the newcomer to a mooring. By the time he again directed the glass to the approaching merchantman, she had raised her house flag. Red, and decorated with some sort o' beast breathin' flames. For sure and certain not the gold lion and crossed swords on a green field that would mark the arriving vessel a Devrey ship.

The morning was hot and getting hotter. He'd removed his jacket and his hat, but Peggety Jack's orders were that he always had to be in proper Devrey livery when he was on the ground. Will jammed his black stovepipe on his head and struggled into his green-velvet cutaway as he climbed down from the tower, all the while shouting "Ship ahoy! Ship ahoy!" at the top of his voice.

The men doing business at New York's taverns and coffeehouses and crowding the city's narrow, twisting streets knew there was a ship coming before Will Farrell did. Jacob Astor maintained a lookout eight miles away, in New Jersey atop the Navesink Highlands, and he had as well a series of semaphore stations between there and his countinghouse on Little Dock Street. The cry of "Ship ahoy!" had been raised ten minutes past. But it was Astor's way to let as little as possible be known by any of his rivals. Only Will Farrell brought news of what sort of ship she was, and the markings on her flag.

He ran the whole way between South Street and Wall Street. The town, always bustling with ordinary New Yorkers, was these days heaving with militia come from miles around to defend her in case the British attacked. Rumors that such an attack was imminent were born, killed, and resurrected at least three times every day. To get to the Tontine Coffee House, where Bastard Devrey was most likely to be found, Will had to elbow his way through the throng. When he pushed open the heavy oak door, he was breathing hard and pouring sweat.

A black man, a waiter wearing a long apron and carrying a shoulder-high tray of mugs of ale, spotted him. "You be looking for someone, boy?"

"Aye. Mr. Devrey."

"Mr. Devrey be upstairs with the traders."

Will fought his way to the back of the room, then took the stairs two at a time. Once before, he'd brought Bastard Devrey news of an incoming ship, and got a copper penny for his trouble. Could be two this time. Ship ahoy!

Bastard Devrey was standing by the window with most of the other traders. He turned and saw Will. "Over here, boy," he called.

The crowd parted and made way for him. Will ran toward his employer.

Devrey waited, his mind racing and his heart starting to pound, though he exercised every scrap of will not to let his excitement show. The lookout had to have been sent by Peggety Jack, and Peggety wouldn't do that unless it was bloody important. Which could mean that a miracle had occurred just when, God knew, he needed it most—the ship Astor's people had announced, the one they were all waiting for, might indeed be *China Princess*, a seven-hundred-tonner with the biggest cargo capacity afloat.

Change his life that would. And it would be good to see the lad again as well. Fourteen Bastard's son Samuel was when he sailed to Canton on *China Princess*. The voyage meant to give the boy a taste of what the business was really about had marooned Samuel on the other side of the world three years now. Celinda would be tickled pink with his return. Not that she'd turn up her nose at the money.

Sweet Christ, he hadn't let himself hope, didn't dare. Now his heart was thumping in his chest loud enough so he feared they'd all hear it. And why not? Given how this bloody war had starved the city for the stuff of trade that was her life's blood, he'd make a fortune on the tea and silk and porcelain in the *Princess*'s hold.

"Mr. Devrey, sir, it's—"

"Hold your tongue, lad! At least until you're close enough so I can hear you and the rest of these rogues cannot."

Bastard Devrey bent over, and the boy whispered his message into his employer's ear. "Peggety Jack sent me, sir. To say ship coming's a merchantman. And her flag's red with a beast breathin' fire."

Devrey kept an iron grip on the lookout's shoulder, so he could stay bent over long enough to get his disappointment under control. The poxed, whore-spawned sons-of-bitches were all staring at him. Waiting. They'd been waiting for some months, salivating over the thought that Jacob Astor had nearly ruined Devrey, that these days all it needed was one more little shove, and the carcass of what was left of Devrey Shipping would crumple and fall to dust. He'd see them all in hell first.

"Is the boy telling you next Sunday's entire Bible lesson, Bastard?" someone called out. "Come, man, share the news."

Devrey released his hold on the lookout. Will resisted the urge to rub his sore shoulder and stayed where he was. Devrey straightened. "I am told," he began, "that the incoming ship is—"

"The fastest merchantman ever to sail, and flies the fire-breathing dragon, the Blakeman flag," a voice announced from the vicinity of the trading room's door. Each man present turned to face the newcomer. "Good day to you, gentlemen. I'm Gornt Blakeman, as most of you know. And the ship that's run the blockade is the *Canton Star*. She was built in China to my exact specifications. Two hundred eighty tons, and crammed to the gunwales with tea, silk, and porcelain. All of which will be auctioned on Pearl Street tomorrow afternoon. I'll be sure and let you know if my captain has word of *China Princess*, Mr. Devrey. You can rely on it."

"Thank you." The words were hot coals in Bastard's mouth. He managed to speak them coolly enough, but he knew his face was blood-red and wet with sweat. "Drinks all around!" he bellowed. "And put them on my account. The heat in this place is insufferable."

A hum of talk began, and a number of the men turned back to the windows, anxious for a sight of this new ship. Blakeman didn't move from his spot in the middle of the room, but gradually the milling crowd closed around him. He was broad-shouldered, dark and lean. Bastard Devrey by contrast had the family's red hair—one of the reasons there were few doubters when Sam Devrey, a lifelong bachelor, admitted to having fathered him on an attractive widow during the Revolution—and he was the shape of a barrel, but both men were tall enough to see over the heads of the crowd. They continued to stare at each other, neither willing to be the first to look away.

Blakeman heard the rattle of glasses and trays as the waiters brought the round of drinks Bastard had ordered. Hell, he'd already won the battle and he was about to win the war; he didn't have to win this skirmish as well. He broke the eye contact, gave in to his thirst, and helped himself to an ale, drinking deep, savoring the bitter tang and the pleasant tingle of the foamy head. Finally he lowered the tankard, waited until the drinks were all distributed, then raised his voice. "Gentlemen, if I may have your attention one more moment." Most continued talking. "I wish to make an announcement," Blakeman called over the din.

Bastard had bent every bit of his will to bringing his emotions under control; now his heart began to pound again. Gornt Blakeman owned a stagecoach company, and he had the exclusive franchise to the two most lucrative routes in the nation, one going north to Boston and the other south to Philadelphia. The year before, Blakeman had sold scrip to raise money to add more rolling stock. Apart from that, Bastard had never seen him among the traders here at the Tontine, and he sure as poxed hell had never heard so much as a whisper that Blakeman owned a merchantman outfitted for the China trade.

"Gentlemen." The last murmur of talk faded. Blakeman waited until he was certain every man in the room was looking at him, then cleared his throat. "I'll buy all outstanding Devrey scrip at eighty dollars per share. Twice what those of you paid who purchased it at last month's offering, and a good deal more profit for those who acquired the scrip earlier. Eighty dollars a share." He had to raise his voice to be heard over the growing hubbub. "Thirty-two pounds apiece, for any of you not patriot enough to think in American terms."

"Paper?" someone asked. Congress had decreed paper dollars as the nation's standard currency soon after the Revolution, but there was no national bank to control the issue, and in New York, coins—precious metal, wherever it was minted—represented the kind of real wealth a man could rely on.

"Cash money in good coin," Blakeman promised. "Paid out at my countinghouse on Hanover Street."

Will Farrell was still standing next to his employer, still hoping Bastard would give him a penny for bringing the news. The stampede of men racing for the door nearly knocked him over.

Chapter Four

MIDDAY AND DARK AS NIGHT, with a scorching wind off the harbor. No rain with it now, though it was bound to come. There was a true midsummer squall brewing. Despite the hour, lanterns had been lit; they swayed in the wind, casting their hellish red light in odd corners, illuminating the seemingly chaotic movement of men and goods.

The porters had shed their official livery and were working in only shirtsleeves and long oilcloth aprons, cursing mightily as they heaved and shoved their way from a pair of ships to the warehouses. *Fidelity,* a coastal schooner that looked to Joyful to be about forty tons, had made it up from the Carolinas and was being unladed at one of Josiah Pendry's two wharves. Next to her, having paid for the use of Pendry's second mooring because he had no wharf of his own, was Gornt Blakeman's *Canton Star.* The merchantman was nearly three times the size of the schooner, and she'd been berthed less than half an hour earlier, but already her hold was being emptied, and her cargo of the luxuries New York never got enough of were on their way to auction. Blakeman had set the time of the sale for the next day.

Joyful stood in the shadows near the warehouse. A porter passed by, close enough for him to smell the rancid musk of the man's sweat and see how the carrying sling cut deep into his forehead. His back was bent under the weight of a two-hundred-pound wooden chest with Chinese markings. Joyful had been two when his parents took him to China. He learned Cantonese from his Chinese amah in six months, and could read, write, and speak Mandarin by the time he was seven. The chop, the chest's marking, indicated DIANHONG CHA— black tea—from Yunnan. The best. Over the next couple of minutes he counted three more chests chopped to indicate they held tea, half a dozen marked as porcelain, and six as silk. And the porters had made only the barest start on the goods in the *Canton Star*'s hold.

His left hand, the one he no longer had, hurt. He felt an almost ir-resistible urge to flex the fingers that had been shot away. Joyful had heard many patients complain of pain in a severed limb and always thought they were imagining things. Now he knew better.

He counted six more chests of black tea. Meanwhile the porters at the next wharf were manhandling hogsheads of molasses and sugar, bales of cotton and wool, barrels of potash, and puncheons of rum. The stuff of everyday life. The silks and porcelains and teas of China were the stuff of dreams.

The rain began at last, pelting down in drops as big as a thumbnail. He was soaked in minutes but ignored it—on board ship you were wet at least as often as you were dry—and concentrated on the pleasure, the rush of excitement he felt watching *Canton Star* yield up her trea-sure. It was almost the same as when he picked up a scalpel. He hadn't expected that.

A gust of wind sent the lantern closest to him swinging in a wide arc. The letters above the warehouse two doors down came into full view—DEVREY SHIPPING—and below the letters a green crest sporting a gold lion above crossed swords. Will Devrey, the company's founder, had adopted those arms in 1697. Should have been shackles and a whip, Joyful thought. Like so many in the New York and New England shipping trade—the Beekmans and Livingstons and Cabots and Lodges—the Devrey fortune had been built on Guinea ships bringing live cargo to the slave market on Wall Street. They said that back then if you passed twenty people on a New York street, five would be black slaves. These days there were nearly a hundred thousand people in the city, and only two thousand slaves. As for the Devrey slave ships, the last one had been put in dry dock before the Revolution. After two slave uprisings and constant rumors of a third, the Council passed a law against importing blacks recently captured in Africa; too dangerous for the close quarters of city life, they said. New Yorkers had to learn to restrict themselves to what were called "seasoned" slaves, men and women who had been whipped into submission, or born into it, on the Caribbean sugar plantations. Such slaves were more expensive and harder to come by, so white indentures from Europe became the household servants of choice. Just as well, Joyful thought. Human slavery struck him as an abomination. Besides, New York's three slave revolts had cost many lives. People who detested you while they slept under your roof were an invitation to disaster.

Before this war the loss of the slave trade hadn't seemed any kind of problem for Devrey Shipping. The China trade, open to the Americans once they were no longer a British colony subject to Parliament's rules, easily took up the slack. Bastard Devrey had built the warehouse Joyful was looking at some four years earlier. Five stories tall, sixty feet deep, and as broad as any two of those damnable twenty-five-foot-wide lots the Common Council intended for the entire city, it was, however, mortgaged from cornerstone to roof.

For all the activity swirling around Joyful, and the thriving commerce that in some ways cushioned New York against the deprivations of war, the blockade was draining Bastard's lifeblood. In addition to mortgaging his real estate, he'd sold scrip that gave investors ownership of nearly forty percent of his company. Like everyone else in the city, Joyful had already heard of the frontal attack Gornt Blakeman had launched an hour earlier in the Tontine Coffee House. By his reckoning, Bastard Devrey had invited it.

A rumble of thunder was followed almost immediately by the crackle of lightning directly overhead, and for a moment everything in the vicinity was bathed in strange blue light. Joyful saw the ship's captain, the man he was waiting for, start down the gangplank. Finbar O'Toole was someone he'd known all his life, the man who had brought Joyful news of his father's death and delivered his legacy. He was also the captain who had run the blockade, and brought Gornt Blakeman's *Canton Star* safely to harbor.

Joyful took a few eager steps forward, then stopped. The Irishman was short and squat, built like a bull, and Joyful had never known him to be afraid of anything or anyone, but he marched down the gangplank like a man headed for his doom, not one who had arrived triumphant after outfoxing the strongest navy in the world.

Finbar's broad shoulders were hunched forward, and his walk had none of the usual seaman's swagger. He carried a small wooden chest about nine or ten inches square, hugging it to his chest with both arms. Why would the captain of a ship being serviced by a dozen porters himself carry one particular chest to shore?

O'Toole got to the foot of the gangplank and hesitated. His beard was as full and bushy as Joyful remembered, though more gray than black these days. Beneath his stovepipe hat, Joyful knew, was a shiny, totally bald scalp. As a child, he used to sit on Finbar's lap and listen to tales of how the Irishman had traded the hair on his head to a leprechaun, but got to keep his beard as part of the bargain.

O'Toole ignored the porters swirling about him and looked round as if he were waiting for someone. He took a couple of steps in Joyful's direction. Close enough now so Joyful could see that the box was made of polished wood—possibly ebony—not the rough stuff of the tea chests, and chopped with a single character, the classic Mandarin symbol of the mythic Chinese fire-breathing dragon. The same sign as appeared on the owner's flag. This box was Gornt Blakeman's private property.

A man appeared, making his way through the dockside crush as if it did not exist. There was menace in his every step, and the porters took pains to move out of his way. Vinegar Clifford had been the public whipper until three years earlier, when the city abolished flogging as an official punishment. Cruel and unusual, the judges said, a violation of the Constitution. Clifford might no longer be in the public employ, but he still clutched his whip, holding it fully coiled under his right arm, close to his body, and he could release it in full snapping fury as fast as an eyeblink. Joyful had seen it on a number of occasions. He took a quick step deeper into the shadows.

O'Toole and Clifford met at the foot of the gangplank. A pair of bulls, looking for a moment as if they might lock horns. They exchanged a few words Joyful couldn't hear, then O'Toole nodded and handed over the ebony chest. Clifford lodged it under his left arm— his right still cradled his whip—and turned and left.

Bloody interesting, Joyful thought. He turned up the collar of his cutaway against the driving rain and strode forward.

"So how'd you know I was captain o' Blakeman's *Star*?"

"I know a lot of things these days. I've become good at listening."

"Because o' that?" Finbar O'Toole gestured toward the black glove.

"Partly that," Joyful admitted. "I've had time to acquire other skills."

"I never 'spected to see you a victim o' your own knife, lad."

They were in the Greased Pig, a grog shop on Dover Street, at a tiny table in the corner, surrounded by a noisy throng of wharf rats who had been laboring since before dawn and were intent on their drinking during this quarter-of-an-hour midday break, the only one they'd have until four o'clock, when their workday ended and it was time to eat. The dockhands concentrated on slaking their thirst, ignoring all else. It was a safe enough place to talk.

"I didn't cut my hand off, Finbar. A blast from a poxed English carronade did that."

O'Toole took a long pull at his grog, fiery rum made right here in New York with sugar brought up from the Caribbean, the result diluted with a half portion of water. "I can see as how folks wouldn't want you cutting 'em up with only one hand, but all the rest o' what doctors do, the purging and cupping and leeching and the like, that don't need two hands, do it?"

"Tell me something, Finbar. In all your days, have you ever seen anyone cured of their ills by the purging and cupping and bloodletting?"

The Irishman shrugged. "Don't go around asking, do I?"

"You don't have to ask. Surgery is what makes the sick well. Everyone willing to calculate experience knows that. It's fear as keeps them from the knife and gives them early death instead. But if people won't trust a surgeon with two hands, they sure as all Hades won't go near one that's single-handed."

"The herbs and simples your ma gave folks," O'Toole said, "they was magic. They cured for sure. I saw plenty o' that afore she died, St. Patrick guide her soul to rest."

Roisin Campbell Turner had been a Woman of Connemara, a member of an ancient Irish healing society like her mother and grandmother before her. It was Roisin who cured the wife of the imperial governor of Canton when the woman's stomach was swollen with a painful growth. In return, her husband, Morgan Turner, was allowed to build a house in Canton itself, where he and his wife and child could live year-round. All the other *yang gui zhi*, the Western foreign devils, had to live above their factories—their warehouses in the Canton trading strip. Moreover, they could reside there only from June to December; the rest of the year was spent at their homes on the Portuguese island of Macau. "My mother's cures worked," Joyful said. "But that's not what I was trained to do. I don't have her knowledge or her skills."

The secrets of the Women of Connemara were passed from mother to daughter, never to a man, not even a son. O'Toole, for all his fierce American patriotism, was Irish enough to understand that. "Very well. But I still don't see what we're talking about."

"Trade," Joyful said. "If I can't be a surgeon, I must be a trader, Finbar. It's the only other thing I know."

"The blockade's put a mighty crimp in trade these days, lad. I ran it this time because the *Star*'s possibly the finest merchantman afloat, but no one can make a regular thing o' running a bloody English blockade."

"I know."

"Then—"

"The blockade won't be in place forever. Already there's a British and American commission set up to talk of peace."

"Talk didn't blow your left hand off. And in case ye ain't noticed, there's like as not to be an army o' redcoats right here in New York sooner rather than later."

Joyful turned and signaled for the bowl of grog. "Nonetheless, peace will come. In the not too distant future, I believe. When it does, I'll need a captain. I want it to be you."

"I'm fifty-three years old, lad. You need a man with more voyages left in him."

"I need a man I can trust."

"Ships cost money," O'Toole said. "More'n two thousand pounds."

Joyful wasn't surprised the Irishman knew exactly how much had been in the moneybag his father sent from Canton. Neither had he ever questioned Finbar's assertion that every penny of what he'd been left had been put into Joyful's hands. A man could be both trustworthy and curious. "The ebony box chopped with the red dragon, the one you handed over on the wharf today, how much did it contain?"

"Don't know anything 'bout any ebony box."

"I was there, Finbar. Filled with silver, was it?" Silver, measured out in a unit called a tael, each equivalent to a thousand coppers, was the trading medium of the powerful hong merchants of Canton.

O'Toole didn't answer. The bowl of grog was passed to them by the men at the next table. Joyful put four copper pennies on the table, and the Irishman refilled both their mugs, then got up and carried the bowl to yet another table. "How are you planning to get a ship? Where's the money for that going to come from?"

"I have the money. At least enough to get things started. I made some wise investments." O'Toole didn't look convinced, but Joyful offered no further explanation. "Gornt Blakeman's making a run on Devrey scrip, buying it up for cash money."

The Irishman lifted his drink and took a long pull, keeping his gaze fixed on Joyful all the while. Finally, he set the mug down and wiped his mouth with the back of his hand. "What do you care? I know Bastard's your cousin, but the way I heard it, there's no friendly feeling between Devreys and Turners."

"None at all," Joyful agreed.

"Then why?"

"Traders thrive by knowing things."

The Irishman shrugged. "Maybe, but you ain't a trader yet. Besides, the *Star* lades near to three hundred tons. There's a goodly amount o' cash money going to come from what was in her hold. Even without what's in the poxed ebony box."

"So you do know what it contains."

Another shrug. "Not for sure," O'Toole said. "I heard it was jewels, but you know Canton, I heard a lot of things."

Joyful's gut tightened with excitement, but his voice was level. "Jewels? Emeralds? Rubies? Where would—"

"Not no poxy colored geegaws," Finbar said softly. "The real thing. Diamonds. Least that's what I was told."

Sooner or later, everything under God's own heaven fetched up in Canton. And if diamonds had arrived in New York on a ship owned by Jacob Astor with his far-flung trading empire, that wouldn't have surprised Joyful. But Gornt Blakeman . . . "Finbar, is there any reason to think Blakeman owns other ships? That he's a bigger trader than he appears to be?"

The Irishman shook his head. "Ain't nothing like that as is talked about in the factories or on the Bogue."

That settled it. Nothing in the world of the China trade could bypass the collective knowledge of the traders' strip and the Bogue, the harbor of Canton. But diamonds? Holy God Almighty, he'd been dealt a card he never expected, and one that made the others he held stronger than he'd dreamed they could be. He couldn't ask for better. Joyful leaned forward. "Finbar," he said softly, "listen carefully. A while ago you said there was no love lost between Turners and Devreys, and I said you were right. Now let me add this. I'm going to be the cousin who owns Devrey Shipping. Not Bastard, and definitely not Gornt Blakeman. Me."

"Indeed? And when's this miracle to come about then?"

"Soon enough. What you've just told me makes it even more certain."

"Known you since you were no taller than your da's knee, lad, and you were always as cheeky as you were smart. But that's a big plan for someone as has one hand and whatever could be made of two thousand pounds. Big enough so maybe it's sheer poxy madness. Leastwise some would say so."

Joyful dropped his voice just above a whisper. "What do you know of the *Fanciful Maiden*?"

"Schooner yer da had back when he was privateering, when we was fighting the godrotting French and their godrotting Indians. What about her?"

"The voyage of '59, when the *Maiden* came back empty and my father said he'd taken no prizes. You know about that?"

"Maybe I do," O'Toole said.

"I know as well," Joyful said softly. "Everything. My cousin Andrew told me."

"Andrew Turner? What's he to do with this? Your da told me he couldn't remember where— Ach, all right. I know what happened in '59. But Andrew Turner and your da were never close. It was your ma Andrew cared for. That's why he took you in."

"I know. Nonetheless, Andrew had the note my father wrote, the one that said where—" Joyful broke off.

"Had, you said. Who's got it now?"

"I have."

"So that's where the money for a merchantman's going to come from?"

Joyful shrugged.

"It's a long odds wager, lad. Made a few o' those in me day, God help me. It's not often they pays off."

"I know. But my ship and getting control of Devrey Shipping, that's going to happen just the way I plan it. I feel it in my bones, Finbar."

"Yer da wanted you to have the tr——, what we're talkin' about. That's how come he told me about it. Said he knew he'd hid it for well and certain, but after the godrotting British finished with him on their poxed prison ship, he couldn't remember where it was. Biggest sadness in his life, that was."

"Then he will rest easier once this is done." Joyful leaned forward. "What's Vinegar Clifford's connection to Blakeman?"

"No idea. Didn't know his name neither, till you said it. Looked to put the fear o' God into a heathen, he did. Rather face an enemy with a cutlass, even a pistol, than a bullwhip."

"I agree. Take my word for it, Clifford's a genius with his whip, and without a trace of pity for his victims. He's called Vinegar because back when he was the town's official whipper, as soon as his victims passed out, he'd revive them with a gallon of vinegar splashed over the wounds. More pain that way."

The Irishman shuddered. "Worst o' the world's devils, them as enjoy other folks' suffering. You think Clifford's workin' for Blakeman now?"

"I didn't think so until this morning. How did you know he was the person sent to claim the box?"

"He knew the password. I was told to wait until we were an hour into the unlading, then bring the box ashore and give it to him as said *bei mat*. Then I answered *nang lik*. Then he said *wing yuen*. Long as he did all that, I'd know he was the right one."

In Cantonese, *bei mat* meant "secret." *Nang lik,* power. *Wing yuen,* forever. Secret power forever. Pretty fanciful, particularly considering Gornt Blakeman wasn't Chinese. "As far as you know, has Blakeman ever been in Canton? He didn't hire you in person, did he?"

The Irishman shook his head. "Never set eyes on him. It was his comprador as hired me."

A comprador was usually Chinese, though the word was Portuguese. Come into use because the Portuguese had opened the China trade nearly a century earlier. A comprador was a facilitator, a man who could move easily in the Asian community but understood the business ways of the Europeans. He was a shipping company's eyes and ears, and counted upon to be fiercely loyal because he had a substantial share in the company's profits, and because the job was customarily passed from father to son. A few compradors were independents, men who worked for any shipper who offered employment on a given day. These men were also trusted to keep the shippers' secrets; nonetheless, they were talking about Canton. *Bei mat,* secret, was written with the symbol for an open mouth.

"Forget about the poxed box and whatever's in it," O'Toole said. "Forget everything about this damned voyage, in fact. Bad joss otherwise."

Joyful knew joss was more than luck, it was fate, something you had to accept. But in New York as in Canton, money trumped luck every time.

Chapter Five

New York City,
Maiden Lane, 2 P.M.

MANON VIONNE WAS TALL and slender and remarkably pretty, with pale gold hair and eyes the color of dark purple pansies. She was also, at the advanced age of twenty-two, unmarried, thus marked for spinsterhood. Which did not seem to trouble her in the slightest in the early afternoon of this summer day. She was smiling and humming softly when she returned to her father's house on Maiden Lane.

Manon came in through the kitchen door, avoiding the shop where Maurice Vionne traded in jewels when he could get them, and more regularly engaged in the smithing of gold and silver. Her father was waiting for her. "You're soaked, Manon. Where have you been?"

"To the Fly Market, Papa. I told you I was going. There was a dreadful storm, did you not hear it?"

She set down her basket as she spoke, and took off her high-crowned straw bonnet and her embroidered shawl, revealing a white-

and-lavender-checked day dress with a high frilled neck and long sleeves with ruffled cuffs. Modest enough, but wet as it now was, the thin cotton fabric clung to her body. That didn't alarm Vionne as much as the flush in her cheeks. Lately, he was more and more convinced his daughter was keeping secrets, and less and less sure what to do about it. Her mother had died eight years before. Vionne was convinced that if his wife had lived their Manon would be married by now, and he would be dandling a grandchild or two. Perhaps a grandson to replace the three sons who had not lived to work beside him as he'd once dreamed, a male heir to learn smithing and inherit his business. "I heard today that Pierre DeFane has a nephew coming from Virginia," he said. "Seems his wife died last year and he—"

"I will be happy to meet the gentleman when he arrives, Papa. I am always happy to entertain your friends, you know that. Now, look at the lovely fish I found at the market." Manon folded back the cloth that covered the contents of her basket and held it up for his inspection. "You shall have a delicious *soupe de poisson* for your dinner."

It was always the same: She never opposed him outright. If she did, he could command her obedience. Instead she was compliant and sunny and seemed to fall in with whatever he wanted. But nothing ever went his way, always hers. You are too clever for me, my Manon. Too clever for any man. And that is the problem. "*Soupe de poisson,*" he said. "I will enjoy that."

Maurice Vionne was perhaps the best known of the town's Huguenot jewelers. He could afford a cook, but like her mother before her, Manon did all the shopping and cooking for the household. It was a considerable savings in the monthly expenses, so perhaps it wasn't so bad that she was a spinster. Besides, she was useful in the shop. In a country without a royal court to support trade in precious stones, smithing was the everyday work that bought their dinners. All the same, trading in priceless stones, that was in the Vionne blood, and Manon had an eye for a jewel as keen as his own. "I will want you to mind the premises later this evening," he said.

"Of course, Papa. Will you not be here?"

"I will be upstairs. With a visitor."

Manon's heart began to pound. She made a huge effort not to let her excitement show. "A customer, Papa? Someone you won't see in the shop?"

Vionne shrugged. "Someone whose business is private. Jewels are often held close to the heart, *ma petite*. You have surely learned that by now."

"Indeed, Papa." Manon knew that more than one widow had come to Maurice Vionne long after business hours, white-faced and morti-fied that she needed to sell her jewelry to get money to live. "Am I to take it you will be receiving a lady?"

Vionne started from the kitchen and didn't look at her when he spoke. "Not a lady, no. Please hold yourself ready just after seven, Manon. Here in the kitchen. I will let my visitor in myself, and call you after I have him settled."

"I will do exactly as you ask, Papa." So! Perhaps Joyful was correct. Nothing in her voice or her manner gave away her excitement, but she could not keep her hands from trembling. Pray God Papa had not no-ticed.

Chatham Street, 4 P.M.

Gornt Blakeman moved quickly through the streets of Manhattan, the smell of the countinghouse still on him. He'd been sitting in a cubby off the main room, hearing the clink of the coins—cash money he'd promised for Devrey scrip and cash money he'd delivered—watching through a crack in the door while the certificates mounted into a higher and higher pile on the clerk's desk. At three he'd had to order the doors closed and the purchases stopped because he was out of ready money. Virtually beggared, if the truth be told. The thought made him howl with laughter. Beggared was he? With what had come in on the *Canton Star*? Not quite. He laughed again, enjoying the looks of the curious passersby. They all knew who he was, every poxed resi-

dent of the city was talking about him this day. Sweet Jesus, but sometimes life was good.

The midday storm had greatly lessened the day's heat; now the sun
was shining and there was a cool easterly breeze. It felt good, fine in
fact, and hunger was making a pleasant anticipation in his belly. Still,
Blakeman paused a few steps before Eugenie Fischer's house.

He looked across the road to the Common, dominated by the new
City Hall, finished two years before. Marble on three sides only, and
plain brownstone at the back. It was a plan put in place by small-
minded men who could not imagine the city growing further north.
But already the city extended well beyond City Hall, the population
moving always deeper into the woods known as the Manhattan
wilderness. These days New York City occupied the full three-mile
stretch of the island's narrow southern tip. As for what was coming . . . The grid laid out in 1811, before the war, showed all of Manhattan—the entire thirteen-mile length, by God!—divided by a dozen
north-south avenues a hundred feet wide, and crisscrossed with a
hundred fifty-five numbered streets, each sixty feet wide. The plan was
for a city of uniform side-by-side lots and straight-sided, cojoined,
right-angled houses that would be cheap and easy to build. No fancy
parks or sweeping vistas in the manner of European capitals. Workers
were what New York City needed if she was to fulfill her destiny.
Thousands of them; Christ, maybe tens of thousands. Seeing the city
develop in just that fashion was one of Blakeman's dreams. Today he'd
brought it a little closer to reality.

The thought made the sap rise in him. He strode to Eugenie's front
door.

Eugenie Fisher had a table for two laid in the boudoir off her bedroom, and she served Blakeman herself from a makeshift sideboard set
up in front of a fireplace not needed in summer. Because, she explained, "I thought you'd want more than the usual amount of privacy, dear Gornt."

"Mmm, yes." Blakeman drank the soup she gave him without much attention. He was more interested in her than in the food, however hungry he'd thought himself when he arrived.

Eugenie was aware of his brash gaze. Sometimes she stared back, but never for very long. And she never gave even the merest hint that she knew what he was thinking. Mostly, she made small talk, an amusing thing she'd read in the Federalist *Evening Post*, or the Democratic-Republican paper, the *National Advocate*. How her maid had been the first to bring Eugenie word that a ship was coming into harbor, only according to her it was a British man-o'-war coming to shell the city. Until finally, "Gornt, I can't bear it. You've been here nearly twenty minutes and you still haven't told me what happened with Bastard Devrey."

"Exactly what I planned to happen. I like your frock." He leaned across the table and fingered the short, puffed sleeve that bared her arm. The fabric was white and thin and felt incredibly soft to his touch. A wide blue satin ribbon caught the gown below her breasts. The dress flowed free from there to her ankles; he could see she'd adopted the latest French fashion and wasn't corseted. He'd heard that in Europe the women adopting this mode actually damped their underchemise so it would cling closer to their bodies. Called it a blow struck for freedom. "I didn't think you were a republican."

"Heaven forbid." She laughed, a tinkling little sound he found himself thinking of many times when he was not with her. "You forget, I was Eugenie LaMont before I married," she said. "French fashion is my birthright. I adore it."

Another part of Eugenie's heritage was knowing when a man wanted to talk of business and politics, and when he did not. It was a skill she had honed during the four years she was married to her handsome lawyer. Dead two years Timothy Fischer was, a victim of the yellowing fever. But her wiles were all the more necessary now that she was a twenty-four-year-old widow and must struggle every month to find the funds to keep her household afloat. "Will your ship have brought me some new silks from Canton, Gornt? If so, I will have another frock made to this same design. Will that please you?"

Blakeman nodded, his mind on other things; Eugenie stood up and took the soup plates away, then busied herself at the sideboard serving the next course. He could see the curve of her buttocks as she moved, and when she stood a certain way, the light from the window showed off the slight roundness of her belly. The fact that she was a lady, not a doxy or a whore, made her boldness wonderfully titillating. "Tell me, will every fashionable woman in the city soon adopt this style?"

Eugenie laughed. "Would you like it if they did?"

"I'm not sure there would be a lick of work done in New York if they did. No man can be expected to keep his mind on business in such circumstances." He got up and went to where she stood and drew her to him. "Today, Eugenie. It's been a marvelous day. Make it perfect."

She let him pull her close, then leaned back so she could still see his face. "Tell me what happened, Gornt. I've been thinking about it for hours."

His hand moved to her breast. She didn't push it away. "Soon as I knew my ship was headed for the harbor, I went to the Tontine and confronted Bastard Devrey, just as I told you I would." His other hand ventured to her buttocks, and when that too was allowed to remain, he began a little pattern of strokes, always exploring a bit further.

"And what did he say?" Eugenie pressed herself against his thigh.

"What could he say? He's all but bankrupt. And as of today I own forty percent of his company. Give me your mouth."

"Gornt, where is the money for all this coming from?"

"That's not your concern. Kiss me, damn you."

"They say you're a pirate. That you—"

He managed to stop her words with a kiss, but moments later she had slipped out of his embrace. Two months and it was always the same.

Eugenie returned to the business of dinner. "Will you have some of this roasted pheasant, dearest Gornt? And perhaps a bit of boiled beef? I told cook no pies because of the heat, but if you—"

He strode to the window. "Come over here. I want to show you something." She stood beside him. "What do you see?" he demanded.

"Ah," she said, looking down into the street. "Two escapees from the Tammany Society next door." She was referring to a pair of feral pigs—the city was full of them—snuffling in the gutter of the street below, and to the building on her right which housed a social club that attracted mostly mechanics and laborers, people of the class that supported the Democratic-Republicans rather than the Federalists.

Gornt chuckled. "Look across the Common."

He meant her to ignore the now decrepit and overcrowded almshouse, she knew. And, of course, the hulk of a building still called the New Gaol, though it had been built in 1766, and the Bridewell, where prisoners with longer terms to serve were packed together like salted fish in a barrel. "The splendid City Hall," Eugenie said. "What about it?"

"Would you like to live in it?"

"On the Common among the Irish ne'er-do-wells and thieves? You are mad, dear Gornt. A touch of the summer heat. Besides, City Hall's not a residence."

"But it could be made so. It could be a palace. And you could be . . . my Pompadour."

Pompadour. A French king's courtesan, never his queen. Her smile was as radiant as always and showed nothing of what she felt. "Mad indeed. But so charming with it."

She wore her dark hair twisted in a coil at the back of her head, and between it and the scooped neck of her gown there was only bare skin. Blakeman placed one finger on her neck. "You wear no jewelry, Eugenie LaMont Fischer. Is it true then that after your husband died you were penniless and had to sell your jewels to live?"

"And is it true that you're a Barbary pirate, escaped from Tripoli when Mr. Jefferson sent American gunboats to attack, and that you have chests of gold hidden in your countinghouse?"

"Not gold," he whispered, putting his arms around her once more. "Diamonds. Emeralds. Rubies. You must come with me some day to that City Hall built by small-minded men and help me select a proper throne room. Bedchambers as well, Eugenie LaMont Fisher, who is driving me insane. Will you do that?"

This time for answer she kissed him. But an hour later when he left, though he'd eaten his fill and his belly no longer growled, Blakeman's crotch was as heavy as it had been when he arrived.

The Manhattan Wilderness
Above the Village of Greenwich, 7 P.M.

By evening another storm had reached the city. The summer dusk turned prematurely to dark; and lightning and thunder boomed and cracked overhead, and rain fell in sheets from the ferocious sky.

The cabin belonging to the woman the town called Holy Hannah was a hovel four miles from the southern tip of Manhattan Island, in the no-man's-land beyond North Street, the limit of the city proper, beyond even the small rural settlement known as the village of Greenwich. The shack sat in a meadow at the edge of the thickly wooded hills that covered most of the island.

Holy Hannah had built the thing herself. The walls were rough planks nailed to tree trunks that had been stuck like posts into the ground; there were places where the gaps between them were as wide as a man's thumb. In winter she collected rags and old newspapers and made a sort of mortar for the joints. Now, in summer, the make-do stuffing had been pulled out to let a breath of air into the windowless space. As for the roof, it was a patchwork of tin and board, and even some bricks that had once come to hand. In this downpour great drops of rain came through the cracks and splattered everywhere. Hannah could as well be standing outside.

She kicked the assorted bits of bedding spread about the floor into a single pile, and covered it with a square of tattered canvas. Then fussed with the pile a bit longer, making sure everything was as well covered as it could be. Another crack of thunder shook the walls.

There was no proper door, only a second square of canvas nailed to a bit of tree trunk acting as a lintel, and left free either side. The force of the rain was driving the makeshift barrier inward, depositing torrents of water at the entrance, churning the dirt floor into a muddy sump. Time was, there were some heavy stones about, good for weighting the bottom of the entry flap; she had no idea where they'd disappeared to.

Her shawl, a thing so old it was no color and no identifiable fabric, hung from a peg on the wall. Hannah grabbed it and put it over her unkempt mane of gray hair, then pushed the canvas flap aside and went into the meadow. You could no longer see the path trodden to the cabin through the high grass; the heavy rain had beaten down every blade equally. Couldn't see much of anything, come to that. Except for the eerie blue-white light that came with each flash of lightning, it seemed like night.

"Hannah, why are you outside? Get back in and stay dry."

She recognized Will Farrell's voice before she could actually see him. Always looking out for her, Will was. His mama died when Will was eight, and without a father as would claim him, the boy had taken to living on the streets. That's where she'd found him, huddling in a doorway on a night when the cold was a thing as could perish a body with some flesh on its bones, much less the scrawny little thing Will was then. Hannah had picked him up and carried him home. There were four or five boys living with her at the time, she didn't remember exactly, and that night they had crowded together for warmth with the newcomer in the heart of the huddle, sustained by their combined heat. The others had disappeared, but never mind. Her boys had always come and gone as they liked, usually without so much as a thank-you or a goodbye. Not Will, though. He was the best of them.

"Get inside," the lad shouted. She spotted his stovepipe hat, floating through the fog as if it traveled on its own. "Get a fire goin', Hannah. I've brought us some proper supper."

She almost couldn't see what he seemed to be dragging behind him, until he got a bit closer and she made out the figure of a second boy, hunched over and wanting to hang back, except that Will had tight hold of him and was pulling him forward.

Another one. Hannah felt her heart lift.

"Do you have a name, then?" Hannah stooped over the brick-lined fire hole in the middle of the cabin and prodded a handful of wood shavings meant for kindling.

"He's Jesse Edwards," Will said. "Told me so when I found him."

The shavings were damp. She kept blowing on them and repeatedly striking new sparks off the tinderbox. Still they did not catch. "And where did that happen to be?"

"Out behind Astor's slaughterhouse on the Bowery. Same place I got that." Will gestured to the large beef kidney waiting to be cooked. "Only I found Jesse first. He was poking around in the pit where old Astor dumps the stuff as smells too bad to do anything with. I told him I knew a better place to look," he added with a sly smile. "But he'd have to turn his back 'fore I'd go and get something from it."

Some months back Will had told Hannah he'd found a way to open the chest behind the slaughterhouse where Henry Astor saved choice bits of carcass he was keeping for himself, or maybe his almighty brother Jacob, who owned half the city and a bit besides. "Told you not to go there too often," she said. "Otherwise he'll think it out, know someone's found the hiding place, and he'll stop using it. We had that mutton chop only a week since."

"Had to make an exception," Will said, getting up to find a log to put on the fire now that Hannah had finally got the kindling going. It was a phrase he'd learned from Peggety Jack. When someone broke one o' Peggety's rules, Peggety would sometimes say he'd not dock the offender's pay after all. He'd say he was making an exception out o' the kindness o' his soft heart, only if there was another time, well, he'd take three times the usual fine. "Had to make an exception out o' the kindness o' me soft heart," Will repeated. "Jesse here was trying to eat that stinking stuff from the pit raw. So I said

I'd get us a bit o' supper and bring him here to eat it. Knew you wouldn't mind."

"Course I don't mind. Birds with one wing need a nest more'n most. But they can sing same as those with two. Ain't you gonna say anything at all, Jesse Edwards?"

"Don't got nothin' to say." The boy mumbled the words into his chest and didn't look at her.

At last the log caught and flames crackled and danced in the fire hole. "Give that kidney here," Hannah said. Will complied, and she took a knife from her pocket and began cutting it into three pieces. "Smell that piss smell," she chortled. "Some folks say you got to soak a kidney 'fore you cook it. But I say the piss gives the kidney flavor. When the Israelites was in the desert and the Holy One, Blessed Be His Name, sent them manna to eat—Book o' Exodus that is—I bet it was kidney with plenty o' piss stink still in it. Manna from heaven, that's what we got here. Get the sticks, Will. How'd you lose your arm, Jesse Edwards?"

"In a battle. Last year."

"You was in the war?" Will's tone betrayed his awe.

Jesse seemed to come alive. "Aye. Aboard Commodore Perry's flagship *Lawrence.*"

Hannah glanced sideways at him. Lord Almighty! Probably the only thing he ever did in his life made him feel a bit special. Though sure as David was a king, only thing he'd got out of it was the loss of one wing. She fixed a share of kidney onto each of three pointed sticks and handed the largest portion to the newcomer. "Don't take but a single arm to do most things," she said. "Like hold a bit of meat over the fire. Besides, the Holy One, blessed be His name, looks after his own. 'Before I formed thee in the belly I knew thee.' Book of Jeremiah. Got any family, Jesse Edwards?"

"Was just me and my ma, then she died and I went to sea."

"And where you been since last year when you was a hero with Commodore Perry?"

Jesse shrugged. "Here and there. Thought I could get work in New

York, but it's the same here as anywhere else, nobody wants me 'cause o' this." He nodded toward the armless shoulder. "Ain't my fault, but—"

"Don't whinge," Hannah said sharply. "The Holy One, Blessed be His Name, helps those who help themselves. Book of Proverbs. He don't hold with whining and whinging." The smell of roasting meat prickled in the air. Not that she'd have minded if there was only a bit of stale bread for supper. Or nothing, come to that. She had long since learned she had much in common with the wild creatures in the woods to the north. She could live off her fat when she must. The Holy One made women tough as they needed to be. Despite years of living rough, she was still as round and solid as a hitching post; still had all her teeth as well. She was forty-five or forty-six, she was never quite sure, and she saw plenty of women younger than she with nothing left but gums. But she had good strong teeth, like all the women in her family, like her mother and her grandmother. How proud of their looks they'd been in their fine taffeta gowns, and dainty leather shoes, and the tortoiseshell combs in their hair. They were . . .

They were dead. No point in thinking on them. Particularly not when now she had two lads to look after. She could all but see the hunger on this new one. The hand holding his bit of kidney over the fire was shaking with it. "Not long now," she said. "Just let it get a bit more cooked, then you can have at it. And we'll see about finding you something as will earn you a few coppers. New York's a fine city for work, and Holy Hannah's got lots of ideas for boys as ain't afraid of it."

By the time they'd finished the kidney, the rain had stopped. Will pulled back the canvas flap and revealed the mottled red and gold sunset sky. "Mackerel sky at night, sailor's delight," he said happily. "Maybe there'll be another ship tomorrow."

"Not likely," Hannah said. "This New York City is Jericho, and there's an ambush against it and the walls are going to come down."

Jesse looked startled. "You said it was a fine city for work and you could—"

"Ssh," Will cautioned. "Don't sass Hannah when she's prophesying. She's not herself then. Sometimes she don't even remember what she says."

"And Joshua set the city on fire," Hannah said softly, staring out into the scarlet sunset. "And the flames shot up as far as the sky, and you could see them for miles around. Miles and miles."

The rain puddled on the well-waxed wood and dripped from the oiled lines and tightly furled canvas of *Canton Star*. "Call this a storm, do you?" Finbar O'Toole shouted, laughing up at the lowering sky. "You must be getting tired." His ship pitched and heaved in New York Harbor. O'Toole smiled broadly at the thought of what it must feel like below, with no fresh air to make it a bit easier to bear. Serves you right, you godrotting bastard.

Ostensibly, he was alone with the three men left aboard now that the ship had been unladed and moved away from the wharf to a mooring in the roads, amid the moldering sloops, schooners, and merchantmen imprisoned in the harbor by the blockade. Most of the crew had been given their wages and let go. But Blakeman had offered his captain an extra quarter percent of the profits of the sale—on top of the three percent that was his payment for the voyage—if he'd remain aboard and take charge of the ship and a few hands to tend her. A month or two, Blakeman said. Fair enough; there was no place on earth Finbar O'Toole was more comfortable than on a ship. And soon as he could get done what needed doing, there really would be only himself and the tars aboard.

O'Toole glanced toward the bow. Tammy Tompkins was on watch, huddled below a tarpaulin awning rigged in the forecastle. The other crewmen were sleeping off their dinners in hammocks on the berthing deck below. As good an opportunity as he'd have, O'Toole decided. He raised the hatch near the mizzenmast and started down the ladderway.

A merchantman was designed to be a seagoing warehouse; everything belowdecks that wasn't strictly necessary to keep her afloat was eliminated in favor of more room in the hold. *Canton Star* was a hundred feet long and pierced for twenty cannon. O'Toole had known he could barely handle three, even with his full crew of nineteen. He'd mounted half a dozen guns before they left China, three to use if he must and three in reserve—for when the bloody barrels burst in the heat o' battle, as they always did. But thank the Blessed Virgin and all the saints, he hadn't fired a shot. He knew when he agreed to captain *Star* and chance a run of the blockade that he couldn't outfight the poxing Royal Navy. His only hope was to sneak past her. And he had. A bit o' seamanship, yes, but mostly sheer poxing luck. Joyful had the notion he was some kind o' miracle worker; the lad had listened to too many fanciful stories at Morgan Turner's knee. Though from the sound of it, 'twas his cousin Andrew as told him the strangest. True enough about the treasure Captain Turner buried, but that Andrew, who'd never been aboard ship in his life, knew where it was when Morgan Turner himself had forgot—that was hard to credit.

The captain's cabin was in the stern, beautifully fitted in wood and brass, and spacious by shipboard standards. It was also one of the few places aboard with a lock on the inside of the door. O'Toole let himself in and shot the bolt. The light that entered through the rain-lashed single porthole was murky and gray, but enough for him to find a small lantern, strike a spark, and get it lit. He held the lantern high, looking at the section of oak-paneled wall that appeared exactly like all the rest, unless you knew exactly the place to press to reveal a small hiding place. That's where the poxed ebony box had been the entire journey. Bad joss, that box. He'd have refused to take it, refused to captain this ship or make this journey, if it hadn't been that doing so solved an enormous problem of his own.

O'Toole lifted the hatch in the corner opposite the secret wall locker and descended the steps that provided the only access to the stores kept below the orlop deck. During a voyage the reserves of rum were kept in that secure region below the captain's cabin. It was also the location of the aft powder magazine. The opening and the stairs themselves were broader than any other ladderway aboard because they had been built to allow for manhandling large kegs above decks.

The rum was finished, doled out in fair and proper rations over the nine weeks of the journey. As for the powder kegs, he'd taken aboard fewer than the magazine held, and far fewer than three cannon would have needed in an all-out battle, much less six. God alone knew what might have happened if that had been discovered. Crew would have hung him from the yardarm. But the only way they'd have known was if there was a battle, and in that case they'd all be dead or captured anyway, and the risk had to be taken. He'd needed space in the after magazine for his own special cargo.

There was a sour smell of fresh vomit. Despite all the dangers, the poxed buzzard was still alive. "*Nei ho ma,* how are you, you sodding Chinese bastard? As bad as you smell, I warrant." O'Toole used his foot to shove aside the false wall behind the empty powder kegs. "C'mon, you *tset-ha tset-ha.* Come out o'there. It's safe enough now."

Time was, when the Cantonese known as Thumbless Wu would have gone for a knife if anyone called him an ugly male stalk. Today he could barely pull himself out of the three-by-four-foot hole where he'd spent the entire crossing, released only in the dead of night when O'Toole thought it safe to let him stretch his cramped legs for an agonizing few minutes. In the first days Wu had spewed forth endless questions each time he saw the Irishman. After a week he'd been too ill to speak. Earlier, when they tied up at the wharf, he began to feel better, but now the storm had made it worse again. He could barely lift his head. Never mind. He was in America; his joss had held. Wu got shakily to his knees and loosed a steady stream of Cantonese curses. Just to prove to himself he was still alive. "*Diu lay lo mo hail! Leng gwai!*"

"Fuck your mother's hole as well, you poxed misery. Sweet Christ but you stink. Here, clean yourself up some." O'Toole pulled a damp rag from his pocket and watched Wu gratefully bury his face in it. The lantern created a shimmer of red-gold light—the hold was lined with copper to prevent a stray spark from setting off the gunpowder—and

O'Toole held it higher to get a better look at the man who'd caused him so much grief and extracted a payment he'd bitterly hated making. Wu's *sam,* a long cotton gown, was encrusted with the sweat and filth of the journey. His *fu,* the long, loose pants worn beneath the *sam,* were equally disgusting. Sweet Christ Jesus, what with his clothes, his long braided queue, and there probably being not another Chinese in New York City, what would happen to the bugger? Not his worry. Finbar O'Toole made a bargain and kept it, and that was him finished. "I'm taking you ashore. *To dei.* Land. New York City. *Nei ming baak ma?* You understand?"

Wu let loose another stream of Cantonese. Mostly curses, but threats as well. O'Toole leaned down so the man could see into his eyes. "Now you listen to me, you yellow bastard. And don't pretend you don't understand English because I know damned well that you do. I kept my word and I brought you here—though Almighty God alone knows why you wanted to come. But you're here and you're alive, which is the greatest amount of joss even a *ho choi* lucky bastard like you could have hoped for. And that's us finished. *Seung dang!* We're square. Paid off my ten thousand and I don't owe you one farthing more. Now keep your mouth shut and come with me, or you'll have to swim or drown."

The small, light boat known as the captain's gig was suspended aft, below the taffrail. O'Toole released it from the davits and quickly and quietly lowered the boat to the water. He glanced around. Tompkins was still in the bow, the two others yet asleep below. Best of all, the rain had stopped and the sky was streaked red with a fine sunset. He signaled and the stowaway crept forward, muttering fierce discontent when he saw he had to descend a rope ladder and get into another boat. O'Toole would have liked nothing better than to have been rid of him earlier when they were moored at the dock, but there were too many people around to chance it then. This was the best way. He helped Wu get a leg over the taffrail and begin his descent. Thumbless

Wu—he used to run the wealthiest and most luxurious gambling house in Canton, but O'Toole had never known him by any other name—used his first two fingers to grip the lines of the rope ladder. He'd always thought the bastard was amazing, even when he owed him most and hated him most. Wu used his forefingers as if they were the thumbs it was said he'd lost at the age of eight, as a result of a gambling debt with a Hakka pirate.

The Irishman turned and saw no one but the man on watch. "Ahoy, Tompkins!" he hailed. "I'm going ashore."

Tompkins turned and started for him. "Give you a hand, Captain?"

"Don't need it. Get back to your post."

This wasn't the navy and O'Toole had never enforced military rules, though he knew Tammy Tompkins had been a navy man before he fetched up in Canton. An insolent bastard nonetheless. He'd pushed too far a time or two and O'Toole had to give him extra watches, even dock his pay on occasion. Probably shouldn't have picked Tompkins as one of his remaining crew, but when it came to handling the lines, the man was as skilled as any tar aboard. When you were going to tend a ship this size with a crew of three, they had to be the best available. Besides, he liked the tar's whistling.

Tompkins raised a hand in compliance, turned around, and went back to his place in the bow, whistling "Old Zip Coon."

O'Toole climbed down to the gig. Thumbless Wu was already huddled in the stern, looking, if it were possible, still more miserable. "Do us a favor," O'Toole said as he picked up the oars. "If you're going to puke, do it over the side."

Chapter Six

THE PINEAPPLE FINIALS had been set atop posts either side of the gate in front of Bastard Devrey's residence in 1706 when it was built. The cobbled path that led to the graceful three-story red-brick house dated from the same period. Very little around the house was the same.

Will Devrey, Bastard's great-grandfather and the founder of Devrey Shipping, was a man of his time. He'd built his house a few steps from the East River docks and the Wall Street slave market that were the foundation of his fortune, installed his wife and children on the upper two floors, and conducted business at ground level. In those days the building across the road was the City Hall, later to be the seat of the American government and the place where George Washington was inaugurated the nation's first president. That venerable edifice had gone to ruin when Congress decamped first for Philadelphia, then for its present home on the drained swamp they called the Federal District. The city tore down the old Federal Building two years past, and the lot housed two brand-new countinghouses now. New Yorkers were short on sentiment when it came to property.

The old Court District for instance, on lower Broadway near Bowling Green. Once it had been the most fashionable part of the city. It was still a charming place to live, but it was surrounded by the clogged lanes and snaking streets of the narrow southern tip of the island. These days the great merchant princes had built themselves palaces in the far north of the town. Jacob Astor's mansion set the standard. It stood in rural splendor on Broadway between Barclay and Vesey streets, and his gardens backed up on Hudson's River. His countinghouse on Little Dock Street, on the other hand, was in the thick of the downtown pandemonium.

New Yorkers with a claim to elegance and social standing no longer lived on Wall Street. And these days only mechanics—craftsmen and shopkeepers and the like—lived above their businesses. Bastard no longer had his countinghouse on the ground floor, but the whole town knew that didn't satisfy his wife. The last time Bastard raised cash by selling scrip in Devrey Shipping, the purpose had been to build a Broadway mansion up near Astor's. Celinda Devrey had been a Clinton. She'd married a man presumed to be able to support her in style, but the war and Bastard's bad judgment conspired to deny her expectations. The Broadway house stood half built and empty, and likely to remain so given the morning's events.

Joyful had been planning this encounter for some time, and he knew he'd never have a better opportunity. Celinda must have given her husband a fair serving of grief with his Wall Street dinner this day. Bastard was as ripe as he'd ever be, a fruit ready to drop into Joyful's hand. All the same, he couldn't simply present himself at the door and wait for a servant to announce him. His cousin was unlikely to be receiving visitors this evening.

It was almost nine o'clock and the rain had stopped. Joyful turned left on the mossy cobbled path that circled the house and approached the set of long windows that spilled light into the shadowy garden. An oil lamp had been lit but the curtains left open. He could see a high-backed chair and a footstool, and a man's legs. Joyful reached for the handle of the casement. It turned easily and opened toward him. "Good evening, cousin."

Bastard did not turn around. "Who the hell are you?" His voice was thick with drink.

"Joyful Patrick Turner, your second cousin, I believe, once removed. At least that's as near as I can work it out."

"Got your hand blown off in this miserable war, didn't you? Not a hellish lot to be joyful about, is there? Go away. Devreys have no truck with Turners. It's tradition. And speaking personally, I care even less for heroes."

"Much as I expected. But I'm not going away just yet. Mind if I pour myself a drink?"

Bastard still had not turned around, but he waved a languid arm in compliance. "Help yourself. The Madeira's excellent but the sack isn't much better than piss. Cellar's gone to ruin in this war, along with everything else."

The simple furniture of New York cabinetmaker Duncan Phyfe was the fashion now. This room's style had the feeling of an earlier time; heavy, rococo pieces in the style of Chippendale. An elaborately carved mahogany table against one wall held a number of decanters. Joyful removed the glass stoppers and sniffed each in turn. When he'd identified the Madeira, he poured himself a generous tot. "Can I get you a refill, cousin?"

"Cheeky sort, aren't you, offering a man his own tipple in his own house."

"Not for long."

"What does that mean? Are you planning to be less cheeky sometime soon?"

"No. It means the house won't be yours for much longer. It will go on the block with all your other assets once Gornt Blakeman squeezes the last drop of life out of Devrey Shipping. As, I trust, you are well aware."

Silence for a few seconds, then, "Come over here, Joyful Patrick. So I can get a good look at you."

He did as he was asked, and took a good look in his turn. Bastard was sweating profusely, his face was bright scarlet, and his eyes were puffy with drink, maybe tears. He squinted up at Joyful, then leaned forward and squinted some more. "Truth, isn't it?"

"What?"

"That we're all redheads descended from Red Bess."

"My mother was also a redhead."

"The beautiful Roisin. Yes, so I heard. I remember now, you're a bastard as well. Christ, what a history."

Joyful shrugged. "My parents married soon after I was born, but it doesn't make any difference. We're not responsible for the past, Cousin. Only the present. And maybe the future."

"My future, as you so generously pointed out, is a bucket of steaming manure. The whole town has the stench in its nostrils. So why should I go on talking to you, Joyful Patrick? This house is still mine, whatever may happen next week or next month." He flailed an arm in the air. "Get the bloody hell out or I'll whip you out."

There was a horse whip hanging on the wall beside the fireplace. Joyful had no idea what it was doing there, and not much fear of Bastard carrying out his threat. "You're in no condition to do any such thing, and I'm not leaving quite yet. No, don't protest. Hear me out. It's in your best interest.

"What you want is to salvage as much as you can from this disaster. But you don't know how, so you're sitting here on what may well have been the worst day of your life drinking yourself into oblivion. And since I warrant tomorrow has worse in store, you'll likely be doing the same for some days to come. And sooner rather than later the sheriff will come to read you into bankruptcy. Then it will be too late."

"Too late for what?"

In spite of himself, Bastard was sobering up, Joyful noted. Give a man a genuine life-or-death choice, and even the fog of alcohol could lift. "Too late for me to help you wriggle out of the mess you're in."

"And how might you do that? Presuming I act before it's too late."

Joyful stretched out his foot and hooked another of the heavy mahogany armchairs closer to Bastard's. He sat down. "It's simple. First you give me a ship; a fast sloop such as the *Lisbetta* will serve very well. Then you make over to me a large part of Devrey Shipping."

A few seconds of silence, then Bastard made a sound between a snort and a chortle. "Well, no reason this family shouldn't finally produce a madman to go along with everything else. No, wait! The crazy old Jew Solomon DaSilva, he was your grandfather. A whoremaster turned gunrunner who nearly burned the city. That explains it. Now get out."

"Solomon set alight my father's privateer, the *Fanciful Maiden,* while she was lying in harbor. But the old reprobate had made a huge fortune for himself before the Huron captured him and tortured him into insanity. And yes, he was Morgan Turner's father and my grandfather. And my grandmother was Squaw DaSilva, who took over her husband's affairs and increased his wealth fourfold. They were a pair of business people as clever as this city's ever seen. My forebears are reasons for you to listen to me, Cousin, not send me away."

Bastard's glass was empty. He waved it in Joyful's direction. "Get me another. You're daft, but I'll listen as long as it takes me to drink it. Then you leave or be horsewhipped."

Joyful poured them both generous refills of the Madeira. "The plan is simple, and that's its greatest virtue. You make over forty-nine percent of Devrey Shipping to me, and keep eleven percent for yourself. That way there's only a small portion of the company can be taken to repay your debts. Whatever happens, the business is safe."

"Jesus God Almighty. You've balls of brass, I'll say that for you, Joyful Patrick Turner. Do you think I care more for the company than my own skin? You've old DaSilva's canniness, all right, and none of his brains. Worse, you've caused me to come sober." Bastard tossed back the drink Joyful had brought him, then lumbered out of the chair and headed for the decanter.

Joyful watched his cousin stagger back to his place beside the empty fireplace, clutching the supply of Madeira to his heart. "It's your skin I'm talking about," he said when Bastard was again settled. "Your life. Good Portuguese wine, not Spanish piss. A home up on Broadway, and—"

"Already have that. Started building it three years past. Before Madison's damned war."

"Yes, but you can't afford to finish it. I'm offering you the chance to change that and take back your rightful place in society."

"On eleven percent of a company whose ships are putrefying in harbor, and will remain so as long as the blockade's in place?"

"On eleven percent, plus a silent partner's interest in my forty-nine percent share. Together we can outvote Gornt Blakeman, but he won't know that until it's too late. It will be a private arrangement and remain so until we decide otherwise."

"You're a madman. What in all Hades do you know about the shipping business? Gornt Blakeman will chew you up and spit you out."

"No," Joyful said quietly, "he won't. You seem to forget, Cousin, that I was raised in Canton. Blakeman's made his fortune in coaching here. He knows nothing of the China trade."

"That's what I thought. As of today I know better. All New York knows better."

"Blakeman was fortunate in his choice of ship's captain who was contracted through a comprador. Gornt Blakeman gambled and won one toss. That doesn't make him a trader of Astor's skill. Or mine."

"You and John Jacob Astor in the same breath. Sweet Christ but you fancy yourself, Joyful Turner."

Joyful stretched out his long legs and crossed them at the ankles, a man prepared to sit awhile. "Allow me to tell you a story. Our cousin Andrew Turner taught me everything I know about surgery. He's a genius with a knife, as I'm sure you know, and when I had two hands, so was I. Not as good as Andrew, but definitely the next-best thing. The cutting trade's about making connections—knowing what will happen when your knife goes in, how to accomplish the task you've set yourself, and get out clean, without severing arteries you can't tie off, or cutting ligaments you never intended to touch. Trade's about connections as well. I speak Mandarin and Cantonese. Time was, I knew every hong merchant by name. These days their sons will have taken over, and I played with most of them when we were boys together. Gornt Blakeman is an outsider who had to hire an independent comprador to find a cargo and a captain for his ship. I will choose a comprador tied so tight to me he'll see my interests as his own. Canton works on loyalty and family ties. I can claim both. What can Gornt Blakeman match against that?"

Bastard took a swig of Madeira directly from the decanter and wiped his mouth with the back of his hand. "Money," he said, swallowing a soft belch. "And after tomorrow's sale he'll have considerably more. I warrant, Joyful Patrick Turner, that you don't have two coppers to rub together. Otherwise you'd have found other allies to help you come after me."

It was a belief that played into Joyful's plan. "Give me the sloop *Lisbetta* and I'll have a healthy stake. You and I, cousin, together we'll make a run on Blakeman's scrip, just as he did on yours."

"You're talking nonsense."

"I'm not. Besides, what other choice do you have?" Joyful reached into his pocket and withdrew a sheaf of papers. "I have the agreements right here. All you have to do is sign them."

Bastard said nothing. Joyful stood up and went to the writing table, where a quill and an inkpot waited. After a few moments Bastard joined him. There was one moment, holding the pen, when he thought of his son in Canton waiting for the war to end so he could come home, thought of the lad's expectations. Then he signed with a flourish. Expectations be damned. His as well as young Samuel's. The bird in the hand was the only possibility since, as far as he could see, there were none in the bush.

Maiden Lane, 9 P.M.

"Marry me."

"I cannot. Not yet."

"You love me. I know you do." Manon reached up and clasped her hands behind Joyful's head. "I can feel the love you have for me. Take me away now, this very night, and marry me."

"You have no shame," Joyful said. They were both whispering because they were standing in the shadows at the rear of the Vionne shop, not far from the door that led to the private part of the house, and Maurice Vionne and his special visitor were in a room above their heads. "I am in love with the most shameless female in New York."

"In all of these United States, more likely," Manon agreed happily. "Now kiss me." He did. "You burn with love for me," she said when the kiss ended. "And I for you. So why—"

"I have every intention of marrying you, Manon Vionne, and teaching you that you do not know everything you think you do. But not yet." Joyful used his one good hand to disengage her arms from round his neck and stepped away.

"My father intends to fob me off on a nephew of Pierre DeFane. He's a widower from Virginia, and he's looking for a wife. Papa will insist I marry him if you don't speak first."

"Manon, I—" He broke off.

"What? You've a secret, Joyful. I can see it in your eyes. Tell me."

"I can't, not yet." The agreements Bastard had signed were in the inside pocket of his cutaway, next to his heart; they felt like fire next to his skin, but they represented a paper claim on a nearly bankrupt company. From being ostensibly without resources he'd become a man with a mountain of debt. He might be the only man who could oppose Gornt Blakeman—for sheer volume of tonnage Devrey's had no rival—but there was yet nothing to brag about to Manon. "Later," he promised. "When I've sorted a few more things."

"But if—"

"Hush." Joyful put a finger over her lips. The sound of a scraping chair and footsteps could be heard in the room above their heads. "I must go. And as for this Virginian widower, I will take a scalpel to the most precious part of his anatomy if he so much as looks at you." He loved seeing her blush. It was one of the many things he loved about her, the pairing of boldness and innocence.

Manon went with him to the door. "I will see you tomorrow," she whispered. "In the usual place. And I'll tell you everything I've been able to find out."

She watched at the door while Joyful slipped into the street, then hurried back to the stool behind the counter. Moments later her father's visitor appeared. He wore a cloak over a ruffled shirt, satin breeches, and a broad-brimmed hat that shadowed his face, despite the fact that it was summer and such clothes were impractical, as well as long out of style.

He swept through the small shop, past the wooden counter and the glass cases displaying Papa's exquisite work. The pierced silver baskets, the intricate rococo cruet stands worked in gold, the candlesticks and coffee jugs in both precious metals—none of them appeared to catch his eye. Papa hurried behind him, then dashed ahead to open the door, bowing the man out. The visitor started to leave, then swiftly turned, his cloak flaring out around his knees, and stared straight at Manon.

She could not keep herself from staring back, at least for a moment. Papa's visitor was Gornt Blakeman, the man the whole town had been buzzing about since morning. Joyful told her he'd followed Blakeman to Maiden Lane and almost danced a jig with pleasure when, of all the shops he might have visited, he had entered the Vionne premises. "I thought he would, I told you so earlier today, but I couldn't be sure he'd choose your father."

"I was sure," she'd said. "If this Mr. Blakeman is as clever as you say, where else would he go but to the finest jewel merchant in the city?"

"Still, it was wonderful joss."

"Our joss," she said. "It's our fate to be together. How did you know he was coming to Maiden Lane?"

"I didn't. The captain of Blakeman's *Canton Star* is an old friend; he served with my father in the War for Independency. He told me he thought he'd carried a fortune in jewels to New York."

"If it's a fortune, Papa will not be able to buy them all. We are not rich, Joyful Turner. And you are entirely mistaken if you believe I cannot be a happy wife unless my husband has chests of gold."

"Nonetheless, chests of gold you shall have. But first you must help me discover exactly what Gornt Blakeman is discussing with your father."

That's when she had changed the subject by proposing to him. As she had done at least a dozen times in the last month.

Manon had not always been so forward. They had been meeting two or three times a week for half a year. The first encounter was in March, a chance meeting at an ironmonger's shop on Front Street. Then there was a second, also unplanned, in the Fly Market. And a few more after that. At first they kept up the pretense that they saw each other accidentally, but by the time Joyful stood beside her on the Battery on the Fourth of July holiday, listening to the reading of the Declaration of Independence that always marked the day, both knew they had contrived their coming together. The crush of the crowd allowed him to take her hand in the one of his that remained, and he'd held it for nearly five minutes. Soon after, he explained that he could not ask for her hand officially, much as he wanted to, because although he had prospects, he no longer had a secure way to earn a living. That was when Manon became the aggressor. She knew Joyful loved her the more for her eagerness, and she took it as a sign of that strength she had always looked for in a man and not found until now.

Papa's visitor was still staring at her. She scared back. Dear God, she would move heaven and earth to discover what Gornt Blakeman wanted with Papa if it would further Joyful's business interests and thus her chance to be his wife.

Blakeman broke the locked glance first. "Your daughter, goldsmith?"

"Indeed. A great comfort to me since her mother died."

Blakeman leaned over and whispered something Manon could not hear. Then the visitor left and Papa closed and locked the door behind him. "What a strange man," she said. "Whatever did he want with you?"

"Business. Nothing to concern you. I thought I heard someone else leave the shop. Had you a customer?"

He must be worried. Papa was always short with her when he was worried. "A gentleman, Papa. He saw the light on despite the lateness of the hour and came to ask about sapphires. I had to tell him we had none, though you were hoping for a shipment of jewels from Paris and Antwerp as soon as the blockade is lifted. That's correct, isn't it?"

"You know it's correct. Who was the gentleman? Perhaps I can interest him in pearls. I've two fine strands left."

"He did not give his name. But I don't think a pearl necklace would interest him. Definitely sapphires, or perhaps emeralds. Did your visitor have something like that to sell, Papa? I'm sure the gentleman will return sooner or later."

"And the blockade will lift sooner or later. And it will snow sooner or later. And it may rain diamonds sooner or later, but I don't think so. You should have made him consider pearls, Manon. Pearls are what we have."

Ann Street, 11 P.M.

Bridey had long since gone to bed, so Andrew Turner answered the bell himself. His heart sank when he saw the black man standing on his doorstep. He was tired, and getting too old for these midnight adventures. "Mother Zion needs me, I take it, Absalom."

"Yes, Dr. Turner, sir. Twice over. One be a man, the other a boy. His grandson."

"Have you stopped the bleeding?" Andrew pulled on his cutaway and reached for his hat as he spoke. His black leather satchel was always packed and ready and waiting by the door.

"Best I could with that turn-and-kit thing like you showed me."

"Tourniquet, Absalom. One word. Good for you. Let's go then. Mother Zion calls and we can but answer."

In most New York churches black worshipers had to sit in the Negro pews, the back row of the gallery. The Methodists, however, had condemned slavery and integrated their services in 1787, but that didn't mean that every member of their various congregations made nigras welcome. By 1801, with the blessing of the appropriate bishop, a number of New York's blacks formed themselves into the African Methodist Episcopal Zion Church. The congregation was called Mother Zion, and the members built their church where they lived, at the junction of Cross and Mott streets, in the section of the city known as Five Points.

The neighborhood got its name from the convergence of Orange, Cross, and Anthony streets, an intersection located over what had been the remains of the old Collect Pond. Time was when the Collect was the only source of sweet water on the island—nearly every well dug on Manhattan yielded a brackish, murky flow—but people said it gave off malevolent vapors that caused yellowing fever. Andrew argued against the theory, but his was a single voice. In 1802 the city fathers filled in the last of the Collect Pond with what they called "good wholesome earth." That left the town at the mercy of a privately owned waterworks, the Manhattan Company, a nest of profiteering vipers who brought shiploads of water from other parts of the state, but laid hollow logs rather than proper pipes and refused to supply water to flush the gutters or clean the markets. Meanwhile epidemics of yellowing fever continued with terrifying regularity, and nothing was done with the broad gutter that had been dug to allow the Collect's overflow access to Hudson's River.

Officially known as Walker Street, the path the gutter traveled became the northern edge of Five Points and was called Canal Street by most New Yorkers. It was a cobbled road running either side of a grass-banked ditch, and for most of the year a small stream of water still trickled through on its way west. People living nearby tossed their garbage into the Canal Street gutter, or dug cesspools that seeped effluent into it. As a result, on a hot night like this one, the ditch sent up a stench that drifted, miasmalike, over all of Five Points.

The horse pulling Absalom's wagon knew the way by itself. The young man kept a loose hold on the reins, and the horse trotted through the star-shaped intersection called Paradise Square though it was no vision of paradise to which Andrew subscribed. The clatter of the wagon's iron wheels on the cobbles cleared a path for them through the crowd of people. Looking for a breath of fresh air, no doubt, and finding instead the stink of Canal Street. Still, it was better than the hovels they called home.

Speculators had bought the little wooden houses of the tanners and free blacks who once lived in the area and strung them together to form boardinghouses for wage earners who couldn't afford better. Built on the swampy land around the old pond, most had started to sag and now hung like brooding hags over twisting alleys and lanes partially paved with broken bricks. Blacks—many free, the rest claiming to be so—lived in the basements. Above them lived the Irish immigrants who had been flooding the city since the 1790s. It was a combustible mix but profitable. The landlords included the mayor and most of the city fathers, but no one made any effort to limit the number of tenants who could crowd into a single room. In Five Points the residents made their own law; still, the district wasn't as dangerous as people said. That was a fiction promulgated by wealthy whites who despised the blacks and the Irish equally, even as they lived off their labor.

Andrew had come for the first time a decade earlier, when these lanes were already crowded but less rowdy. He'd been treating a patient on Chambers Street, and when he left the house, a black man was waiting for him. "Be a blessing o' God if you be coming with me for just a bit o' time, Dr. Turner. Cissy Fish, she be needing you real bad."

Andrew was accustomed to being recognized, and to the fact that the city's poorest knew he never turned them away. He followed the man and was led to the basement of a church he later learned was Mother Zion.

The woman called Cissy Fish had fallen into a cesspool and been attacked by rats. Her face was pretty much eaten away, along with both her hands and one foot. Andrew knew at once that she was so thoroughly poisoned that no matter how carefully he cleaned up the wounds they would turn black and fester. She'd die in agony within a few days and there was nothing he could do to stop it, but she was pregnant, close to term, judging from the size of her, and when he put his ear to her stomach, he heard the child's heart, strong and steady. He didn't waste time talking about the options, simply grabbed a scalpel and cut the child out of her, allowing the shock and the rapid blood loss to make a quick and merciful end to the mother's life. The baby was a little girl; she lived, and her father, Zachary Fish, Zion's minister, named the child Andrewena for the man who had saved her life. Since then, whenever his scalpel might be useful to a member of the black community in Five Points, someone would appear on Ann Street and bring Dr. Turner to the cellar of Mother Zion. Never the sanctuary.

The entrance was low enough so he had to stoop to get in, half hidden on the church's Mott Street side, and this night guarded by two burly black men he'd never seen. One swung open the door and Andrew stepped inside. A couple of lanterns made a splash of light in the corner where his patients, a man and a young boy, lay side by side on the floor. Zachary Fish stepped out of the shadows to greet him. "You're a welcome sight, Dr. Turner. Thank you for coming."

Andrew grunted a reply and dropped to his knees beside his patient. Not as easy to do these days. He winced, then forgot his discomfort when he examined the unconscious boy. Someone, Absalom perhaps, had covered him with a horse blanket. It was soaked in blood. Andrew peeled it back. A wad of bandages had been wedged in the boy's groin. They were as bloody as the blanket. Andrew lifted them.

Absalom had come to kneel beside him. "Be no way I could get a turn-and-kit on that, Dr. Turner. Leastwise, none I could see."

"Jesus God Almighty . . . No way, Absalom. You did everything you could." Andrew put his hand on the boy's heart. Much too fast, and thready. He was in shock, and barely alive. But he was young and strong, and the wound had clotted over before he bled to death. Might be he'd live, but doubtful that he'd give thanks for that dubious blessing. His testicles and penis had been removed.

The older patient, the boy's grandfather, had lost the bottom half of his left leg. It had been roughly chopped off just below the knee. The tourniquet had stopped the bleeding and the man was awake, staring up at Andrew. "How be my grandboy?"

"As well as he can be. He's strong. He'll fight to live."

The man looked to be somewhere around fifty. He had the ebony skin that marked him as a pure African black, probably from the Sugar Islands. Quite possibly an escaped slave. "Blackbirders?" Andrew asked.

Blackbirders were slave-catching gangs. Many of the members came from right here in Five Points, impoverished Irishmen who'd been recruited to look for runaway slaves they could haul back to their owners. The ringleaders, who generally lived elsewhere, paid the birders half the bounty and kept the rest. The Irish put up with this arrangement not because they were fools, but because it required the cooperation of a magistrate to certify that the nigra in question was indeed a runaway slave. Like most city officials, the magistrates were Protestants. They had, if possible, less use for Catholic Irish than for blacks.

The man didn't reply to the question; he was watching Andrew prepare his saws and scalpels. Better to give him something else to think about. "I take it this was the work of birders?" Andrew repeated.

"Not exactly."

"What's that supposed to mean? They did it or they didn't."

The wounded man turned his face to the wall. Reverend Fish spoke for him. "Weren't the birders this time, Dr. Turner. It were the man as organizes a goodly number of them. Francis Xavier Gallagher. F.X. Has a butcher shop on the Bowery, but he comes often enough to Five Points."

"Too often by the look of it. A butcher . . . I warrant he did this with a cleaver."

"Aye," Absalom said softly. "Not the boy, though. F.X. be using a carving knife on the boy."

Andrew continued preparing his instruments and attempted to keep his tone neutral. "You were there?" He did not pretend to understand the intricate loyalties and alliances that made life possible in this place.

"No, sir. F.X. and his leather-apron boys be over on Orange Street. Place they always meet. I be looking in the window."

Leather-aprons were butchers' helpers. They took their name from the ankle-length leather covering they wore to protect them from the blood of their trade. Other blood as well, from the sound of it. "Nothing you could do, Absalom?"

"Nothing at all, Dr. Turner. Too many leather-aprons with F.X. Only thing I could do be to watch, and make sure we could bring our folks back here to Mother Zion when the leather-aprons be done."

"I understand," Andrew said. He had been searching for a particular needle. He found it, and a length of catgut. He'd tend to the boy first; sew up what was left of his scrotum, being careful to leave a hole for the urethra. "We'll clean up the wounds and do some stitching." Jesus God Almighty, he sounded positively cheerful, but there was no point in letting on that however many times he thought he'd seen the worst, something like this could make the bile rise in his throat and required every ounce of self-control to prevent him retching. "May well be that both your patients will survive, Absalom."

"I be surviving." It was the grandfather. His voice was soft and weak, but his words were not. "I be definite to survive. But F. X. Gallagher . . . It not be so definite about him."

Half an hour later Andrew was done. He and Zachary Fish drove out of Five Points in the old trap. The soft clop of the horse's hooves on the mostly dirt streets between this northerly neighborhood and Andrew's comfortable home on Ann Street to the south made the only sound in the nearly midnight dark. The heat was only slightly less formidable than that of midday, and the air was still thick and full of moisture. For a time neither man spoke, both enjoying the slight breeze caused by the movement of the wagon. After a while Andrew asked about his namesake.

"Andrewena be fine," Fish said. "She'll be sorry she missed you, but I believe a ten-year-old should be abed at such an hour." He sighed. "Though I warrant it won't be more than a few years and she'll be thinking of marrying and setting up on her own."

"Indeed." They married young in Five Points, and bred until such time as either the breeding or something more lethal killed them. "Greet her for me."

"I be doing that, Dr. Turner."

The two men had exhausted the only bit of ordinary life they had in common. More silence, until Zachary Fish said, "There be something else." His voice was a soft sound in the night.

"Yes, Reverend?"

"I hesitate to mention it because I don't be exactly sure . . ."

"Not being sure is a condition of existence, Reverend Fish. We have to act anyway."

"Yes, I believe that be a fair statement. That conversation we had some months past, Dr. Turner . . ."

"Last year, I believe. Something about a regiment being raised from here in the Five Points."

In the starlight Andrew could see Fish's nodding head. "You remember I told you it be a Connecticut man seemed to be doing the organizing?"

"I do. Someone you've never seen, you said. And you didn't think he was acting for our government."

"That be right. Didn't think so then and don't think so now. All his activity was with the whites, so I don't be likely to have any particular confidences. Thing is . . . lately seems there have been suggestions made to my people. No one will admit it straight out, but I do hear things."

"Signing up volunteers for the Committees of Defense," Andrew offered. "The city's awash with men prepared to defend her if the British invade."

Fish looked straight ahead and kept his loose hold on the reins. "Not defense of New York City, no sir, Dr. Turner. They don't be signing we coloreds up for that."

"I see. So you think this man from Connecticut is perhaps acting for the enemy?" During the Revolution the British had offered any black who would fight for the king his freedom when the war was won. No surprise that plenty had taken them up on it, but those Negroes who survived the fighting had mostly gone to Canada. Like Cuf, the mulatto that Squaw DaSilva had raised alongside Morgan. Cuf fought beside Morgan and Andrew with Washington for the cause of independency, but in the end they'd made no place for him in their new republic. The way Andrew heard it, Cuf went to Nova Scotia after the war. "The redcoats up to their old tricks?"

"No," Reverend Fish said. "I don't think it be the British as are trying to enlist my people in their cause this time. Nor the man from Connecticut who be here last year. I believe the recruiters to be working for someone right here in New York. I'm still trying to learn his name. That's why I haven't yet brought you the information. But seeing as you're here . . ."

"I'm grateful, Reverend. And if you find out any more—"

"I'll let you know, Dr. Turner. I promise."

The East River on the Brooklyn Side, Midnight

The schooner was called *Le Carcajou*—the Wolverine—and her figurehead was a carving of the beast, mouth agape and fangs bared, claws ready to strike. She slipped silently up the inlet on the flood tide, flying only the mainsails of her two masts. Rigged thus, she was maneuverable but not fast. Silence and stealth mattered, not speed. *Le Carcajou* had made this voyage under various flags. At the moment she flew none.

Gornt Blakeman stood on the rocky beach below the cliffs that sheltered the cove and waited until the vessel dropped anchor. Then he lit the lantern he carried and waved it right to left four times. As soon as he'd done that, he extinguished the flame. A few minutes passed. Blakeman heard the soft splash of a dinghy being lowered, then the rhythmic sound of oars cutting through the water. "*Bon soir, mon ami,*" a voice called out. "You have not, I hope, waited long."

"Lower your voice. And I've been here five godrotting nights in a row. I was beginning to think you weren't coming."

The man rowing the dinghy beached it, got out, and waded to the shore, tugging his small craft behind him. "*Alors, ça suffit,* there is a tide here, *bien sur.* But not one that comes this high. At least I don't think so. What is your opinion, *mon ami?*"

"I have none. I don't know a damned thing about boats and water."

"Exactly. So you will keep a civil tongue in your head when you address a seaman who has run a blockade from Nouveau Orléans to here. A thousand miles at least, and His poxed Majesty's poxed Royal Navy on the prowl for most of it. Not the easiest of voyages, monsieur. It will, I hope, be worth the while of myself and my companions."

The moon had set, but there was enough starlight for Blakeman to see the man wore a shabby jacket and breeches, and an eye patch as well as a bandanna tied around his head. Christ, the costume wanted only a parrot on the shoulder. "Don't try to disguise your profession, do you?" And before the pirate could answer, "And I know another who ran the blockade for six times the distance. And brought me a fortune in silks and porcelains in the bargain. So what did you bring, Monsieur Tintin?"

"Congratulations, *mon ami.* I take it the ship you spoke of, the one from Canton, has arrived. You will see a fine profit, I'm sure." And never mind that it's a damned sight easier to run a blockade on the high seas than along the coast. I am not here to see who can piss the furthest, Monsieur Blakeman. "Now, we have much to discuss, have we not?"

"You have the agreement of Lafitte and the others?"

Tintin shrugged. "Jean Lafitte is many miles distant, monsieur. I am here."

Friday, August 19, 1814

Chapter Seven

THE DANCING KNAVE was crowded in fair weather and foul. This hot and squally summer night was no different. Men filled the large room where the smell of tobacco mingled with that of rum, and the soft clack of the gaming counters didn't quite drown out the sweet voice of a young woman accompanying herself on the hammer dulcimer. "Young maidens beware at the Pilgrim Street Fair . . ." Not to worry. There were few women in the gaming salon, and quite probably no maidens.

Men were gathered at various tables, some playing at cards, some at dominoes, others at dice. Occasionally, one would gather up his winnings or shrug off his losses and make his way to the adjacent room known as the Ladies' Parlor—each "lady" young and charming and beautifully gowned, and smelling of Hungary Water or Devrey's Elixir of Violets. They amused themselves with cards and dominoes (no dice, they were inappropriate for ladies), and there was no sense of that fevered intensity that prevailed across the wide entry hall. In the Ladies' Parlor a harpist strummed softly in one corner, interrupted by the occasional tinkle of feminine laughter. Neither tobacco nor rum were permitted. Instead small glasses of Madeira were available, or tea in capacious porcelain cups and coffee in others half the size. The air of gentility was further served by the fact that everyone pretended not to notice when a man tapped a bared shoulder, or perhaps simply nodded, the chosen woman rose, and the pair disappeared up the stairs.

The Dancing Knave had six small but tastefully furnished working bedrooms on the second floor. Each had a heavy velvet curtain in front of the door and equally thick curtains at the window. It was occasionally possible to hear moans, shrieks, the rhythmic bouncing of a bed, or the sound of slaps on bare flesh as a gentleman indulged his taste for spanking or being spanked—but it was all muffled. The Knave's ladies were a world apart from the four-copper hot-pocket girls of Canvastown, or the tuppenny Mollie O'Hannigans of Five Points, or the even cheaper prostitutes who walked the streets of the notorious Corlear's Hook to the south, offering to lift their skirts right there in the open. The Dancing Knave was not unique; there were discreet parlor houses in other reputable sections of the town. But none could approach the elegant ambience of this pleasure palace that stood alone well north of the populous city.

When the British took Nieuw Amsterdam from the Dutch in 1664, the thickly settled part of the town ended at Wall Street, while the Voorstadt—the out-city where the storehouses and the farms could be found—extended a half mile to the north. The rest of Manhattan was wilderness. When the colonies declared independence 112 years later, New York City had spread as far as Canal Street. In the chaos of 1776, Tories who still swore loyalty to the king fled with only such goods as they could pack. Among them were the heirs to the large De Lancey estate, a country house built by a former governor of the province. His land began at Canal Street and extended north to Kips Bay, two miles further up the shore.

Few Tories had been more hated than the De Lanceys. One of the first acts of the postwar Common Council was to put their property on the block. Most of it was bought by a group of businessmen who named themselves the Delancey Street Consortium, dropping the French spelling and pronunciation. The consortium planned grand private houses and dignified squares for their newly acquired holdings, a neighborhood for the best of New York society, but the idea gave way first to internal squabbling then to war. In 1812, when the woman calling herself Delight Higgins arrived from Canada, she was able to buy three of the newly mapped but undeveloped lots on Rivington Street for just under seven hundred dollars, or a little less than two hundred and seventy-five English pounds. In the panicked atmosphere that accompanied the declaration of war, none of the sellers had bothered to ask where a woman like Delight—not long since run out of York as a whore, and worse, a mulatto bitch who did not know her station—would come by such a sum in cash money.

In fact, the purchase took every last penny Delight Higgins had managed to bring with her in the form of gold coins stitched into the hem of her frock and the lining of a canvas satchel. Nonetheless, a glorious house was built to her exact specifications. When it was finished the rooms on the ground floor were paneled in luxurious mahogany, with fittings of finest brass, and the most talented joiner in New York had been called in to create a hidden balcony, a small and secret aerie from which it was possible to observe everything happening on the gaming floor. The hawk's nest, Delight and the man who had financed the building of the house and become her silent partner called it, and it was so cleverly concealed high in one corner of the main salon that it was all but unnoticeable.

There was no access to the nest from the gaming floor. The narrow set of stairs that led to the balcony was concealed in a passage between the aerie itself and Delight's private third-floor rooms. "My hawk flies only between my bed and his perch," she'd said when she first showed her partner the arrangement. Back then he'd been satisfied, but lately both his plans and his desires had expanded well beyond the Knave. Delight suspected as much, though she pretended not to care.

"A good night," she said when she joined him, slipping silently into the small space in a shimmer of dark red silk and a heady wave of scent, the silver pendants at her ears sparkling in the dimness. "I'm glad you didn't let the rain keep you away."

"I've long since learned I don't melt." He spoke softly, cautious even though the men below were intent on their gambling.

"Not even for me?"

"Ah, that's different," he said. "I always melt for you."

No, not always. Less and less often these days. But she wouldn't say so.

The balcony was barely big enough for two. Delight turned and pressed herself to him. His arms circled her waist from behind. Nestled together in that manner they could both look down on the gaming floor. After a moment she lifted his right hand and placed it on her breast, just to the side of the diamond brooch pinned in the cleft. "This kind of weather is always good for business," she whispered. "See how generous the gentlemen are being?" A percentage of every wager belonged to the house. Good hard coin, Delight knew, was frequently the most effective aphrodisiac.

"From the look of it, tonight they're not all gentlemen."

"You mean Tintin?" she asked, conscious that his hand was still where she had placed it, but he had initiated no further caress.

"The fellow with the eye patch and the bandanna," he said.

"Tintin," she repeated, pressing her hips closer to his. "At least that's the name he gave." Ah, better. She could feel Adam rising, and the hawk's thumb had begun to circle her taut nipple. "Forget his looks," she said. "He had coin, not paper. Enough to make him a gentleman in my eyes."

"Fair enough," he whispered directly into her ear. "But five coppers will get you ten he's a pirate."

"Tonight he's a fine New York gentleman. The kind I like best; he's been losing for an hour." She moved her buttocks against his groin. "And look who's playing with him."

"Finbar O'Toole. The hero of the hour because he brought *Canton Star* to port."

"Indeed. So it's as I promised. The brave captain hasn't been in New York for twenty-four hours and, like everyone who matters, he comes to the Dancing Knave."

"Exactly as you promised," he agreed, not bothering to add that he had never required much convincing; the club always seemed a likely investment. The loan had been paid back long since, and every week he collected four percent of the Knave's profits. They had each kept to the exact terms of their agreement. Becoming her lover was something apart from business. Still, there was a special excitement to taking her like this up in the aerie, with the sound of the gambling continuing below. She'd permitted it only twice before, but he had the feeling she might do so again tonight.

As usual, she read his mood. "I shouldn't go far from the gaming floor on such a busy night," she whispered, turning in his arms meanwhile. "So what do you think we should do?"

He answered by pressing her hard against the wall, pushing up the skirt of her gown, feeling the red silk slide seductively over her long thighs and narrow hips. Nothing else was required but that he loose himself. Delight was in every detail dressed like a lady. Her pantaloons were the sort worn by the town's most elegant and respectable women, without a crotch, in the interests of health and sanitation.

Only a few of the substantial number of coins the man who called himself Tintin had brought with him remained on his side of the table. The rest had been shoved across to Finbar O'Toole. It was, however, once more the pirate's turn. *Eh bien.* Tintin knew as well as any man alive that everything in life could change on a single throw. He picked up the leather cup, shook it vigorously, then let the dice roll across the green baize surface. Three of the four lamps in the chandelier above his head had burned out. A servant had hurried over to replenish the oil and light them again, but Tintin had waved the man away. Now the single lamp yet lit cast just enough light for him to see that he had thrown a pair of ones, the lowest possible score. "*Merde! Tous les saints* bear witness! I will give a silver chalice to the Church of *Saint Sépulcre* if my luck changes."

"And who might that saint be?" O'Toole had been fortune's darling for the past hour. Coins were piled in front of him. He scooped the dice back into the leather cup, clapped his palm across the top, then began the up-and-down jiggle that had preceded each of the session's winning throws.

Tintin took the pipe from his mouth. "You are all heretics here in New York. It is the holy Church of the Holy Sepulcher in the Holy Land. Where the Holy Savior was laid in the tomb after the bastard Jews crucified him. Only a Protestant would not know such a thing."

O'Toole continued moving the dice cup up and down. Slowly. Still not ready to throw. "Careful who you're calling a Protestant. The name's Finbar O'Toole, born in County Galway and baptized in the True Faith before my first taste o' mother's milk. And have you been to see this Holy Sepulcher Church in the Holy Land?"

"Course not, how would I get there? *Jetez les dés!* Throw the dice. You win again, of course. But not until you throw."

"And if you've not been to the Holy Land, and don't know how you'd get there, how is it you'll be giving this chalice to this church where Our Lord was three days in the tomb? If your luck changes, o' course."

Tintin was halfway across the table before the last word was spoken, holding O'Toole's shirt in a bunched knot beneath his neck, his face only inches from the Irishman's. "You accuse me of breaking a vow? You will die, man from Galway."

The Irishman didn't struggle against Tintin's grip. "Aye, no doubt I will. But not tonight, you pirate toad." O'Toole's right hand came up and hovered close to the other man's neck. It held a knife. "Let go of me or your blood will be all over Delight Higgins's table."

"Delight doesn't tolerate fights on her premises, gentlemen. You are both newcomers here, but I assure you, the rule is strictly enforced."

The woman's voice was low and melodious, but it hinted of iron in its sheath of silk. "If you want to fight, you go outside. Let him go Mr. Tintin. And you—Captain O'Toole, is it not? The man who brought *Canton Star* to safe harbor this very day? Welcome to the Dancing Knave, Captain." Delight nodded to the chucker-out standing just behind her. "I assure you, Mr. Clifford's bullwhip is not meant for decoration. Give him the knife, Captain. He'll give it back when you leave."

O'Toole couldn't turn his head, but he could see the huge man standing behind Delight Higgins. Sweet Savior and all the saints, it was the man as had come to the dock to collect Gornt Blakeman's ebony chest. This time the long leather thong hung free, ready to snap. And Vinegar Clifford wasn't wearing a proper cutaway and a stovepipe as he had that afternoon; a black singlet and leggings showed every bulging muscle.

"Mr. Clifford, help the gentleman in the eye patch to sit down. Then take Captain O'Toole's knife out back to be sharpened and shined."

Clifford put his bearlike hand on Tintin's shoulder. The Frenchman shoved it away, but at the same time he released his hold on O'-Toole's shirt and sat down.

"Excellent," Delight said. "Now, the captain's knife, if you please, Mr. Clifford."

The whipper took a step forward. O'Toole handed over the knife.

"Thank you," Delight said. "I truly appreciate your cooperation, gentlemen."

A crowd had gathered when it seemed there would be blood spilled. They were openly disappointed.

O'Toole still held the dice cup. Delight took it out of his hand, at the same time leaning forward so her breasts were inches from the Irishman's face.

He swallowed an excess of spit. God Almighty, make any man's mouth water she would. Her tits were practically under his nose, magnificent, and the color of golden honey.

"A wager, gentleman," she said. "To add spice to the evening's entertainment. Everything on the table against this." She unclasped her diamond brooch and laid it between the few coins scattered on the Frenchman's side of the table and the coins in tall stacks in front of Finbar O'Toole. The grumbling voices of the customers surrounding them quieted and faded away. She had everyone's attention now. "One throw each, my friends. Highest roll takes it all."

"Fine for you and me," O'Toole said. "This one," he nodded toward Tintin, "doesn't have a big enough stake to make the wager credible."

A man stepped out of the crowd. O'Toole blinked. Holy Virgin and all the saints. "If the gentleman will permit, I'll stake him." Gornt Blakeman flipped a gold ten-dollar piece onto the table in front of Tintin. "You agree, sir?"

Tintin glanced at the coin, then turned his single eye toward Blakeman. "To what? This is not much of a stake, monsieur."

"It will stand for a thousand. I've an auction to take place tomorrow on Pearl Street worth many times that, as most of the town knows. If you happen to have missed that local gossip, I assure you Captain O'Toole here can warrant it's true. He brought my ship to harbor." Blakeman looked at the Irishman for confirmation.

O'Toole hesitated. Blakeman and Tintin might be strangers, and then again, they might not. Could be they were somehow in league against him. Why else would Gornt Blakeman be involved? At the moment he had less need than most of Delight Higgins's diamond brooch. The thrill of the wager then? Didn't Finbar O'Toole understand that! Still, it didn't seem to fit Blakeman's character.

"No question about it," he said, giving in to the need in his belly, the lure of the gamble. "After tomorrow Mr. Blakeman can back his wager with cash money."

"*Eh bien,*" Tintin said, leaning back, tapping the stem of the pipe against his yellowed teeth, his good eye staring straight at the other man, and nothing to be read in it but the calculation of the moment. This wager linked the three of them, Blakeman and the Irisher and himself. And the half-breed bitch. He'd seen hundreds of her sort on the block in the caves where he and Lafitte and the others divided their plunder and sold the live treasure for which they had no use. Hands tied behind their backs, stripped naked, waiting to see who would buy them and how they were to be used. Would she look so proud then? *Certainement non.* But it was Blakeman who was to be dealt with now. Perhaps the bitch would come later. "And if we win, monsieur? *Maintenant,* now, you stake ten dollars and I have not much, but at least four times that."

"If we win," Blakeman said easily, "I add my thousand to the pot, and you and I split equally."

"And if we lose?"

"We lose."

Tintin nodded. "*D'accord, monsieur.* I agree. But I roll the dice."

"I've no quarrel with that." Blakeman took a step back, into the shadows, away from the glow of the single lamp overhead.

Delight went first. She rolled a four and a three. There were loud calls of approval from the onlookers.

Finbar O'Toole rolled a one and a two. His jaw went rigid, but he said nothing.

Tintin dropped the dice into the leather cup, shook them, murmured a curse and a blessing, then spilled the dice onto the table. A five and a two.

"A tie!" Delight said. "We two must roll again." She sounded genuinely pleased, as if entertaining her customers, all now whooping and cheering, was more important than winning the bet. She picked up the dice, shook them, and rolled two fives.

Tintin fixed her with his one eye and leaned forward to claim the cup. "*Alors, mademoiselle, comme vous dites, vous et moi . . .*" He scooped the dice into the receptacle, shook it briefly, and tipped it over. Only a pair of sixes or a six and a five would see him the winner. He threw a three and a four.

The crowd exploded in hoots and whistles. Delight wore a silk drawstring bag around her wrist and she loosed it and held it open. Finbar O'Toole pushed the coins inside. Delight picked up the brooch: three leaves and a stem, studded with diamonds and a few tiny pearls.

"No flower," the hawk had said when he gave it to her to mark the first anniversary of their bargain. "Your beauty supplies that."

She turned to Blakeman. "Will you fasten this in place for me?"

Their eyes met and held for a moment. He smiled and slipped his finger between her breasts to safely fix the jewel to the red silk. "My pleasure, Miss Higgins."

"No, Mr. Blakeman, the pleasure is mine. Shall I come tomorrow to Pearl Street to claim my thousand, or will you bring it here?"

"I'll bring it to you personally," he promised. "Tomorrow evening." Then he turned and very deliberately stared up at the aerie.

Still in the hawk's nest, Joyful was convinced he couldn't be seen from where Gornt Blakeman stood. But the nature of that upward glance had made it a safe wager the other man knew he was there.

"Not you, necessarily," Delight said. "Blakeman guessed that the balcony was there, a place from which someone could observe the gaming. It's not an unusual feature in clubs such as this."

"Possibly," Joyful said. "But I think we should be very aware of Mr. Blakeman." It was past three in the morning, and they were in her bedroom. The Dancing Knave was closed, the ladies slept alone in the second-floor rooms, Vinegar Clifford was in the bed that every night was trundled into place by the locked and barred front door, his whip at his side. Delight was eyeing her own bed with longing. Seated at her dressing table, she could see it reflected in the mirror, Joyful stretched on top of the counterpane, still fully dressed. "You're not tired?" It wasn't the question she wanted to ask—*Will you stay the night?*—but it was the only one she permitted herself. She was a fool. She should never have given in to him in the nest. Having eaten his fill, he was no longer hungry.

"A bit tired," he said. "But I think I'd best sleep on Greenwich Street tonight. I've business in the Fly Market tomorrow. I wouldn't want to be late."

The previous autumn, when he'd quarreled with his cousin Andrew and moved from Ann Street, Joyful had rented a room at Ma Allard's boardinghouse. At first he slept there only one or two nights a week—a respectable cover, he called it. During the past three months she could count on one hand the times she had wakened in the morning to find him beside her.

"Why the Fly Market? Is your new profession to be a butcher?" she asked. "Or a fishmonger perhaps?"

"Business," he said curtly.

"As you wish." Her tone revealed nothing of her anguish, or the fact that every time she looked at him she saw him as she had in that astonishing moment when he leaned out of the shay to sweep her to safety.

She'd not been sure he was real until he reached down and plucked her out of the street, the shay still thundering ahead, and Delight feeling that she might fall and be crushed beneath its wheels. Her bonnet had fallen off and her hair tumbled free—as it did now when she removed the pins that held it in place all evening—but miraculously she'd managed to hang onto her canvas valise.

"Look," he'd said when they had cleared Canvastown, "if you've no place to stay, we can try to find you a boardinghouse. I know a landlady or two who might not mind being wakened at this hour for the chance to rent a room."

They were on Broadway by then, at Wall Street, passing by Trinity Church, where every Sunday upright Christian gentleman who made money from the brothels and bawdy houses six days a week nodded in agreement when the preacher railed against them on the seventh. She'd put her hand on his arm, so he had to turn and look straight at her, see her clearly in the glow of the streetlights. "And will one of these obliging landladies be likely to rent a room to me?"

Joyful's friend Barnaby Carter had made a sound that was something between a snort and a sigh. Joyful held back for a moment, then admitted, "In this part of town, probably not."

"That's what I presumed. It's why I was where you found me."

She remembered the silence between them, the beating of her

heart, and the sound of the horse's hooves clattering over the cobbles. Joyful spoke: "My name is Joyful Patrick Turner, I'm a ship's surgeon. My friend Barnaby Carter has a warehouse on Pearl Street. It would do at least until morning." And when Barnaby protested, Joyful said, "We can't leave her on the street," overruling everyone else in that way she would come to know so well.

He took her the first time right there in Barnaby Carter's warehouse, in the same shay in which he'd ridden out of her dreams and into her life. Barnaby went upstairs to his wife, and Delight turned to Joyful and offered her mouth and he took it, and everything else beside. Quick the first time, slower and better the two times after. "What an extraordinary woman you are," he whispered when the morning light seeped in under the big doors, reminding them the world remained to be dealt with.

Tell him, a voice in her head had whispered. Tell him how you used to busy yourself doing chores in Clare Devrey's kitchen whenever he was there, come to visit the sister born twenty-two years before he was, whom he was just getting to know in that first month back in New York after Canton. Tell him how it was back when you were little Laniah stoning the hearth, or scrubbing the pots, listening to him talk about how he'd come home to be a doctor. Dashing out to get more coal or a few logs, and rushing back praying he hadn't left in the meantime, just so's you could go on breathing the same air he did. Tell him how not a day has passed since you ran away with his niece Molly that you haven't dreamed of him. The words wouldn't come.

They still hadn't come. Not from that day to this.

Joyful got off the bed and came to stand behind her, putting a gentle hand on her shoulder, as if he were remembering too. She fussed with the stud of her left earring, meeting his glance in the mirror. "Delight . . . My dear, listen to me."

"I am listening. But this earring has become troublesome." Time was when she'd have asked him to loose the stud for her. Out of the question now. For months she'd told herself it was because of Joyful's need to adjust to life with only one hand, to find a replacement for the surgery that had once been his passion, that he had seemed to cool toward her. She could fool herself no longer. Damn him to hell, she didn't want to. "I've been thinking about the night you rescued me."

"It was a good night. I'll always remember it that way."

Her heart plunged at the goodbye in the words. "Oh my, what am I thinking of!" The words rushed out of her, sounds meant to turn back the tide. "It's so late and I'm so tired. Go on back to Greenwich Street, Joyful. We can talk tomorrow." She was unable to keep the shiver from her voice, and hated herself for the weakness. "You're coming tomorrow, aren't you?"

"Perhaps. I'm not sure. Delight, listen . . ."

She turned to face him. "Very well. Speak your piece." At least four times in the last month she'd been sure he meant to say it was over between them, and worked all her wiles to see that he did not have the opportunity to say it. She was tired of that game. Say what you want, Joyful Patrick Turner, and the devil take you. The last man who saw me cry was Jonathan Devrey; I was ten years old and he was fifteen. You won't be the next one. Say whatever you want.

"I think . . ."

"Yes?"

There was a pause, as if he'd changed his mind at the last second. "This Tintin," Joyful said, "I think he may be somehow connected to Gornt Blakeman. I think that business tonight with the wager was somehow for my benefit. If Blakeman comes again, keep a close eye on him. Let me know what you see."

Relief flooded through her. "Yes, of course I will. I'll tell Mr. Clifford as well."

Joyful shook his head. "No, don't say a word to Vinegar. Not about Blakeman, or about Tintin for that matter. I think the whipper is in league with Gornt Blakeman as well. I know that at least he runs errands for him on occasion."

"What sort of errands? How do you know?"

"It's a long story, and as you said, it's late and you're exhausted.

We'll save the details for another time. Meanwhile, be your usual clever self and keep me informed."

"I'll do that," she promised as she lifted her face for his good-night kiss.

Chatham Street, 5:30 A.M.

Eugenie slept fitfully, her hand pressed between her thighs, conscious of the emptiness beside her in the bed. When she woke, it was with the unrelieved ache that had become her constant companion since she was widowed.

Damn Timothy Fischer for freeing the wanton spirit in his eighteen-year-old bride, then dying four years later and leaving her with nothing but debts and a constant hunger she was terrified to satisfy lest it destroy her status as something to be desired because it was difficult to obtain. Damn Gornt Blakeman as well. No, double damn him. May he rot in hell for indulging his need to brag, thinking that would more quickly gain him access to her bed. In reality, if she had not so soon realized how much she had to gain by refusing him, he would by now be her lover.

Eugenie felt a touch. It was far too early for her maid to come to wake her. And that stroke along her cheek—a man's hand. Her heart thumped. Gornt? Would he be so brazen?

"Madame, *vous ne dormez pas*. I felt you stiffen at my touch. I stiffen as well." There was a small chuckle that only served to stoke Eugenie's growing terror. "But that is not why I am here. Open your eyes, Madame Fischer. We have business to discuss."

Eugenie opened her eyes. Her gasp threatened to become a scream. Tintin placed his hand over her mouth. "*Ne criez pas!* I am here on business, madame. If I wanted something else, I would have it by now."

He took his hand away and Eugenie scuttled to the other side of the bed. Tintin did not try to stop her, only noted the way the lace of her nightdress reached from her ankles to her neck but somehow left more exposed than covered. *Eh bien,* what would it be like to lie between those luscious thighs? He'd been watching her before he let her know he was there. He could smell the heat of her dreams. No husband for two years. She would shriek with pleasure. *Tant pis,* he was there on business.

"What are you doing here? What do you want with me?"

"I have brought you something." He reached into the pocket of his satin coat. Earlier, when the dice would not fall for him, he had been tempted to put this treasure on the table. Then Blakeman had pushed himself into the picture, and, *merci à tous les saints,* the locket had not been lost to his foul luck.

Eugenie looked at the bijou swinging from his hand.

"Where did you get that?!"

"From a gentleman who made a bargain, madame. Your late husband."

Eugenie reached out and snatched the bauble from his hand. Tintin let it go.

It was impossible, but yes, it was Timothy's mother's locket. Timothy's father had given it to her as a betrothal gift, a gold oval with the letter *M* for Mariah inlaid on the front in pearls. And there on the side were the teeth marks said to have been made by baby Tim himself. "But it was given to a . . . a gentleman in New Orleans. A business matter. I myself sent word to say that my husband had died and to ask for the locket's return. That was two years past."

"At your service, madame." Tintin bowed with exaggerated formality. "I am sorry to have been delayed in bringing your treasure back to you." He would never have risked a thousand miles of blockaded coast simply on the chance that Gornt Blakeman's scheme might succeed. But coupled with the likelihood that Monsieur Timothy Fischer's widow would be as willing to do business as Fischer himself had been . . . That had been a gamble worth taking.

Eugenie looked at him, as if seeing for the first time the eye patch and the bandanna. Timothy had spoken of a pirate and a distant place near New Orleans called Barataria Bay, where clandestine slave auctions took place by candlelight in hidden caves and great wealth was to be had if only one were sufficiently daring. Holy heaven, it was true! "Turn around."

"Why?"

"Because I wish to get out of this bed."

"And why should I deny myself the pleasure of observing that?"

"Turn around, damn you!"

Tintin chuckled and faced the window, listening to the rustle of the sheets and her soft steps on the Turkey carpet. Some pleasures were best kept separate from business. But the mulatto bitch who thought herself good enough to make a wager with a white man and win, that was another matter.

"Very well, you may turn back." She had put on a negligee made of the same lace as her nightdress.

"Now, madame, we must talk. Perhaps we can sit?"

"Not in here." Eugenie led him from her bedroom to her boudoir, the adjoining parlor where just yesterday Gornt had bragged of his challenge to Bastard Devrey, and she had schemed for a proposal of marriage. Now, in less than twenty-four hours, everything might have changed.

Chapter Eight

THE DUSTING was a fine excuse. A woman came to scrub and polish three times a week and another once a fortnight to deal with the laundry, but in the frugal Vionne household the women of the family had always assumed a large share of the daily tasks. Now, with dear mama gone to her reward, there was only Manon. She carried her basket of cleaning cloths and scented oils and waxes into the room above the shop that served as her father's study.

A tall bookcase stood on the wall opposite the windows, but the shelves did not provide enough space for all papa's collection. Books of every size and shape were piled on the floor. This time of year, with no fire in the fireplace, there were even books on the hearth. Her hope was to find among them some notes papa might have made the night before when he received Gornt Blakeman. No such good fortune. The top of his desk was clear of everything but his loupe and more books.

Manon selected a soft chamois cloth from her basket and dabbed it with comfrey-scented beeswax, then began polishing the top of the cherrywood desk. It had been made by a local craftsman to her father's exact specifications, and it glowed with the patina of many decades of use and care. How many times had she seen papa spread a dark blue velvet cloth on this surface and carefully place upon it one or another sparkling treasure dug from the earth or wrested from the sea? When she was little, papa would often carry her up here and set her on his lap while he examined some precious stone that had come into his possession, a treasure that would remain with him only until he could find a buyer. "We are the temporary guardians of all this beauty, *ma petite* Manon. We must take the opportunity to appreciate it." Then he would show her how to hold the loupe to her eye (she was too little to screw it in place and free both hands) and peer through it into the depths of a topaz or an emerald, even a diamond, and see the fire dancing within.

His loupe was usually downstairs in the shop, but this morning it lay on the desk. He must have brought it up here the night before, but there was no sign of any jewels or of the soft square of velvet.

But that could be a good sign! She had frequently seen her father use the velvet spread-cloth to wrap jewels that had recently come into his possession but which were not yet to be put on display in the shop. On such occasions he would lock the gems in a small wooden case, then lock the case in the bottom left-hand drawer of the desk. Always. Papa was a great believer in the sacred quality of routine. And inevitably, when the chest and the drawer held something of value, the tiny keys that unlocked them were placed on a chain that Papa slipped over his head and wore beneath his shirtfront. At other times the keys were in the little depression at the back of the desk that was meant to hold an inkpot.

The two small silver keys winked up at her from their regular place, proving beyond doubt that nothing was wrapped in the velvet cloth, and nothing hidden away in the locked chest in the locked drawer. Manon's disappointment was a physical thing, rising up to flush her face. But if he'd locked nothing away, where was the velvet square?

She heard a step on the stairs, picked up the chamois, and venting her frustration on the desktop, rubbed so energetically that she knocked one of the stacks of books to the floor. They fell with a loud clatter.

"Books are too valuable to be treated so, Manon."

"I know, Papa. I am sorry." She knelt down and began gathering up the leather-bound volumes. One had fallen open. Manon could see the French words engraved in gold on the spine. *Six Voyages . . . en Turquie, en Perse, et aux Indes* by Jean Baptiste Tavernier, a great gemologist and world traveler. Papa had often used it when teaching her about the history of precious stones. Published in Paris in 1679, it had been the prize of his father's collection. "The Tavernier! Oh, I really am sorry, Papa."

"I know, *ma petite*. Do not fuss. No harm has been done." Manon had snatched up the Tavernier. Vionne knelt and picked up the other two volumes. When he did, Manon saw the square of dark blue velvet; so it had been in use to mark a place in *Six Voyages*. Without thinking, she had used a finger to hold the book open the way it fell. The heading of the page facing her was *Le Grand Mogul: le plus grand diamant dans tout le monde*—the Grand Mogul: largest diamond in all the world.

A Meadow Just Below Canal Street, 11 A.M.

Midmorning and the heat already fierce. Canton was hot as well, but in China, Thumbless Wu was a man of power and wealth who could command shade and fans, and cool scented baths. Whatever he wanted to eat appeared almost as soon as he thought of it. In this *diu ngoi gwok* city of the foreign ghosts, except for the bits of disgusting *gwai* food he found in the foul drainage gullies that ran through each street, he starved. Even the hole on the *diu suen* ship had been better. At least the *diu* Irish had brought him food some times. But no *fan*. No *fan*. Ahyee! How could he live without *fan*?

It did not seem possible he could sweat more or shake more or puke more, but Wu continued to do all three. Lying on his belly and retching into the grass on the edge of a field beyond the city streets, he would have wanted to die, except for what he saw ahead of him. A field of flowers, bright red and with their faces open to the sky. With such heat and sun they would soon drop their petals. The round pods left atop the stalk would burst with ripe seed. The man walking among the red flowers was obviously interested in the same calculation. Ahyee! *Ho wan.* Finally, good luck. All gods bear witness if he lied. Wasn't this exactly what he had come to this barbarian land to find? The red flowers—poppies, in the *diu suen* speech of the *diu suen* foreign devils—poppies and an apothecary who knew how to make their seed into the black sticky stuff that produced white smoke. He knew this man was an apothecary; he had seen his shop. And now he had seen the red flowers. No *fan,* but he could not die now. Wu felt another wave of nausea rise in his throat and gave himself over to yet another bout of the shivering heaves that produced nothing, but he was smiling.

Chesapeake Bay,
Aboard the British Warship H.M.S. Griffin, *11 A.M.*

"So, General, we are agreed?" The admiral leaned over the map spread across the wardroom table and rested his finger on the little village of Benedict in Maryland, on the nearby Patuxent River.

The general commanded a fighting force of forty-five hundred, but at the moment his troops were aboard twenty warships. It was the admiral's job to get them to the place they could be best used, and he was the senior officer for this part of the operation. Nonetheless, the two men had conferred as equals since the previous month in Bermuda when they decided to sail for the Chesapeake. The area's extensive shoreline and her large cities were without any fortification; the American secretary of war didn't believe in fortifying cities. "There's no barricade can match a bayonet," he said often. The British general concurred, but only if one had a great many men to wield the weapons. The Americans did not. The entire Federal District and much of Maryland were a plum ripe for the picking. The immediate issue was where to land the troops.

The general studied the area the admiral's tapping finger indicated. "Benedict? You're quite sure?"

"We can take it easily. Our spies tell us there are supplies to be had, including plenty of horses, and it's forty-five miles from their so-called capital city."

"And Baltimore?"

The general was still of two minds about which city to attack first. The admiral was not, but that would be the next engagement. He was a methodical man who preferred to settle one encounter at a time. "Baltimore remains a possibility, General. There's another road from Benedict leads directly there. And we've sympathizers among the Marylanders who will be happy to provide guides."

"Very well. Benedict it is. And either Baltimore or Washington to be their Waterloo."

The admiral smiled. "Perhaps not quite of such import, General."

"Perhaps not. But it will finish the job." Wellington had defeated Napoleon at Waterloo; now only the defiant Americans stood between Britain and the world dominance that was her divine destiny.

An orderly was summoned. Three days' rations were to be cooked aboard and distributed—three pounds of pork and seven and a half pounds of bread per soldier. "I trust it will be enough," the general said after the man left. "As long as this Benedict is as easy a target as you say."

The admiral smiled. "Not to worry. I'm told President Madison's wife Dolley sets a fine table at the Executive Mansion."

New York City, Noon.

"He won't have me." Jesse Edwards shuffled along Broad Street, ignoring the storerooms and shops that had once belonged to the wealthiest of the Dutch burghers who founded the town and called it Nieuw Amsterdam. There was a hard lump of something in the boy's path, and he kicked it ahead of him while trying to resist Holy Hannah's forward tug on his left arm. "He'll take one look at this," he jerked his head in the direction of the stump of his right arm, "and say no thank ye, I'll not be needing any freaks."

"The Holy One, blessed be He, helps those as help themselves. Proverbs. Look at all these places." Hannah gestured to indicate the countinghouses either side of the wide street. "When I was a girl, they was businesses below and rich men's dwellings above. Now rich men live as far away from the stink of their money as they can manage, and there's so much business in the town, nearly every inch of Broad Street is taken up with it. Course he'll have you, Jesse. Why not, when it's Holy Hannah's idea?"

"You mean he'll be feared you'll put a curse on him otherwise?"

"Never! Vengeance is mine, saith the Lord. Book o' Deuteronomy. Holy Hannah don't curse folks. All she does is sometimes make a suggestion as to what might please the Holy One, blessed be his name."

Broad Street had been an early Dutch canal, dug to let ships come inland from the East River and offload into the yellow-brick warehouses that fronted either bank. The rich burghers who lived above the warehouses used the canal as a sewer, counting on the tide to flush it clean twice a day. As it turned out, the Dutch were more industrious than nature and the tide could not cope. Eventually, the burghers and *huisvrouwen* found themselves living beside a stinking ditch so disgusting they had no choice but to pave it over and create what was then the widest street in Nieuw Amsterdam. Hannah pulled her charge along Broad and Dock, narrow and twisting side streets, and hurried him along to Hanover Square. "That's the place right over there. Quite a few like it these days, but when I was a girl Devrey's was the only shop of its kind."

The gold-lettered sign said DEVREY'S PHARMACY, FINE PERSONALS. It hung at right angles to a door set in a small house built catty-corner to the road, below an overhanging eave that protected the entrance from the weather. How many times had Hannah gone through that door? Too many to count. Mama used to buy her Number Seven Cologne from Devrey's. Once the fine ladies of the town again had money to spend after the Revolution, Devrey's new cologne attracted a goodly share of it. The pharmacy also sold face powder and wig powder and scented soap. Lord Almighty, what was the point o' thinking on any o' that now? "Come along, lad. Leave that kick-about bit o' rubbish you've trailed all the way here and come inside."

A bell tinkled when they pushed the door open, just as it had when she was young. The pharmacy smelled exactly the same, sweet and bitter in equal parts. Straight ahead, on the shelves behind the counter, were the tall glass jugs and ewers containing the many colored elixirs that Clare Devrey had simpled into being with the mysterious skills it was said she'd learned from her Irish mother, Roisin.

The short, broad man standing behind the wooden counter in front of the apothecary bottles was Clare's son. Thirty-some. Ten years younger than Hannah, but she remembered seeing him as a child, skating on the Collect Pond in winter and flying kites on the Common in autumn. You're a foolish old woman, Hannah. Oh that today you would listen to my voice. Psalm of David. Today, not yesterday and not tomorrow. "Good day to you, Jonathan. I've brought you a message. And a messenger."

Jonathan Devrey stood exactly where he'd been when she opened the door. Good God, Holy Hannah with her flyaway white hair and her shapeless rags and those blue eyes that seemed to stare straight through a man. What could she want with him? "What message is that?" His voice spiraled up into a squeak. "I didn't ask for any message." All the town knew Holy Hannah had the gift of prophecy. But what had that to do with him? Except to bury his parents who died together in 1805 when the sleigh they were in overturned and dropped them into the freezing waters of Hudson's River, he'd not been in a church since he was a boy. Besides, Hannah Simson was a Hebrew. What business could any Jew god have with him?

"The Spirit of the Holy One, blessed be His name, breathes where it will, Jonathan Devrey. You need not ask for a message to get one."

Jonathan had been pasting labels on small containers of Devrey's Elixir of Well-Being, a thick and bitter brown tonic that was the most popular of the simples sold in the shop. Now he started shuffling the bottles about as if the exact manner in which they were set out on the counter was of vital importance. "Very well, go ahead, tell me what you've come to say. Then get on with you. You're not good for business, Hannah. No customer will come in while you're here."

"Won't take long," she said. "Molly sent me."

He wasn't surprised. As soon as she'd walked through the door, he'd suspected it would have something to do with his twin sister. From the day sixteen years earlier when she disappeared, every worrying thing that happened to him seemed to be about her. Why not a visit from Holy Hannah as well? "Molly's been gone a long time. What's she got to say to me now?"

"Says you're not to worry. Says she understands."

"Understands what? I had nothing to do with whatever happened to Molly. No one has ever accused me of—"

"Molly says she's at peace and you shouldn't worry. She forgives you."

"I'd nothing to do with it." Jonathan was shouting now, unable to help himself. "Whatever took Molly and Laniah, it was no doing of mine."

Hannah had to bite the inside of her cheek to keep from laughing. Laniah a young mulatto slave who had belonged to Clare Devrey and her family, vanished the same time Molly did. Most folks thought the pair had wandered off into the Manhattan wilderness and starved or drowned, or got sucked into the quicksand that could be found in many spots in the woods. Poor Jonathan—all these years he'd been so busy denying responsibility for his sister's disappearance, it never occurred to him that no one really thought he bore any blame. New Yorkers were too practical to worry about a crime when there was no reason to think one had been committed. "Molly says she doesn't mind that you have all this"—Hannah waved her arm to indicate the pharmacy—"and she has nothing. She is happy you are successful."

Jonathan took a deep breath. "Fine, I am glad to know my sister is at peace. Now, please go. And take him with you."

It was the first indication that Jonathan had noticed the boy, who was busy making himself small behind Hannah's back, and she took the opportunity to haul him forward so he could be plainly seen. "His name's Jesse Edwards. Fought in the war, he did. Jesse here was with Commodore Perry. Tell him, Jesse."

"On the *Lawrence*," Jesse mumbled.

Jonathan was intrigued in spite of himself. "That so? Perry's flagship?"

"Till he left for *Niagara,* aye."

"The great battle on Lake Erie?"

Jesse nodded.

"From the size and the age of you, I'd guess you were a powder monkey. Dangerous work, lad. Is that how you lost that arm?"

Jesse nodded yet again. Near enough to the truth so he figured even Holy Hannah wouldn't accuse him of lying.

"Well, you don't brag on it. I'll say that for you. Very well, you're a hero then. Here." Jonathan held out a bottle of Devrey's Elixir of Well-Being. "Have one of these. Make you feel better than you can imagine. Everyone in town says the same. Costs three pennies a bottle, but no charge for you, seeing as how you're a war veteran and a hero and all."

Hannah still had hold of Jesse's collar, and she shoved him forward. "Go on, take your present. But that's the last thing you should expect from Mr. Devrey for free. He'll pay you a wage for your work, and you touch nothing else, you hear. Otherwise—"

"Hold on! I never said anything about the boy working for me. I have no need of—"

"Course you have need. I told you I brought a message and a messenger. Molly says you're to begin delivering things to folks as want 'em. Save those as live in the outer wards the trouble of coming here to Hanover Square. It's a fine idea now that the city's grown so much you're not in the center of things. Molly says Jesse's to work every day but the Christian Sabbath, and to have a wage of four shillings a week. Coin money, mind. And you give him a cup of hot milk and ale when he arrives in the morning and another at midday."

"I don't—"

"Molly says he's also to clean the shop once a week and sweep outside the front door twice a day. And he can do things like see to those labels you were busy with when we arrived. You'll get good value for money, Jonathan Devrey. Your poor dead twin sister says so."

Jonathan was beginning to doubt that any of this was a message from beyond the grave. That Molly and Laniah were long dead there could be no doubt, but Holy Hannah probably knew as little about what happened to them as the next person. As for this one-armed powder monkey, everyone knew Hannah took in waifs and strays and usually put them to work in the town. Probably they brought their earnings back to her. Nonetheless . . . A delivery service. He knew of no shop in the entire town that offered such a convenience, and could be the lad would be useful in other ways. "Can you handle a broom with one arm, Jesse Edwards?"

"Aye, sir. I can."

"And you could stick a label to a bottle as well?"

Hannah shoved the boy forward once more. "Don't just say you can, Jesse. Go on, show him."

She'd pushed him right up to the wooden counter. Jesse used his left hand to smear some of the thick paste on the back of one of the labels, then used that same hand to pick up a bottle of Elixir and put the neck between his teeth. After that it was easy to pick up the label and stick it on.

"I'll be fluttered," Jonathan said. "Good for you, lad. Neat and quick as if you had two arms and the hands that go with them. Very well"—he leaned over the counter and put out his right hand; Jesse took it with his left—"you are hired. Can you start now?"

"Course he can," Hannah said. "And you might want to think about getting him some livery as well. Your expense that will be, mind."

Livery. Well yes, it might be a good idea. Show the town he was as important as his miserable cousin Bastard, that would. "I'll consider it."

"And he's to have four pennies right now. An advance against his first week's wages."

"I don't see—"

"Molly said so. Only I think she meant it to be five pennies."

"Very well, four pennies." He reached into the cash drawer below the counter.

"Five," Hannah insisted. "I'm sure that's what Molly said."

Jonathan counted five coppers into her outstretched hand, careful not to touch the dirt-encrusted skin. Jesse looked on and didn't say a word.

As soon as she left the shop, Hannah ducked into the alley beside it. Mustn't let Jonathan Devrey see her cackling with laughter. Messages from the dead indeed. What kind of prophesying would that be? No, this day's work was just natural Simson canniness.

Her great-great-grandfather had been a West Indies trader and an elder of Shearith Israel, the synagogue where the town's Jews worshiped to this day. By 1720 he had become the first provisioner to supply the Jewish community here and in the islands with meat that was butchered in the proper rabbinical manner and stamped KASHER. His sons had gone from butchering to supplying not just Jews but the whole town with foodstuffs. By the time her father came along, there were entire sections of New York City markets, baker's stalls and greengrocers and fishmongers and the like, owned by her branch of the family Simson. Knowing about business was in her blood. She'd done Jonathan Devrey a good deed this day. Never mind that he thought it was— Holy heaven! What sort of being was this?

Thumbless Wu stared at the creature who was staring at him. A *gwai nui sing,* he realized after a few seconds, a foreign ghost woman. His only concern was that she not try and take what he was eating. Wu wasn't strong enough to stand and run, but he half turned away, clutching the lump of moldy green bread to his chest.

Blessed be the Holy One! Must be some kind of Indian, though far fewer of them came into the town these days, and he didn't look like any she'd ever seen. Didn't matter. He was starving. Otherwise he'd not be gnawing on that disgusting bit of whatever it was that Jesse had kicked here all the way from Broad Street.

There were five major markets in the city. The Fly Market at the foot of Maiden Lane was the oldest of them, but it had been vastly improved since it was first established in Dutch Nieuw Amsterdam. Back then it took a license issued by the authorities to sell meat in the town. How else could the population be protected from dog passing itself off as beef, or feral cat in the place of chicken? These days the city fathers went still further to guard the food supply.

At the Fly Market the butchers' stalls were sheltered beneath a slate roof held up with substantial brick pillars; there was yet another roofed-over area for the sale of fish. Women sold produce at tables whose locations had been claimed by their mothers and grandmothers, and passed on as a matter of legacy. Competition for custom was fierce, but the ultimate stamp of approval was bestowed only by New York's wealth of public employees. There were inspectors of quality, markers and sealers of weights and measures, overseers of the porters, packers, and cullers, even one officious man whose job it was to be certain no oysters were sold between June 1 and September 30, when it was said they were not healthy.

As if any sane person would eat an oyster left to fester in this searing summer heat, Manon thought. She patted her forehead with a lace-trimmed handkerchief, and tried to appear interested in the wilted produce at the stall of Elsie Gruning. More important, she tried to appear uninterested in Joyful, standing beside her, also trying to look fascinated by the carrots and onions.

Elsie watched the couple, smiling, enjoying the little romantic conspiracy in which she'd been playing a part for many weeks. The beautiful golden-haired girl—Elsie had known her since she was little and her mama came to buy Elsie Gruning's fresh-picked produce—like a princess she was. And the handsome young man, so tall and strong. Such a pity about his hand. Ach, not so important. It could have been some more necessary part of him. He was no less a man for the loss of a hand. And see how he cares for the girl.

"You look so distressed," Joyful murmured. "What's wrong? Has your father—"

"It's not papa. At least not only papa. I—" Manon broke off. The Widow Tremont was two stalls away, buying a crock of honey. She was a mantua maker, a pillar of the Huguenot community, and she'd been chasing after Papa since Maman died. She'd love nothing better than to go running to *dear* Monsieur Vionne with a bit of gossip, passed on because, of course, she had only his good name in mind.

"Mevrouw, the carrots . . ." The old Dutch politeness still came naturally to Elsie. Her grandparents had been Hollanders, and both Dutch and German remained as common as English on the many farms of West Chester and Long Island. "Your papa will not believe— *Ja kum nau,* I am wasting my breath. You do not care about carrots today. Mijnheer, look—" She sensed another customer approaching her stall and paused.

The shopper, a dusky woman dressed in shabby, shapeless clothes with a shawl pulled halfway over her face, approached to within a couple of feet, then halted. Elsie waited a moment to see if she was going to ask about the carrots—New York's poor frequently bargained for the produce the gentry didn't want—but this one simply looked at Mevrouw Manon and her gentleman friend, then turned and disappeared into the crowd. As for the man and the girl, like mooning calves they were, right here in the open. It could lead to nothing but trouble. "Look over there, mijnheer . . ." Elsie prodded Joyful with one of the carrots judged not worthy and nodded in the direction of the large wooden building across the way.

The double doors to Abraham Valentine's coopery were wide open. Joyful could see barrels of every size stacked in neat rows and apparently no one keeping any kind of watch over them. Elsie leaned forward. "Mijnheer Valentine left a few minutes ago," she murmured. "Him he left in charge." Her nod indicated a small boy sleeping soundly between two large oak kegs just outside the door.

Joyful nodded his thanks, then took Manon's arm. "Come. Hurry."

"We cannot," casting a quick look over her shoulder and noting gratefully that the Widow Tremont was still occupied with paying for her honey, "I mustn't be seen to—"

"Hush. Come quickly and no one will see us. Elsie will keep lookout for us. You will, mistress, won't you?"

The woman wiped her sweaty face with a bright red handkerchief and bobbed her head in the direction of the coopery.

Joyful hurried Manon across the gravel path, past the sleeping boy, and beyond the displays of finished kegs and barrels to the darkened rear behind Valentine's lathes, and the piles of staves and iron bands that were the tools of his trade. He found the sweet smell of fresh wood shavings almost overpowering. The smell of Manon as well, the smell that was uniquely hers, along with the lilies-of-the-valley scent of Hungary Water. He'd known other women who used the same scent, but before Manon, none he wanted forever. He drew her close. "I can't bear how troubled you are. What has happened?"

"I don't know how to explain"—the words muffled, spoken with her head pressed to his chest. "You know nothing of jewels, so it will be hard for you to understand."

Joyful put his hand beneath her chin, turning her face up to his, wanting to speak of other things, not wanting her touched by what he must do to secure their future. "What is the name of the purple gem that's the color of your eyes?"

"Amethyst."

"Yes, that's it. I saw one once in Canton. You will have amethysts after we are married. I will send word to China that I will pay any price for the most beautiful such jewels to be had."

"Joyful, please. You must listen to me."

He let her go. "Yes, of course I must. It's about Blakeman's visit Thursday night, isn't it? Manon, does your father suspect about us?"

"Papa suspects nothing. He is a dear man, a wonderful man, but I can make him think anything I want. No, don't smile like that, Joyful. You believe I am speaking women's foolishness. I am not. But we are wasting time. Mr. Blakeman, his visit last night had something to do with the Great Mogul." And when she saw his look of puzzlement, "It is a diamond. The largest in the world. Almost two hundred carats. This big." Manon held up her hand and made a circle with her thumb and forefinger and saw Joyful's eyes widen. "Like a pigeon's egg," she added.

He shook his head in wonderment. "How can a diamond be such a size?"

"It was even larger before it was cut. According to Tavernier, eight hundred carats. He saw the diamond in India in 1649. By then it had been cut, and the lapidary who did the job made such a mess he was not paid but fined by the Mogul emperor who owned it."

Joyful put his hands on her shoulders and peered into her lovely face, feeling the heat of his wanting her even as he knew he must remain absolutely cool, avoid at all costs the one wrong move that would lose him everything. "Did Blakeman sell your father this fantastic diamond?"

"Of course not! Where would Papa get the money to buy a treasure of that sort? That's the part of this business that so troubles me. A diamond such as the Great Mogul . . . Joyful, no one in all New York could afford to buy such a stone. Not even Jacob Astor. It is a jewel for a king, or an emperor. If Mr. Blakeman brought Papa the Great Mogul, the only plan can be to cut it. And I cannot believe my father would agree to do such a thing."

Jesus God Almighty. He was beginning to see the pieces moving around in his head, forming themselves into different patterns, varied options. "The stone . . . What did you say it's called?"

"The Great Mogul."

"You believe Gornt Blakeman wants your father to cut it, so it can be sold to various very rich men? Men like Jacob Astor?"

She nodded, eager for him to understand and grateful that he did. "Yes, exactly. What else can he want? I think—"

"Manon, if you are right, if that's what Blakeman's after, would your father do it?"

"No! That's what I'm telling you. I know he would not."

"Why not?"

"Because he has not the skill. Papa is a wonderful goldsmith. Gold and silver, they speak to him . . . no, they sing. With precious stones it is his knowledge that is important. He understands their rarity and their value, so he can buy and sell them with skill. But as a a diamond cutter . . ." Manon shook her head. "He has some training, but very little practice. The Great Mogul is one of the world's rarest treasures. To attempt to cut it and fail, have it shatter into splinters . . . Papa would never forgive himself. It would destroy him."

"Then he cannot intend to do it."

"But what can he intend, Joyful? What can this Gornt Blakeman want with Papa? And how did he come to have the Great Mogul in the first place?"

He laid his hand alongside her cheek. "I think I know, but I'm not sure yet. And I don't know exactly what role your papa is to play in the scheme. But this is wonderful information, my love. No, don't shake your head, it is. It puts me—us—well forward of where we were. And I'll look out for your papa."

"You promise?"

"Of course I promise." He laid his palm alongside her cheek, feeling the silkiness of her perfect skin, not trusting himself to kiss her, because he might not stop.

Manon felt his need. So many times in these past weeks, when her frustration at his reluctance to ask for her was at its worst and the circumstances made it seem possible, she'd almost forced the issue. She could simply yield to him now. If she pressed herself against him—but here, like this . . . His right hand was still pressed to her cheek. Manon reached for his black glove and raised it to her lips and kissed the wrist that ended in nothing.

In the alley behind the coopery the woman in rags who had seen them near the produce table caught her breath. She watched through a tiny window that hadn't been washed in so long it provided only a shadowy view, but she could see well enough to know the blond girl had kissed a part of Joyful Turner he had never allowed her to touch. Delight Higgins shuddered and pulled the shawl closer, seeking warmth to dispel the chill in her heart.

Chapter Nine

New York City, Pearl Street,
Barnaby Carter's Warehouse, 1 P.M.

IT WAS SUNNY OUTSIDE but semidark in the cavernous building where normally every variety of coach and carriage was on display. There were none to be seen now, only the huge and heaving crowd—mostly men, but Joyful noted a goodly number of women—filling the place, and spilling out the open double doors that led to the street.

"Lot forty-seven. Three more chests of tea." The auctioneer stood on a makeshift block, a line of empty kegs overlaid with boards at the far end of the warehouse where no daylight could reach, lit by half a dozen huge torches tipped with flaming pitch. "Straight from Canton despite the almighty British navy, blast them all to Hades. Take a good look at this delicious and wholesome treasure, ladies and gents. You're not about to see more anytime soon." He kept talking while the chests were manhandled into place by the porters. They wore nothing but homespun shirts and leather breeches, and still dripped sweat. Every other man in the place sweltered in his woolen cutaway coat. The city's she-merchants, females who had moved from ordinary shopkeeping to owning large storehouses and dealing only in wholesale, were not the sort to adopt the latest French fashions and give up their corsets and petticoats; they were swaddled in heavy taffeta and brocade. The place reeked of overheated flesh and sweat-soaked cloth. And something else—the indescribable musk of a lust for goods and profits. That hunger had been building since the day before, when *Canton Star* sailed into harbor. Now it was a frenzied storm of desire driving prices almost beyond reason.

The auctioneer used his long pointer to indicate the chop on the tea chest nearest him. "They tells me this mark here means black tea from a place they calls Yunnan. And you clever folks wouldn't be here if you didn't know that's the finest tea in China. So what am I bid, ladies and gents? Who'll start me off at forty dollars each chest? You there in the front, madam, I see you. Do I have forty-five? Indeed. Fifty then. Sixty? Yes sir. Against the she-merchant with the premises on William Street. Surely you're not all done?"

"Eighty," a voice bellowed from the rear. Another yelled that he'd pay a hundred. Moments later the hammer came down on a bid of one hundred and ninety-five dollars each chest for the lot of three. Sold to the man known to provision Archibald Gracie's private stores.

"Gracie does himself well, doesn't he?" a voice said in Joyful's ear.

"Why not? President of the Tontine, takes the lion's share of the trades. How have you been, Barnaby?"

Joyful had been ignoring Barnaby Carter for months, since he came home with one hand rather than two, but he'd known there would be no avoiding him today. Not once the broadsides that went up all over town announced the venue for Blakeman's auction as Carter's premises. Not as unexpected as it might be, considering the amount of business the two men did together in the ordinary way of things. Blakeman's coaching routes to Philadelphia and Boston were the most lucrative in the nation, but they traveled along rough and rutted highways from hell. His rolling stock required constant renewal;

Gornt Blakeman and Barnaby Carter each needed the other to stay in business. "How have you been, Barnaby?"

"Well enough, Joyful. But I could do with a game of billiards."

"You mean you think you might beat me now I'm one-handed, since you seldom could when I'd two." He had practiced using the glove to support his cue stick. It was awkward as bloody hell.

"I'd like a chance to try."

"Sometime soon, old friend. That is, if you'll be able to spare the time. Look at this." Joyful nodded at the jammed warehouse. "Never seen such a crowd in here before. Are you planning a permanent switch to auction hall?"

It was not as far-fetched a notion as it might have been a few years back. These days New York had outgrown the informal arrangement that allowed each type of commodity to be traded at a particular inn or tavern—real estate at the Exchange Coffee House, goods and shipping cargoes at the Merchants'. Since Independence, businesses had sprung up with no purpose other than the sale of whatever came out of a ship's hold. Most of the auction venues were in fact here on Pearl Street, because it was hard by both the wharves and the counting-houses. Auctioneers, on the other hand, were for hire all over the town.

The one Blakeman had found to conduct his sale was a small wiry man, agile and with a booming voice. Most important, he was fast. While Carter and Joyful talked, the auctioneer arrived at the crying of lot fifty-one, half a dozen bolts of shimmering silk in rainbow colors that glowed and glistened in the light of the flaming torches. Moments later the hammer fell and the fabric had gone to a consortium of the city's finest mantua-makers—all women—whose representative paid an astonishing seven hundred dollars. Still, it was less than Blakeman might have gotten had he used a regular auction house. None of those would have permitted a single buyer to represent a group of competing merchants, to avoid bidding against each other and driving up the price. It was a rule the city's tradespeople broke at their peril; the penalty was to be banned from future public sales. Worth the risk today, probably. God alone knew when another ship would arrive from Canton.

Or perhaps not God. Might be that the information lodged with Jacob Astor.

The great man was standing off to the side of the auction block. As far as Joyful could tell, he had bid on nothing. Come simply to see what *Canton Star* had managed to get through the blockade, and because, like every trader in New York, scenes like this were what he lived for.

Barnaby disappeared, summoned by one of the porters. Joyful saw his chance and began edging toward Astor, trying to attract no attention. Not too difficult in these circumstances; everyone was concentrating on the goods, and the auctioneer, and the drama that took place as each lot was cried and the bids spiraled ever upwards.

Now he was close enough to see Astor's narrow mouth and beaklike nose. The eyebrows were black, the hair, cut to earlobe length. Naturally white, it seemed. Joyful could see no traces of powder on the exquisitely hand-stitched lapels of the great man's cutaway. He was short and stout, and said to be over fifty, but there was nothing soft or aging about Jacob Astor. Simply standing beside him, Joyful could feel the man's strength.

He had written the note before coming here, after he'd left Manon at the Fly Market, while he thought about the diamond she described. *No one in all New York could afford to buy such a stone. Not even Jacob Astor. It is a jewel for a king or an emperor.* The crush of bodies kept pushing him closer. Near enough now so he could jostle Astor's arm, or just slip the note into the man's pocket. Too risky. What if he never checked, simply put the coat in the hands of his valet?

Astor bumped his hip. An accident, Joyful told himself. There was a second bump, and he would swear Jacob Astor had pinched his thigh. He looked down. Astor's hand was extended palm up, ready to receive the note that no one other than Joyful himself knew he had written.

Jesus God Almighty, the man was a seer. Joyful's fingers were trembling when he pressed the piece of paper into Astor's hand. The older man was cool as ice. His expression never changed and he never looked at Joyful. His fingers curled around the bit of paper and made it disappear. Seconds later he was gone.

Finbar O'Toole was also at the auction, his face impassive as the bids soared and the amount earned by his daring and seamanship climbed ever higher. Joyful picked him out of the crowd and watched him for a time, then transferred his attention to the man who had crafted this drama.

Gornt Blakeman was seated to the rear of the auctioneer in a chair placed on yet another makeshift dais of kegs. He was caped and hatted, his face in the shadows, legs sprawled in front of him. One hand rested on an elaborate gold-topped walking stick. The effect was that of a king on a throne.

The last lot was cried soon after three. Now the business of paying for it all began. There were four cashers with quills and inkpots, seated at side-by-side tables near the entrance to the warehouse, ledgers open in front of them. An iron-banded chest sat beside each man. The coins dropped into the chests with a constant clatter, mounting in hills and valleys that every once in a while a casher leveled with the side of a hand grown black with the filth of so much money. A small group of head porters stood next to the tables, checking receipts against lot numbers and, once convinced of ownership, waving the treasure out the door on the backs of the lesser porters in their charge.

Gradually, the place began emptying, and the worst of the crush was transferred to the street, where cartmen and those who'd hired them jockeyed for the best position to load the bought-and-paid-for goods. Standing in the dimness between the doors and the cashers' stations, Joyful saw one porter, a man who seemed far too old for this sort of work, stagger and fall to his knees, clutching his breast. He started for him, but the man struggled to his feet, heaved up his load, and headed for a cart.

The lines in front of the money takers finally came to an end. The last buyer, a short, heavyset woman with an astonishing amount of chin hair, had succeeded in capturing one small lot of silk ribbons and paper fans. She paid a bit over thirty-one dollars for her goods, twelve guineas English. The casher who took the money bit hard on each coin before pronouncing it the genuine article and dropping it into his chest. Despise the British most of them might, but every New Yorker knew there was no currency more to be prized than English silver.

The woman's booty fit into a foot-square wooden box, and she carried it herself, passing close by Joyful. Delight had hired Bearded Agnes some six months after the place opened, to look after the frocks and furbelows of the Knave's ladies, and Agnes had become a kind of auntie to the lot of them. Stern but always fair, she went about her duties as if she were unconcerned by the contrast between herself and the pretty young things in her charge. Joyful knew better. Bearded Agnes had sneaked into the hawk's nest one night to ask in a hushed whisper if there was some way he could permanently cut away her disfigurement. "You or your cousin, perhaps?" He'd had to say that neither of them could help her, that he'd been with his cousin when another woman with the same complaint had come looking for a cure and been sadly turned away. *Something gone awry in the makeup of her, Joyful. But nothing I'd know how to excise with a scalpel.*

Bearded Agnes drew level with Joyful, then passed him by. Joyful watched her openly—Agnes incurred curious glances wherever she went—but she ignored him. He turned his head slightly, so his line of vision included Gornt Blakeman. As he'd suspected, Blakeman was eyeing them both. *Know who she is, don't you, Mr. Blakeman? And, I suspect, you know who I am. Or you think you do.* He took a couple of steps in Blakeman's direction and nodded. Blakeman looked surprised at first, then nodded back. Agnes had disappeared meanwhile. "A fine day's undertaking, sir," Joyful said touching the brim of his stovepipe. "My congratulations."

Blakeman bowed. "Some of us can claim only to be businessmen, Dr. Turner. Neither hero nor surgeon."

"That's as may be, Mr. Blakeman. In my case the description of surgeon no longer applies." Joyful held up his gloved left hand.

"The cruel fortunes of war, Dr. Turner. But a man of your talent will surely rise above them. I noticed you present throughout the sale."

"I was here as an observer only, Mr. Blakeman."

"Might I ask on whose behalf?"

"My own, sir."

"Indeed."

Their eyes met. Blakeman abruptly turned away and went over to the line of cashers, studying each ledger in turn, making notes meanwhile on a bit of paper. "In round numbers, something over twenty-five thousand pounds sterling," he announced finally. "To be precise and patriotic, let's call it two hundred and seven thousand American dollars." He turned and said in an even louder voice, "Will you accept that figure as accurate, Captain O'Toole?"

Finbar O'Toole stepped out of the shadows, his glance roving over the four chests. "Fair enough, I expect."

"Excellent," Blakeman said. "And if I calculate correctly, that makes your share six thousand seven hundred of our proud United States dollars." He began counting out coins, accumulating a hefty pile of silver and gold, and finally pushing it all in O'Toole's direction. "Did you bring a sack, Captain? Perhaps you need the loan of one. I, as you can see, came prepared."

Blakeman reached behind him to where a store of sturdy homespun moneybags waited on a table. "Will this do, sir?" O'Toole nodded. Blakeman handed the bag to one of the porters, now standing around waiting for his day's wages to be paid. The man took it, held it open with one hand, and swept the coins into it, then tied it tight closed, but it was Blakeman himself who passed it to O'Toole. "Your due, Captain. Well earned."

"Not quite." Joyful stepped forward. "These were in the pile you counted out before this fellow here dropped them." He dropped to one knee and picked up four coins that had fallen to the dirt floor and been kicked beneath the table by the porter. It was the man's private dodge, not Blakeman's, but there was no doubt whatever that Blakeman had seen it happen and said nothing.

"So, Dr. Turner"—Blakeman turned to face him—"not just a war hero, but eagle-eyed with it."

Joyful started to say something, then felt Finbar's hand on his shoulder. "That money you're holding belongs to me, I believe."

"So it does." Joyful handed over the four coins, then nodded to Blakeman and turned and followed the Irishman out the door.

Behind him he heard Blakeman's instructions that each head porter be paid fifteen coppers for his day's work, ten to the under-porters. "And twenty dollars to the auctioneer. A fine job, sir. I thank you." Not a word about Barnaby Carter. A professional auction house would have taken one percent of the profit. Barnaby, since he could not exist without the business of Blakeman Coaching, was to get nothing and like it.

"I suppose I should thank you for getting back the money that godrotting porter tried to steal."

Joyful shrugged. "Why bother?"

"What's that supposed to mean?"

"Only that it makes no difference if you have a few dollars more or less, Finbar. It'll all be gone in a matter of weeks—or days, more likely. Depends on where you do your gambling."

"I'm not gambling," O'Toole protested. But he did not meet Joyful's gaze.

"It's a disease, old friend," Joyful said softly. "There's no talk of it in any of the medical literature, but I'd warrant my soul it's a sickness as real as yellowing fever or dropsy."

"Do I look sick to you?"

"Your symptoms aren't the kind that show in the body. How much of your life have you spent waiting for the turn of a card or the fall of a die, Finbar? A third? Two-thirds?"

O'Toole took a long pull of the ale he was drinking with his dinner of mutton chops and beans. "Depends on how much of my span I've spent aboard ship," he said. I don't gamble when I'm at sea, lad. Never. Not just now I'm a captain. 'Twas the same when I was an ordinary tar. The ocean calms me, calms the poxing itch."

"An itch. Is that what it is?"

The Irishman shrugged. "Only way I know to describe it. What about you then? No vices? Hero and healer, is that what they'll write on your gravestone?"

"Not likely. And I've vices enough." Jesus God, yes. But the lack of control was what separated him and O'Toole "We're not talking about me."

"What then? Why did you want to get Gornt Blakeman thinking on you by pushing yourself forward the way you did? Not for four poxing coins, I'm sure o' that."

"Let's say I'd like him scratching a bit as well. Finbar, back in Canton, either on the trading strip or the Bogue, did you ever hear talk of a diamond big as a pigeon's egg called the Great Mogul?"

"Not unless the talker was full of white smoke." The devil opium. In Canton, since the British began bringing the stuff in from India so's to have something to trade for Chinese silk, four of every ten men were said to be addicts. "I don't think a diamond like that could— Holy Mother of God, you're talking about the jewels in Blakeman's private chest, aren't you?"

Joyful leaned forward. "Lower your voice. I'm not sure that's what was in the chest. It may have been. May. That's all."

O'Toole looked down at his plate, busied himself with his mutton chop, then pushed the food away. "Something else I've got to tell you. Fellow who came after that poxing box. Used to be the town whipper, you said."

"What about him?" Joyful took a swallow of the tall ale in front of him, considering Finbar over the tankard's rim.

"He's the chucker-out at a fancy parlor house out at the edge of town on Rivington Street."

"That has to be the Dancing Knave," Joyful said evenly. "More gaming club than parlor house."

"Caught the fever yourself, have you?"

"No. At least not the way you mean."

"You're talking about a different sort of wager."

Joyful nodded, then leaned forward, something in him shamed by not being entirely straight with the man his father would have trusted with his life, but not ready to tell him everything despite that. "Finbar, I've got a ship. To make that Caribbean voyage."

"I don't believe it."

"It's true. The sloop *Lisbetta*. You can get a look at her up at—"

"I've no need to get a look at her. She's one o' Devrey's."

"Indeed." The papers Bastard had signed were still in the inside pocket of Joyful's cutaway.

"So? Bastard Devrey just handed her to you? Out o' the kindness o' his heart?"

"Something like that."

The Irishman shook his head. "Not good enough, lad. I'm bloody sure there's not a chance Bastard Devrey would trouble himself to do a favor for any man named Turner. What's his reward to be?"

"Salvation."

O'Toole pulled an ivory toothpick from his pocket and began working on the bits of mutton stuck in his teeth. "Is it Jesus Christ you think you are then?"

"It's complicated, Finbar. You'll have to trust me."

O'Toole got to his feet. "I may be a gambling fool, lad, but I'm not stupid. I don't captain for them as tell me lies to my face. If you don't trust me enough for the truth about your poxing cousin, you sure as hell shouldn't trust me to run a sloop past a Royal Navy blockade, find a treasure as was buried some fifty years past, and bring it back and hand it over. If Bastard Devrey's giving you a sloop, he can poxing well give you a captain to sail her."

Front Street, 4 P.M.

Delight wore a pale yellow gown, trimmed in cream-colored lace, caught below her breasts with a wide blue satin ribbon that matched the one on her high-crowned straw bonnet. The same shade of blue satin faced her cream-colored parasol. As exquisitely dressed as any New York lady, she walked with her head high, though her eyes were modestly cast down. Or so it seemed. In reality, her glance took in everything.

Word was that sometimes the blackbirders did their filthy business in broad daylight; that's why it was her custom to take Vinegar Clifford with her when she had to do some errand in the town. Today, when she was ready to leave, he wasn't to be found, a problem she would deal with later. Stay alert, Delight. Be ready to run if you must.

Dear God, why had she come back? In York, Canada, where the trouble started—a jealous wife and an equally envious owner of a club that supplied boy whores and wanted to branch into Delight's end of the business—a gentleman had offered to take her to London. Instead, New York, the town of her youth, had drawn her back as if it had her heart on a string, as if she could ever find what it was she'd lost here. *Dearie my soul, Miss Molly, is you sayin' we be goin' all the way to Canada where the devil French and them fierce Indians is?*

None of that way of talking was left in her mouth now. Thanks be to God. *You can go on speaking like a little slave girl, or learn to speak proper English and let no one think they're your better.* That's what Cuf said after she and Molly got to Nova Scotia.

She had learned Cuf's lesson well. By the time Laniah turned herself into Delight Higgins, she spoke as well as any lady alive. But New York remained a dangerous place for people of her sort. The newspapers were never short of notices offering hefty rewards for capturing this or that nigra, many described as light-skinned, like her. But whatever shade of black or brown you might be, unless you could produce a paper that said you were born free or officially manumitted, the blackbirders could take you, and be legal about doing it. There wasn't a magistrate in the city who would find for a nigra without papers over the claim of a white. Besides, most disgruntled owners weren't fussy about whether the slave being returned to them was the one they'd lost.

"Don't worry," Joyful had said the one time she spoke to him about the danger of the blackbirders. "Just get word to me and I'll come and sort things out."

Dear God, how long had she trusted in his promises, spoken and unspoken? And despite everything that followed—even becoming her lover—he never once recognized her as little Laniah. In the Knave she was Delight Higgins in her fancy gowns and her jewels, his for the taking whenever the mood might strike him. Outside of that special, secret place she was only another darkie who barely cast a shadow. Outshone by a golden girl who'd never felt a switch across her back, or had to use her body to make her way.

According to Elsie Gruning, Manon Vionne was the girl's name. She had offered the information willingly enough when Delight said she was a laundress looking for work, and thought the young woman might be a kind employer. "*Ja*, kind she is. And she might hire you. Call at the goldsmith's on Maiden Lane." A darkie to do the white girl's washing—that was the way of things. That in her foolishness Delight Higgins had really believed Joyful Turner loved her—that would be a cause for astonishment. She'd stood at Elsie Gruning's table, trying to ignore the anguish that thrummed in every part of her, and over the way, beneath the roof where the butchers plied their trade, a big, red-faced man had held a wood pigeon by the feet, the bird madly fluttering its wings in a hopeless quest for freedom, then lowered it to his chopping block and brought his cleaver down on the bird's neck. Delight had put up her hand, as if she could feel the creature's pain.

She could feel it still.

It was after four now, and the sun yet blazed in a cloudless blue sky. She turned into Scrivener's Alley, the short passage between Front and Little Dock streets, where most of the town's clerks-for-hire could be found. Usually, the city's alleys were dank and shaded; by law they need only be wide enough to accommodate the withers of an average size horse. This one was broad enough to admit sunlight. Delight kept her parasol open as she walked on. The last house on the left was the residence of Silas Danforth, Master Scribe, according to the brass plaque beside the door.

Slyly Silas, he was called by those who knew him best. "You go see Slyly Silas Danforth in Scrivener's Alley," the black brewer who delivered kegs of ale to the Dancing Knave had told her a few weeks before. "He'll see you right, Miss Delight."

"Now why would I be wanting a scrivener?" Keeping her tone light, not letting the brewer see the hope and the fear at war in her belly, threatening to escape into her eyes. "It's cash money at the Knave; I don't keep accounts here." While she spoke, she'd pressed into the man's palm the coins to pay for the week's supply of ale.

The brewer's hand had closed over hers, imprisoning her slim, pale gold fingers in his large black fist. "I know 'bout you," he'd said softly. "I can always tell them as ain't entirely secure inside their skin, them as is looking over their shoulders for the white man with the whip or the blackbirder with the chains. Slyly Silas Danforth in Scrivener's Alley. Say you be sent by Tap-a-Keg Jonah and he'll see you right. Cost a bit it will, but you be sleeping a whole lot better after than you do right now."

It wasn't the same as being on the registry of Negroes born free and those officially manumitted, but it would be better than the nothing she had right now. Of course, if Joyful were to live with her openly, everything would be different.

Dear God but you're a fool, Delight Higgins. You might as well still be Laniah the slave girl for all you've learned. She closed her parasol with a snap and used it to knock on Slyly Silas's door. No reply. She tried the handle. The door wasn't locked; the scrivener's tiny office, however, appeared to be empty.

Delight waited for her eyes to adjust to the interior dimness, then looked around to be sure Danforth wasn't sitting somewhere in the shadows, enjoying himself at her expense. The room was just big enough for a desk and two chairs, and a low table beside the street door. She'd come here twice before, once to make her request and once to pick up the goods she'd ordered, but on the second visit Slyly Silas had sent her away empty-handed. Not ready, he explained, the press of custom. If she still wanted the papers, she'd have to return to get them. What she wanted was to scratch his eyes out, but she'd said she would be back in a week.

There was a small handbell on the table. She picked it up and gave it a vigorous shake. "Delight Higgins," Slyly Silas said as he pushed aside the dusty yellow cretonne curtain that separated his business from his house and entered the office. "Freewoman born in Nova Scotia in 1780. Daughter of Lizzie James Higgins and Cuf Higgins. Also free."

Danforth was short and bloated, with a rounded paunch that stuck out in front of him, short black hair, and dark, protruding eyes. His two front teeth hung over his lower lip. Like a rat's, she thought, a sly, self-satisfied rat. "Born in 1784," Delight corrected. As for claiming Cuf as her father and inventing a wife for him, considering her purpose, she was sure he wouldn't mind. "That's what we agreed."

"Oh, did we? I must have erred then. I can do the papers over if you like. Take another week or two and cost a bit more. But you won't mind that, will you? Miss Delight Higgins isn't any ordinary nigra, she's a woman of property."

"Indeed she is, Mr. Danforth." You won't provoke me into an outburst, you poxed bastard. I can be so cool my breath will turn you to ice and freeze you solid right where you're standing. "A few coins more or less is not any mind to me. Nonetheless, I'll take the papers as they are."

Delight reached into her drawstring bag for the money she'd counted out and wrapped in muslin before she left the Knave. Born in '80 as he'd written, or in '84 as she'd asked, it made no difference. She wasn't sure of her real age anyway. She'd guessed she might be shaving off three or four years with the birth date she'd chosen. *Must be that Clare magicked you up a youth potion when you were a lass.* That's what Cuf used to say. *The years go by, but you don't look any older.* Cuf was well into his sixties last time she saw him, with his hair gone entirely white and his skin—mulatto tan like her own—a web of creases. She didn't bother to tell him the only thing Clare Devrey ever gave her was the back of her hand, or the flick of the woven willow switch she kept conveniently hanging by the kitchen door.

"I have your money right here, Mr. Danforth. If you'll just let me see the papers, we can conclude—"

"You mustn't be in such a hurry, Miss Higgins. A day like this, when it happens the whole town is well occupied with the unexpected bounty just come from Canton, and you and I are fortunate enough to be alone in this quiet spot . . . Why rush off?"

"I will decide how I spend my time, Mr. Danforth. Now, do you have what I've come for?" Ten guineas she'd paid him when she placed her order, add to that the eighteen she had in her hand and his fee for the papers that said she was a free woman was one hundred dollars. She gave Vinegar Clifford twenty dollars a month, and he was among the most generously paid workingmen in the city. The youngest and prettiest girl in the Ladies' Salon might earn thirty coppers on a busy night. Slyly Silas was an extortionist, but he was surely a wealthy one. "For my part, I have what I owe you right here." She let him see the roll of coins.

"A woman of business," Slyly Silas said. "Comes directly to the point." The yellow curtain had closed behind him when he came in, now he reached up and pushed it open. "Very well, we will waste no time on idle chatter. What you've come for is in here. Come and claim it, Miss Delight Higgins."

"I prefer that you bring the work out here, Mr. Danforth. That way I can get a good look at what I'm buying before I pay for it."

"It's flawless work, Miss Higgins. You know that or you'd not have come to me. None of your kind would come to me unless they knew that in return for giving me what I ask, they get what they must have."

"I still want to examine the goods."

A smile spread across his rat-like face. "So do I, Miss Higgins. So do I."

The chill started in her belly and moved toward her throat. Slyly

Silas continued to hold the curtain aside, waiting for her to pass into what she now realized must be an empty house.

It was fifteen years since she'd spread her legs on anyone's say-so but her own. Slyly Silas Danforth would not be the one to make things the way they used to be. He would not resurrect Laniah, who ran away from Nova Scotia four years after she got there, because she was tired of being expected to wait hand and foot on Molly Devrey, despite the fact that Laniah was the only one who knew secrets Molly would sooner die than have exposed. Only one way she could survive in York once she was there, on the streets at first, finally in the best parlor house in the town. Until one day she sat herself down in front of the mirror that belonged to the woman who ran the place and recognized two things. First that she was truly beautiful. And second that she had two choices, to be a whore or a mistress of whores.

There had to be other scriveners in the city who could do what Slyly Silas did as well as he did it. As for the thirty-some dollars she'd already paid him, even after she paid Joyful his share, she earned three times as much in a week. The devil take the money and Danforth beside. She opened her mouth to say so.

The scrivener spoke first. "They tell me there are lots of blackbirders in the city these days," he murmured, still smiling. "And more to come. A fine business, blackbirding. Pay a tidy sum those bounty hunters do for information about any nigra as doesn't have freedom papers."

Damn you to hell, Joyful Patrick Turner. Damn you for eternity for letting me believe what was never true, that you meant for us to be together always. Damn you and damn that yellow-haired vixen you prefer to me. *Never let a white tormentor see how they make you feel, you're just marching to their tune if you do.* Another lesson learned from Cuf. Delight walked past the scrivener into the room in the rear. When he came after her, she imagined she could feel his hot devil's breath on the back of her neck. She did not have to imagine his hand on her buttocks.

Chapter Ten

New York City, 5 P.M.

BLAKEMAN HAD EVERY INTENTION of going to Eugenie after the sale. Instead he found himself riding his horse all the way uptown to Rivington Street, conscious that there were twice as many soldiers in the city as had been there the day before. Mostly Yorkers, the blue-and-buff-clad New York state militia whose long history went back further than the colonial wars with the French and the Indians, but men from some of the New England regiments as well. Blakeman felt his gut tighten. He was closer than he'd dared dream to getting everything he wanted. An attack by the British now could raise patriotic sentiment where none previously existed, and that could scuttle him.

Forty minutes later he reached the Dancing Knave. He tethered his horse at one of several empty hitching posts and rang the bell hanging beside the door. It was still very early for these ladies of the night. He settled back against the porch railing to wait.

Bearded Agnes poked her head out of a partially opened door, her black whiskers hidden by the frame. "We're closed until seven. Glad enough we'll be to see you then, Mr. Blakeman. Be sure and return."

"I'm not looking for entertainment. I've private business with your mistress."

"Miss Higgins is indisposed. She'll be available later this evening as well."

"I'm sure that's true for every other man in New York, but I think she'll see me now. I have a thousand dollars that belongs to her." Blakeman held up one of the smaller moneybags he'd filled earlier at Barnaby Carter's warehouse, thrust it close to the cracked door, and jiggled it so the coins made a clinking sound. "One thousand exactly. Don't you think you'd best tell her?"

Agnes opened the door wider and stepped aside. "You can wait in there." She jerked her head to indicate the now empty Ladies' Parlor, then left! Minutes later she reappeared. "Follow me, sir."

She took him to a small room on the third floor. It was elegantly furnished, with a decidedly feminine air, the delicate furniture painted white touched with gilt and upholstered in pale silk. "Miss Higgins will be with you shortly. Meanwhile, feel free to take your ease."

There was a decanter on a spidery-legged table under a window. Blakeman removed the glass stopper and sniffed. A fine Malmsey from Spain. He found a glass and poured himself a tot, downed it quickly, then poured another.

"I'm pleased you have discovered the refreshments, Mr. Blakeman."

Delight Higgins stood in a doorway he had not noticed. She wore a silk dressing gown the color of green apples, with a swirling skirt and a tight bodice held together with a line of bows. The gown's deep neckline exposed the curve of her spectacular breasts. "Afternoon, Miss Higgins. Your wine is as delicious, or perhaps I should say it's as beautiful, as everything else in this place." He lifted his glass in a toast, then took a long drink.

"Agnes tells me you brought my winnings."

"Right here." He offered the moneybag. Delight took it.

Eugenie would have colored prettily and looked away, letting him see that his nearness disturbed her. Delight stared straight at him. "If what I'm told concerning the day's events is accurate, Mr. Blakeman, you'll hardly miss these few coins. I believe your sale was very successful."

"It was, I'm pleased to say."

"And I'm pleased to hear it. Particularly since I believe you have incurred a further debt."

"And what might that be?"

"I returned home less than an hour ago and discovered that I've lost my chucker-out. I understand Vinegar Clifford has removed himself and his bullwhip to your employ for double the wage I paid him. Forty dollars a month, Mr. Blakeman. You might be thought to have the crown jewels hidden away in your countinghouse."

Blakeman had turned back to the Malmsey and was pouring himself a second tot. He missed the wide mouth of the glass and a few ruby drops spilled on the table's painted surface. "Nothing so dramatic," he said, glad to hear that his voice didn't show how she'd startled him. "The times are restive. I found myself in need of Mr. Clifford's skills. However, I apologize for pinching him from under your nose. Is there some way I can make it up to you?"

"I'll set my mind to thinking of one, Mr. Blakeman. I can usually—" A ripple of laughter from somewhere downstairs interrupted her. "My ladies," Delight said. "I sent Agnes to your auction and she came home with a box of ribbons and fans. The ladies are having a fine time deciding who is to get what."

Blakeman turned to face her. "But you will not participate in the division of the spoils?"

Delight shook her head. "I have other ways to amuse myself."

"About that debt . . ." He was close now, near enough to smell her perfumed skin.

She did not move away. "What about it, Mr. Blakeman?"

"I am a man who pays what he owes, Miss Higgins. In coins or in kind. I have a suggestion for you. Might you be interested in hearing it?"

"I might be." His face was inches from her own, but Delight didn't yield. A long, hot bath had gone some ways to removing the stink of Slyly Silas rutting over her, but nothing would erase the memory. Over the years, during the countless times when she was on her back because she had to be, she had one sustaining fantasy. She thought of her sex as a bear trap, a thing of iron with savage teeth, destroying the invader even as he entered. If Gornt Blakeman wanted to risk his manhood to her death grip, why should she stop him? "I am prepared to listen to most suggestions. If they are profitable."

She expected him to touch her, but he did not. Instead he retreated to one of the room's elegant little chairs, still clutching his glass of Malmsey. "What if I were to offer you the control of every whore in the city, Delight Higgins? Would you be able to manage them?"

She laughed out loud, unable to suppress her reaction even as she saw his face darken with anger. "Every whore in the city, Mr. Blakeman? The Corlear hookers, the Canvastown hot-pockets, and the Five Points Molly O'Hannigans? *All* of them?"

"All of them." He'd suppressed his anger, sounded cool, and charming with it. "And, not to imply that any house in New York is on a par with the Dancing Knave, the ladies of the other parlor houses as well."

"What a remarkable notion. Taken all together, have you any idea how many there might be? Has anyone?"

"Not now, no. But soon I will have. In the interests of good order and general health and well-being, it might be better to have the entire trade confined to one area of the town. And of course registration will be required."

"Required by whom?"

Blakeman shrugged. "That's not important just now. You still haven't answered my question. Can you manage what will be a very large and thriving business, Miss Higgins? As well as you see to this smaller enterprise?" He nodded his head toward the burble of laughter still coming from somewhere beyond the little parlor. "I admire your understanding of the notion of the carrot and the stick."

"Many more carrots than sticks, Mr. Blakeman. It makes life considerably simpler."

"But when necessary, Miss Higgins . . . ?"

"When the stick is necessary, yes, it is used."

"And on a wider scale?"

"You're serious, aren't you?"

"Entirely serious. Never more so."

Good God. "Then I will tell you that I can do whatever I need to do, Mr. Blakeman. Whatever is in my best interests, and those of"— she hesitated, unsure how to characterize the relationship that seemed to be on offer—"of my colleagues."

"Excellent," he said softly. "I believe we have an understanding, Miss Higgins."

"I believe we do, Mr. Blakeman."

"In that case I'll be bold enough to go a bit further. Now that Mr. Clifford is in my employ, he confirmed some information I only suspected. About what I'm told you call the hawk's nest."

"It can't have come as a great surprise," she said with a small shrug. "Such arrangements are useful in places like the Knave."

"Indeed. But the identity of the hawk? Mr. Clifford mentioned a name. I found it . . . unexpected."

Delight waited. So did he. After a few seconds she took a step closer and removed the now empty glass from his grip. "More wine, Mr. Blakeman?"

"Thank you."

Her stomach was churning and her hands shook as she poured the Malmsey. Fortunately, her back was to him and he couldn't see. When she could trust her voice, she asked, "Unexpected in what way, Mr. Blakeman?"

"Heroes," Blakeman said softly, "upstanding men of medicine . . . In the public mind such things are not associated with whoremongering."

"In that case the public must be made up entirely of fools." She knew she had confirmed Joyful's identity as plainly as if she had spelled out his name. Delight turned and lifted the glass of wine she had poured for her guest. "I am suddenly struck by a great thirst, Mr. Blakeman. You'll forgive me if I drink some of this."

"I will find the remainder all the sweeter for that fact, Miss Higgins." Blakeman rose and went to where she stood.

Delight took a few sips of the wine, then held what was left to his lips. When the glass was empty, she put it down and began undoing the ties of her dressing gown one by one. When she got to the last, she paused. A recklessness and a fury were rising in her, unlike all that had gone before. *You keep yourself cooler than that icicle hanging from that tree, little miss Laniah. Listen to Cuf, because he knows. Cool as ice, that's how you win.* But some coals could not be extinguished. Some rage was beyond suppression. Some betrayals demanded a fiery vengeance.

Joyful never recognized her. Not in Barnaby Carter's shay. Not in this place they'd built together. Not in her bed. Not last night when he was so enthusiastically fucking her in the hawk's nest. Not today in the Fly Market. She had opened herself to him in every possible way, and Joyful had never cared enough to realize that she was part of his past as he was part of hers. She was a convenience. Beautiful and available, and black enough inside and out so she should expect no more. Because—time to tell herself the truth—she had never been part of Joyful Patrick Turner's plans for his future.

"Perhaps you should consider, Mr. Blakeman, that what you're calling whoremongering is not the only . . . shall we say the only vulnerability to be exploited?"

Gornt realized that she was giving him something special, and that it might be more valuable than she realized, considering how little she really knew of his intentions. "And what might another be, Miss Higgins?"

"A young lady. I believe her name to be Manon Vionne."

There it was then, the other piece of the puzzle. A woman, the jeweler's daughter as it happened. That's why Delight Higgins was betraying her lover, and that's how Joyful Turner knew whatever he knew. "Ah," Blakeman said. It was a sound of great satisfaction.

"Ah," Delight echoed.

She undid the last tie, the green dressing gown fell open, and he reached for her. Delight allowed herself to melt against him. The bear trap waited.

Maiden Lane, 5 P.M.

"Excellent, *ma petite,* as always." Maurice Vionne ate the last mouthful of his dinner of duck stewed with onions. "You are as fine a cook as your *maman* before you. I said as much to Pierre DeFane just the other day."

"I am flattered by your praise, Papa. I take it, however, that Monsieur DeFane cares about my cuisine only on behalf of his nephew, the widower from Virginia."

"Of course. DeFane is well married. You know Madame DeFane, surely."

"Surely," Manon agreed. A tiny bird of a woman with the claws and the destructive instincts of a hawk. "And when is this nephew to present himself in New York?" She would meet him a time or two, maybe even permit him to call on her here rather than simply see her in the company of others. That would show Joyful he had to stop shilly-shallying.

"As soon as he can. It's very difficult to travel these days. We're told there are British warships in the Chesapeake who land troops at will, and harry the roads and the surrounding farms."

Her father sounded truly worried. Suddenly, the matter of Mr. Madison's war seemed to Manon to be more urgent than whether she could maneuver some unsuspecting widower to serve her ends. "It seems a terrifying prospect, Papa. The British can't really make us colonies again, can they? So many soldiers and militia in the streets, and sometimes, in the market, one hears dreadful things."

Vionne pushed back from the table and stood up. "Dreadful indeed. And perhaps true, at least in part. But for myself, I do not think the redcoats will prevail, however much damage they do. We were a morsel too big for them to swallow in '76 and so we shall be now. In-dependency, *ma petite* Manon, once and for all time. That is how it must be. Never doubt it."

She was surprised at the vehemence in his voice. "Of course, Papa. I am sure you are right."

"Yes, and about you as well. You would do well to remember always that your papa has only your best interests at heart. Now, please hold yourself ready to produce some refreshments in the next hour or so. I am to have a guest."

"The man you saw last night, Papa? He is to return?" Her heart began the same fierce tattoo that accompanied any thoughts of what she might do to speed the time when Joyful would consent to ask for her hand. Or even, perhaps better, whisk her away without bothering to get permission. "I can—"

"I told you to forget about last night's caller. I am expecting a col-league, Mr. Frank of Water Street."

"The Hebrew goldsmith, Papa?"

"Yes. We'll offer him some wine, and perhaps a few cakes. Nothing too fancy, Manon."

"Yes, Papa. I will do exactly as you say."

Half an hour later when she carried the tray of wine and small cakes to the shop, she found her father conferring with another man as well as Mordecai Frank the smith. "Ah, come in, my dear. My daughter, gentleman. Manon, may I present Mr. Frank, whom I be-lieve you have met, and his friend, Mr. Simson."

Manon knew Samson Simson as well, but only by reputation. He was an attorney, the first Jewish gentleman to be a member of the New York bar. Why would Papa and Mr. Frank want a lawyer? None of her thoughts showed on her face. She smiled and nodded and dropped a graceful curtsey. And though she tried hard not to stare at the book all three had been bent over when she arrived, she knew it was the Tavernier.

❦

Maiden Lane, 10 P.M.

"Your daughter, sir," Blakeman said. "Manon. I want her."

Vionne's eyes were heavy with sleep—he'd been in bed when an insistent hand on the brass knocker of the front door summoned him to his shop—and now they opened wide with astonishment. "You want my Manon? For what?"

"What do you think? For a wife. I am unmarried and nearly forty. Past time, wouldn't you say? As soon as the banns can be called. A matter of a few weeks, I believe."

"But—"

"Yes? But what?"

"You don't know her. Last night . . . I don't think you'd ever seen her before."

"Quite true." Blakeman wore boots and satin breeches, as on the previous evening, with a ruffled shirt and a hat with an outsize brim. He had removed his hat when Vionne let him in. Now he leaned forward, putting his face directly in the glow of the small oil lamp the goldsmith had lit. "Here, get a good look at me. Am I such an unpleasant prospect as a son-in-law?"

A jutting chin, glittering eyes. Not handsome exactly and not young, but the look of a man who would always get what he wanted. Vionne glanced at the entrance to the private part of the house. He'd wager his last pearl necklace Manon was standing a few feet away, ear pressed to the door and listening to every word. She would have heard the ruckus Blakeman made trying to get in and come downstairs. Vionne swallowed hard. Dear God, if only her mother were here . . . "I would not expect my Manon to marry a man, any man, purely on my say-so." Too bad she had to hear that. It would make her all the more impossible to manage. Gornt Blakeman was not a man to be trifled with. "You must return at a more regular hour, sir. And perhaps—"

"She's a virgin, isn't she? I told you last night she was the finest gold in your possession. A treasure to be guarded." They'd been the last words he whispered to the goldsmith as he left, and only half in jest.

But that he might marry the goldsmith's daughter and do good for himself while doing ill to Joyful Turner—that hadn't occurred to him until Delight Higgins mentioned the girl's name. In fact, the idea came to him in the mulatto's bed. "As long as you can guarantee she's untouched, I will require no dowry." Blakeman paused, waited for a response. Instead, Vionne kept looking at the door to the private part of the house. Must be he thought the girl to be listening—a bad habit and one he'd have to break. "I want sons, sir. I require them. Huguenot women are known to be good breeders. Have you sons, Mr. Vionne? Does she come from good stock?"

"My wife, God bless her memory, gave me three sons, Mr. Blakeman. All born healthy and alive. Unfortunately, two were lost to the cholera, and one was trampled by a runaway horse."

"That's all right then. Come, goldsmith, you should be smiling. Have you had a better offer for your goods? I can support her, as you know. And my connections . . ." Blakeman waved an expansive hand. The shop was deep in shadow, but they both knew what exquisite and expensive trinkets lined the shelves. "It will be no bad thing to be my father-in-law, sir. Speak to your daughter. Then arrange the banns."

Blakeman turned and left the shop. Vionne stared after him, then went to the door to the private quarters and pulled it open. There was no sign of Manon and no evidence she'd been there listening, but she would not have remained demurely in her room. *Tighten your grip on her, Maurice.* Almost the final words his wife spoke as she lay dying. *Take Manon in hand, otherwise she'll take you.*

Vionne sighed, closed the door, and turned back to the shop to lock the street door and extinguish the oil lamp, but for a moment he let his glance rove over the lustrous gold and silver creations he had so long labored to produce. What would it mean to an artisan like himself to be connected to a man like Gornt Blakeman? A little shudder traveled from his spine to his scalp—the tall-dream shivers, his dear dead wife used to call such feelings. *You're a fine man for dreaming, Maurice Vionne. Good thing I'm the practical one.* And Manon? She was a blend of them both. Might she be practical enough to find the notion of marriage to a man like Gornt Blakeman more intriguing than she apparently did the suit of Monsieur DeFane's nephew?

Upper Broadway, 11 P.M.

Back in Germany, Jacob Astor had been the son of a village butcher. He was rich as Croesus now, and in America a quarter of a century, but he still spoke English with a thick, guttural accent and a foreigner's syntax. "So, you come by me very late, Dr. Turner. Usually, I am by now in my bed."

"But you were willing to keep the appointment, sir." The note Joyful passed Astor at the sale said he would call at 11 P.M. and that it was in Astor's best interest to see him. It also gave the address of Joyful's boardinghouse, in case Astor wanted to put him off. He'd sent no such word.

"*Ja*, very willing," Astor admitted. "Curious I was."

"So am I. This afternoon, Mr. Astor, at Blakeman's sale, when I passed you the note, you seemed to expect it. How was that possible, sir? Are you possessed of some extraordinary mystical power? Is that the secret to such magnificence?" Joyful waved a hand to indicate everything around them.

The rest of the country accused all New Yorkers of excessive spending and ostentation, but nowhere in the city—probably not in the nation—could there be another man who lived like Jacob Astor. His mansion in this countrified northern end of town was staffed by Chinese servants, the only persons of their race in New York as far as Joyful knew. Astor had brought them over on one of his merchantmen before the war. The butler who let Joyful in had the flat features of a *nongmin*, a Han peasant, but his employer had dressed him in the elaborately embroidered black satin gown and crimson silk trousers of a prosperous hong merchant.

For Joyful, seeing the butler was like having a window on his past suddenly opened. *"Chi le fan meiyou?"* he spoke the traditional greeting in proper Mandarin. Have you eaten rice today?

"Chi le. Chi le." The butler said. Eaten. Eaten. The words repeated twice for emphasis in the Chinese manner, and always the answer, even if the speaker were a half-starved rickshaw driver. In this case, however, it looked to be true. The man was plump and round, and beaming at Joyful. *"Nin guixing?"* May I know the honorable gentleman's honorable name?

Joyful would wager ten hot dinners and his cue stick that Astor must have told him who and what to expect, else the butler would have been shocked to have a New York *yang gwei zih,* a foreign devil, address him in his own language. Instead he was smiling and entirely self-possessed. "*Wo xing* Turner," Joyful said, giving his surname first, because that was the way it was done in China: "Turner Joyful Patrick."

"*Wo xing* Wong. *Wo xing* Ah Wong."

Ah was a diminutive, used in China for only the most trusted servants. The man was indicating his high standing in the Astor household.

"Ah Wong," Joyful said with another bow.

The butler bowed back. "Prease forrow me," he said, obviously proud of his English. He turned to lead the way, and Joyful saw that his queue, his braid, had been extended with silk to hang halfway down his back. Jacob Astor's Chinese butler was as splendid as everything else in the place.

The entryway was vast, with a marble floor and gilt columns and walls lined with mirrors. It had proved to be a proper prelude to the study where Astor and Joyful now sat: large enough to be a ballroom, two stories high, and decorated with elaborate frescoes depicting hunting scenes. The tables were made to look like elephant ears or boar tusks—for all Joyful knew, they *were* elephant ears and boar tusks—and the chairs were carved to resemble lions and tigers. His host was seated across from him, in a chair carved to look like a snarling tiger, with the fearsome beast's head forming a canopy over Astor's. The tiger's mouth was open and the great teeth seemed ready at any moment to snap shut on a victim. Magnificence indeed.

"All this," Astor waved an arm to indicate the room and everything beyond it, "from much hard work it comes. And a little good fortune. And also, Dr. Turner, the power of seeing. Observation." Astor tapped his temple to indicate his eyes. "With these only."

"Observation?"

"*Ja.* Nothing else."

"Forgive me, sir. I don't believe it."

"But it's true. Let me explain. You can no longer be a doctor or a surgeon," he gestured toward Joyful's missing hand, "but nothing else you do yet. You have been seen frequently at the docks. When I am told this, I think about your father. I know he was many things, but he finished his life in the Canton trade. His son was raised in China. I too am a trader. I trade in many things. Property, here in New York, you know that, no?" Joyful nodded. Everyone knew that Jacob Astor spent hours prowling the edges of the city, buying what seemed unlikely plots of land that always turned out to be the next place every New Yorker wanted to live. "And furs I trade," Astor continued. "Many furs. First they came. But now, also the silks and porcelains and tea of Canton. Everyone knows these things. You as well, Dr. Turner. So, when like me you appear at Blakeman's sale, but you buy nothing, I observe that we are both there for curiosity only. After a time you come beside me. A little, what shall I say . . . stealthy. It must be that you intend to speak to me, or to pass me a note. Speaking would attract attention, which already you have tried to avoid. I decide it is to be a note. And because I remain curious, I put out my hand."

"I am impressed, sir."

Astor smiled. "*Ja,* a little, so am I. What is your scheme, Dr. Turner? You must have one or you would not be here."

Careful now, Joyful reminded himself. It was like playing cards with the midshipmen. You mustn't show all your cards at once, but you have to make it seem as if that's exactly what you're doing. "I believe in simplicity, Mr. Astor, so I will come straight to the point. I am now the majority holder of Devrey Shipping scrip, and thus, de facto, the owner of the company. I wish to make common cause with the most powerful trader in the nation."

Astor's tone was mild. "A sick dog, Devrey Shipping is, full of fleas and disease and a long time taking to die. But it is my competition, so if you speak the truth, you are my enemy." Joyful started to say something and Astor held up a hand to forestall him. "I think you have come here because you do not want me to think of you or your company as my enemy. And I think perhaps it is true and you are not. But am I sure? No, Dr. Turner, sure I am not. Please, convince me."

"Two words should be enough. Gornt Blakeman." Joyful thought he saw a flash of interest in the other man's eyes.

"So. A great victory he has had, a great day. I congratulate him. But fear him I do not, Dr. Turner. My best information says only one merchantman he has, the *Canton Star*. I have a fleet."

"So have I, now."

"You, or Devrey's, I should say, have eight merchantmen. All are rotting in the roads. One East Indiaman too. Apparently, still she is captive in Canton. As for me . . . I own four ships meant for the China trade. Two are idle. The other two are"—he hesitated—"gainfully they are employed."

"As privateers, I warrant."

The older man shrugged. "I am a loyal American, and I wish to help my country in her time of need. Attacking the enemy's shipping is a good way. As good as sailing with the navy"—he nodded again toward Joyful's missing hand—"and much more profitable. Come," he stood up. "Let me show you something, Dr. Turner. Please, over here."

Astor led his guest to an almost life-size bronze statue of the Greek god Atlas, holding up a globe of the world. The globe was made of ivory-colored parchment stretched over an iron frame, the continents etched in position in dark sepia tones. The globe was discreetly pierced, and lit from within with some kind of lantern. Jacob Astor extended one finger and set the contraption spinning. Joyful could not look away. Shafts of light appeared to fly from the earth's interior toward the great beasts that populated the study. His host touched the globe a second time and it stopped turning. They were looking at North America. "So, here is our United States," Astor said. "Much bigger now that President Jefferson bought the French Louisiana, no?"

"Very much bigger."

"And here is what President Jefferson wrote to me about that bigger country." Astor took a letter from a nearby shelf and handed it to Joyful.

The letter was dated April 11, 1808. *All beyond the Mississippi is ours exclusively, and it will be in our power to give our own traders great advantages over their foreign competitors.* Joyful stopped reading and skipped to the signature. *Thomas Jefferson,* it said, *President of the United States.*

"Here I have a trading colony." Astor tapped the western edge of the North American continent. "Astoria. A year ago I sent men to find a better route between Astoria and here." His finger rested on St. Louis in the Missouri Territory.

"And did they find it?"

"*Ja,* Dr. Turner. I think they did. A pass through these mountains"—his short, stubby finger had moved to the Rockies—"where wagons can go without so hard a journey. So after this miserable war is over, many can travel from here to here." The finger traveled from New York through the Oregon Territory to the colony he'd named Astoria. "And Astor's ships will trade with ease, everywhere." Once more the globe spun at Jacob Astor's touch and shafts of dancing light illuminated the surroundings. "Everywhere," he repeated. "And from Astoria my merchantmen will not have to go around Cape Horn." Astor's pointing finger dropped to the southernmost tip of South America. "They can go straight across the Pacific Ocean to China."

"And the goods will then travel overland to New York? Using this passage you've discovered?"

The older man snorted with laughter. "No, no! That would be stupid, *hein?* Better Astoria becomes a big city like New York, so I can trade there directly."

He couldn't make it plainer. Joyful Turner was nothing more than a mosquito perched on the mighty tiger's luxurious coat, a small annoyance to be flicked off with the swish of a tail. Nonetheless, it was too late to back off now. In fact, it was time to show another card. "Tell me, sir," Joyful said, "do you consider your Astoria to be part of the United States?"

"*Ja,* of course. I am a patriot, Dr. Turner. That is why presidents write to me."

"And because you finance them," Joyful said quietly.

Astor smiled. "A little money," he admitted. "For President Jefferson, and now for President Madison. To help with the war effort. I must do this because we have listened to stupid men, and now we have no Bank of the United States to buy bonds and issue credit. So that task falls to Jacob Astor and a few of his friends. I will make a profit, *ja,* Dr. Turner, but still I am a patriot. Come, we will again sit." Astor led the way back to the other side of the room and once more seated himself beneath the open-mouthed tiger.

The wager had been both called and raised; it was time for Joyful to show his hand. "I believe you are a patriot, sir. Otherwise I wouldn't be here. Whatever the difficulty, I would have found some way to take my information directly to Mr. Madison."

Astor leaned forward, one hand tapping impatiently on his thigh. "You know something. What?"

Joyful's mouth was dry and his stomach knotted. He could so easily be wrong. Andrew could have been mistaken. Manon could have misunderstood Blakeman's business with her father. He took a deep breath. "I believe that Gornt Blakeman is soon to offer you an opportunity to do something extraordinary, something that can make you fortunes yet undreamed of, Mr. Astor, but not on behalf of our young nation. Quite the opposite."

Astor fixed his visitor with his dark and intent gaze, saying nothing.

"What if I were to tell you," Joyful continued, "that Gornt Blakeman has in his possession a rare stone, a diamond worth a king's ransom. And that I am all but certain he plans to come to you with a scheme to offer this jewel to a foreign court."

Astor leaned back. His face was shaded by the overhanging tiger's head, and Joyful could no longer see his eyes. "If, Dr. Turner, you were to make such a statement, I would ask first how you came by the information."

"And I would tell you that I cannot say."

"Then why should I believe you?"

"Because it is a matter of honor, and there is a lady involved. But as to the information, I have no reason to lie about such a thing."

Each man took the other's measure in silence. Suddenly, Astor leaned forward and grasped Joyful's left wrist. "I warrant this makes you a patriot as well, Dr. Turner."

Joyful hated to have his wound touched; he steeled himself not to jerk away. Finally, having inflicted as much discomfort as he chose, Astor released his grip. "A true patriot, Dr. Turner. So I shall tell you more than anyone else knows except, I hope, President Madison. All this hysteria in the streets, the soldiers . . . New York is not about to be invaded. Our enemy goes somewhere else—but do not think we are safe. Our United States is in more danger than ever before. In fact, I have to the president sent word. He must leave the Executive Mansion."

"The British will attack the Federal District?" Joyful could not keep the dismay from his voice. "You're certain?"

"No, not certain. Only it is what I think. I have arranged so here in New York I will know first if it happens. Now," Astor reached over and tugged on a bell rope that had been fashioned to look like a leopard's tail. "Brandy we must have, Dr. Turner. And I will tell you more of my story, and you will tell me what you can of yours. Without, of course, you violate a lady's honor."

Finbar O'Toole pulled evenly on the oars, his rhythm easy and practiced. The Inner Harbor was flat as a lake, a splash of bright moonlight laying a path for the gig to follow. He could see his ship, riding at her mooring in the roads. There must be a current running out there.

Close to midnight and he still had the whole of his six thousand seven hundred, except for a few coppers gone for drink. He'd not been near the Dancing Knave. Hadn't even taken a hand of cards when there was a free place at a table of players in one of the numerous taprooms he'd visited during the evening. Not restraint and sure as hell not good sense, spite was more like it. A sickness indeed. He bloody well wasn't sick. And if he was, how come Joyful Turner was prepared to let him captain a fine sloop like *Lisbetta*? Presuming Joyful really had any say in the matter. Why would Bastard Devrey give his cousin a ship to go off on the kind of fool's errand O'Toole suspected this treasure hunt to be? A share in whatever was found, probably. But over half a century had gone by since that suspect voyage of the *Fanciful Maiden*. Why should whatever Morgan Turner buried still be wherever he'd put it? And what about the small matter o' the poxing British blockade? Couldn't last forever, Joyful said. True enough. But Bastard Devrey was hanging on by a thread, and the dogs were snapping at his heels. Odds were, he'd fall and be torn apart well before the Royal Navy sailed off and these waters were safe enough for a voyage to the Caribbean.

Holy Mother of God, what was going on?

Canton Star was abeam her portside neighbor, a sloop that had been so long a prisoner in the roads she looked like a ghost ship, all peeling paint and tarnish. The bowsprit of Blakeman's merchantman was aimed directly at the sloop's midsection. From this distance it appeared *Star* had not yet made contact with the other vessel, but it was a close thing.

The sloop was the property of a small-time coastal trader whose name O'Toole didn't know, and whoever he was, he'd be no more'n a gnat's bite to the likes o' Gornt Blakeman, especially now. But Finbar O'Toole was captain o' the *Star*. If she did damage to anything afloat, however worthless, it was his responsibility. "Ahoy, Star o' bloody Canton!" he hailed. "Ahoy, sailor o' the watch!" He picked up the stroke, pulling so hard on the oars he soon had no breath left for shouting.

❧

The forward anchor had gone adrift. No damage done, there was still some distance between the *Star* and the sloop. It was a simple matter to pole off the other boat and secure the anchor line. O'Toole did the job first, then silently approached the forecastle, where the tar on watch was supposed to be. He was there all right. Tammy Tompkins—flat on his back, slack-jawed, snoring, and dead drunk. He had to be, otherwise he'd not have slept through the trouble or the fixing of it.

If this were the navy, Tompkins would be summarily hanged and no questions asked. It was not, but O'Toole wanted the man dead.

He went below and retrieved the red woolen bag that hung in his cabin and was standard fitting on any ship. When he returned topside, the cat-o'-nine-tails—a black leather handle and nine short, knotted cords—was in his hand. The first stroke caught Tompkins between his shoulder and the side of his neck. He woke screaming and rolled away quick enough to catch the second stripe on his back. "What are you doing? You daft old bastard! This ain't the poxing British Navy! You can't flog me! I'll kill you first!" Tompkins scrambled for purchase on the deck, rolling below the foremast. "I'll kill you!"

"Off my ship!" O'Toole roared. "Get off my ship or you're a dead man!" He saw the knife that had materialized in Tompkins's hand, but ignored it, just went on swinging the cat, occasionally landing a blow. Meanwhile, Tompkins thrust and thrust again, trying to dodge the stripes O'Toole was raining down on him but get close enough to slash the Irishman's flesh. The cat held him away. In moments the tar's shirt was in shreds, and his chest and one side of his face was slick with blood. "Get off my ship!" O'Toole howled. "Off! Off! Off!"

Tompkins twisted and turned, half crouching, half rolling. His goal was the bulkhead, and he finally reached it and grasped the gunwale. Pulling himself up exposed his back to two more vicious stripes. He ignored them and clambered over the side of the ship, descending by the futtock shrouds, hurling curses while the cat continued to belea-guer his head and shoulders.

O'Toole swung the cat until Tompkins was out of reach, then dropped it and stood where he was, chest heaving, until he could breathe without pain and the red haze of fury in front of his eyes had begun to clear. He was aware that the two other crewmen had come up from belowdecks and stood by the forward bulkhead, watching him. He bent down, scooped up the cat, and turned and pointed it at one of them. "You"—he was still gasping for air—"take over the watch." Both tars were red-eyed. It must have been a three-man raid on the rum, with Tompkins drawing the short straw and having to at least pretend to stand watch. Now his blood was a dark brown stain on the heavily buffed boards. O'Toole pointed the cat at the second sailor. "Swab the deck before you go below."

"Tompkins can't swim," the first tar muttered.

The Irishman had already started for the ladderway that led to his cabin. He stopped, turned slowly around, and looked at the man who had spoken.

"Then he'll drown," O'Toole said. "He was drunk on watch. He deserves no better."

"Don't matter none." The second tar was leaning over the side. "He's taken your gig, Cap'n."

By then all three had heard the splash of the oars as Tammy Tompkins made for shore.

Saturday, August 20, 1814

Chapter Eleven

New York City,
Hanover Street, 2 A.M.

GORNT BLAKEMAN had been planning to find somewhere better to live than the private rooms above his countinghouse for over a year, even if it was only a temporary stop between present arrangements and those that would be suitable for the future he planned.

Months he'd spent putting the pieces of the puzzle in place: enlarging his coaching business, maneuvering to get a big enough share of Devrey Shipping so he could negotiate on a more equal footing with the Boston shipowners whose alliance was crucial to his plans, waiting for *Canton Star,* praying that Finbar O'Toole was really the man to bring her safely through the British blockade, and when indeed his ship arrived in triumph, holding his breath to see if she had brought him the one thing he truly wanted, the treasure that would make his dreams a reality. All that had taken priority over domestic arrangements.

As for tonight, he could have returned to Delight Higgins's bed. It was a good deal more luxurious than his own, and God's truth, she knew enough ways to pleasure a man to ward off boredom. Nonetheless, he'd had enough of her. There was something unyielding in the she-witch, something that made him feel she was the aggressor even as she lay beneath him. Christ, how did women like that keep from constantly being with child? They must have ways. She must have them. Else those slim hips and that taut belly would long since have become permanently misshapen and spread.

Eugenie would not have stopped a child from coming, even if she knew how. Why should she? She'd been a respectable married woman. Despite that, in four years she'd given Timothy Fischer no heir. She must be barren. A pity, all things considered. As for the rest . . . Would it be the same with her as with Delight Higgins? When he finally had Eugenie—and he would have her—would he discover the same flinty core? Hard to say. And the yellow-haired beauty the mulatto had served up sauced with so much venom, Manon Vionne, the goldsmith's daughter? A virgin. He was sure of it. Spirited, judging from her father's reaction to the proposal, but never mind, he'd mold her to his liking. Build them a proper house as well, up near Astor's. Or maybe make the City Hall into a palace. Eugenie would be close enough so he could have her as well as a wife. Something to please him while Manon was bearing his sons.

The door of the taproom next to the countinghouse swung open, and a body was hurled into the street. "No drink without coin, you miserable bastard. You can die of thirst for all I care."

The ejected man slid on his rump just short of Blakeman's boots. Blakeman extended a leg to kick the drunk out of his path, then stopped.

"Got to find Gornt Blakeman," the seaman muttered. "Lives around here. They told me . . ." He stopped speaking long enough to vomit into the gutter, then wipe his mouth with the back of his hand. "You'll find Blakeman on Hanover Street, they said."

"Mr. Blakeman to you. What do you want with him? What's your name?"

"Tammy Tompkins, that's me. Genuine war hero. Sailed with Admiral Perry, I did. Did my share. More'n my share. Had enough o' guns and blood and sawing lads in half while they was still alive."

"Yes, well it appears you've had enough of something." The man was filthy, badly cut up, and his checked shirt was in tatters. Blakeman had seen such wounds before. "You've had a taste of the cat, probably well deserved, but what's that to do with Mr. Blakeman?"

"Sailed all the way from Canton on his ship, I did. And stayed aboard on his personal request. Now I got to find him."

Blakeman leaned down, ignoring the sour stench of vomit and sweat. It had been Captain O'Toole's job to select the three tars he wanted to keep aboard. Looked as if he'd made at least one bad choice. "What's your business with Mr. Blakeman?"

Tammy Tompkins squinted up at the face now hovering some six inches above his own. "Not your lookout. I got to . . . Say, I know you. You're Bla— Mr. Blakeman. I seen you when we came into harbor."

"Say that I am, that still doesn't tell me why I shouldn't roll you into the gutter and go on my way."

"Don't you be doin' that, Mr. Blakeman. No sir. Not when I got valuable information you should have."

Tompkins struggled to his feet—Blakeman pointedly offered him no assistance—and staggered a bit until he found a hitching rail he could lean against. "Valuable information," he repeated. "Worth a bit it is."

"Worth not summoning my chucker-out to finish the flogging that seems to have been started aboard my ship? Which you doubtless deserved."

"Didn't do nothin' deserves no cat. Should o' been let go ashore, like I asked. Had to take watch instead. Cap'n now, he goes ashore whenever he bloody well pleases." Tompkins began rhythmically kicking the toe of one boot against the upright of the hitching rail.

"Is that your information? That Captain O'Toole comes ashore as he chooses? That's hardly worth your time, much less mine." Blakeman started to walk past the tar. Tompkins put out a hand to stop him and Blakeman quickly brushed it off. "Keep your filthy hands away from me. And either tell me something important enough to make me stand here and listen, or get out of my sight."

"It's important. I swears it. But you can't 'spect a bloke to spill his guts for nothin' but a smile, can ye? Even the likes o' poor old Tammy Tompkins deserves a bit o' somethin' for all the trouble he's took to come and tell you what he knows."

Blakeman reached into his pocket and found a few coppers. Tompkins smiled and extended a horny hand to receive them, then looked up disappointed.

Another search through his pockets produced a guinea. More than he'd intended to offer, but the only other money he had easily to hand. Blakeman dropped the coin in Tompkins's outstretched palm.

"Bless me! That's fine, sir. Glad enough to tell you about the Chinaman, I am now."

Blakeman suppressed a sigh. A wasted guinea.

"Knowed he was aboard, I did, for some weeks," Tompkins said. "Would o' reported it right away, 'cept I saw how he was what you might call a personal guest o' the cap'n."

"Guest? What are you talking about?"

"A stowaway, Mr. Blakeman. On the *Star*. A Chinaman down in the after magazine where the gunpowder was, and the rum. That's how I knowed. 'Twas my job to organize bringing up the rum whenever it was wanted. Took three o' us to manhandle them kegs up through the cap'n's cabin. First couple o' times weren't nothin' you might call notable, then, third time I think it was, I smelled something awful. I moved some things about, and there he was, huddled back in a little corner. I'd o' raised the alarm right then, 'cept I figured the cap'n had to know. Seein' as the only way to get down to the after magazine is through the cap'n's quarters."

It could be true. Blakeman struggled to assess the possible threat to two props of his plan, the box and the cargo. But he'd already sold the cargo and reaped the profit, and the box and its treasure were unharmed and in his possession. So what could a Chinese stowaway have to do with him? "You have to be mistaken."

"No sir, Mr. Blakeman. Saw him with me own eyes, I did, first night we was in harbor. Cap'n brought the stowaway above decks and rowed him ashore his own self. I swear it."

Greenwich Street, 5:30 A.M.

The note was delivered by a small black lad who handed it to Joyful without a word. *Come at once. Bring your kit. The boy will show the way.* It was signed simply *A. T.* "Did Dr. Turner give you this?"

"I don't be knowing his name. Dr. Turner, he be a cutter?"

"A surgeon. Yes."

"Then prob'ly that be him."

Joyful had come to the door in his shirtsleeves when his landlady summoned him. He turned and headed up the stairs, long legs taking them two at a time. "Wait for me. I'll return straight away."

Moments later he was back, wearing his cutaway and carrying the black leather satchel that contained the tools of his trade. Correction, his former trade. "Is Dr. Turner all right?"

"Don't be knowin' that," the boy said.

"What do you know?" Joyful put on his stovepipe and led the lad out the door.

"Only as I be supposed to bring you to Mother Zion."

"In Five Points?" The boy nodded. Joyful was not surprised. Andrew had began his doctoring in the almshouse hospital years ago, and he'd been treating the poor ever since. "What's your name?" Joyful asked.

"Joshua."

"Very well, Joshua. How did you get here?" The sky was flushed dawn pink and the street was silent, and empty of any kind of transport.

"Runned all the way."

"Yes, well you're younger than I. And fortunately not too heavy for Mary Jane to bear the added burden."

Joyful stabled the piebald mare at Foster's Livery, a few steps from the boardinghouse. She was old but serviceable. It took no time to saddle her. Joyful swung himself up, then reached down for the boy. Moments later they were trotting north up Greenwich Street headed for Five Points.

Joyful smelled blood as soon as he entered the church's cellar. He had shrugged his coat off and opened his satchel before his eyes adjusted well enough to the dimness to see Andrew bent over a table in the far corner.

His cousin was stitching, from the look of it. "Choose a patient and get started," Andrew called out. "Those you can probably help are over here by the window."

Joyful had to pick his way over the bodies of a dozen black men to get to the spot Andrew indicated. Three appeared to be dead. At least two others were soon to be, and there was little he or Andrew could do about it. But just below the grimy, head-high slit of a window that let in a modicum of light from the street, there was a man with his hands pressed to his face, moaning. Joyful dropped to his knees beside him.

A few feet away Andrew finished sewing up the man he'd been attending and moved to another. "Leave me, Absalom," Joyful heard him say. "I can do this with Joshua's help. You go and assist my cousin, Dr. Turner. He has only a single hand, so you must supply your two in place of the one that's missing."

Joyful's patient had lost an eye, gouged out in a fight from the look of it. The eyeball was hanging by a few strands of sinew and one distended artery that fortunately had not been severed in the attack. He'd have bled to death by now otherwise.

He turned to get a scalpel from his satchel and found there was no need. The young man Andrew had called Absalom had already selected the best one for the task and was holding it out. "This be the one, don't it, Dr. Turner, sir?"

"The very one, Absalom. My cousin has trained you well."

Absalom grinned and began preparing sutures.

Joyful held the scalpel in his teeth while he moved the stuffed glove that supplied for his left hand into position below the hanging eye to act as a support, making sure he didn't cut through the man's cheek and add to his troubles. Damn, he didn't want to cut the glove either. "There are cloths in there on the right." He jerked his head toward the open satchel. "Fold a few into a pad and give it to me."

Absalom was quick as well as clever; it was done in a few seconds. "Well done, Absalom. Now give this fellow one of those dowels to bite on. Yes, that's it."

Joyful swabbed enough blood out of his good eye so the man could see. He was staring at the surgeon in terror.

"This is going to hurt like bloody Hades," Joyful said cheerfully. "But with any luck you will neither bleed to death nor be poisoned by your wound. And when I'm done, you'll still have one good eye. Think on that. Quite a few of that lot over there"—he jerked his head in the direction of the inert bodies by the door—"have not been anywhere near as fortunate. Now bite down as hard as you can on that bit of wood and we'll get started."

Five minutes later he'd cut away the eyeball, tied off the severed blood vessels, and stitched the eye closed. "Neat enough so you won't frighten small children after it heals," Joyful said. The man, however, had passed out and didn't hear him.

It took the better part of the morning for Andrew and Joyful to patch up seven of the wounded and pronounce six others dead. Joyful was only formally introduced to the man Andrew called Reverend Fish when he and his cousin were led from the cellar-turned-surgery to a small room off to one side. There was a pitcher of ale and some biscuits waiting for them.

"My cousin, Dr. Joyful Turner," Andrew said. "Joyful, this is Reverend Zachary Fish, the minister here at the African Methodist Episcopal Zion Church."

"I be pleased to meet you, sir," Reverend Fish said. "And very grateful for your assistance this day."

Joyful shook the minister's hand. "Glad to have been able to help. But I'm left wondering about the wielders of those very effective knives that made ours necessary."

"As am I." Andrew poured ale for himself and the other two men. "There appears to have been if not a war, at least an all-out battle. With F. X. Gallagher's men, I presume."

Reverend Fish shook his head. "That may come, but this was an engagement of a different sort. Black man against black man," he said softly. "Warring gangs with allegiances that be important only to them. We do not, it seems, have enough violence visited upon us from outside, so we must be doing evil to ourselves."

Silence for a time, broken by Andrew. "The first time I cut into the flesh of a Negro, Reverend Fish, I realized that we all bleed the same color. It should therefore not come as a surprise that we all lay claim to the same idiotic vices."

"I think—" Joyful was interrupted by a loud knock on a door that led to the street.

Fish got up, opened the door a crack, and stood speaking in low tones to someone neither Andrew nor Joyful could see. After a few moments he turned back to the two doctors. "My neighbor, Mr. Patrick Burney, has urgent need of a physician. He lives quite nearby, so he knew you gentlemen were here . . ."

Fish left the request unspoken. Andrew started to rise. Joyful extended a restraining hand. "I'll deal with it. You were here and working well before I arrived." The older man was ashen with fatigue. "Go home, Cousin Andrew. Get some rest." He turned to Reverend Fish, "You'll see that he does?"

The minister nodded. "Absalom be taking him back by wagon. If you could hurry, Young Dr. Turner. I believe the need be pressing."

Outside, the sunlight was blinding and the noise of the street came as a shock. Joyful had arrived in Five Points in the relative hush of dawn; It was past noon now.

The district was a mass of horses and pushcarts and wagons and people. In addition to the rolling stock used to transport and display commodities, there were countless women carrying trays of goods slung from their necks with leather straps. Each one hawked her wares while elbowing aside neighbors to the right and left.

Reverend Fish had sent Joshua to guide Joyful to where he was needed. The boy darted into an alley between the church and a rickety wooden building. Joyful had no idea where he was, but his guide apparently did. The boy stopped beside a door painted bright yellow with a large green cross splashed across the top half. Joyful remembered hearing tales of the gangs of Five Points, how they identified their territory with symbols of one sort or another. "Mr. Burney," Joshua said, "he be in here."

"Thank you. Joshua, you must wait. I'll never—"

"No fear, Dr. Turner. The lad will wait on ye." Burney had magically appeared at the door, opening it only a crack and motioning Joyful inside before he slammed it quickly shut, throwing a pair of bolts and sliding a large bar into place. "Upstairs," he said.

Joyful followed him up three flights of creaking stairs, the passage so narrow his shoulders brushed the walls either side.

"She's in here." They had reached what seemed to be the top of the house.

"She?"

"My daughter Brigid Clare. She's three."

Burney threw the door wide open and stood aside. Joyful knew what to expect. The child would be burning with fever, suffering from one of the many illnesses that beset the young, whether they lived in a slum like this or in a mansion like Astor's. Damned little he'd be able to do for her; cupping and bleeding and administering tincture of mercury, but they never cured anyone of anything as far as Joyful knew.

They were in an attic with barely enough headroom for Burney and not enough for Joyful. The child lay on a pile of rags in one corner of a room that had been created by erecting three walls under the eaves. The smell of dirt and damp was overwhelming. There was something else as well, something dead and rotting swiftly in the heat.

Joyful crouched and went to the child. Every muscle in his body ached after the hours of surgery. "Hello, Brigid Clare."

He put a hand on the little girl's forehead. She was cold, remarkably so, considering the sweltering heat. And clammy. Shock? Joyful lifted one of her eyelids. The whites were bluer than they should be. She was covered with an assortment of rags, and he reached beneath them for the hand closest to him. There was no resistance. He pulled the hand free. The pulse was faint, thready, and he noted the nail beds were blue as well. Definitely shock. And no damage apparent to the parts of her body he could see. Joyful lifted the blankets. Both legs looked normal. He turned to Burney. "How long has she been like this?"

"All morning. Ever since she got bit."

He should have guessed. "A rat?"

"Yes." Burney nudged something with the toe of his boot. "This one here. I bashed him stone dead while he was still on her."

"Where?" Joyful opened his satchel while he waited to be shown the wound.

Burney stepped forward and moved the coverings aside. "Her backside. Right here." He rolled the child on her side; she made no protest. "Did what I could, but it weren't much. Sucked out some o' the blood, and put a bandage on the place where the flesh was torn. Then, when I heard there was doctors next door, occurred to me . . ."

"Yes. I understand. Let me see." Joyful leaned over to study the wound. It was ragged, and oozing but not gushing blood. "You say you sucked blood from her when it happened?"

"Right away. That's what we did in the old country. Me ma, she always sucked the poison out o' rat bites."

"Mine did the same," Joyful said. Irish common sense, Roisin would have called it. "You did the right thing." He was probing the wound as he spoke. The child moaned once. "I'll clean this up, cut away the ragged edges, put in a few stitches," he said. "You'll have to help me. I've only one hand."

"I know," Burney said, kneeling beside him. "Not to worry."

"Not to worry indeed. You've already done the best that can be done for her."

Ten minutes and he was done. Brigid Clare had sniffled a bit and gasped once or twice. Now it seemed to Joyful she was warming up, and she looked more alert. "There's a good chance she'll recover." He stood up as well as he could in the low-ceilinged space, feeling the blood race back into his legs, making them tingle. "Most important thing is not to let the injury become septic." Joyful had shaken a generous amount of powdered yarrow into the wound before he stitched it. Now he reached into his satchel, retrieving an ampule of a thick dark green oil. "It's a cleansing balm," he explained. "You should change those bandages morning and night. Put a little of this on each time." Peppermint and sumac steeped in camphorated oil. Roisin had never given him any formal training in her Woman of Connemara skills—that wasn't permitted—but some things he'd learned simply by being around her.

Burney put out a hand to take the balm, then pulled back. "I've no money to pay ye."

"Doesn't matter. Take it. For Brigid Clare's sake."

The Irishman snatched at the vial. "Good of ye. And good to help Reverend Fish."

"Do you know him well?" Listening to Andrew and the minister, he'd have thought the Irish and the blacks to be deadly enemies.

"Well enough." Then, as if he could read the thoughts of the other man, "Don't make a lot o' sense nigras and whites hating each other, not when we're all poor and jumbled in together here."

"No sense at all," Joyful agreed. He started down the stairs, and Burney came after. They'd reached the last landing before the barred door when Joyful felt the other man's hand on his shoulder. "I know who you are," Burney said.

Joyful wasn't sure he knew what the man meant. "Yes, well . . ."

"I mean I know you were with Perry. One of the heroes of Erie."

"There have been many battles since then and many other heroes. Besides, I didn't fight. Just patched up those who did."

"Still," Burney said. "Are we going to win, do you think, Dr. Turner? Will we stay independent?"

"I think so. Yes."

"Sure, that's what I think as well. Glad to hear an educated man like yourself agrees. The United States for all time. That's why I don't exactly see why they're formin' the regiment."

"What regiment is that?"

"The one as is going to be the army of the new country. I reckon 'tis a daft notion. But they're payin' three coppers when you sign up, and promisin' there'll be ten per day when the army is fully established. Brigid Clare's ma died when she was born. Me and me little girl, we're alone here. A man does what he must, Dr. Turner."

"Yes, he does." Burney was no longer looking him straight in the eye. "I understand. Still, it would be useful to know who it is raising this regiment."

Burney looked up the stairs, as if he thought someone might have appeared to overhear them.

"I was christened Joyful Patrick," Joyful said. "We Irish have to look after each other, especially when something's downright foolish. Like talk of a new country. A name, Mr. Burney."

"Can't say for sure. Could be the same man who said as how you had to be watched."

Joyful managed to conceal his surprise. "Gornt Blakeman. He's the one who's raising the regiment, isn't he? And the one who said I should be watched."

"Not him exactly; it were F.X. Gallagher. Comes to the same thing." Burney turned the small bottle of oil over and over in his fingers. "And he said to keep a lookout for the lady as well."

"What lady? Damn it, man, I need to know."

"This stuff's going to help my daughter get well, isn't it?"

"It is. What lady?"

"The goldsmith's daughter. Mistress Vionne."

Anger made the blood at his temples throb. Joyful yanked on Mary Jane's reins and headed her south. The horse obediently turned onto Broadway, but not before casting a reproachful look over her shoulder. Joyful patted her shoulder. "Sorry, old girl, it's not your fault." They were far enough north so he could give the mare her head after that, bend forward and let her run out. In minutes they were in the ever increasing crush of carriages and wagons and pedestrians of the churning city at the tip of the island, and he had to rein her in while his thoughts still raced. The bloody bastard. If he harmed Manon, Joyful would take him apart with the one hand he had left.

It was getting on to one o'clock, and Hanover Street was thronged with people. Most were crowded round the countinghouse door below the sign that said BLAKEMAN COACHING.

The fury born in Five Points was a thing of ice now, cold enough to allow for calculation. If Gornt Blakeman was in his countinghouse or in the private rooms above them, Joyful would confront him and have the whole thing out right now. He and Bastard had the majority shares of Devrey scrip and would buy him out or force him out. As soon as he'd done that, he'd talk Delight into letting him raise a mortgage on the Knave. Someone at the Tontine was bound to like that investment. He might even be able to get enough to finance the *Lisbetta*'s voyage to the Caribbean.

And what if Blakeman was somewhere else? According to Manon, the Great Mogul had not been left with her father, so either Blakeman kept it on his person, or he'd hidden it here on Hanover Street, probably in his private quarters on the upper floor. What a coup that would be: steal the bloody thing right out from under the poxed bastard's nose, and use it to fix an alliance with the king of traders himself.

Joyful pushed his way into the countinghouse and was instantly immersed in the hubbub. One clerk was shoving away a clutch of people who seemed intent on crawling over his tall desk while another was shouting, "Told you already, Mr. Blakeman's not here and we don't know when he'll be back."

One question answered, and more of an opportunity than he might have imagined. The countinghouse was chock full of suppliants who knew that, as of yesterday's sale, Gornt Blakeman had become a man with a great deal of ready coin.

"It's my little one as needs . . ."

"Worth his while, no doubt about that. Shells peas with one touch. Greatest invention since . . ."

"Married to his third cousin, I was. He'll want to see me right now."

The clerk standing at the desk in the back of the room raised his voice above the tumult. "Get out, all of you! He's not here and we've work to do."

An old woman with one side of her face eaten away by the pox shoved her shawl clear of her head so her disfigurement was more easily seen. "How would you feel if this was you? Wouldn't you try and ease your way a bit with a few coppers a rich man wouldn't miss?" At least a dozen voices shouted agreement.

"A few coppers. He'll never know they're gone."

"He's not here, I tell you. Why won't you . . ."

Joyful sidled along the edge of the room, skirting the chaos. A heavy velvet curtain hung six feet to his right, and logic said the curtain shielded a stairway to the private quarters overhead. If Blakeman had really stashed the diamond on Hanover Street, the stairs would be well guarded.

He'd taken his medical satchel with him when he tethered Mary Jane on the street; it was his excuse for being here if he was challenged. He'd been summoned to a sickbed. Sorry, he must have mistaken the address.

At the curtain now, and still no sign of the guard he was sure Blakeman must have posted. Joyful used the stuffed glove to sweep aside the curtain and slipped quickly behind its folds, every sense alert, waiting to be challenged. There was no sound except for the incessant demands of the throng in the countinghouse, somewhat more muted now, thanks to the thick curtain. Dark as night as well. He sensed rather than saw that he was in a narrow passage facing a flight of stairs.

He started to climb, moving slowly, alert for a squeak that would summon the watchdogs Blakeman had set to guarding his huge diamond. Unless, of course, it wasn't here. On his person then. Or— The creak he'd anticipated came. Sounded to him like all the gunpowder in creation going off at once, though he knew it was only a small noise in the darkness. Joyful froze, waited. Nothing. Could be no one was here because the diamond was hidden somewhere else. Or it was nowhere within thousands of miles. It might well be that Manon had misunderstood, and the fabulous Great Mogul, diamond of the ages, was in the court of some sultan or pasha on the other side of the world.

Another stair. Christ, how many were there? He stretched the glove straight ahead of him, counting on the extended sense he'd developed these last months. He wasn't disappointed. He knew that he was one step from the top landing, and that he'd encountered yet another velvet curtain. Joyful took a deep breath, listened carefully, and heard nothing. He pushed the curtain aside. A sliver of light came from below a closed door. He reached for the handle; it turned easily and the door opened without a sound. Holy Jesus Christ, it could not be this easy.

Joyful peered into a gloomy room. One window faced the street. The other on the opposite wall. Both were heavily draped. He listened to the steady rumble of noise from the countinghouse below—no change of pitch to indicate that anyone had raised an alarm—and something else. He'd wager his soul it was the sound of a stream of piss hitting a china chamber pot, stopping and starting. As if whoever was relieving himself was having difficulty.

Blakeman's private quarters were a single room, stretching back into deep shadows. The front end was dominated by a surplus of heavy furniture—chests and tables, and a bed hung with still more velvet. By the bed he saw the man obeying the call of nature: Vinegar Clifford, wearing his working outfit of black singlet and leggings. He was hunched over a delicate-looking chamber pot painted with bright pink roses. It was the first time Joyful had seen the whipper without his weapon at the ready.

Clifford's whip lay on a table a few feet distant. Both his hands were hanging on to his cock, and not simply to aim his stream. Seen in profile, the whipper's face was contorted in pain, and he was groaning softly under his breath. Given the gingerly way Clifford was handling himself, it was in the genitals he felt the attack. Any odds you cared to name said the strained trickle of piss was flecked with blood, and letting it flow meant suffering the tortures of the damned. Getting his own back some might say. Vinegar Clifford, not long since the most feared man in the city's jails and almshouse, was suffering the terrible burning agony the simple need to urinate caused when you were a victim of the French disease.

Joyful was as sure of his diagnosis as if he'd examined the patient and heard the list of symptoms. Secondary syphilis, with attendant renal disease. Probably a few months after initial contagion was signified by a painless chancre on the penis that soon disappeared. Nothing painless about this stage of the malady.

Excellent, suffering was a fine distraction.

Joyful took a few steps into the room. If he could get to the back of the crowded chamber, he could hide until such time as the whipper went back to his post downstairs guarding the entrance to the upper floor. As soon as he left, Joyful would search for the ebony box. If he didn't find it, he'd wait for Blakeman to come home.

Clifford was still intent on his own business. A large chest provided Joyful cover for a few feet, a tall armoire did the job for another few. Then he was in the open again, skirting the table where Clifford had left his whip. The other man's back was to him, the ropy shoulder muscles twitching in spasms of misery. The groans had become a steady, tearful whimper. Too bad some of the poor sods who'd felt the sting of the lash and the vinegar bath that followed it couldn't be here to watch.

Joyful took another step, and something hit him from the rear; he cried out in surprise. Clifford cursed and twisted round, looking for the source of the sound, then doubled over with the pain of the sudden movement. "Who's there! I'll flay the hide off—"

Not a chance. Joyful dropped his satchel and stretched his hand toward the table. As soon as he changed his position, the loose floorboard that had sprung up and hit him clattered back into position. Joyful ignored it, feeling the thrill of triumph when he beat Clifford to the whip by something less than a heartbeat. It uncoiled in his hand, the long lash puddling on the floor at his feet. "Stay where you are, otherwise you'll have a taste of your own medicine."

"Jesus poxing hell. It's Joyful Turner, isn't it? What are you doing here?"

"I might ask you the same. Aren't you supposed to be at the Dancing Knave about now? Miss Higgins won't be pleased to know you're looking after Gornt Blakeman's business instead of hers."

"Don't matter none to me what that nigra—what Delight Higgins thinks. Work for Mr. Blakeman now. And he didn't say nothing about you coming here."

"Fair enough. But does Blakeman know you're so racked with pain every time you piss that anyone can gain access to his private quarters?"

"That ain't none of your business. No skin off your nose neither."

"Maybe not. But how much more of that agony can you take?" Joyful nodded toward the chamber pot. "A man has to piss sometimes, Vinegar. Even you."

"That ain't none o' your business neither."

"Illness is my business. Your waterworks are damaged. I can fix them." He tucked the whip under his left arm and reached for his medical bag with his right.

The whipper eyed him with something close to terror. "I ain't letting you take a knife to my privates!"

"I never said anything about cutting. I'm a doctor as well as a surgeon." Joyful swung the bag toward him, undoing the buckle. He needed his gloved stump to hold the bag open while he rummaged for what he wanted. The whip dropped to the floor. Clifford ignored it;

there was no question what mattered most if it came to a choice between a man's cock and his whip.

"Here's what you need." Joyful extracted a brown glass bottle, tightly corked, and put it on the table. "This will help with the pain when you piss. Take a swallow when you first feel the need to go, and try to wait a few minutes. The pain won't disappear, but it will be considerably less."

"Truth?"

"Why would I lie?"

Clifford reached for the bottle. Joyful snatched it away. "Nothing's free in this world, Vinegar. Not even medicine."

"How much?"

"In coin? Nothing. It's information I'm after."

The whipper's glance darted to the whip lying on the floor between them. "What kind o' information?"

"The box you collected from Captain O'Toole. Where is it?"

"Don't know nothin' about any bloody box."

Joyful moved to return the bottle to his bag. "Lies are a waste of time, Vinegar. I was there. I saw you take the box."

Clifford made a small move toward the whip. Joyful stepped on it. "Of course; a man in your condition wants more than relief from pain. You want the illness to be cured before your cock shrivels up and falls off."

"Falls off! Jesus, I never heared—"

"There's plenty you never heard. Not your line of country, is it? It's mine, though. That's why I can say for certain that this"—Joyful extracted a small green-glass vial from his bag—"*this* will cure you. This yellow powder may taste like cat vomit, but sprinkle a bit on your tongue morning and night for a time, and not only will your cock stay attached to the rest of you, peeing will no longer be painful and there'll be no blood. I guarantee it."

Clifford stared at both bottles with open longing. Forty dollars a month was useless if his cock fell off and left him no kind of man at all. "I got the box on the dock, just like you say, and brought it straight to Mr. Blakeman. He paid me five dollars, but as to what was in the box . . ." The whipper shook his head. "Ain't got no bloody idea. And that's the truth."

"Why send you? Blakeman could have simply collected the thing and be done with it."

"No sir. He couldn't do that. You know about medicine, Dr. Turner. But I know about men of standing. Been doing their dirty work for years. Men of Mr. Blakeman's sort have to keep their hands clean. You going to give me that stuff or ain't ye?"

"In a minute. I've one more question. Where's the box now?"

Clifford shook his head. "I've no idea. Don't want to know neither. Blakeman's paying me twice what I earned working at the Dancing Knave. Long as I can piss without going through hellfire, I'm content. Now, do I get the stuff or don't—"

"Get out, all of you!" The bellow from below stairs penetrated two thick curtains and one door. "I'll have the law on the lot of you otherwise. Mr. Clifford! Get down here! Bring your whip!"

Clifford hesitated, looking toward the stairs and the summons from Gornt Blakeman, and at the brown bottle and the green sitting on the table. Joyful made up his mind. "Here," he said, pushing the medicines forward. "Just remember that when you need more you're to come to me." He'd specified small doses, but he'd stake his soul Clifford would believe the more he took the faster he'd get well. "Meanwhile, keep your eyes and ears open so you've something to report in payment."

"That window over there," the whipper said, jerking his head toward the rear wall. "It overlooks a private yard. And there's a tree with a branch you can probably reach if you lean out far enough." He crouched down to reclaim his whip. Joyful kicked it in his direction. Clifford grabbed it and stood up, at the same time whisking the two glass bottles into a drawer on his side of the table. "Hurry. I'll give you as long as I can, but Blakeman's sure to come up here sooner rather than lat—"

Another booming yell from below. "Mr. Clifford!"

The whipper ran for the door.

Joyful hesitated. There were shouts from below, and sounds of scuffling feet. Clifford laying about someone with the whip, no doubt. Joyful headed for the rear window, threw his bag out first, then climbed into the tree. He hated heights. It used to make him dizzy just watching the seamen maneuver high above his head in the rigging, but the tree was close enough to the building so he wasn't conscious of the drop. Climbing down with only one hand was twenty times more difficult than he expected, but he got to the ground with only a slight scrape to his cheek and pulled his watch from his waistcoat pocket. Two o'clock. Probably too late to find Manon at the Fly Market. And though he now had urgent business with Delight—if Clifford had bedded any of the women at the house when he was contagious, they would have to leave—he couldn't face the thought of that just now. These days every encounter with Delight was a reproach to his conscience. Moments later he was astride his mare and headed toward Greenwich Street.

The bottle of laudanum was a loss, but fortunately he had two spare back in his room at Ma Allard's. There was only one more of the small bottles of tansy powder, but not much to be bothered about there. Tansy was useful for cleansing wounds, but God knows, no cure for the French disease. Physicians and quacks alike had been trying to find one for centuries with no success. But the stage of the malady currently afflicting Vinegar Clifford, ex–official whipper of New York City, would end of its own accord in a matter of days or possibly weeks. Both Joyful's experience and the medical literature said so.

Syphilis began with visible sores, at which time it was most easily spread. Next it passed into an acute stage involving agonizing pain, then after a short time retreated for months or maybe years, coming back to kill the victim usually well before his appointed span. Meanwhile, the tansy powder would do Clifford no harm, and the laudanum was a proper treatment for this acute period. As for giving the whipper false hope, Joyful felt no guilt about it. His oath of medicine did not require him to tell a man his death was going to be sooner rather than later and ugly when it happened. As for what he'd gained and what use Clifford might be to him in the future, he'd have to wait and see. It would all depend on his joss.

Chapter Twelve

New York City,
the Foot of Maiden Lane, the Fly Market, 2 P.M.

CUSTOMARILY, Joyful met her here between noon and one. Manon had arrived at the market a little before twelve on this Saturday and waited nearly two hours, but he never appeared. She dared not stay too long; Papa had been watching her all morning, asking repeatedly when she planned to leave and when she would be back. "You need not fuss yourself about such things," she'd told him. "I will look after the household arrangements, Papa. Just as I always have."

Vionne had mumbled something about unmarried ladies needing to take special care of their reputations, then gone off to his shop, but he'd come back into the house three times to see what she was doing and inquire about the marketing. He acted as if he wanted to say something, but couldn't make up his mind to do so. Wanted to pass on the proposal of marriage from that odious Gornt Blakeman, no doubt. As if she would ever consider such a thing.

In her heart Manon truly believed her father wouldn't force her to marry Mr. Blakeman, despite the financial advantages of such a union. But right now, she was quite sure, he was waiting anxiously for her return and telling himself he would know no peace until she was someone's wife and no longer his sole charge. Dear heaven, he might even take it on himself to come looking for her, and her basket still held only a single turnip and a few greens for salading. Small comfort such a dinner would provide.

Manon flew about the market, spending five coppers on the hindquarters of a plump rabbit the butcher skinned while she watched, then a ha'penny more on half an ounce of mustard seed from the spice monger's stall. A nice *lapin à la moutarde* would improve Papa's temper. But it would do little for her own. Where are you, Joyful? How can you have deserted me today of all days?

As she'd expected, her father was waiting when she returned, standing by the kitchen door and muttering that she'd been gone a long time. "I do not understand why I cannot do things as I have always done them, Papa. Why are you besetting me this way?"

Vionne mumbled something about her well-being and his responsibility and returned to his shop. Manon stirred up the kitchen fire and began preparing her braise of rabbit with mustard, though her mind was definitely not on her cooking.

Holy Hannah had told Jonathan Devrey to put his new messenger in livery. This old thing didn't seem like livery to Jesse Edwards. Not the proper sort like Will had, with Bastard Devrey's coat o' arms right there on the collar. This was just an old brown cutaway coat with a few moth holes, and much too big for him. It was Holy Hannah as sharpened a twig and used it to pin the empty arm into the pocket so it didn't flop about. The way Will told it, he'd been taken to a genuine tailor and had his green cutaway and waistcoat made up bespoke-like. His stovepipe hat didn't come halfway down his head and perch on the tops of his ears neither. Course Jonathan Devrey didn't have a fancy house on Wall Street. According to Hannah, Mr.

Jonathan, as he was supposed to call him, lived above his shop same as ordinary folk.

Sign o' the Hungry Babe, he'd been told. Tavern right at the top end o' Maiden Lane. The sign hanging over his head had a picture of a wee babe with its mouth wide open like it was squalling for food.

The barmaid seemed to be squalling for what Jesse brought as well; she grabbed the four bottles o' Devrey's Elixir of Well-Being and tucked 'em right down her dress. "Just here t'ween me tits," she told Jesse, whisking off his hat and planting a big kiss on the top of his head. "And next time Mr. Devrey sends you, make it your business to come when we're not so busy as we are now. I'll take you out back and show you what I think o' this new delivery scheme." She grabbed for his crotch. "Didn't lose the jewels along with the arm, did ye, lad? No, praise God. Cock's right where it should be, and standing up to say hello to Bess as well. Next time, little man. I'll be yer first and get ye started proper."

The men standing by the long counter saw and heard the whole exchange and guffawed loud approval. Jesse, too red-faced and flustered to say anything, escaped into the street, then realized he'd forgotten the hat the barmaid had taken off his head and had to go back and claim it. Bess was waiting for him, but he didn't see his hat until she snatched up her skirts and revealed it gripped between her legs in their striped knitted stockings. "Come and take it, lad! Bess deserves a bit o' pleasure for all the hard work she does."

He grabbed for the hat, and the barmaid spread her legs and let it drop. His hand connected with the brush between her plump thighs. He jumped back, then bent and swept his hat from the floor to his head, as the whole taproom erupted in laughter. Jesse turned and fled.

He hadn't gone ten steps when another young woman was hailing him. Jesus God Almighty! What a job o' work this was turning out to be. He went to where she stood beside the gate at the end of an alley that ran beside a little brick house with a goldsmith's shop at street level. "Yes, miss. Are you wanting something?" Right pretty this one was, with a pearly white smile and eyes like purple pansies. Spoke like a proper lady as well.

"I haven't seen you on Maiden Lane before. What's your name, lad?"

"Jesse Edwards, ma'am. Work for Devrey's Pharmacy, I do. Delivery boy."

"That's exactly what I'm after. I'll give you two coppers, Jesse Edwards, if you take this to Ma Allard's Boarding House, number forty-seven Greenwich Street. You're to put it straight into the hand of the gentleman whose initials are written here." Manon held out the folded and sealed note with "J. P. T." written on the front. "No one else, mind. And if you wait until he has read it, I promise you'll get another copper for your trouble."

Three coppers! What would Hannah say when he brought her those after doing only two days' work? He could tell Mr. Jonathan he'd had to wait for Bess the barmaid, seein' as how she was busy and all. "Right, I'll do it, ma'am. Who am I to give it to again?"

Of course the lad couldn't read. Silly of her to have expected anything else. "A gentleman whose initials are J. P. T." She pointed to the letters, then saw his look of puzzlement and shook her head. "Never mind, simply show the note at. Ma Allard's. But mind you, don't give it to anyone else. Only the tall red-haired gentleman himself. Otherwise you won't get that extra copper."

"I will do exactly what you say ma'am. Never fear." Jesse snatched the note, pocketed the money, and took off running, waiting until he'd rounded the corner to stop a passerby and ask the way to Greenwich Street.

"Jesse Edwards. As I live and breathe."

"Dr. Turner. I never thought . . . Lady just said I was to give this note to a gent with the 'nitials J. P. T. Said he, I mean you, would give me another copper for bringing it."

"Did she now? And where did you find this lady who was so sure of my generosity?"

"Near the tavern, sir. One by the Sign o' the Hungry Babe. Mr Devrey sent me and—"

"Bastard Devrey sent you?"

"No, Dr. Turner. It's me friend Will as works for Bastard. I'm in the employ o' Mr. Jonathan Devrey as has Devrey's Pharmacy in—"

"Hanover Square. Yes, I know." He'd visited Clare a few times when he first got to New York from Canton, but Joyful had never been close to his sister, her husband, or their twins. The girl called Molly and her young slave disappeared about a month after Joyful came home. As for Molly's brother, Jonathan, Joyful knew him only well enough to know he was disagreeable. "Someone at the Hungry Babe gave you—"

"No sir, Dr. Turner. I was at the tavern 'cause I had to bring some o' Mr. Jonathan's Elixir to the barmaid. After I left the Hungry Babe, the lady stopped me beside the goldsmith's shop. Pretty as anything, she was, sir. And she gave me two coppers to bring this, and said you'd give me another when you got it."

Of course. Manon. He should have realized. Joyful reached into his pocket, found a copper, and handed it over. "Goodbye then, Jesse. Thanks for bringing this." Joyful started for the stairs, then paused. Sweet Christ, he'd taken off the boy's arm; he had to still be surgeon enough to ask how the lad was faring without it. "How are you keeping, Jesse? Wound giving you any trouble?"

"Not much, Dr. Turner. Me shoulder aches a bit sometimes. And there's others when I'd swear it was me elbow or me wrist was giving me gyp."

"I know, Jesse." Joyful held up the black glove. "I feel the same plenty of times. Could swear it's the fingers of my left hand that are causing me pain. Not much to be done for it, I'm afraid."

"Holy Hannah, sir, she gives me some leaves to chew on when it hurts bad. Says she learned 'bout 'em from the Indians used to be up there in the woods near her place."

"Is that where you're living? With Holy Hannah?"

"Yes, sir. Right good she is to me too. Good to everyone. Will Farrell, he's been with her longest, but just now she's nursing some kind o' Indian."

"An Indian? Really?" They were standing in Ma Allard's front hall. As far as Joyful was concerned, the only thing motherly about his landlady was her nosiness; she was certain to be somewhere close by with her ear pressed to a door. "I'm sure you're mistaken, Jesse," he said loudly. "Holy Hannah's a loyal American, she'd not have any truck with Indians. Now you'd best get back to work." Joyful hustled the boy onto the street while he spoke, but kept hold of his shoulder. "Listen, lad," he whispered when they were outside, "tell Hannah it's dangerous to have an Indian living with her now. There's much feeling against the Canadians because of the war. Someone will be sure to think whoever it is a spy for the British, and Hannah along with him."

"I'll tell her, Dr. Turner. Anyway, this one's the strangest Indian you ever did see. Doesn't wear a scalplock. Just a braid down his back. And don't speak no proper English neither. No matter what Hannah gives him to eat, he don't seem to know what it is or even to like it much, hungry and weak as he is. Fan, he keeps saying. Fan. We take turns fannin' him sometimes. But it don't seem to help."

By the dovecote at three, today, Saturday, the note had said. *Or eleven tomorrow at the Bowling Green. Imperative.*

There were a number of dovecotes in the city, but the one Manon meant was located in the center of a tiny garden next to the Jews' Mill Street Synagogue, a ten-minute walk from her father's house. The dovecote was an exquisite conceit painted snow white and the blue of a robin's egg. They had stopped to admire the graceful birds and the lovely building on one of their earliest meetings.

Joyful was on Mill Street before three and waited until nearly four. Manon did not arrive. She must have found it impossible to get away; she'd not have disappointed him otherwise. He cursed himself for not managing to get word to her earlier when she'd have expected to meet him at the Fly Market, and for not telling her yesterday about his arrangement with Bastard Devrey. He'd felt guilty about that ever since. The Chinese-inspired belief that the gods were always watching, waiting for a man to slip, held him back. Damn you for an ignoramus, Joyful Patrick Turner, damn you to hell.

Samson Simson came out of the synagogue, his stovepipe already on his head, not in his hand as it would be had he been visiting a Christian church. Joyful knew him. Both men touched the brims of their hats. Simson then walked on.

The street was again deserted. Joyful hung about a few minutes more, pretending to admire the charming garden and the dovecote. Then, accepting Manon had been unable to come and he could not see her until the next day, he reclaimed his mare from where he'd tethered her and headed east toward Pearl Street.

Maryland,
The Hills Above the Village of Benedict, 4 P.M.

The two men lay on their bellies, looking down on the British encampment. "What do you reckon," the first man whispered. "Six or seven thousand?"

The second man shook his head. "Fewer than five. But that'll be plenty if every battle's like this one."

The village had put up no resistance; the inhabitants merely fled, taking with them most of the horses.

"Won't be this easy if they're planning to take New York," the first man said with a native's pride.

"Maybe so, but that's not where this lot are headed. Fleet will sail right into the harbor when it's New York they're after."

"So what do you reckon, Baltimore or Washington?"

The second man, the one who was making notes to take back to Jacob Astor, shrugged. "Can't say for sure. Except that there's nothing for them in the Federal District. Baltimore's a much bigger prize."

"But it's not the capital."

Another shrug. "Has to be something to be capital of, if that's to matter."

"We'll wait and see then?"

"We'll wait and see," the other man agreed.

New York City, the Open Country
Above the North Street City Limits, 6 P.M.

Holy Hannah's shack appeared at the far end of the field. Like an apparition, Joyful thought. Like something you'd see at the Bowery Theater, a bit of scenery painted on a curtain.

Hannah was bent over in the long grass to the side of her rickety cabin. No sign of Jesse or the other boy Jesse said was living with them. No sign of the Indian either. If that's what he was.

Apparently Hannah had dug herself a well since he was last here. On that occasion Andrew had been summoned and brought Joyful with him. They were to tend a lad who had fallen out of a tree. The patient was stone dead by the time they arrived—he'd cracked his head wide open—but Joyful distinctly remembered one of Hannah's other boys being sent to fetch water from a stream.

The bucket was full. Hannah hauled it up, straightened, then tipped the contents into a jug at her feet and dropped the bucket back down the well. "Whoever you be," she called without turning around, "you don't be doing yourself any good just looking. You want something, come and ask Hannah straight out."

Everyone said she had second sight.

Joyful moved the mare forward a few paces. The nearest tree had a marble marker screwed into its trunk that said FOURTEENTH STREET, evidence of the Common Council's determination to level the island's hills and impose a grid of numbered streets and avenues on the wilderness. He swung out of the saddle. Fourteenth Street had a branch low enough for the reins, and he made them fast, then walked toward the woman. "Hello, Hannah. Do you remember me?"

She turned at last and squinted into the westering sun. "Joyful Patrick Turner. Course I remember you. They tell me you're not doctoring these days, that you're after making your fortune instead. Your Dr. Turner cousin never made himself a fortune. Storing up treasure in the heart of the Holy One, Blessed Be His Name, is Andrew Turner. He's not a Hebrew, but he's doing *mitzvot*. Don't s'pose you know the meaning o'that, Joyful Patrick. Good deeds. Doin' things way the law o' the Almighty says they should be done. Treasure where it can't be taken away."

"I do the best I can, Hannah. And you, I hear, are still taking in every stray that comes along. Jesse Edwards told me there was an Indian as well."

She shrugged and didn't meet his glance. "Folks come and go at Hannah's. Everyone knows that. I hear you be the one as turned Jesse into a pigeon with one wing."

"I cleaned up what the British guns left behind."

Hannah nodded toward his black glove. "That happened same time. Least that's what Jesse said."

"Told you the story, has he?"

"Only after he seen you on Greenwich Street. Came running back here soon as he could to tell me Bag-o'-Bones was a danger to us. Danger from an old Indian like Bag-o'-Bones, that don't make no sense."

"Bag-o'-Bones, that's what you call him?"

"Aye. Can't tell us what his real name is. Don't speak no English."

"Let me have a look at him, Hannah. Could be I know a bit about his language."

Hannah cocked her head and looked straight at him. Joyful felt a need to stand taller. Her eyes were an extraordinary shade of blue and her gaze was the sort that looked right through a man. "Bag-o'-Bones is sleeping. Come back another time. He—"

"*Diu lay lo mo hail. Leng gwai.*" The shout came from the direction of the shack. "*Ah si. Ah si.*" Cantonese. The roughest sort, the language of the streets. Fuck you all and I need to shit.

"He's not sleeping now," Joyful said. "He's telling you he needs to relieve himself."

"Is he now? Well, he knows where to go. All Indians know—"

"He's not an Indian, Hannah. And I don't for one moment believe you ever thought he was."

"Aye," she said, matter-of-fact about having lied to him. "At first I did. Then I got a better look at him."

A man pushed aside the flap of oiled cloth that served as the cabin's door and staggered out. Hunched over, and barely able to walk, he maneuvered himself around to the far side of the cabin. Moments later he returned. Joyful was waiting for him.

"*Chi le fan meiyou?*" Joyful asked. Have you eaten rice today?

"*Chi le. Chi le.*" Eaten. Eaten. But the man was staring at Joyful with eyes full of terror.

"*Bu chi le. Bu chi le,*" Joyful muttered. "You haven't eaten rice. not in some time from the look of you. And stop staring as if I'm a ghost. I'm a flesh-and-blood *yang gui zhi,* a foreign devil who happens to speak like a proper Middle Kingdom person."

"*Bu chi le,*" the man admitted softly. "*Bu chi le fan.*" No rice.

"*Bu chi le fan,*" Joyful repeated. "That's the problem, isn't it? You've eaten no rice in God knows how long." Bag-o'-Bones indeed. He was starving, nearly to the death. Joyful turned to Hannah. "What have you been feeding him?"

"Whatever I can get, same as the rest o' us. He don't eat much, though. I keep trying to tell him he needs food more'n anything else, more'n being fanned for instance, for all that's what he keeps saying. Fan. Fan. I say eat, eat. But he won't listen."

"He's Chinese. *Fan* means rice in his language. It's life's blood to him. Nothing else is proper food."

"Rice," Hannah said with astonishment. "What am I to do about that then?"

It was dusk by the time Joyful reached the corner of Broadway and Barclay Street. This time he didn't approach Astor's imposing front door; he went round to the tradesman's entrance. A young Chinese girl answered his ring. "Ah Wong," Joyful said, *"tsai jia ma?"* Is he here?

The girl's eyes opened wide in surprise, but she quickly regained her composure. No doubt the servants had all heard the tale of the New York foreign devil who spoke the language of the Middle Kingdom. *"Tsai. Tsai,"* she said. *"Qing nin deng yi deng."* Ah Wong was at home. The honorable gentleman should wait a little wait.

The girl hurried away with the painful, small, and unsteady steps that bespoke her bound feet—her golden lilies, as they were called in China. A young man came into the kitchen, the butler's son perhaps, dressed in a traditional gray cotton *sam* and *fu,* and tall for a Chinese, with exceptionally broad shoulders. He bowed respectfully and hurried away without speaking, but Joyful suspected the young man too knew about the *yang gwei zhi* who had a civilized tongue in his head. Moments later Ah Wong appeared. He also wore a loose gray cotton jacket and trousers, not the embroidered silk of the previous night. He asked politely if Joyful had eaten rice that day. Joyful said he had. And that he hoped Ah Wong had done the same.

"Chi le. Chi le." Eaten. Eaten.

In his case, Joyful was sure, it was true. "There is another," Joyful said, "also a man of the Middle Kingdom, who has not eaten. They offer him only foreign food. He is starving." There was no rice to be found in the city these days. It was grown in the Carolinas, and coastal shipping was as prey to the patrols of the Royal Navy's blockade as was everything else.

Joyful was convinced the man who had brought Chinese to serve him had to understand that for these people to be without rice was to die; a man of Astor's prescience was bound to have laid in an ample supply. If not, Ah Wong and his brood would be wasting away, but there was plenty of flesh on the bones of the butler and the little serving girl and the young man. More than there probably would be had they stayed in China. *"Bu fan. Bu fan,"* Joyful repeated. No rice.

"Hen chuo. Hen chuo," Ah Wong said. Very bad, repeated twice to show how bad he thought it. "Swallowing the bitter sea."

"Bitter indeed." There was no real reason the man should give him rice in this time of scarcity, but Joyful was counting on what he knew of the Chinese character.

Ah Wong would give him rice for the sake of *guanxi,* to bind their alliance. In China good *guanxi* made all business—indeed, all survival—possible. Joyful had to be the first and only foreigner the butler had met in New York who spoke his language, a fluent Mandarin that could only have learned as a child. Joyful knew that for Ah Wong he was a link to this foreign place which might prove as useful as being employed by a man of Jacob Astor's wealth.

"Eh. Deng yi deng." Wong hurried off. He had told Joyful to wait a little wait, and something would be forthcoming. And he'd spoken in ordinary terms, not the flowery honorifics of his first meeting with the butler, or of the little servant girl swaying on her golden lilies. He and Ah Wong had become equals of a sort, conspiring to do something that one way or another might someday further both their interests.

The butler returned, followed by the young man Joyful had seen earlier. *"Ta jiao Wong Hai."* His son's name was Hai. *"Ta de shenti hen zhuang."* The honorable gentleman should note that the son was in good health and of a superior size to most men.

Hai carried a burlap bag of rice—about two or three pounds of it, Joyful guessed. A substantial quantity under the circumstances, but nothing that required the impressive breadth of the lad's shoulders, not even considering he carried a small iron cooking pot as well. Nonetheless, Ah Wong kept pointing to the rippling muscles to be seen beneath Hai's *sam. "Liqi hen da. Hen da."* Very strong. Very strong.

"Very strong," Joyful agreed. The rice was clearly local, the burlap stamped CAROLINA—probably shipped from the South before the blockade was put in place—but the pot looked to have come from China. The family Wong would not have trusted the foreign devils to have proper utensils to prepare the food that kept them alive and would have brought a supply of rice cookers with them.

Ah Wong issued instructions to Hai Wong, and the son carried the rice and the pot out to where Joyful's horse waited. Joyful turned to follow, but Ah Wong put out a hand to stop him. "This too," he said in his singsong English. Then, in Chinese: "For my brother from the Middle Kingdom." Joyful wasn't quite sure if his story had been believed, or if Ah Wong thought he had some other reason for wanting rice. It didn't matter. Only *guanxi* mattered. The something else was a set of chopsticks, and a twist of paper containing a spoonful of tea. "*Chi . Chi,*" Ah Wong murmured. Eat. Eat.

"*Chi. Chi.*" Joyful agreed. "Tomorrow and a few days after as well. Your brother from the Middle Kingdom thanks you. So do I."

"*Fan* is the Mandarin word for food as well as for rice," Joyful told Hannah. "Rice is life." They were watching her latest stray use Ah Wong's gift of chopsticks to push the grains straight from the cooker into his mouth. The rice was hot and steaming, cooked by Joyful over a small fire Hannah built out of doors, beside what Joyful had mistakenly thought to be a well; it was actually a brick-lined cistern ten feet deep, designed to catch rainwater. About half full thanks to the summer storms.

"And do all China peoples have no thumbs, like this one?"

"No. He may have angered the wrong person. He says he's called Thumbless Wu. I reckon he's been like that for some time." Despite the missing digits, the man handled the chopsticks with ease; it was an adaptive skill he'd have needed years to perfect.

Joyful thought he saw the man's eyes turn in his direction, but only for a moment. Wu's attention quickly returned to the cooker of rice. He ate half of it, then stopped, saving some for another meal. "*Tsi bao,*" Joyful said. "*Tsi bao.*" Eat your fill. He held up the bag of rice. "You need to get your strength back. I will leave this for you when I go. You can cook yourself more when you like."

"Make him do it for himself," he told Hannah later as he prepared to leave. "You'll never get it right. And don't say anything around him you don't want overheard. He may not speak English, but I suspect he understands it."

"How does that come to be? If he's a China man like you say, how did he get here?"

"I'm not sure, but I'd venture he came on *Canton Star.* I can't think of any other explanation."

"Gornt Blakeman's ship as ran the blockade?"

Joyful nodded agreement.

"And you think Bag o' Bones learned English on that passage?"

"No, I doubt that. He's a Cantonese. Canton's a trading colony, China's window to the West. He'll have had plenty of opportunities to learn English."

"So why did he come to New York?"

"I have no idea," Joyful admitted. "None at all."

Hannah considered for a moment. "He's got a knife," she said. "I seen it. Weak as a sick kitten he may be, but he still hones that knife with a stone every day, and uses it to shave his scalp. Everything but that braid."

"That's his queue. No Chinese will ever cut it. When the Manchus defeated the Ming Dynasty in 1644, they made it a law that every man in the country had to have a shaved head and a queue. Without that braid, Thumbless Wu can't return to the Middle Kingdom. That's what they call China, by the way, a place between heaven and earth." Hannah raised her eyebrows. "If he cuts his queue, he can never be buried with his ancestors."

"It's not him bein' buried as bothers me. You reckon he's any kind of danger to my boys?"

Joyful considered. "Whatever has brought him here, it's nothing to do with any of you. He might steal you blind and leave in the middle of the night, but I don't think he'd do any of you physical harm."

"I'm not worried about him thieving," Hannah said with a shrug. "Wouldn't be the first time. And there's not much to steal. I'll let him stay."

"Good. He should start getting stronger now he's eating rice. If you have any meat to spare, you can give him a bit of that as well. Or some pot herbs or salading. I'll try and come back tomorrow or the next day and see how he is. Maybe by then I can get him to tell more of his story."

Rivington Street, 10 P.M.

The small door at the rear of the Dancing Knave led to the cellar where Tap-a-Keg Jonah deposited his wares once a week. Joyful used his key. The door, whose iron hinges were kept well oiled on Delight's express orders, opened soundlessly. He slipped inside. Normally, he had no reason not to be seen going into the Knave by the front door like everyone else. Tonight was different.

He made his way up the cellar stairs. The rear hall was deserted. He moved quickly toward the front of the house, pausing to look into the Ladies' Parlor. One girl sat alone playing a hand of solitaire. The others must all be upstairs in the bedrooms. She glanced up and saw him. "Good evening, Dr. Turner."

"Good evening, Cecily. How are you?" A plump and pretty fair-haired little thing, she looked perfectly well. But looks were no guarantee of anything.

"Perfectly fine I am, Dr. Turner. Bit bored, though." And with a cheeky little smile: "You wouldn't care to spend half an hour"—she'd started to say "upstairs," but thought better of it—"playing cards?" she finished instead.

"Can't right now, I'm afraid, Cecily. I'm looking for Miss Higgins."

"Right behind you." Cecily dealt herself another hand.

Joyful turned; Delight was standing at his shoulder. "I need to talk to you," he said quietly.

"Later," she said. "Upstairs?" It was a plea as much as a question.

Joyful shook his head. "I can't stay." And seeing the flash of disappointment that touched her eyes: "I'm sorry. Business. But I do want to talk to you."

"Yes, well, not here. Cecily, you can't be trying very hard if you're the one left when all the others are chosen. Perhaps you smell unpleasant. Go upstairs and wash."

The girl flushed bright red, but got up and headed for the stairs, sidling past them, careful not to look at the man all the girls swooned over, though they knew he was their mistress's lover. Delight watched her go, then led the way into a small room off the entry hall that served as a private office where sometimes she conferred with customers, usually refusing the credit they were asking for. There was an oil lamp on the table, the flame kept economically as low as it could be without going out. Delight turned the little wheel that lengthened the wick and the place brightened considerably. She saw the bruise on Joyful's cheek. She couldn't keep herself from touching the mark. "What happened?" she asked, caring though she didn't want to.

"I had a disagreement with a tree branch. Delight, Vinegar Clifford's gone to work for Gornt Blakeman."

She shrugged, careful not to let him know how it made her feel to hear him speak the name of the man she'd invited to make him a cuckold. "I know. I have already replaced him with three Irish lads from Five Points."

"You're always ahead of me," he said. "But there's another concern. Clifford has the French disease. The lasses could be infected—"

She looked at him, appalled. "You think any one of my ladies would have given herself to Vinegar Clifford?"

"I know it's against your rules, but—"

How could he think that because a woman whored to survive she might willingly give herself to an animal like Clifford? "No," she said. "Not against my rules. It's against theirs."

"I could examine them if you like . . ."

She shook her head. "It's entirely unnecessary. The young Irishers maybe, if I don't keep an eye on them. But the whipper? Never."

"Very well, if you're certain."

Delight nodded. It was growing easier by the minute to live with what she'd done. Particularly when Joyful again said he couldn't stay and left without even accepting her offer of a glass of wine.

Sunday, August 21, 1814

Chapter Thirteen

New York City,
Scrivener's Alley, 8 A.M.

YOU HAVE EVERYTHING ready, Mr. Danforth?" Eugenie wore an old-fashioned, tight-waisted frock with a wide skirt and a snug bodice. It covered her from neck to ankles, and her bonnet had a thick veil that covered her face.

"Everything, madam. Exactly as required."

Slyly Silas busied himself collecting the documents he'd prepared for her, keeping up the pretense that he didn't recognize her. *I'm not that much of a fool, Mistress Eugenie. Used to see you, I did, back when I was doing work for your late husband. Timothy Fischer always wanted his paperwork to be the very best, and to drop into his hand, so I delivered the goods to the house on occasion. That's why he came to me, and it's why he picked you, a lady as might have been courtesan to some king over in Europe. Doesn't make a ha'penny worth o' difference that I recognize you, Eugenie LaMont Fischer. Too high on the shelf, you are, for the reach of Slyly Silas, and he knows it.*

Her money, however, was another matter. Danforth put out his hand and Eugenie counted twelve coins into his palm. "Forty dollars, as agreed," she said. Lord help her. The servants wouldn't be paid for another six months. And what about her bill at the butcher's? At least four months overdue and sure to go four months more. Ah, but when this investment produced a profit . . .

"Exactly right, madam." Danforth had to bite his tongue to keep from trying to weasel a bit more out of her. Might have done, if he hadn't caught sight of that fellow as was waiting for her when she came two days past to place the order. Patch over his eye, bandanna round his head, sort o' hiding himself 'neath the canopy of that smart little chaise she was driving. A pirate for sure. Slyly Silas was far too canny to get on the wrong side of a pirate.

Eugenie longed to get out of the stuffy little room and away from the leering of this disgusting scrivener, but she longed still more not to have to come back anytime soon. She took the time to examine the documents.

There were six sets, each neatly inscribed with a fine quill writing on thick paper, produced in triplicate as the law required, and each set clipped together with a straight pin. The top three claimed the missing slave to be "a male nigra upwards of five feet." None of the papers specified how many inches upwards. "Has dark eyes and black curly hair." Plenty of those about. "Answers to Pompey," one document said. Two others assigned the names Nero and Caesar. The nigras would deny having those names, but that did not figure to weigh overmuch with the magistrate. Everyone knew that the first thing a runaway did was drop his slave name for something that sounded properly white and Christian. You could call a sow a steed and it remained a sow, but the nigras couldn't be expected to know that. The other three documents indicated the runaways to be women. One even specified a "comely mulatto." That had been Tintin's idea. Eugenie thought it unwise to be so specific, but he insisted. Getting hold of the nigras that matched the descriptions was his part of the bargain. "Thank you, Mr. Danforth. These are excellent. I may return for more before too much longer. For now, I bid you good day."

Danforth swung the door open and bowed her out, then rushed to the window and pushed the curtain aside a crack, just enough so he could watch her lift her skirts and climb into the chaise. Driving herself, Eugenie was, as she'd done on her first visit. Didn't want anyone knowing where she'd been, not even a servant. The pirate being the exception. Wasn't with her today, though.

Slyly Silas jerked the curtain all the way open, letting the daylight stream in. Eugenie might want more documents. She'd said so. Where would she get them if not from Slyly Silas Danforth?

For most New Yorkers Sunday morning was time for church, and Maurice Vionne and his daughter were not exceptions. Ten o'clock found them in their customary pew in the French Church of the Holy Spirit, founded when the Protestant Huguenots first fled Catholic France for the safety of Nieuw Amsterdam. L'Église du Saint Esprit continued to conduct services in the French language, but since 1804 the rite had been that of the Anglicans. It was a Protestantism perhaps not quite as austere as that which the Huguenots had brought with them, but its services were equally long-winded.

It was nearly quarter to eleven and Manon estimated the service to be less than half done. The preacher was droning on, reading psalms. She leaned over so she could whisper in her father's ear. "I must go, Papa."

"How can we go? There is still—"

"You stay. I will go." A woman in the pew behind shushed them, but Manon ignored her. "We will give less scandal that way."

"But . . ." The woman shushed again and Vionne let his protest trail away.

Manon turned to give the scolding woman the sharpest glance she could muster, then leaned even closer to her father and put her lips right against his ear. "It is a lady's concern, Papa."

"Ah," Vionne breathed. He patted her hand, then quickly withdrew

his. A husband and father for a quarter century, he could still be un-
nerved by women's fluxes and flows.

"With him that had a proud eye and an ambitious heart I would
not eat," the preacher intoned.

"Go," Vionne whispered to his daughter. "Go, go."

Manon had been careful to insure that she was seated at the end of
the pew. She rose, clutching tight the lacy shawl that was her head covering and gathering her skirts to prevent any swishing sound, and hurried up the aisle.

"In the morning I put to death all the wicked of the land," the
preacher cried out as she left.

French Church Street was between William Street and Broadway, a little less than a quarter mile from Bowling Green. Manon arrived at the
park five minutes before eleven, breathing hard. She'd walked as
quickly as she dared without actually running. The watch did not pa-
trol after sunrise; nonetheless, a lady running through the streets
would attract attention. She dabbed her cheeks with a lace-trimmed
handkerchief, turning swiftly in the middle of the small green oasis
and enjoying the faint breeze made by the swinging skirt of her frock
of lavender silk.

One man had apparently chosen not to say his prayers this Sabbath morning. Manon spotted him a little distance away, near a
bronze statue of General Lafayette astride a rearing steed, apparently
intent on the inscription though he didn't look the sort who could
read, and altogether too common for fashionable Bowling Green.
Was he here before she arrived or did he come in after she did? She
couldn't remember. But he was no one she recognized, so he would
pass no tattle on to Papa. On the other hand, it appeared there would
be no rendezvous, and thus no tattle. Joyful was still nowhere to be
seen.

Dear God, what if that one-armed boy simply took her two coppers and never delivered her note? Then she saw Joyful on the walkway

straight ahead, his long-legged strides bringing him to where she stood.

Joyful spotted Manon at almost the precise moment she saw him. They hurried toward each other and met beside a small bandstand, painted white, gleaming in the late morning sun. Later that day there would probably be a concert. Pretty ladies in the latest fashions would stand beside elegant gentlemen in stovepipes and gray cutaways, and there would be talk and smiles and a bit of flirting, and enthusiastic clapping when the band played stirring patriotic tunes. Now there was only the pair of them.

He had to make a physical effort not to take her in his arms. Joyful touched the brim of his hat. "Good day, mistress. What an unexpected pleasure to see you."

Manon clutched her shawl close and nodded her head in a prim greeting. "Good morning to you, sir." Joyful was looking over her shoulder now, toward the man who had been so interested in the exploits of Lafayette. She saw the direction of his glance and murmured, "I don't know him. I don't believe he knows us. Joyful, that mark on your cheek, what happened?"

"It's nothing. As for that fellow over by the statue, I suspect he knows us all too well." The stranger had turned and was looking at them. Joyful offered her his arm and Manon took it. He led her down the walkway, and after a few steps chanced a quick look over his shoulder. The man was looking straight at them, but when Joyful turned, he spun around, pretending interest in a display of flowers. Joyful pulled Manon off the path and around to the rear of the bandstand. He drew her close, exulting in the scent of roses that always seemed to surround her. The shawl that covered her hair slipped to her shoulders, and he pressed his cheek to the golden braid coiled round the top of her head. "Manon. My sweet Manon."

The embrace lasted only a moment, both of them conscious of how much they must accomplish and how little they had. Manon pulled away, tipping her face back so she could look at him. A few ringlets had escaped from her coiffure. He curled one around his finger. She lifted his hand to her lips, kissing his palm, feeling again that tingle that whenever they touched started at her toes and worked itself up to the back of her neck. "You got my note," she said when she let his hand go. "I was so afraid you might not."

"I did. Your messenger was a powder monkey aboard Perry's ship. I'm the one took the poor little blighter's arm off. He works at Devrey's Pharmacy these days, and you can trust him with messages anytime. I was at the dovecote yesterday."

"I'm sorry, I thought I could get away, but I could not. Papa has taken to watching me like a falcon circling its prey." She must tell him about Blakeman, about what he'd said to Papa, but other things first, the things that were important to Joyful. There was so little time. "Joyful, Papa had another caller the night before last. A Mr. Mordecai Frank. He's a Hebrew and a goldsmith. Like Papa, he sometimes deals in jewels. I'm sure Papa invited him to talk about cutting the Great Mogul. But when I went to bring them some refreshment, another man was also there. He was introduced as Mr. Simson, a lawyer. I believe him to also be a Hebrew."

"Samson Simson. He was just leaving the Jews' synagogue when I was waiting by the dovecote."

"That's an astonishing coincidence!"

"Perhaps. But his presence with Frank at your father's may indicate that they were talking about something other than Blakeman's jewel. Some matter of property possibly."

"No. It was the Great Mogul. The Tavernier was on the counter, and when I came in, the three of them were bent over it like schoolboys at their lessons."

"Very well." He'd think later about what roles Mordecai Frank and Samson Simson might play; for now there were more pressing concerns. "There's something I should have told you. It's about Bastard Devrey. I—" He heard the crunch of boots on gravel and whipped off his hat, craning his neck to see over the railing of the bandstand. He pressed the stuffed glove on Manon's shoulder, pushing her into a crouch.

The man who had been by Lafayette's statue was headed toward them, peering anxiously in all directions. Not Patrick Burney as Joyful had thought at first, but probably an Irish laborer. *Me and another fellow lives down here. S'posed to keep an eye on you, and on her when we can.* Since the man had been at Bowling Green before Joyful arrived, he had to have followed Manon here. Joyful's mouth filled with the metallic taste of rage.

Manon sensed his mood and looked up at him anxiously.

"Ssh. Stay down." He mouthed rather than whispered the words. The man hadn't seen them duck behind the bandstand. He was obviously still looking for them as got closer. Joyful bent and spoke directly into her ear. "Stay here. Don't move." He crept silently to the edge of the structure, positioning himself so he could see but not be seen. *Only s'posed to let F.X. know what you do. Not do ye any harm.* Gallagher's instructions according to Burney, but from Gornt Blakeman more likely. He'd show the bloody bastard a bit about harm.

The Irishman stood on the path, looking around with a bewildered expression. After a time, he shrugged and started to walk away. Joyful sprung out of his crouch and hurled himself at the man's back. The pair of them fell to the ground, rolling across the gravel walkway and onto the grass. Joyful was the taller by at least half a foot, and the better fed. He finished on top and half rose so he was kneeling on the stranger's chest, his right hand at the man's throat. "Who sent you? Why were you spying on us?" The reply was burbled nonsense. The pressure on the man's windpipe made sensible speech impossible. Joyful eased his grip, but only slightly. "Who sent you?"

"Don't know . . ." More pressure on the windpipe. The man choked and wheezed, then, when he was again allowed to speak, "Got me instructions from one o' F.X.'s leather-aprons. Can't tell you nothing else. It's the truth, on me mother's soul."

Joyful took his hand away and got to his feet. "Stand up. Come, there's nothing wrong with you a glass of ale won't fix."

The man stood, staggering a bit, grasping his throat and wheezing.

"Sure and you're him . . ." Stertorous breaths between the words. "Dr. Turner . . . what saved little Brigid Clare Burney's life."

"I'm the man you've been told to spy upon."

"No, it's the lady I'm after watching. Five coppers a day," the man mumbled, not meeting Joyful's gaze. "It's three wee ones I've got, and another on the way."

"What's your name?"

"Desmond Mulligan. Mully, they calls me."

"Very well, Mully," Joyful reached into his pocket and came up with a shilling. "Here's the equivalent of twelve coppers. Call it two days' pay. So you're now earning eleven pennies a day, and six of them are from me. I'm outbidding F. X. Gallagher and whoever's behind him. That means you're loyal to me, not F.X., correct?"

"Jesus, Mary, and Joseph"—Mulligan blessed himself with a hurried sign of the cross—"it's a better wage than I've seen since this poxed war started. But F.X. is a nasty piece o' work. I can't be seen—"

"Mr. Gallagher doesn't have to know a thing about our arrangement. All I ask is that you keep your ears and your eyes wide open and report back to me."

Mulligan still hadn't taken the shilling, but neither had he taken his eyes off it. "How am I supposed to do that, Dr. Turner? Worth me arms and legs if F.X. was to—"

"I've seen what the butcher and his boys do with their cleavers, Mully. But could be you'll be sent to follow me sometime. Or you could find an excuse to switch assignments with Burney. That could happen, couldn't it?" Mulligan nodded agreement. "Excellent. So once and a while it may happen that you and I are in the same place at the same time. In the meantime, all you need do is keep your wits about you, so you've something to tell me if the occasion presents itself. When it does, you'll collect whatever's owed you at the rate of sixpence a day. Take the shilling as two days' wages in advance. Do we have a bargain?"

Mulligan nodded and snatched the coin, then turned and ran off. Joyful watched until he'd gone through the gate leading to Broadway. Manon came out from behind the bandstand to join him. They were totally alone, and she brushed a bit of grass from his coat, then touched the mottled blue-green bruise. "Is that how you got this? Fighting with men of that sort?" And when he simply smiled and shook his head: "Why did you give him money, Joyful?"

"Only a shilling. To insure he's on our side, not against us."

Manon was rapidly calculating all the implications. "You knew from the first he was here to spy on us. But how could he have known we'd be in Battery Park?"

He had no intention of telling her she was the one who had led Mulligan to their meeting place. "He was following me and guessed where I was headed."

"Not on his own account, surely. Joyful, who is behind this?"

"Gornt Blakeman. Because I'm now the owner of Devrey Shipping—"

"But that's wonderful!" Her eyes sparkled with delight, then narrowed.

"What?" Joyful demanded.

"Friday night. Quite late, I think it was nearly ten, Gornt Blakeman arrived and brazened his way into Papa's shop. I heard the ruckus and came downstairs and listened at the door. Mr. Blakeman asked Papa for my hand."

Joyful bit back the curse that rose to his lips. "And what did your father say?"

"That he would not promise me without my consent. So far he's said nothing to me of the proposal."

He relaxed a little, but only for a moment. Whatever else he might be, Gornt Blakeman was a very wealthy man. "If he does mention it, will you consent?"

She laughed softly. "Must you ask?"

For answer he wrapped his arms around her waist, pulled her close, and kissed her again, restraining himself, not wanting to frighten her with the depth of his hunger. Manon brought up both hands and put them either side of his face, pressing closer still, and parting her lips. He could taste all of her, all the sweetness. He lifted her slightly off the ground, feeling her body slide against his, the softness of her belly and her thighs, feeling his control slip away. She dropped her hands to his shoulders and pulled back. "Joyful," she whispered, "Joyful."

He set her down and let her go. "I'm sorry."

She put a finger over his lips. "Don't be. I'm not. I wondered why Mr. Blakeman was suddenly so convinced he must have me. I think Papa did as well. Now I know. It was to harm you."

"Any man alive would want you. But I'm part of Blakeman's reason, no doubt about that."

"Anyway, it doesn't matter," she said. "Now that you're the owner of Devrey's, you can tell Papa we wish to be married. Gornt Blakeman will have to find some other woman to supply him with sons. I think it's really a brood mare he wants. He asked Papa if I came from good stock. I do, you know. Mama had three sons. I shall give you at least that many, and . . . Joyful, what is it?" And when he did not respond: "You will ask for me now, won't you? You've said right along you must have something to offer, but if you own Devrey's Shipping—" She broke off, staring at him, waiting for the words that did not come.

Somewhere nearby a clock chimed the hour. "Half eleven," Joyful said. "Your father will be worried."

"Furious, more like." She spoke quietly. All these weeks and months she had been so sure. Had she made herself a fool? Mistook dalliance for devotion? "You're right, I must go. But first, please answer my question. Do you mean to ask Papa for me?"

"Dear God, Manon. Of course I do. It's only that right now—" It wasn't simply how much remained to be worked out. Blakeman and Astor, and a company with more liabilities than assets, and—God help him—everything at the Dancing Knave. He must at least speak to Delight before formally committing himself to . . . He saw the disappointment in Manon's eyes, saw the tears she was too proud to shed. Damn them all, and hang the time. "Can you stay long enough for me to explain?"

Her heart began a fierce thumping made up of one part exultation and one part doubt. "I will stay. I must."

It took him a few minutes to run through the nature of his

arrangements with his cousin. "All I've really done so far," he finished, "is make myself responsible for Bastard's mountain of debt. But I have a plan, Manon. I've met with John Jacob Astor as well."

Her eyes opened wide in surprise. "With Astor? What did you discuss?"

He shook his head. "Not now. You must go."

She stood on tiptoe to kiss him one last time. "This week," she said just before she turned to go, "I will be at the Fly Market every day at noon. Come when you can."

She'd thought to go round the back to the kitchen entrance, but her father was waiting by the open front door. "So," he said.

"I am sorry, Papa. I was delayed. I will begin the dinner immediately."

She tried to push past. Vionne put out a hand and stopped her. "First, tell me where you have been." Manon said nothing. "Look at you. Your hair is loose. Your dress is stained with grass. You are like . . . like . . ." Good God, she should be married, no longer his responsibility. "See what you look like," he repeated. Angry with her, and with himself because he'd never made her behave.

"Like what, Papa?"

"Like a harlot." The word burned his mouth, but Vionne could think of no other.

"I will pretend I did not hear that." Manon tried again to move past him.

Vionne took a step to the right so he was still confronting her. "Manon, for heaven's own sake. I am your father. I want only the best for you. But you leave the holy house of God to . . . To do I know not what. Tell me where you have been."

"I cannot. If you do not let me go to the kitchen, your dinner will be much delayed."

"I have asked the Widow Tremont to cook for us. She is in the kitchen even now. And from today she will do all the marketing."

Adele Tremont, mantua-maker to the city's most elegant women, had no need of additional employment. She was here because she'd set her cap for Maurice Vionne from the moment his wife died. "I see. And I, Papa? What am I to do?"

"You are to go to your room, Manon. You are to remain there and to think of the shame you are bringing on me and on the memory of your dead mother. And of how unlikely it is that, if he manages to get here from Virginia, the widowed nephew of Monsieur DeFane, or anyone else for that matter, will be interested in soiled goods."

Pearl Street, 3 P.M.

Because it was the Sabbath and not a workday, the dinner hour of the town was promptly at three. The enticing smell of a chicken roasting before the fire drifted down the stairs of Barnaby Carter's premises and tickled the noses of each of the five men gathered in the semidark at the rear of the cavernous warehouse.

The carriages normally on display had been returned to their customary places as soon as the Thursday sale ended. The men were seated in the shadowy interior of a large coach of the sort built to make the run between New York and Boston. Indeed, the man speaking had the sound of Massachusetts in his speech. "In Boston, gentleman, we are in a deplorable situation. Our commerce is dead, our revenue gone, our ships are rotting at the wharves. We are bankrupts, and it's plain the so-called federal government has not the wherewithal to protect our coast. Once we have effected the arrangements we propose, it is imperative that we never allow our treasury to become so depleted. Every citizen of our new nation must contribute—"

"Surely, sir, you are not suggesting that we should tax our citizens. That is exactly what . . ."

Gornt Blakeman, sitting with one hand pressed to his chin, did his best to look attentive as he listened to New Hampshire's objections to any sort of taxation. In fact, the entire, apparently endless argument, bored him. Not a ha'penny's worth of brains among them all: Boston, Concord, or the pair from Hartford. Too bad the Rhode Island fellow hadn't managed to join them today. He was far and away the most sensible of the New Englanders. Damn! Lucretia Carter must be a fine cook. That chicken smelled blissful. No wonder Barnaby looked so discontent at having to stand guard by the door of his warehouse while his dinner cooled in the rooms above.

Concord was still pressing his point. "It should be possible simply to apply a tariff to imported goods and—"

"Some tax on general income is bound to be required." The elder of the two men from Connecticut had a booming voice. The younger shushed him even as he nodded agreement with the point raised.

Blakeman felt the sensation of pins and needles in his left buttock and shifted his position as far as the cramped conditions allowed. They had been sitting here the best part of an hour. Bloody waste of time. The discussion of how a central authority was to raise revenue was pointless as well as premature. The real issue was whether a few strong and capable men would seize the initiative and act on it, or try to cajole an entire legislature into seeing things their way. In New York, at least, the answer was clear. Blakeman cleared his throat. The others turned to him. "We must have power before we can determine how to exercise it, gentleman."

"Ah, Mr. Blakeman"—Boston again—"I thought the cat had stolen your tongue."

"I simply choose not to contribute to a discussion I believe to be taking place before its time. If we do not—"

"What of your pirates, eh?" The booming voice of the elder of the two Hartford men, his deafness excuse for interrupting as well as shouting. "Got 'em wrapped up as you promised? Going to 'stand and deliver,' as they used to say?"

"I believe, sir, that was 'highwaymen.' But I assure you, I am in close touch with the Baratarians." According to Delight, that fool Tintin couldn't stay away from the Dancing Knave, and he could practically see her salivate each time he mentioned his plans for putting her in charge of every whore in the city. He'd do it too. Control, that was the thing. Not this madness called democracy.

"The Baratarians," Boston said. "Does that mean Lafitte has agreed to attack United States shipping once our scheme is in effect? I ask, Mr. Blakeman, because he has never done so before."

"He has never before, sir, been offered letters of marque from a separate American nation." That was the real issue and the one they were all still tossing back and forth as if it were a potato too hot to touch. Fools, the lot of them. The continent was enormous. Plenty of room for two nations, probably more if it came to that.

The younger Connecticut man winced. "It may not be necessary to go so far, gentlemen. After all—"

New Hampshire made his move. "Perhaps we can settle all this at a convention."

Blakeman clenched his fists, but not so the others could see. Damn the man to hell. A convention. The blasted things could go on for years.

"A convention," New Hampshire repeated. "That's the proper way to decide these matters. We shouldn't be traveling all the way to New York in these dangerous times, and meeting in secret. We need to call a convention and openly discuss our ideas for . . ."

Blakeman watched him. Go on, say it, you liverless toad. Our ideas for secession. New England and New York to form a separate nation.

". . . our ideas for how to proceed," New Hampshire finished lamely.

"I expect we are the logical venue." One of the Hartford pair, the soft-spoken one this time. "I mean, being in the middle, as it were, Connecticut's a sensible choice."

The others agreed. Even Blakeman nodded. Never mind that he intended it would all be settled well before any convention could be summoned, in Hartford or elsewhere. Once New York had claimed the freedom that was rightly hers, made a swift and separate peace with Britain, and sent her merchant ships back to sea, the New England states would trip over each other in their haste to form a new confederation.

"So how did it go then?" Carter asked when he closed the door behind the last of the men to slip quietly from the warehouse to the all-but-deserted street.

"Well enough," Blakeman said.

"They're all with you?"

"With us, Barnaby. With us." Blakeman clapped a hand on Carter's shoulder. "You and the other mechanics, you do know this is how it must be? We cannot allow Madison and his War Hawks to steal our livelihoods, can we?"

"Course not," Carter agreed.

Blakeman left and Barnaby went upstairs, but despite the lusciousness of Lucretia's chicken dinner, he had little appetite.

Canvastown, 6 P.M.

"Cue ball to take the red to pocket three." Joyful curled the top half of himself across the top end of the eleven-foot billiards table in the rear of McDermott's Oyster House. "One carom on the way to the pocket," he added. A carom was a strike and a rebound that hit another ball.

Barnaby stood to the side, eyes fixed on the table, leaning on his stick. His head was wreathed in the smoke rising from a cigar clamped between his teeth. "Double the bet says you can't make it a triple." Given the position of the four balls in play, a triple carom would earn thirteen points, the maximum possible in a single shot.

Joyful looked up. "Maybe. But not a chance unless you back off a ways. No wonder Lucretia let you out after dinner. Glad to see the back of you and get that noxious smoke out of her house."

"A fine Connecticut cigar this is," Barnaby protested. "Not your cheap pipe tobacco from the South. That's the stuff makes your eyes water." Not counting Joyful and himself, every man in the place had a pipe stuck in his mouth. Nonetheless, Barnaby took the cigar from between his teeth and stubbed it dead on the wall behind him. Didn't want to put Joyful off, not when he'd refused to go near a billiards table for so long. The British were bastards, all right. But did that make Blakeman's scheme right? He had to talk to Joyful about it.

"Pocket three," Joyful repeated, working the stick repeatedly through the inert fingers of the glove.

Barnaby took a step backwards, so it wouldn't seem he was staring. "How about that wager?" he asked.

Joyful put his head down again, concentrating on the shot, deciding whether to take up Barnaby's challenge. Normally, he'd have said yes instantly. What was holding him back today? As far as he could recall, in every game he'd played with both hands, the only thing his left did was steady the cue stick. So why was it so damnably difficult to do the same with the glove? Because it didn't feel natural, that's why. Bloody hell, it probably never would.

The perfect moment when you felt as if the stick were simply an extension of your arm, and when every ball on the table was far too big to miss, wouldn't come. He straightened and stepped away from the table, walked around a bit, loosening up, using the opportunity to examine the positions of the two red and two white balls from a variety of angles. "You're on," he said after a final squint at the lie. "One scratch of the cue ball and a triple carom, two reds and a white." He chalked the cue for the third time. "Thirteen points against thirty coppers. You'd better have it in ready coin, Barnaby me lad. I'll not be doing with promises."

An oil lamp hung directly overhead, adding its smoke to the general miasma. Joyful blinked to clear his eyes, once more stretched across the upper right corner of the table, and inserted the stick through the immobile fingers of the glove. He slid it back and forth a few times, just to get the feel of things, and took his shot. The cue ball spun across the table, hit first a white and a red, sent them ricocheting into opposite pockets, then shot back to bank left, caromed off one more white, and pocketed the final red.

Carter hooted with delight. "You did it!"

Joyful was still bent over the table. He cocked his head and looked up. "You're sounding awfully happy for a man who just lost thirty coppers."

Barnaby's grin stretched the width of his face. Joyful replied with one of his own.

McDermott's Oyster House was more bawdy house than tavern or fishmonger's, but it lived up to its name in that there were plenty of oysters in evidence, and no officious city inspectors hanging about to say August, a month without an *r*, was the wrong time of year to be selling them.

Two young blacks stood at a wooden table by the front door, dancing in place and keeping up a steady stream of talk while they pried apart the nearly smooth shells of the Long Island blue points as fast as the customers could toss them down their throats. "Come along, gents," the patter went, "shuck 'em, huck 'em, swallow 'em down. A penny for four. Best in town."

"Best place to come for oysters this time of year," Joyful said, choosing a particularly fat and succulent example. He bent his head back and tipped the shivering creature into his mouth. It was grand. Briny and rich and clean-tasting, with no hint of spoil. "Got these today, did you?" he asked the nigra lad nearest to hand.

"Yes sir. Not more'n two hours past. Shuck 'em, huck 'em, swallow 'em down, gents. You got three more coming, sir." The boy's feet shuffled a lively rhythm on the sawdust-covered floor. "Penny for four. Best in town."

Joyful put his coin on the table and picked up a second oyster, nodding to Barnaby to claim the other two. They made their way across the room to where a woman tended a row of tapped kegs, dispensing pewter tankards of dark beer with a dense, creamy head. "The beer's as good as I've tasted anywhere, as well," Barnaby said.

"Fresh oysters and good beer. Is that why you wanted to come all the way over to Canvastown?"

"McDermott's table always gave us a good game." Barnaby was staring into his beer, not looking at Joyful. "And it's where we played that last time, before you went off to war."

The night he'd met Delight. Barnaby had probably forgotten all about that incident. "So you figured it was the right place to come for the start of a new era?"

The other man's head shot up. "What do you mean? What kind of a new era?"

"My hand, Barnaby. That's all." Joyful held up the glove. "What did you think I meant?"

Carter looked around before he answered. No one was paying them any mind. "Joyful, this place . . . You think it's true about your father?"

"Depends. Which particular truth did you have in mind?"

"That rumor says he set the fire back in '76. When Washington and his troops had to withdraw and let the redcoats occupy the town."

"I'm not sure. He never talked about the Revolution, not the war. But if he did light that blaze, it was on Washington's orders."

"Yes. A true patriot, Morgan Turner."

"I think so. Barnaby, what's this all about? Not billiards and oysters, is it?"

Carter tipped his head back and downed the last of his beer. "Not here. Come outside."

Half an hour later the shay turned onto Greenwich Street, the old horse knowing her way and Carter needing to keep only a loose hold on the reins, though he still had to keep his eye on the road. Joyful was glad of that, glad Barnaby hadn't watched his reactions to the tale, a confirmation of everything he'd already suspected. "Barnaby, you're sure they were talking about secession? Planning a conference to ratify it?"

"No, I'm not sure. I couldn't hear everything. Joyful, it's worth my livelihood if Gornt Blakeman finds out I've said anything. I can't exist without his business. You know that."

"Of course I do. You know I'll keep your confidence. But I need to ask two more questions. First, why did you tell me?"

"Everyone's talking about how you've been spending a lot of time at the docks. The fellows say you're setting yourself up to go into the China trade. Makes sense, seeing as how you were raised there. But if it's true, after what's happened this week, it's Gornt Blakeman will be your main competition. I figured you'd want to know."

Not just that, Joyful thought. It's because you're uncomfortable with the notion of what he's doing. That's why you were asking about my father—measuring yourself against Morgan Turner, and measuring me as well, if it comes to that. I've no doubt you're faithfully reporting what's being said among all the mechanics at Tammany Hall, and that's what counts. "That brings me to my second question. What about the others, like yourself—craftsmen, small-business owners, the ones you say Blakeman's enlisted in his scheme? Are they all convinced it's the right thing to do, get out now and the devil take the union of the states?"

"Hard to say. It's attractive, of course. This war's been devilish hard on mechanics; we're the ones have suffered the most. The rich, men like Jacob Astor, they can wait it out. The poor are poor no matter who— What is it?"

Joyful had grabbed his arm. "Hold up," he said softly, straining to see into the deceptive shadows of the early evening. "I'll get out here and . . . No, better still, drive me right to the door."

Carter obliged, still not knowing what it was Joyful had seen, or thought he'd seen. They pulled up in front of Ma Allard's door, and Joyful claimed his cue stick from the corner of the shay and jumped down from the rig. "Goodnight, Barnaby. A fine game," he said, speaking at the top of his voice and elaborately tipping his hat. "My compliments, sir. You offer more competition when I've only one hand. We must do it again soon."

Carter leaned down, spoke softly. "Joyful, you really mean me to leave?"

"Absolutely old friend," he said, matching the quiet of the other man's tone. "And Barnaby, don't worry. You did the right thing by telling me. And I'll keep your confidence."

Carter nodded, clucked to the horse, and the shay moved off. Joyful tucked his stick under his arm and made a great point of fumbling for his key, whistling softly under his breath all the while.

"Dr. Turner."

"Aye. Who wants me?" He didn't need to turn around. He'd spotted Clifford's distinctive barrel build from forty feet, despite the fact that the whipper was huddling in a doorway across the road.

"It's me." The whipper came to stand beside him. "Vinegar Clifford," he said loudly. "Your patient, what's come to see you on a medical matter."

They were, it seemed, both talking for the benefit of whoever might be lurking in the shadows of the summer dusk. Dangerous times. And Gornt Blakeman at the center of them, a spider spinning an even larger web than Joyful had imagined.

"Come inside then, Vinegar Clifford, and we'll see if this one-handed surgeon can cut away what ails you."

"No cutting. I told you before, I ain't going to let you take a knife to me private parts."

They were in Joyful's room, he had his bag open and a scalpel in hand. "That's easy to say, Mr. Clifford. But I gave you a week's supply of medicine yesterday, and here you are looking for more." Got a taste for laudanum, Vinegar have you? Why not? The pure thing's a sight better than anything you can buy in the town. If he's still following Clare's old recipe, even Jonathan's three-penny elixir is only sixty percent laudanum and forty percent water. The stuff in that brown bottle I gave you was one hundred percent pure. "Did you take it all in one dose or two?"

The whipper shuffled from one foot to the other. "Neither," then, sheepishly, "Three, I think. It hurts terrible bad. Need to piss again right now, I do, Dr. Turner. Without the brown stuff, I can't see how I'll manage."

"With considerable pain," Joyful said. "As you did before. Very well," he stretched out a foot and hooked a chamber pot from under the bed, nudging it in Vinegar's direction. "Get your prick out and let's see if the condition is the same."

"Now?" The whipper was still eyeing the scalpel.

"Of course now. Not ashamed of your equipment, are you, Mr. Clifford? Perhaps your cock's not as intimidating as your whip."

"Course I ain't shamed. You saw me yesterday, didn't you? You know I've plenty of meat in me britches. Besides, you're a medical man. Not supposed to make judgments about that sort o' thing." He had loosed his buttons while he spoke. Now he gingerly withdrew himself, putting the whip under his arm so he could use both hands.

Joyful pushed the chamber pot closer. "Go on. Have at it, Mr. Clifford. I need to see your stream before I can be sure your condition warrants more treatment."

Clifford gritted his teeth, hunched over the pot, and produced a small trickle of urine, then groaned and stopped. "Holy Jesus in heaven, I can't. Not without the medicine. The pain's something fierce."

Joyful took a bottle of laudanum from his bag. "This will make it easier, won't it? You know that for sure now."

"I do, Doctor Turner. And I'll not forget your kindness in—"

Clifford reached for the laudanum and Joyful snatched it away. "Not so fast, Mr. Clifford. Payment is required."

The whipper pulled up straighter, a touch of the old cockiness in his glance, still willing to try and strike a bargain. "What about the yellow powder? The stuff as will stop me cock falling off."

"Used all of that as well, have you?" Joyful fished in his bag for his last green bottle of tansy powder. Years before, Andrew had discovered a woman up in Yonkers in West Chester whom he swore was the finest simpler in the land. The day Joyful took his medical degree, Andrew had driven the younger man to her farm and introduced them. Like his cousin, Joyful had been getting his medicaments from Yonkers ever since. Half a day's journey there and back, and God knew how he'd find the time at the moment. Still, it was worth it. The whipper might play the innocent, but he'd not have come here without something to trade. "You've been greedy, Mr. Clifford. That's why you need more medicine so soon."

"Sooner I can get well the better," the whipper muttered. "Can't say different to that, can ye? It's plain common sense."

"A sprinkling on your tongue morning and night, the dose I prescribed, will do the job. But you need to take it for more than a single day. A week at least." Like one of those pleasure garden acts, always give them a reason to come back. "So what have you brought with you to make the purchase?"

Joyful held the two bottles in plain sight. Meanwhile the whipper's need to answer the call of nature overcame his fear of the pain. He bent forward, and a few more drops of urine dripped into the pot. "Jesus," he muttered, his face red and scrunched with pain, sweat beading on his forehead. "Blakeman's been meeting with someone."

As he suspected. Though it was no more than he'd already had from Barnaby Carter, it was confirmation. "Meeting with whom? When and where?"

"Last night," Clifford said. "Late it was. And he only took me with him part o' the way."

Christ. The meeting Barnaby was reporting on had taken place earlier that day. "Last night? What was Blakeman doing today?"

"Don't know nothin' about today. He went out and left me at the countinghouse. Only took me with him yesterday cause by the time he went out it was late and dark. Just part of the way, like I said."

"Part of the way to where, Mr. Clifford?" Joyful pulled the cork on the bottle of laudanum and poured some of the viscous brown liquid into his dosing spoon.

"Over in Brooklyn Village. We took the ferry, than hiked up the coast a bit. After that he left me to wait in a tavern. Came back near an hour later and we came home."

"Up the coast exactly where?"

"Can't say."

"What was the name of the tavern?"

"The Buxom Wench," Clifford said. "Please . . . I can't hold back much longer."

Joyful's oath demanded that he do no harm, and those were real tears streaming down the whipper's cheeks. But how many of his victims had wept and shrieked with pain when Clifford added a splash of vinegar to the misery of flogging? Joyful felt no pang of conscience about the delay when he leaned forward and tipped the dose of laudanum into his patient's open mouth.

Lower Marlboro, Maryland, 8 P.M.

It was still stinking hot. Even now when the sun was almost below the horizon, the pair of them were itching and sweating.

Astor's agent wore a townsman's woolen cutaway and trousers. "Heat's damnable," he said, jerking his head toward the column of redcoats they were tracking, "but worse for the likes of them."

The second man wore buckskins and a broad-brimmed hat, and carried a long rifle with brass fittings and a polished oak stock. He jerked his head to indicate the flotilla of British boats moving slowly up the Patuxent, flanking the army on its right, fully visible from the hill that was their lookout point. "Makes you think the navy's a better berth, don't it?" There had been only enough horses left at Benedict to allow the general officers and their staffs to ride. The rest of the redcoats in their heavy woolen uniforms with packs and weapons strapped to their backs were on foot, strung out across the countryside in a long double file, their boots tramping in perfect unison.

"Navy's better until you get a taste of the cat," the first man said. He pulled back from the brow of the hill and consulted his notes. "I reckon we've covered some twenty miles. At least we will have by the time they get where they'll have to stop for the night."

"And after that?"

"Either the Federal District or Baltimore."

"You're still not sure?"

"Not yet." The man in city clothes was a professional surveyor, but neither he nor his companion carried any maps. It would finish them to be caught with such evidence. Even the few scrawls the surveyor had made in his notebook as they traveled might have had them hung for spies. "We won't know for sure until we're at Upper Marlboro," he said, consulting the map that existed in his mind. "That's where the road divides. One direction for Baltimore, one for Washington."

"How long till they get there?"

"A few hours' march still. They won't go the distance this night. They'll have to make camp soon as it gets dark and start again in the morning."

"Could be they'll have something else to contend with before that." The man in buckskins was a marksman who knew he could pick off any number of redcoats before their inaccurate muskets found the range. He'd start with the officers. Soon as there was any kind of offense by the Americans, he'd join in and . . . Ah, Christ. He was whistling past the graveyard. They'd seen no evidence of any kind of defense. There were a few American gunboats nearby, but they were hiding. Too outnumbered to be any use. Bloody British navy probably knew where they were, and couldn't be bothered doing anything about it. They had bigger fish to fry. "Could be we'll send a welcoming party to greet them," he insisted. Whistle louder, that's the best thing.

"Could be we will," the first man agreed. "But given the way Madison's generals have handled everything else so far, it's not bloody likely."

❧

New York City,
The Dancing Knave, 11:30 P.M.

There was a smell about the place at this hour. Joyful had noticed it before. It was the smell of money, of course. By now large sums had been won and lost. The losers stank of fear and disappointment, but they were overpowered by the musk of the winners. Like stud bulls they were, snorting, permanently erect, deciding which female they would have first.

As soon as they'd had enough of the tables, the men drifted to the Ladies' Parlor to examine their options. Some would sit with two or three of the girls for a time, enjoying their tinkling laughter, playing a game of cards perhaps, letting the girls each win a few pennies, then they'd make a selection and command their choice upstairs with nothing more than a look. Others were more direct, making a quick choice as soon as they entered the parlor, nodding peremptorily in a girl's direction, knowing that here in this place at this moment, whoever he was, he was a king and his command was law.

Or so Delight allowed them to believe.

Joyful stood near the entrance to the Gaming Salon, dressed like a customer in a scarlet waistcoat and a striped cutaway. Delight had seen him come in and knew immediately that this was not a usual visit: the hawk always wore black in his aerie. She had avoided him ever since. Just as well. His business tonight was not with her.

Gornt Blakeman was playing at cards with a man who had been a regular since the Knave opened. A trader, Geoffrey Colden, was one of the original Buttonwood signers; he also served on the Common Council. Colden sat facing the door to the entry hall, and he nodded when Joyful approached. "Good evening to you, Dr. Turner."

"And to you, sir. Mr. Blakeman," Joyful said, acknowledging the other man.

"Dr. Turner." Blakeman kept his back to Joyful and continued to concentrate on his hand. "My trick," he said, and swept two cards toward him, then laid down the king and queen of clubs, "and a common marriage to declare." He moved one of the ivory counters used to keep score. "Do you play bezique, Dr. Turner?"—still not turning around.

"I do, Mr. Blakeman. At sea there are long periods of nothing whatever to do. Every game gets a try."

"Perhaps you'll play in my place then, Dr. Turner?" Colden laid down his hand. "I see the young woman I've been waiting for."

A buxom dark-haired girl had descended the stairs from the bedroom floor and gone into the Ladies' Parlor, signifying she was again available. Her name was Rosa Maria, and Delight had told Joyful in detail of her special skills—*a Portuguese, incredibly strong, squeezes the life out of them*—and how many of the men would have no one else.

The trader got up and hurried away. Joyful went round and took his seat. "With your permission, Mr. Blakeman."

"Delighted, Dr. Turner." Then, smiling now that they were facing each other: "Delight, that's the most important word hereabouts, isn't it?"

"Wise men all recognize it as such."

It was Joyful's turn to deal. He could see Blakeman watching him, wondering how he was going to manage with one hand, not doing anything that might make the task easier. "Adaptive creatures, humans," Joyful said. "I'm sure you've noticed that as well."

"Not being a man of science like yourself, I might have missed some of the manifestations, Dr. Turner."

"Joyful, please. Gentlemen should be on friendly terms when they wager."

Blakeman leaned back, tilting his chair so it was supported only on the two rear legs. "Frankly, I prefer to gamble when the odds are high enough to tempt me."

Joyful didn't answer, only gathered the cards in front of him: a double piquet deck, sixty-four cards, the usual four suits, but with everything from two to six removed. He used the glove as a stop, building the stack of cards against it, then cut the deck and deftly shuffled the second half into the first, then did it again. And a third time. Then he pushed the cards toward Blakeman to be cut yet again.

"Cleverly done," Blakeman said. "Apparently, surgery is excellent training in dexterity."

"In many things. About those odds . . . Will you agree to a dollar a point, Gornt?" He'd not been invited to use Blakeman's Christian name. Pushing the proprieties, but not too far, because he had first offered the familiarity with regard to himself.

"A rich wager—Joyful." There was only a slight hesitation before Blakeman used his name. "I accept. In fact, let's make it two dollars a point." Blakeman took a stack of guineas from his pocket and laid them on the table. The coins were silver, winking softly in the subdued light of the salon. "Agreed?"

"Agreed." Joyful placed his own stake on the table. His coins were reichsthalers, gold ducats, the currency of the Holy Roman Empire. Much rarer than British guineas and considerably more valuable. There was no change in Blakeman's expression, but a certain hardness came into his eyes.

Joyful dealt three cards to his opponent and the same to himself, then two each, then three again—eight cards per hand. He turned over the seventeenth card, the one that determined which suit would be trump. It was the ace of diamonds. He set it beside the remainder of the deck, the stock, never taking his eyes from Blakeman, but seeing no reaction. If diamonds being the trump suit meant anything, the other man hid it well. They picked up their hands, Joyful fanning his awkwardly, almost dropping them. Blakeman smirked, but recovered quickly and made his face impassive. He played the first card. "Knave of hearts," he said softly. "The dancing knave."

"In that case the trick belongs to me." Joyful let a glimmer of a smile show. He had to lay his hand facedown on the table to select the card he wanted, the one that would claim the trick. In bezique there was no requirement to follow suit in this early part of the game; face value was all that mattered. He played the king of spades and used the glove to nudge the pair of cards to his side of the table. "I declare as well a common marriage." Joyful selected two more of the cards from his hand, a king and queen of clubs, laid them down, and took three from the stock. He'd drawn two more queens and a ten. Every one a diamond. He now held five trump cards. He looked up, his face showing nothing. "Your play, Gornt."

Blakeman took his stock card. Joyful watched him as if he were seeing him from somewhere far distant and at the same time very close, as if he were operating and all the intricacies of the surgery, every step he must take and each thing he must accomplish, was writ large before his eyes. The game, the night, whatever he wanted, it was all his. Tonight it was his joss to win. He knew it deep in his gut, but knew too this was a battle only, not the war.

Thirty minutes later there were three times as many ivory counters on Joyful's side of the table as on Blakeman's. A crowd had gathered round them, the players in the gaming salon knowing both men at least by sight, knowing the talk of the past few days, sensing that more than cards was being played, and considerably more was at stake than money. One of the Knave's new chuckers-out, Preservation Shay, was nearby, keeping watch in case a tense game led to trouble. Being from Five Points, Preservation Shay would have imbibed the ability to sniff out a potential fight with his mother's milk.

Blakeman took his third trick of the hand in play and claimed the right to make a declaration. "Double common marriage for twenty points," he said, laying down the two kings and the two queens of clubs. He took the appropriate counters. "Shall we double the wager?"

Out of the corner of his eye Joyful picked up another onlooker, come from the far side of the room to stand behind Blakeman: Vinegar Clifford, carrying his whip and in working dress. He hated him, Joyful knew, precisely because he needed him. Because if there was trouble, Clifford would be required to act for his employer, and against his desperate self-interest. Not to worry, whipper. There's to be no trouble. Not tonight. This is only first blood, neither of us wanting to show too much or cut too deep.

Blakeman was still waiting for Joyful's reply to the suggestion of higher odds, both of them knowing the money meant nothing. "Agreed," Joyful said.

Delight had joined the crowd around the table, standing exactly midway between the two men. Blakeman took the next two tricks. Then Joyful trumped the king of spades with the seven of diamonds and said quietly, "I declare a double bezique." His cards were spread facedown in front of him, and without looking he selected four and turned them over. Two queens of spades and two knaves of diamonds. Five hundred points. The highest possible single score.

Blakeman pushed his remaining coins to Joyful's side of the table, then drew a handful more from his pocket and flipped them onto the pile in front of his opponent. The coins in front of Joyful would support a laborer's family for five years and it was, both men knew, only the tiniest part of what was at stake. Blakeman stood up. "Congratulations, sir, you play better with one hand than most men do with two."

"In Canton they'd say it was my joss to win tonight. That the cards fell for me and skill had nothing to do with it."

"Would they? I'll take your word for it, since I've never needed to go there in order to profit from the place. Goodnight to you, Joyful."

"And to you, Gornt."

Blakeman walked up the stairs toward the bedrooms, though he had not stopped by the Ladies' Parlor to select a companion. Clifford followed his employer out of the Gaming Salon and took up a position at the foot of the stairs, clutching his whip and staring straight ahead.

A couple of the other players indicated a willingness to take Blakeman's place at the bezique table, but Joyful gathered his winnings and stood up. "Another evening, perhaps, gentlemen. Thank you." He headed for the front door. Delight appeared at his elbow, smiling, and offered him an oversized goblet, the bottom filled with brandy, the dark brown-gold color attesting to age and quality. "The house offers its congratulations and claims its portion, Dr. Turner."

God, but she was magnificent. She wore a purple gown, caught with a pink satin ribbon below her incredible breasts, the dress made of cloth so fine her honey-colored skin showed beneath it, and cut in the latest fashion so it skimmed her body and emphasized every lush curve. Joyful felt the sap rise in him; the smell of her and the smell of money and success blending into a heady perfume that was almost overwhelming. He took the brandy and tossed it back in one large swallow, welcoming the fire that chased from his throat to his belly, feeling every part of him aflame, and knowing that it would take nothing more than a nod of his head, for her to take his arm and accompany him up the stairs with everyone watching. The one woman in the place who was not for sale.

He would have gone with one of the whores without a second thought, happy to be able to satisfy the natural hunger the evening had raised in him. Because it was Delight, because of everything that had gone before, he knew that if he did it would be a betrayal of Manon that would haunt him forever.

Delight took the empty goblet from his hand. Joyful produced a handful of the golden reichsthalers. "The house share," he said, seeing the question in her eyes, wanting to be kind, knowing there was no way she wouldn't take his rejection as a public insult, but incapable of doing anything else. "It's late and I'm tired," he said softly. "Good night."

Delight turned and headed for the stairs, following where Gornt Blakeman had led.

Monday, August 22, 1814

Chapter Fourteen

New York City,
The Dancing Knave, Soon After Midnight

DELIGHT'S WHOLE BODY ached. Blakeman had used her hard, but she'd want it no other way. Tenderness was no part of what she felt for Gornt Blakeman, or any man, come to that. Not now, and not ever again.

She went downstairs, thinking since it was already Monday morning the crowd might have thinned, but the doors to most of the second-floor bedrooms were shut when she passed (indicating they were in use). There were as well still a goodly number of players in the Gaming Salon, and more coming from the look of it. Preservation Shay was in some kind of altercation at the front door.

Delight started for him, saw who it was who wanted entry, and paused by the Ladies' Parlor. The two other chuckers-out were both there, amusing themselves playing games with the ladies. She summoned them to her. "Stay here where you can see me. Come if I call you." Then she went to the door.

"It's all right, Preservation. I will deal with this." She turned to the man who was insisting on being admitted: "You are not yourself, Captain O'Toole. Come in if you like, but perhaps it's better if you rest upstairs for a time. I'm sure I can find a lady to keep you company until you feel better. Which do you prefer, yellow curls or brown?"

"Neither." O'Toole pushed past her, heading for the Gaming Salon. The two lads responded to Delight's gesture and stepped into his path. "Got plenty o' coin," O'Toole said. "More'n enough." His words were slurred and his gait unsteady, but his grip on the moneybag he was waving under their noses was firm enough.

"I'm sure you do," Delight said. "But here at the Dancing Knave gentlemen who are feeling the effects of their tipple are asked to wait until they come to themselves before they chance their luck." Drunks caused nothing but grief at the gaming tables, and Irish drunks were the worst of all. "Where do you choose to wait, Captain O'Toole? Upstairs in one of our comfortable rooms? Or somewhere off the premises?"

Preservation Shay took a step closer. She made a small motion that held him off for the moment, and waited for an answer from the Irishman. O'Toole said nothing, just turned and stumbled toward the front door. Very well, she'd given him a choice and he'd made it. Just as well, perhaps. "Please come back and see us soon, Captain. When you are more yourself."

She watched O'Toole stagger into the street, then shut the door. There was a chuckle behind her; Delight turned and saw the pirate Tintin standing at the foot of the stairs, laughing. "Too drunk to know what he's missing," he said, jerking his head in the direction of the upstairs rooms. "Two of your ladies are available for the price of one this evening, or so the bearded hag told me. I chose a red hair and a yellow. It was fine sport, though I admit"—his glance raked her from head to toe—"I have a taste for the dark meat of the bird."

"I'm glad we were able to please you, Monsieur Tintin." Anything as long as it kept him away from her. The last two times Tintin was at the club he had shadowed her every move, always looking at her in that same insolent way. It didn't matter, Delight reminded herself; customers always thought she was simply a more expensive version of one of her ladies. She didn't care what they thought, as long as they left their money behind. And she had Slyly Silas's papers now, the next best thing to actually being listed on the roster of free blacks. "If you will excuse me. I am a bit unwell this evening. The gaming tables are still busy. I'm sure they will amuse you almost as much as the two ladies did."

Tintin stood between Delight and the stairs. He did not move aside. "Shall I tell you what would really amuse me?"

His eyes told her what he had in mind. Delight forced herself not to let her rage or her disgust show. "I can guess, monsieur," she said quietly. "But tonight it is not to be." She nodded toward the chucker-out, still shadowing her every move. "This is Preservation Shay. I keep him always at my side. A wise precaution, don't you think?"

Tintin looked the young man up and down. Muscles, yes. But he did not move as one accustomed to staying out of the range of a blade. Tintin's knife would make fast work of this Preservation Shay. *Oui*, but there were the other two. *Eh bien*, the bitch was right. Tonight it was not to be. Soon though. He was tired of waiting, and now that Eugenie had the documents, he would arrange things so it was no longer necessary. "Good night, Mademoiselle Delight. Sleep well."

"Thank you, Monsieur Tintin. I'm sure I shall."

Bloody mulatto bitch, damn her to hell. Normally, Finbar O'Toole wasn't much bothered by the color of anyone's skin, man or woman. Wasn't the outside that mattered, he'd long since discovered. 'Twas the good o' a woman's heart, or the courage o' a man's. But tonight Delight Higgins was a mulatto bitch and he wished her dead. Or worse. Ah, sweet Mary and all the saints, 'tweren't the fault o' Delight Higgins he felt as he did. 'Twas the fact that he'd never before been turned off a ship. Never gave cause before poxed Thumbless Wu forced him to carry a stowaway.

Now, that was a bad thought. A thought as proved the effects o' all the rum he'd poured down his gullet this day were wearing off. Couldn't have that. Couldn't let his anger and his shame have free rein. His soul would sink into a black pit if he did that. His heart would explode in his chest with fury. The remedy was more grog. A great deal more grog.

He looked around and realized he'd walked from the distant reaches of Rivington Street as far south as Bowery Village. Plenty o' grog shops here where farmers and such like came to sell their goods shy of the market tax they must pay below the Common. The signs of the Duck and Frying Pan, the Pig and Whistle, and the more elaborate placard of the Gotham Inn hung nearby, but the closest was the Bull's Head Tavern, straight across the street. Apparently, the landlord wasn't one to worry about his health or that of his customers. Everyone knew disease traveled on the nighttime breezes, but the curtain of the tavern had been pushed aside and a welcoming golden glow spilled into the road.

O'Toole paused long enough to pat the moneybag strapped to his bare chest and hidden by his shirt. Safe it was. And thanks be to Blessed Mary and all the saints, he'd had sense enough to distribute a share o' coins in his pockets, so no need to go into the stash 'twas best no one knew he had. Six thousand bloody dollars, by the Holy Name o' Jesus. The most part o' it anyway. Still his. A miracle, that was. And maybe a good thing the mulatto bitch hadn't let him into the Dancing Knave this night. He stepped from the shadows into the path of yellow light and followed it inside.

Aye, a good place, and good joss as brought him here. The stink o' the rum was strong enough to make a man drunk just from breathing. Place was a butchers' rest, he remembered. Pens out behind for the cattle brought over from the farms of Long Island or West Chester, rooms for the cowmen to sleep after they got here, and the city's official slaughtering sheds a few steps away. Men steeped in that much blood and beef would accept nothing less than the strongest rum a landlord could provide. "Grog!" he shouted as he took a seat at a table near the door. "Double ration and make it quick."

Four double rations later he felt no better. Couldn't do anything right this night. Not even get drunk. "Bloody Blakeman," he murmured. "All bloody Blakeman's fault. May he rot in hell."

"Easy there." A man slipped into the seat across from his. "Doesn't do to be talking about your betters like that, Captain Finbar O'Toole. Doesn't do at all."

"Who in bloody hell are you? And what do you care who I talk about?"

"Seaman, same as yourself. Least I was. And a man o' New York who knows there's some folks you can curse aloud, and others you can't." The stranger nodded toward a large rotund man seated at a nearby table. "Heinrich Ashdor he was when he came. Henry Astor now. Owns this place and pretty much everything round about. A very important fellow. Has a brother who's more important still—Jacob. I warrant you've heard about him. But ye might not know the man as is sitting next to old Heinrich—F. X. Gallagher. From Ireland, same as yourself, but much better placed in this city than you are, Captain O'Toole. As for Gornt Blakeman, he's an important man as well. Tend to stick together, that sort does."

"Even so. Not your lookout who I curse or where."

"Aye, but we seamen should look after each other, same like the rich folks. Mercy!" he called out. "Two more double rations o' grog. My friend here's still thirsty."

"What's mercy to do with it? You pays for your grog, it's yours. Nothing to do with mercy."

The other man chuckled. "That's the barmaid's name. Sort o' appropriate, wouldn't you say?"

"I might. Or I might ask what your name is, since we're on the subject."

"Folks call me Peggety Jack." He stuck out a wooden leg. "No reason you shouldn't do the same."

His face was as wrinkled and brown as an apple been in the stores too long, and the one tooth was all he seemed to have, hanging over his lip like a fang.

Mercy arrived with two more glasses of grog. O'Toole raised one in a toast. "Here's to your health, Peggety Jack."

"And to yours." The other man lifted his glass in reply and took a sip. "Tell me, what's your quarrel wi' Gornt Blakeman?" he said, keeping his voice low.

"None o' your bloody business."

Peggety Jack shrugged. "Don't matter none. All the same, bring a man's ship through a godrotting British blockade, and make him richer than he was by the sale o' more'n two hundred tons o' China tea and China silk . . . seems odd you'd be cursing him two days later. Got your fair share, everyone says. Blakeman paid you off soon as the sale was done, while half the town was there to see it."

"Aye. Never said he didn't."

"Then what's your squawk?"

"I told you, it's none o' your business."

"Maybe it ain't. Or maybe it is. In a sort o' way. Friend o' Joyful Turner, ain't ye?"

"His da was a friend to me. What's that to do with anything?"

"Nothing," Peggety Jack assured him. "Nothing at all. Just repeatin' the gossip, I am. Tell you what I think. Only a guess, mind. I think you and Blakeman had a falling out and you're not captain o' *Canton Star* any longer. Am I right?"

"Know a lot as goes on down by the docks, don't ye? I mean for someone is up here with the butchers."

"Sometimes don't prove nothin' where a man drinks. You're up here with the butchers this night as well."

"Aye, so I am."

"And not captain o' *Canton Star* no longer neither."

O'Toole shrugged.

"So what'll you be doin' next then? Not too many berths available these days. Not even for a captain as can outfox the Royal Navy."

"Ain't too many I need." O'Toole raised his hand to signal for more rum. "Only one."

"True enough. Does that mean you've got the one lined up?"

"You might say."

Mercy brought the grog. Seemed to O'Toole he was drinking three for every one Peggety Jack got through, but somehow all the glasses on the table were emptied soon enough.

"What's the name o' the ship then?" Peggety asked. "The one you're going to be captain of now as you ain't workin' for Gornt Blakeman."

"Never you mind. She's a fine sloop. That's all you need to know. As fine a sloop as ever sailed, and we're going on a treasure hunt."

"Oh, are you now?"

"Aye. If you weren't so long in the tooth, Peggety Jack, old as Methuselah I reckon, I'd offer you a berth. All the way to the Caribbean we're going."

The old man leaned back in his chair and studied the Irishman. "Tell you what that sounds like to me," he said softly. "Seein' as how you're right and I'm old as any man in this city ain't already dead. And seein' as how when you was in the Revolution you served under Morgan Turner. And how it just so happens there's talk that Morgan Turner buried a treasure some time afore that war, after the last voyage o' the *Fanciful Maiden*. Seein' as all that's the case, I'd wager a fair sum you're planning to take your fine sloop, whichever fine sloop it may be, and go after what some calls the thrice-back treasure."

O'Toole shook his head to try and clear it. Sweet Mary and all the saints, he was too drunk to think straight, and too sober not to know this was a dangerous conversation. "Don't know what you're talking about."

"Aye, ye knows. I can see it in your face, Finbar O'Toole." Peggety leaned forward, both hands clutching a mug of grog, rheumy old eyes fixing the Irishman in an intent stare. "Listen to me, you set out on that voyage, it's a lee shore you'll sail by. Waste o' time and effort and sailors' lives."

"You're daft. No man alive can say as Finbar O'Toole don't know better'n to sail by the lee shore."

"I say it. Because seems like you don't know the thrice-back treasure was found long since. The Jews got it. Fitting that is. Now drink up and I'll take you to where you can sleep safe for what's left o' the night."

Maryland,
an Encampment at Upper Marlboro, 11 A.M.

Still no sign of any American defense. The British heard only the sound of exploding powder in the distance. "That will be the gunboats," the general said. "They're blowing them up lest we take them."

The admiral waved a dismissing hand. "Not worth the navy's time and trouble. Nothing but barges. Look here, this is the way to do it." He had accompanied the army ashore because he was familiar with the territory. He bent over a map. "We avoid the nearest bridges. They're sure to be the most heavily defended. But if we go eight miles further up the Eastern Branch of the Potomac, north by northwest"— his finger traced the route as he spoke—"we can come into the Federal District from above. The river's a good deal more shallow at that point; your troops can ford if they must."

"That assumes your map as well as your memory is accurate. And that we have decided for Washington rather than Baltimore."

"I think we must decide so. Washington is the heart of this absurd enterprise."

"Just what do you believe to be absurd, Admiral? This war?"

"From their side, yes, of course it is. Barges with a few gun emplacements to oppose the Royal Navy. Hubris in the extreme. But I meant this pretentious exercise in sovereignty. Destroy what they call their capital, that'll give them a more realistic notion of exactly who they are."

The general sighed. "That's as may be, sir. But I'm told this Federal District is little more than a few buildings on a drained swamp. I do not choose to spend the lives of my men for such a paltry return. Baltimore is an important city of many thousands, with businesses and a port and—"

"And it will have no particular significance for the Americans living in other cities. Whereas Washington . . ." The admiral let the words trail away, intent on his own vision of glory.

The general settled himself in one of the leather camp chairs that had been set up in the command tent. It was, he feared, to be a long and hot and difficult argument, but it was not one he was prepared to concede.

New York City, the Fly Market, Noon

"Every last nubbin o' it," Holy Hannah said. "Down his gullet."

Joyful was not of a mind to worry about Thumbless Wu and his supply of rice. He kept craning his neck, looking for Manon. "How'd you know to find me here?"

Hannah shrugged. "Just did, that's all. You said he'd die without rice. Where am I to get more then, since it's all gone?"

"I think I'd best see to that. I will, Hannah, soon as I can. If not today, tomorrow."

"Better be today," she said. A few women came by, the baskets on their arms full to overflowing with meat and pot herbs and fresh milk and cheese, the products of the lush and verdant countryside which New York could not be deprived of by any British blockade. The women pulled their skirts aside so as to have no contact with Holy Hannah. "Today," Hannah repeated, ignoring the snubs she was well used to. "Otherwise forget Thumbless, he'll be Bag o' Bones again."

"Not that fast," Joyful said. There was still no sign of Manon. He wanted to go to Elsie Gruning's booth and ask for her, but not with Holy Hannah following him about. "Go home, Hannah. I'll come later today if I can, and certainly by tomorrow."

"And you'll bring more o' that rice?"

"If I can," he repeated.

"You better had come," Hannah whispered, stretching upward and pressing her mouth close to Joyful's ear. "Sooner rather than later, you hear?"

"Hannah, it's more than Wu you're worried about."

She settled back on her heels and shook her head. "Can't be talking 'bout it here. You come out to Hannah's. Then we'll see."

He started to demand an explanation, but was distracted by the sight of Finbar O'Toole hurrying toward him. "What in God's name are you doing here?"

"Looking for you. Have to talk to you, lad."

"Everyone seems to be telling me that today. Hannah here as well." He turned to look for Holy Hannah, but she wasn't there. He thought he spotted her disheveled mane bobbing through the market crowd, but the vision was already too distant for him to be sure. "Wait here," he told the Irishman. "I'll be right back."

"Don't fail me, lad. Important it is."

"Yes, I heard you." Finbar O'Toole's idea of something important was likely to be more relevant to his concerns of the moment than were Hannah's. But Manon trumped them both. "Wait here," he repeated. "I'll return shortly."

Elsie Gruning was at her usual place. "Too wet it's been for the onions," Joyful heard her say. "But this kale be full of goodness, mevrouw. See how dark it is. *Ja*, three pounds at least you need."

He waited while she stuffed great wads of thick and crinkled dark green leaves into the customer's burlap bag and took the coins due her. Then, after the woman had taken her kale and left, he spoke. "Good afternoon, Mistress Elsie."

"Good afternoon, mijnheer." Elsie lowered her voice. "The *juffrouw*, she be with you?"

"Not today, Elsie. That's what I came to ask you about. Have you seen her?"

"Not since Friday last, mijnheer. Today the Widow Tremont came. Made sure I should know she was buying for the household of Mijnheer Vionne and they always got the best."

"But Mistress Manon always—"

"*Ja,* I know. But today it was the Widow Tremont. I thought perhaps you and the *juffrouw* had—" She broke off. "I do not mean to give offense, mijnheer."

"None taken, Elsie. Listen, if you see her, will you give her a message for me?"

"*Ja,* sure, mijnheer."

"Tell her I'll keep trying. Say I'll come to the market this week as many days as I can."

"I will tell her, mijnheer."

"And say that if we keep missing each other, she should try the dovecote and—" Joyful broke off. Finbar had tired of waiting and was coming toward him. "I must go, Elsie. Thank you."

Nowhere in public, Finbar insisted; there wasn't a taproom or a grog shop that he considered safe enough for what he had to say. They went instead to Joyful's Greenwich Street room. The Irishman refused the single chair and sprawled on the bed, supporting his bald head on the brass headboard, keeping only his muddy boots on the floor, and pressing his fists to his temples and moaning every time he moved.

"Sweet Christ, Finbar. I can get drunk just breathing the fumes you exude." Joyful threw open a window. "Has to be a goodly amount of rum still sloshing around in your belly for it to make such a stink."

"A goodly amount," O'Toole said grimly. "That's fair enough. 'Bout the only thing as is."

"What's that supposed to mean?"

"Reason I got blind drunk, poxed Gornt Blakeman threw me off his ship."

"Why would he do that?"

"Gave a tar a touch o' the cat."

"Did you now? Well, that's your right, at any rate." Joyful had seen men flogged to the death. A much less frequent occurrence in the American navy than in the British, but the law of the sea remained in force whatever colors a ship flew. "Why should Blakeman want to be shut of you for that? Who was it?"

"Just a tar. Nimble-footed as a monkey in the rigging, and whistles better'n most men fiddle, but he—"

"Name's not Tammy Tompkins, is it?"

"How'd you know that?"

"A lucky guess. He was aboard *Lawrence* with me. Whistling was his long suit. Bit of a shirker sometimes, but he could reef sail faster and tighter than any man aboard. Tammy Tompkins. I'll be buggered. Seems as if all that crew as are still alive are showing up in New York."

"Seamen circle from one port to another like water spinning down a bunghole," O'Toole said morosely. "No surprise in that."

"Probably not. But why should Gornt Blakeman give a hoot in hell about you taking the cat to Tammy Tompkins? Good God . . . You didn't kill him, did you, Finbar?"

"Course I didn't kill him. Not even close. Wanted to, I admit. He was drunk on watch and fell asleep. But he was well able to steal my gig and row himself to shore when I was done with him." Finbar snorted in disgust, then grabbed his head. "Holy Mother o' God, paying for my sins, I am," he muttered. "Forget Tompkins. Got something important to tell you 'fore I croak."

"You won't croak, Finbar. That's an informed medical opinion." Joyful drew the chair closer to the bed and sat down. "Let me make it a bit easier, since you're a man in distress. I expect the person we should be talking about is a Cantonese rogue called Thumbless Wu."

O'Toole sat up a bit straighter, wincing at the intensity of the pain the movement caused. "Met him, have you? Can't say as I'm surprised."

"Why not?"

"Ain't likely to be another man in this city as speaks the language of that blighted *tset-ha tset-ha*. Not much cause to wonder if he found you. Or you found him."

"Neither as it happens. Holy Hannah found Wu and I met him at her cabin."

"Holy Hannah? What's Thumbless Wu got to do with her?"

"Hannah takes in strays. Wu was starving. It seems you don't feed your stowaways particularly well, Finbar. Even those you invite aboard."

"Wu tell you that?"

"No, he's told me nothing. As for him being a stowaway on *Canton Star,* how else would he get here? The rest was just a guess. You're too good a captain to have a stowaway aboard and not find him. Unless you chose not to."

"Well I didn't starve the bugger. Whatever he says. Not any more'n I flogged the life out o' that blighted bastard Tammy Tompkins."

"The whole world's doing hard by you, is that it, Finbar?" And when the Irishman shrugged: "Where's your money? Did you have to leave it behind on *Canton Star* when Blakeman ran you off? Want me to go and get it for you, perhaps? Is that what this is all about?"

"Took me money with me," O'Toole muttered.

Joyful thought for a moment. "But you don't have it now, is that it?"

"That's it. Not what I came to see you about, though." The last thing he remembered was Peggety Jack showing him the way to the shed where he spent the night. *You'll be safe here, Captain O'Toole.* He could probably find the old bastard and indeed he would, but there was no way on God's green earth he'd be able to prove Peggety Jack took the moneybag and left him nothin' but the few loose coins remaining in his trouser pockets. Not as full o' grog as he'd been, and in a blind stupor to boot. "Money comes and money goes. Nothin' new in that."

"You need a berth, that's why you came. You're prepared to sail the *Lisbetta* to the Caribbean."

"No, lad. That's exactly what I'm not prepared to do. I may be a fool, but I'm not a liar or a cheat. Whatever you think. And for the sake o' the log, I didn't take a single strip off Gornt Blakeman's back by giving Thumbless Wu a hidey-hole aboard *Canton Star,* not a single strip. Shared me own grub with him. Took meals in me captain's cabin and brought him a portion o' that. Not that he ate much. Never saw anyone be that seasick afore." Despite everything, O'Toole smiled at the thought.

"Yes, and starving for rice."

"Course he was. But I daren't give him any. I start asking the cook to make rice on a ship wi'out a single Chinaman aboard as anyone can see . . ." He shrugged.

"Fair enough. But I think we're wandering down herring alley, Finbar." It was a sailor's term for going astray when you went ashore. "You say you've lost your money, but you won't captain *Lisbetta*. And that whatever made you bring Thumbless Wu to New York on Gornt Blakeman's ship, it's nothing to do with me. So what exactly is it that was so private you wouldn't talk about it except here in my room?"

O'Toole sat up and instantly bent over, holding his pounding head in his hands. "First, for the sake o' log, like I said, I haven't any idea why the *tset-ha tset-ha* wanted to come to New York. I brought him because I owed him a hundred taels of silver. No way I could pay that. Thumbless agreed to cancel the debt if I brung him here. Whatever else he gets up to, it's nothing to do with me."

"Very well. But I believe we still haven't gotten to the part that bears on me."

"No, lad, we have not. Be warned, you aren't going to like it."

"I've been told things I didn't like often enough before this. I doubt I'll die from one more."

"Aye, well, remember that when you hear this one. The treasure ain't in the Caribbean any longer. Wherever your da left it, 'tis not there now."

"I see. How do you know that?"

"Fellow called Peggety Jack told me."

"Any reason you should have been talking with this Peggety Jack about something I told you in strictest confidence?"

"'Tweren't like that," O'Toole said. "He talked to me. I admit I don't remember a lot o' what we said, but I swear on my mother's soul, I never mentioned the treasure. Not the *Fanciful Maiden* neither. 'Twas this Peggety fellow what brought up both of 'em. We were at the sign o' the Bull's Head on the Bowery. And he says to me, 'Goin' after the thrice-back treasure, are ye? 'Taint there. The Jews got it.' That's what he said. On my mother's soul, lad."

As far as Joyful knew, only he and his cousin Andrew knew about the "twice around and thrice back" legend that was at the heart of the enigma of Morgan Turner's treasure. For his part, Joyful was entirely certain he had not repeated those words to another human being.

Ann Street, 3:30 P.M.

"Extraordinary," Andrew said. "Truly." They were in his front room. The windows were all open—Andrew didn't hold with the notion that disease was carried on the humid currents of summer air—and because it was nearing the dinner hour, the smell of good cooking mingled with the city heat. "I give you my word, from the day I got hold of the damned note until the day I handed it to you, I might have looked at it twice, perhaps three times. No more. And I sure to God Almighty never spoke of what your father had written. Not to anyone. Alive or dead."

"I didn't think it likely, but I had to ask."

"Yes, of course you did." Andrew sat silent for a few moments. "Occurs to me," he said finally, "the thing we don't know is where that piece of paper had been between the time your father wrote the words and the moment I took it out of Caleb's dead hand."

"I've thought the same thing. And there's no way we're going to know, is there?"

"None I can imagine."

Joyful walked to the open window, looked outside for a time, then turned back to his cousin. "One other thing . . ."

"Yes?"

"Finbar said this Peggety Jack told him the Jews had it and it was fitting that they did."

Andrew shook his head. "I'm afraid I can shed no more light on that than the other. Unless he was referring to your grandfather. Solomon DaSilva. Since he was a Jew, I mean."

"That occurred to me as well. But I can't make the connection."

"Nor can I. Doesn't put us much further forward, does it?"

Joyful pursed his lips, thought for a moment, then changed tack. "Different subject," he said, "in its way more vital."

"Yes?"

"There's a young woman . . ." He saw Andrew smile and felt himself blush, the red intensifying when he realized he was behaving like a lovesick puppy rather than a mature and battle-hardened man. "Her name is Manon Vionne."

"The goldsmith's daughter? Pretty lass, I've seen her. And an up-standing family. I approve."

"Her father doesn't."

"Why not? You're a hero and the son of a hero, a medical man to boot. What possible—"

"I shouldn't say he doesn't approve of me. What I mean is that I'm sure he would not."

Andrew stared at him a moment, then shook his head. "You've not made a formal request for the lady's hand, have you? In God's name, Joyful, why not? It's high time you married."

"I have no means to support a wife. Not yet." The steady income from a brothel was not something he could reveal to either Andrew or Maurice Vionne.

"I see. But you're telling me all this for a reason, Joyful. What is it?"

"I am concerned for her safety. If her father should turn her out."

"Turn her out? Joyful, I think I had best not ask what is behind that worry."

"It's not what you think; I give you my word. But if my fears are realized, may I bring her here to stay? Only until I can marry her and give her a home of her own." If Vionne insisted that Manon marry Gornt Blakeman, and she refused to do so, all hell could break loose.

"Of course. How could you think otherwise? Besides, having a young woman in the household to fuss over—Bridey would think she'd died and gone to heaven."

As if summoned by the speaking of her name, Bridey tapped on the door, then opened it to announce that dinner was ready, and of course she'd set a place for Dr. Joyful, who definitely looked to her as if he could use a proper meal.

Pearl Street, the Private Rooms Above
Barnaby Carter's Warehouse, 5 P.M.

Lucretia Carter—Lucretia Hingham before she married—had never thought, after she became Barnaby's wife, to use her skills in what her mother and her aunt had called "the female arts." Not until this war made business so difficult, and Gornt Blakeman didn't pay them what he owed. After that, she'd no choice. "What's a body to do, Miss Delight? The times are terrible hard."

Lucretia's voice was like nails scraping on glass, but Delight was accustomed to it by now. She came frequently to the room above Barnaby's warehouse. "Indeed they are, Mrs. Carter. And you do perform a much needed . . . Do stop sniveling, Felicity." Delight turned to the girl beside her. "Drink your tea. It will strengthen you. And take this." Delight offered her handkerchief. "Your own is too sodden with tears to be of any use."

Felicity, who had been weeping off and on since she first confided that "Granny hadn't come to visit" for two months, took the square of linen and used it to soak up another rush of tears. Lucretia leaned forward and patted the girl's knee. "It's going to all be over before you know it, dearie. Haven't the other girls told you how quick I am? Thorough as well, of course. In these matters"—the screech rising to an almost unbearable pitch—"One must be thorough." *Scrape up, down, and side to side, Lucretia. Otherwise you can't be sure you've got it all. A babe might be born despite your efforts, maybe missing an arm or a leg or even a head, missing the part you scraped away without getting it all. So the poor woman is worse off than when she came to you. Terrible for business, that is. Word does get around.* "No half measures," she promised. "Don't you worry about that."

"I can't stand pain," Felicity wailed. "Never could. And Cecily told me—"

"Cecily is a fool," Delight said. "A very pretty one, but a fool nonetheless." She removed another little brown bottle of Devrey's Elixir of Well-Being from her drawstring bag and emptied it into the girl's tea. The third dose today. Pray God they'd soon take effect. Otherwise the whole town was bound to hear the screams. "And do consider, Felicity, that you have only two alternatives—Mrs. Carter here, or a bouncing babe whose papa is a total mystery to you." She did not add that the girl would also have nowhere to live, since there was no place at the Dancing Knave for a pregnant whore, terms of employment that had been made clear the first day Felicity came to work. No parlor house, not even one considerably less prestigious than the Dancing Knave, would take her with a big belly, much less a squalling brat in tow. The Hook it would be then.

"Let's get started, shall we?" Lucretia drank the last of her tea and stood up.

Felicity made a halfhearted attempt to protest. Delight pulled her out of the chair. Sweet little thing, Felicity. Thin and delicate, and all those red-brown curls. The gentlemen adored her. Too bad she wasn't more careful about flushing out her sex after every customer the way she'd been taught. Well, she wasn't likely to forget after today. "Come along, Felicity. We mustn't keep Mrs. Carter waiting." Quite docile the girl was now, all her consternation replaced by a dreamy look. Ah, Jonathan, one thing you did learn from your mother and your sister— how to make the town's best laudanum tonic. Wouldn't I love to see your face if you knew the identity of your best customer. Impossible, of course; Agnes would continue to be the one to buy the Knave's supply of Devrey's Elixir of Well-Being.

"Here we are then. Everything's ready." The room where Lucretia Carter practiced her art was furnished with a high and narrow brick platform topped with a straw mattress—"Mr. Carter made that arrangement for me. Such a thoughtful man"—and a table containing the tools of Lucretia's trade: three nails, each almost a foot long and forged so thin they were little more than stiff threads. Lady nails, they were called. "Mama's these were before me," she confided to Delight. For maybe the tenth time. Then, with a little giggle: "Oh, the tales they could tell." She always said that as well.

Felicity had become as uncoordinated as a rag doll. It took the two of them to hoist her atop the bricks, and get her frock and her petticoats rolled above her hips and her legs in the proper position. No need to take down her pantaloons since they were respectably crotchless. The girl was humming to herself. "Bend your knees, Felicity. Yes, that's it." Delight spread them apart. "Have you light enough, Mrs. Carter?"

"Oh, yes, Miss Higgins. Plenty. Do it mostly by feel, I do. After all these years." It had never been her intention to do it at all. She'd hated growing up in a house where mama and mama's sister were never through with ladies who first wept and begged, then when they got what they wanted, screamed the very roof off the place.

Delight took her customary place at the top of the narrow bed, slipping one arm below Felicity's shoulders.

Lucretia waited until the other woman was in position, then spread Felicity's sex with one hand, and used two fingers of the other to withdraw the wad of seaweed Delight Higgins had inserted the previous day. A right miracle that was. Opened the ladies up so wide it made it almost easy to get the nail in and do the job. Seaweed, who would have known? Mama and Auntie certainly had not. "Seaweed, Miss Higgins. I do declare."

"Yes, Mrs. Carter. You do." Every single time I come, you do declare. But you'll go to your grave knowing no more than you know now. It does what it's meant to do. Never you mind that it was Roisin Campbell Turner who taught the secret to her daughter, and Clare Turner Devrey who used to send me to every beach in New York looking for the special orange seaweed. And once I had the temerity to bring back not orange but brown . . . *Switch the skin off your back I will, you little fool. How would you like it if it was you lying with your legs spread and your womb was so tight nothing could get in . . .*

Lucretia reached for the longest and thinnest nail.

Delight put a hand over Felicity's mouth to stifle the inevitable screams of agony. It was easier with the seaweed and the laudanum, but never easy. Never that. And all so a girl could avoid starving to death, and men could have their pleasure whenever they wanted it. "Go ahead, Mrs. Carter. Get it over with. We're ready."

Good God, what if Gornt Blakeman were to make good on his offer and she really were given charge of every prostitute in the city? A license system he'd said, to promote good order.

Lucretia inserted the nail. Felicity's first shriek fought its way out despite Delight's restraining hand, and she struggled to tear herself out of her employer's grip. Delight made the usual soothing noises while tightening her hold on the girl's head and shoulders. "Do be quick, Mrs. Carter."

"I'm doing my best, Miss Higgins. Quick but thorough." *Scrape up, down, and side to side, Lucretia. Otherwise you can't be sure you've got it all.*

There were hundreds, maybe thousands, of prostitutes in the city. How could Gornt Blakeman come to hold that much power? But if it did happen . . . Delight saw a selection of houses, different standards in each one, each meant for a different class of custom. Better to get even the hookers under a roof. She'd need half a dozen Mrs. Carters, and every scrap of orange seaweed the beaches of New York would yield.

"There, that's it. You're all done, Miss Felicity. That wasn't so bad, was—"

"Save your breath, Mrs. Carter. She's passed out."

"Just as well, isn't it?" Lucretia held out her hand and Delight passed over the two shillings she was due. "She's sure to bleed some tonight and tomorrow," Lucretia said. "You will be sure to keep her abed until the flow stops. And no . . . no gentleman callers for at least three weeks."

"I will do exactly as you say, Mrs. Carter." One reason the Dancing Knave had the prettiest whores in the city—if you had to be scraped out, Miss Higgins herself looked after you and you got an entire fortnight to recover from the procedure. Delight told herself that's why she took the trouble to use the seaweed, and allowed her ladies such a luxurious amount of time before they must again entertain customers. Because it insured that she always had the best girls in town. Nothing to do with being softhearted, or knowing all too well what drove women to whoredom.

Delight went to the window and tapped on the glass. Preservation Shay heard the signal and nodded. She saw him come into the building and began drawing on her lace gloves as she went back to the table where Felicity lay. "I've no doubt we'll see each other again soon, Mrs. Carter."

"No doubt, Miss Higgins." Who would have imagined that she would talk to a half-nigra woman as if she were a social equal? Mama and Auntie always refused to perform their services for nigras, but if Lucretia Carter turned away the custom of Delight Higgins, she and Mr. Carter would be in a sorry way. All the same, hard as things were, Lucretia was not comfortable with the story Mr. Carter had told her last night. Wormed it out of him, she had, when he came up from downstairs half an hour after her lovely Sunday dinner had gone stone cold, and he could barely force himself to eat three bites. Having their prosperity restored by going back on their word to the rest of the states—it didn't seem right.

Preservation Shay, who had been sweet on Felicity since the first day he came to work at the Dancing Knave, came into the room and lifted the girl as if she were a precious bit of porcelain and carried her down the stairs. Delight Higgins said goodbye, and Lucretia Carter wished her a good day and looked forward to their next meeting.

Imagine, a whore being treated like a princess. A mulatto no less, and one who wore a frock Lucretia herself couldn't afford if she scraped the unwanted babes out of the womb of every woman in New York. The modern world was surely an extraordinary place.

Chapter Fifteen

New York City, the Woods Above North Street,
Holy Hannah's Cabin, 8 P.M.

WU SAT ON THE GROUND, leaning his back against a tree and watching the woman called Han-nah draw a bucket of water from the cistern. Watching the *yang gui zhi* who spoke the language of the Middle Kingdom. Ahyee! The most dangerous foreign devil in this place.

He and the foreign ghost woman were speaking their own speech now. Wu could overhear only a few words and understand no more than half of those. Easy to move closer, but that would put the rest of his plan at risk. Some distance away the two boys were playing a game that involved throwing a knife so its tip stuck in the ground, showing off the various ways it could be done. He had seen boys in China playing a similar game. Not him though. Never games. Never games. Third Son Wu—he could not now remember any name he'd been given before he became Thumbless—had always worked on the junk with his father. The gamblers came by night and by day, and his earliest memory was distributing the mahjong tiles to the newcomers. Eventually he learned to count the money. Then to gamble himself. Until he paid a debt with both thumbs and decided to forget everything he'd learned and start over again. Not on the junk, on land.

Never gamble. Never gamble. Only make a place where others can let the tiles and the money run through their fingers. Thumbless Wu became an important man, a rich man who would be an ancestor. Then the British brought the white smoke from Calcutta to Canton, and he watched others become even richer.

Ahyee! Great chests of wood, each one packed with forty big balls of the sticky black stuff that miraculously became white smoke. Forbidden. Forbidden. The emperor says so. Never mind. The chests are sold on a secret island in the River Pearl, and the buyers, all civilized men of the Middle Kingdom, pay the English traders in silver, which the traders take to Canton to pay the hong merchants for tea—ahyee! always so much tea—and silk and porcelain. Everyone happy. Except the emperor. Except Thumbless Wu.

Men, it turned out, would pay more and sacrifice more to be allowed to draw in white smoke than to gamble, and when their brains had drifted away with the smoke, they had no money left for other pleasures. But when Thumbless Wu formed a secret society to oppose the hidden places where those who once gambled went to suck in white smoke, the men who bought the chests that came from Calcutta made every man of the Middle Kingdom who traded with them for the precious black balls swear that Wu Thumbless would have none of what they bought. Those who defied the rule they killed. So. So. When the last of the traders who dared to do business with him was dead, it was clear. To be the richest man in Canton, to be an ancestor, Thumbless Wu must first become this filthy thing reduced to begging for rice. Until here in New York he could find his own source of white smoke.

Good plan. Good plan. In Canton he had met men who had been to Calcutta, and he learned that the black balls began when the special red flowers dropped their seed. But how to make the seed into the sticky stuff that could be sucked into the lungs as white smoke, no one could tell him that. Then he heard the American sailors brag that in New York there was everything that could be desired on this earth. Since men without number desired the sticky black stuff that made white smoke, it followed that the red flowers could also be found in America, as well as someone who knew how to make them into the precious black balls and pack them forty to a chest and send them on a ship to Canton. The rest would be done by Thumbless Wu and his many brothers and cousins and uncles, and their junks that stretched end to end in the Bogue and sailed up and down the coast of the Middle Kingdom.

He had come far and suffered much. He would not give up everything he had gained merely to satisfy his curiosity about what the red-headed barbarian with the civilized tongue was discussing with the foreign ghost woman.

Wu moved, slowly and cautiously; each little bounce along the earth took him nearer the trees. Soon the voices of the *yang gui zhi* were only a distant noise that sounded to him like throat clearings.

"Look down there, Joyful Patrick Turner," Hannah said. "Tell me what you see."

The cistern was not very deep. "Water," Joyful said, peering over the mixed jumble of boulders and pebbles that surrounded Hannah's hole in the ground. "And some leaves, and possibly a drowned animal or two that had the misfortune to fall in. What's this to do with me?"

"Told you, I did. Something shining. Very valuable. Coming over the water."

"That's as may be, but not from this filthy cistern." Joyful turned aside, took off his hat and tucked it under his left arm, and found a handkerchief with his right to wipe the sweat from his forehead. Something shining coming over the water. The Great Mogul? But how did Holy Hannah know about it? And what did she know? He had no answers to those questions, but he was sure that wherever Manon's diamond came from, it was not this rat hole of a cistern. "We're on an island, Hannah. The sea's all around us. Why does your something shining have to come from these few inches of standing water?"

"The Holy One, blessed be He, told me to ask. What do you see?" she repeated.

"Nothing," Joyful admitted. "I see nothing shining and nothing valuable. And if Almighty God is speaking to you, I respectfully suggest He could be a damned sight clearer."

Hannah shrugged. "Then the message don't be for you. And as you'd do well to remember, Joyful Patrick Turner, 'the Lord will not hold him guiltless that taketh His name in vain.' Book o' Exodus. One o' the holiest books."

"The one that tells about the Children of Israel going forth from Egypt, isn't it, Hannah?"

"Aye."

"And the Egyptians chased the Children of Israel, and they wandered forty years in the desert. Never been easy to be a Jew, has it? So why would I be told the Jews had something that belonged to me?"

"The Lord parted the sea to let the Israelites pass, and drowned the Egyptians that came after them. That's all in Exodus as well. And don't matter what you was told. Not unless the teller had some sense in him, and whatever it was really belonged to you, not someone else. Look into the cistern, Joyful. Tell me what you see."

"Nothing, Hannah," he said, sighing. "Nothing different than I saw before."

"Not meant for you then." There was an air of finality to her words. Joyful didn't think he could change her mind with argument or cajolery.

She bent over to heft the jug she'd filled with water. It was a great brown thing that held twenty gallons at least. Mighty heavy for an old woman. Joyful took the jug from her. "Jesse or Will should be doing this for you." He glanced over to where the two boys were playing mumblety peg.

"The lads do their share," Hannah said. "And mostly they work from dawn to past dark. Ain't many chances they get to play."

"Thumbless then. Where's he got himself to, by the way?" The man had been sitting on the grass a few minutes before. Now Joyful couldn't see him.

She shrugged. "Thumbless don't be strong enough to lug around jugs o' water. Once he is, then he'll go. As for where he is right now, probably went to do his business out in the woods behind. Does that often enough. Less, mind you, since he been eating that rice you brung."

"It's what he's accustomed to. Agrees with his digestion."

"Did you bring more?"

"Not yet."

"Said you would."

"Yes," Joyful agreed. "I'll try and get more and bring it back." Tomorrow perhaps, or even the next day. Let Wu build up enough of a hunger for the stuff to make him more cooperative. Knowing that the man had convinced Finbar to allow him to stow away on the *Canton Star* was not the same as knowing why he'd come.

There was no way Thumbless Wu could keep up with a man on horseback, but he'd never intended to. There was still light enough for him to follow the prints made in the soft earth by the horse's hooves. He worried that he'd lose the trail when they got to the paved roads of the city, but at least he knew what the horse of the barbarian with the red hair looked like. He would recognize it if— Ahyee! His joss was marvelous this day. The gods were truly smiling on him. The place the barbarian was going was here at the very edge of the town.

The trail of hoofprints led around to the back of a large and imposing house. Only a mandarin of highest standing would live in such a house. But if the barbarian had business with such a mandarin, he would go in through the gate facing the street. Instead he had tethered his horse in the rear, beside a brick wall that when Wu peeked over it revealed a small garden of luscious fruits—pears trained to climb the walls, and apple trees marching in precise rows up the middle of the square. Even better, there was a young girl working in the garden. And she was not a *gwai nui sing,* a foreign ghost woman like the one called Hah-nah. This was a civilized girl swaying on proper golden lilies.

While he watched, a young man, also a civilized person, but tall the way those from the far northwest of China were, came out. He was carrying a small burlap sack on a shoulder broader than the task required. *Fan.* The thought made Wu's mouth water. He fingered his knife, but knew that even with it he was no match for the young man tall as a *gau leng* Manchurian, and the even taller *yang gui zhi* barbarian who came out of the house behind him. The girl bowed herself respectfully out of their presence and went back into the house. The two men went to where the barbarian's horse was tethered and spoke for a while, using proper Mandarin, the Chinese being especially courteous to the man with the red hair, calling him Lord and bowing repeatedly, even though the barbarian kept telling him not to do so. "But I am honored by your presence, Lord. We all are." Over and over, as if he were the barbarian's servant.

They spoke about the war, who was winning and who was losing, and how soon the mandarins on both sides would talk their way to peace. Thumbless Wu knew about the war. He knew that to get to America it had been necessary for *Canton Star* to sail past the fighting ships of a mighty navy, and that from the moment he set foot on the *diu ling* boat he was at the mercy of the *diu ling* barbarian captain he thought of as O-too. Never mind. Never mind. He was here. And he had found the apothecary and the red flowers. And now—all gods bear witness to the quantities of incense he would burn in thanksgiving for his marvelous joss this night—he had discovered civilized people. He did not mind when he saw the young one who looked like a Manchurian put the *fan* in the saddlebags of the barbarian with the red hair, and he felt no anxiety when the barbarian mounted his horse and rode away. He was quite sure he was in a place where he could make *guanxi,* and once he did, *fan* would follow.

Wu waited until the tall young one went into the house and the girl tottered back out on her golden lilies. She made his mouth water more than the *fan.* "Psst . . ." Wu hissed at her.

The girl turned to the sound. When she saw him, her eyes opened to become too big for her face, like a small animal, startled in the night when it was caught in the glow of the lanterns of a junk coming to the shore.

"Psst . . ." Wu said again, and beckoned her to him.

Hanover Street, 8:30 P.M.

Vinegar Clifford, wearing his working uniform of black singlet and leggings, stood motionless with his arms folded, the bullwhip dangling uncoiled from one huge fist. Gornt Blakeman's countinghouse was old, the ceiling of the front room low, the exposed beams darkened with the smoke of the many open fires that had burned on the hearth before the Franklin stove was installed. The two tall desks stood waiting for the morning when the clerks would return and conduct Blakeman's business. For now the whipper was alone, standing guard beside the narrow staircase that led to the private quarters.

The thick door on the landing was firmly closed and no sound escaped from behind it.

The upstairs room with its surplus of heavy furniture was already full of black shadows, the only relief a pool of yellow light cast by a single oil lamp burning on a table. Gornt Blakeman and his guest sat inside the circle of light, and though he knew they were secure and well guarded, Blakeman spoke in a voice barely above a whisper. "It is a time for men of vision, Mr. Astor. Men who can see the glory that lies ahead."

"*Ja,* perhaps. Also a time it may be to hang for treason."

"I do not believe that, sir. I don't think you believe it either."

Jacob Astor shrugged. "I know what I believe, Mr. Blakeman. It is to know what you believe that I am here at your countinghouse."

"Very well, I will tell you." Blakeman's face looked strange and fantastic in the lamplight. As if, like the dragon on his ship's flag, when he opened his mouth flames would shoot forth. "First, I cannot see that it is treason for a man to consider how best to protect his fortune, indeed his very ability to earn his living, from fools who put it in peril. That such fools have been elected to their office does not seem to me to enter into it."

"Three responses there are to that. One is that here in New York we made a solemn agreement. Both documents we signed, Mr. Blakeman, the Declaration for Independency and later the Constitution. We joined the United States. By what right do we unjoin?"

"The same right as was declared in that first document you mentioned. Because, 'in the course of human events,' as they put it, 'it becomes necessary.' And personally, Mr. Astor, I signed nothing. Neither is your name on the document."

Astor sat in a large, velvet-covered chair with a gilt frame, primly upright so his feet could touch the floor. The chair was not only uncomfortable, it was rather more grand than this crowded room under the eaves deserved. *Ja,* but Blakeman's chair was grander still. A throne. *So, der Kerl wollte König sein.* The man would be a king. How long had he nursed this dream? "The people of New York, Mr. Blakeman, the mechanics and the ordinary workers you must have for your scheme to succeed, they are all republicans these days, against the British and for the French. They support President Madison and his war. Your man downstairs, big he is, terrifying even. But all the city he cannot keep in line with his whip."

"True, Mr. Astor." Blakeman's voice was if anything even softer. "But Vinegar Clifford and his whip are not the only means of enforcing order. I can call on others if necessary."

"The militia is here to defend the city against the British. When you say 'March!' you think they will put one foot in front of the other?"

Blakeman waved a dismissive hand. "Not every man of New York is a member of the militia. Security will not be a problem. Take my word for that."

" *Ja,* perhaps. But how can even this great city stand alone among the nations of the world? It is a fantasy, Mr. Blakeman. Almost I might say a delusion."

"No, Mr. Astor. It is not. You forget, perhaps, that before there were these so called United States, there were Athens and Sparta, and later Florence and Venice . . . the great city-states of history."

"*Ja,* history. Ancient history. Now, in modern times, it is—"

"In modern times things are different, I agree. I never said only New York, Mr. Astor."

"So? Who else? Men from Massachusetts?"

"Some," Blakeman admitted. "Still more from Connecticut. And perhaps Rhode Island."

"New England hotheads."

"That's what the British called them thirty-five years ago when they met in Pennsylvania to talk rebellion. Look where that led."

"To where we are," Astor admitted. "To the Union now you tell me we must leave."

"So that we can survive, sir. So fools cannot lead us by the nose to our inevitable defeat and impoverishment."

"And the rest of the world? How, please, will they not see this as an act of supreme disloyalty? Why should they again trust to keep their word those who would do such a thing?"

"Indeed, Mr. Astor, that is where you come in."

This time Astor said nothing. Blakeman knew the moment had come. He rose and for a moment disappeared into the shadows at the far end of the room. When he returned, he carried a leather box about as big as a man's fist. "Prepare yourself, Mr. Astor. I am about to show you one of the wonders of the world."

Astor had to struggle to maintain the placid expression that had served his business interests so well for so many years. Not because of what he was about to see. He was sure he knew what the box contained, and he had no particular interest in precious gems. His heart was pounding because it appeared that everything young Turner had told him was true. Which meant the risks were enormous. The syndicate he'd formed to support the war effort had purchased millions of dollars' worth of government bonds. If there were to be, to all intents and purposes, no United States government to redeem them . . . *eine Katastrophe.*

The box opened with a snapping sound. "One of the wonders of the world," Blakeman repeated, whispering this time. "Here, have a look."

Astor leaned forward. The diamond lay on a black-velvet cushion, and immediately it seemed to gather to itself all the light in the room. All of it was drawn to the heart of the rose-cut stone, each of the diamond's facets splitting the rays and throwing them back like so many bolts of silent but splendid thunder. "*Du lieber Gott,*" Astor murmured. "A diamond as big as a large walnut. Never have I even heard of such a thing."

"A royal diamond," Blakeman said quietly. "A diamond that belongs in the crown jewels of a great ruler."

"So in this new country of yours, you will be a king? An emperor perhaps?"

"Not a bit of it. I'm not that much of a fool, Mr. Astor. You yourself pointed out how republican are the sentiments of the ordinary folk of the city. At first I may need to, let's say, vigorously convince them to go along with how things are to be—and be assured I'm prepared to do it—but business thrives on peace, not unrest. No, we will offer the people of New York a society where every man is the equal of every other, where those who work will never starve, and those who do not can go to their grave the paupers they deserve to be. I will be no king, Mr. Astor, and certainly not an emperor. I shall be the governor of this province. Each of the others, Rhode Island and Connecticut and Massachusetts, they will have governors as well. And from among them we will choose a president."

"And this president, he will have this?" Astor nodded toward the diamond still shimmering between them.

Blakeman shook his head. "A thing like this only causes trouble. Best if we get it out of our new country sooner rather than later, as soon as we make our peace with Great Britain and our ships are allowed to sail unmolested. And might I remind you that within our union we will have twice as many ships as will be left in the remaining United States, even if you include their entire navy."

"*Ja,* that of course is true." Take New York and most of New England out of the Union and you cut out the country's mercantile heart, certainly seventy or eighty percent of its seafaring trade. What would be left? A few southern plantations, some riverboat traders, and the rest wilderness. Great some day, *ja,* but now . . . Without the Northeast, the United States was a joke. "The jewel, Mr. Blakeman. Still I do not understand."

"International acceptance, Mr. Astor. That is the thing our new nation will need, and it's what the diamond will obtain for us. It's the answer to your concern, sir, that we will be pariahs, outcasts never to be trusted. You, Mr. Astor, will see that does not happen."

"How is that to be, Mr. Blakeman?"

"You will write to the Holy Roman Emperor, Francis II of . . . of Hungary, I believe."

"Emperor of Austria," Astor supplied. "And king of Hungary and Bohemia."

"That's the one. Speaks German, they tell me, so you're the natural one to correspond with him. And because the letter comes from a New Yorker of such splendid prestige and influence as yourself, this emperor, this king of kings, will accept our magnificent—nay, our priceless—gift, and we will be . . . How shall I put it? We will be anointed. We will be a nation."

"*Wunderschön,*" Astor murmured. "It is a plan of such . . . such audacity, Mr. Blakeman, that words I cannot find to comment."

"Audacity? Yes, I suppose it is. But we can only thrive over here if we understand the Europeans over there. I trust, Mr. Astor, you do not forget that."

"I do not, Mr. Blakeman. You may count on the fact that I do not forget most things which are important."

"I never meant to imply that you did, sir. My apologies." Damn!

Bend over, Mr. Bloody Astor, and I'll lick your German-English-American arse for you. Anything to be sure you're my ally and not my enemy. "Indeed, it is because I know that your reputation is as great abroad as it is here that I am asking you to arrange these matters."

Astor didn't say anything. He leaned forward and stared at the diamond for what seemed a very long time.

The box had never left Blakeman's hand, and he was growing weary, but he waited until Astor had pulled back before he snapped the lid shut. "So, Mr. Astor," he asked softly, "are you with us?"

"It is not a decision a man makes in a few minutes, Mr. Blakeman."

"Perhaps not, but time, sir, is not on our side. The New Englanders are pressing me."

Ja, and you want to be able to tell them that you bring to the table the richest man in America, so they will give you more respect and you will be chosen president when the governors make their selection. *Das ist doch ganz klar, nicht?* Yes, entirely clear. Only exactly how he should reply was not clear. "Say that I write this letter you suggest. And say we find a way to get the letter where it must go, despite the blockade—"

"I've a ship as has run the blockade before." But not the captain who made it happen. God rot his wretched hide. Still, there are other captains, some bound to be as good as O'Toole.

" . . . given the natural way of men's unbelief, what do you suggest I tell them?"

"About the diamond?"

Astor jerked his head in an impatient nod. "*Ja, ja.* Of course about the diamond."

"It's called the Great Mogul and its story is well known among collectors of the world's great gems. Fellow called Jean-Baptiste Tavernier saw it in sixteen-something, in India. Next thing we know, it was in Persia."

"But it is not in Persia now. How does it happen, Mr. Blakeman, that the Great Mogul is here in New York, with you?"

"Because, Mr. Astor, by the time I became involved, the Great

Mogul was in Canton. Everything finishes up in Canton sooner or later. A man like yourself surely knows that."

"*Ja*. But I too have business in Canton, and it never—"

"Aye, so you have. But this time my joss was better than yours. I knew somebody as knew somebody, as knew somebody else. And word came to me that the first somebody was in need of a great deal of money, and desperate enough to offer a treasure at a tenth its value. I'm sure, sir, you know that last year I sold scrip in my coaching business."

Astor nodded.

"Supposedly, I needed cash to buy more rolling stock, since I'd just been given the exclusive right to the route between New York and Philadelphia. Truth is, I got the coaches on a promise, and used the money to arrange for the purchase of the stone, and to finish outfitting the fastest merchantman afloat and lading her with the kinds of goods as set the city agog just three days past. So now, Mr. Astor, you know the whole story. How much longer do you think you'll need to decide if you're with us?"

"Not very much time, Mr. Blakeman. A day or two, perhaps three." Once he knew whether Madison was safe, what the British army was planning—news that might be on the way to him even now—it would be easier to deal with Gornt Blakeman. "First, one other thing occurs to me. You have told me the story of the Great Mogul is well known. But why should the emperor believe this diamond to indeed be the Great Mogul?"

"For one thing, sir, as you have seen, the stone is its own best argument. It is magnificent, is it not?"

"That we have established. Truly magnificent it is."

"Very well. In addition, I have taken steps to document its pedigree. There will be a certificate of authenticity written by the city's finest jeweler. He will swear that this stone is genuine, and that it matches exactly the description in the book by the great Tavernier. I expect to have the certificate tomorrow. Then we will have a copy made and send it with your letter."

Astor stood up. "So, Mr. Blakeman, a man of foresight you have shown yourself to be. One who thinks of everything. I have no doubt it can be profitable to do business with such a man."

"Is that a commitment, sir?"

Astor smiled for the first time since coming upstairs to Blakeman's private quarters. "Not yet, sir. A few days, as I said. I will send you word and we will meet again. Now . . ." He gestured toward the door to the stairs. "You can please insure that I am permitted to leave without tasting the whipper's kiss."

Blakeman accompanied him to the door, opened it and called softly down the stairs. "My guest is leaving, Mr. Clifford. Show him out."

"Yes sir, Mr. Blakeman."

He waited until he heard the front door close behind Astor, then Blakeman again shut the door that led to his attic. He wanted to shout out loud with triumph, but he only raised his voice slightly and pitched it to the dark far corner of the room. "So, what do you think?"

"I think you've got him." Bastard Devrey came out of the shadows into the lamplight. "I think you baited the hook and threw the line and reeled him in."

"He'll join us? You genuinely believe so?" He didn't really need Bastard's affirmation, but it wouldn't hurt to hear it.

"I absolutely believe it. He knows this war is squeezing the life out of every man of property in the nation. Why in God's holy hell would he not join us? He's a business man, same as you and me."

"Not exactly the same as you," Blakeman said.

"Don't ride me, man. Don't make me sorry for the bargain I've made."

"Now why should you be sorry for that, Bastard Devrey? You had to choose between Gornt Blakeman and your upstart young cousin with only one hand and not many more coins. You chose me, just to prove your brain wasn't entirely addled by your run of bad luck. Why in hell's name should you be sorry for that?"

Rivington Street, Near Midnight

Sweet Mary and all the saints, according to Joyful he'd smelled like a spilled keg o' rum hours before, and though he'd had a fair amount since, Finbar O'Toole was still mostly sober. God help his sorry soul. O'Toole blessed himself with the sign of the cross and muttered a pious incantation, then put his hand in his pocket to be sure the coin was still there. A single golden lady, last bit o' money he had. Spent everything else that godrotting Peggety Jack, may his soul be damned to everlasting fire, had left him on rum mostly, and a few hands o' cards. In the normal way o' things a guinea was silver, and worth twenty-one shillings, some two and a half dollars American. But a golden lady, that was twenty dollars probably, though there were some as would give more. All there was between Finbar O'Toole and a pauper's grave. Didn't make much difference when he couldn't manage to get drunk whatever he spent.

One lucky roll o' the dice, that's all it would take. Holy Savior, hadn't he seen it happen times enough? Even to himself on occasion. One lucky roll o' the dice or turn o' a mahjong tile and there you were, a rich man again.

The Dancing Knave shimmered in the starlit dark of semideserted Rivington Street. Candles in every window and no curtains to hide their glow. A beacon it was, and from the look o' things plenty had homed in. There were carriages parked up and down the street, and at least half a dozen horses tethered to nearby hitching posts. O'Toole mounted the steps that led to the front door and lifted the brass knocker.

"Good evening, sir."

"The same to yourself." O'Toole squinted into the brightness of the vestibule. New lad this, brawny enough but young and without that air of menace as hung about the chucker-out as used to be here. "Where's Vinegar Clifford got himself to?"

"He's no longer in Miss Higgins's employ. I take it you wish to join us, sir?"

The sounds of the tables, the clatter of dice and the ruffle of cards, reached him from the Gaming Salon only a few feet away. O'Toole's palms began to itch. "Aye. That's my—"

"Just a moment, Preservation. The gentleman is an old friend as you recall." Delight came to the door and spent a few seconds regarding her latest caller. "You seem in better form than you were last evening, Captain O'Toole. I'm glad you decided to return. Step aside, Preservation. Let the captain come in."

O'Toole was extra conscious of his movements. Very straight. Very steady. One foot after t'other. No point in letting her change her mind and decide he was drunk after all. Didn't want to get chucked out now he'd come this far. He fished the golden lady out of his pocket. "One roll o' the dice, Miss Delight. One lucky roll, that's all 'twill take."

"Happiness," Delight said softly, "is always one roll of the dice away. Isn't that your experience, Captain O'Toole?"

"You might say, Miss Higgins. You might . . ." The word suddenly evaded him. He had to think on it for a few seconds. "You might shay," he mouthed at last. "Yesh ma'am, you might shay."

Damn the man! He was as drunk as he'd been the evening before, only this time he'd fooled her long enough to get in. Delight looked to her chucker-out, then paused. Each and every gaming table in the salon was surrounded by a clutch of players. The Ladies' Parlor was empty, while every one of the little rooms on the second floor was occupied. A night of rare profit, and one thing sure—Finbar O'Toole would not go quietly a second time, not now he'd actually gotten in. It would take all three of the Irish lads probably. They'd get the job done, but not until they'd made a ruckus that would draw the attention of every man in the place. Expensive pleasures, Delight had long since learned, were best enjoyed without time taken to consider their cost. "I wonder if you might not like to rest a bit before you visit the gaming tables, Captain O'Toole. I have exactly the right lady in mind to keep you company. She's an infallible lucky charm. Any number of gentlemen have told me so. Preservation, go and find Cecily and bring her here at once."

"I think she's busy up—"

"Here. At once." Delight moved closer to O'Toole and put her arm through his. "You will adore Cecily, Captain O'Toole. I guarantee it. Beauty and luck besides. What more can a man ask?"

Ah, hell. Why not? He was more tired than he'd realized. And there was nothing to rob him of, so he could let the lass pleasure him, and sleep for a bit, and worry about naught. When he woke up, the tables would still be there. And as long as he still had his golden lady . . . "Tell you what, Mish . . . Miss Higgins," he held out the coin. "You keep this for me. So's I can roll the dice whenever this young lady and I are . . . When I'm enough rested."

Delight took the coin. Preservation appeared with a yellow-haired girl who was still adjusting the ribbons of the dressing gown she'd wrapped around her plump nakedness. "Here she is, Miss Higgins."

"I was with a gent as always leaves me a bit extra," the girl sputtered. "How come I—"

"Because I said so. And because I trust you to handle those as need a bit of coaxing." Handle, Delight thought, was indeed the word. "You'll thank me, Cecily," she murmured as she gave O'Toole a gentle shove in the girl's direction. "You'll be at least fifty coppers richer, I'll see to that, and I've no doubt it will be over before you can blink. Take him up to the third floor, the little bedroom beside my private parlor." She didn't usually allow her business activities to spill into her personal quarters, but just now that was the only bed other than her own that was empty.

Tuesday, August 23, 1814

Chapter Sixteen

Brooklyn, the Inner Harbor, 1 A.M.

IT WAS WELL KNOWN that there were ghosts aplenty in the shallows of Wallabout Bay off the Brooklyn coast. During the Revolution, the notorious British prison ships had been anchored here—hundreds of men packed together in reeking holds, starved, regularly beaten, afflicted with cholera and dysentery, and since only two at a time were allowed on deck to relieve themselves, forced to lie day and night in their own filth and that of their neighbors. The rotting wooden hulks of some of the ships yet remained. Sailors swore that some nights, out on the water, you could hear the cry that greeted every dawn in those fearsome years, *Prisoners, turn out your dead!*

Tintin's oars slipped rhythmically in and out of the water, and he did not turn his head as he rowed past the skeletons of those vessels of horror. Eugenie did not look either. She sat in the small boat's bow, facing the pirate. Feeling herself all but naked.

"So," Tintin asked, "*qu'est-ce que vous pensez,* Madame Eugenie? The clothes are more comfortable, or less?"

"Infinitely less comfortable, Monsieur Tintin. I would not like to be a man all the time."

"Ah, but no one would take you for a man, madame. That is a deception we could not sustain. A lad. *Un garçon.* At the very start of his manhood."

"It comes to the same thing," Eugenie murmured. The shirt with its ruffled stock and the cutaway coat were not so bad, but she could not force herself to look down at the tight trousers. Her maid had hastily stitched her into them, drawing the fabric skintight in the back where the seam would be covered by the coat. The result was to make a clear outline of her hips and her legs. It was as if she wore nothing at all. Meanwhile she must keep her head entirely upright or the stovepipe hat would probably fall off.

"We are almost there, madame. Now, please, be entirely silent."

Tintin turned the rowboat into the mouth of a long and narrow cove. Halfway up its length there was another inlet, and another off that. She soon had no idea where they were, and when the narrow hull of the two-masted schooner appeared, it seemed to Eugenie to have materialized from nowhere. She tipped her head back to read the name painted with many flourishes along the side. *Le Carcajou.* The Wolverine.

Tintin made the rowboat fast to the pirate ship. A man appeared above their heads and dropped a rope ladder. "You go first, madame," Tintin said. "I can best assist you that way."

He extended his hand and smiled, yellowed teeth gleaming in the light of the sliver of new moon. Eugenie shuddered, but not so that it showed. A lesson she had learned from her husband—never show weakness. She took Tintin's hand and allowed him to help her find her footing on the lowest rung of the ladder.

"Now," he said softly, "imagine what it would be like to try and do this with your skirts and petticoats flapping around your ankles."

Eugenie could not answer; her jaw was clenched too tightly. I can do this, she told herself over and over. I can do this. One rung and then the next. Each time conscious of how slippery were the leather soles of the boots which, like everything else she wore, had belonged to Timothy. There had been no way to alter the size of the boots; she'd had to stuff the toes with crumpled sheets of newsprint and be satisfied. I can do this. I will not scream because Tintin has his hands on my backside. Supposedly to assist me up this wretched ladder. One more rung. I can do this. I must do this.

The grinning face of the man who had dropped the ladder and watched her entire painful ascent was finally level with hers. "Welcome aboard, laddie. It's not every night we— Whoa, what have we here? Not exactly what it looks like, eh?"

He had pulled her onto the deck by then, and Tintin had come aboard just behind her. "You may look, *mon ami*," he said, "but you may not touch. We have business with the la——, with the boy. Very private business."

The second pirate laughed softly. "Too bad. I could fancy some pleasant company. All what you brung us so far ain't too happy to be here."

"Where is he?"

"Below."

Tintin considered, then made up his mind. "We too shall go below. Come, *mon petit garçon,* I have something to show you."

"You said I would get my money as soon as we came aboard your ship. I do not choose—"

"My ship," Tintin leaned in close enough so she could smell his foul breath. "As you say. And I remind you no one knows where you are. So for tonight we do what I choose, *non?* It is better to smile politely and speak softly, *garçon.* Much better."

He turned, and Eugenie, knowing she had no choice, dutifully followed him.

The deck was a shambles of half-coiled lines, and stacked boxes and chests, and empty bottles that rolled treacherously close to her feet in the clumsy boots. The pirate who had lowered the ladder followed her, and she spotted a few others at various places on the deck. One, sprawled a little distance away, wasn't dressed like the rest. He wore regular seaman's clothes, checked shirt and oiled breeches, and in another setting she'd have thought him an ordinary tar.

The sailor was apparently convinced by her disguise. "Brung another recruit, have ye?" he called out. When no one answered, he began to whistle. Eugenie knew the tune. Timothy had sung it whenever he was in particularly high spirits. *Once was a man with a double chin who played with skill on the violin . . . played in time and played in tune . . . wouldn't play nothin' but "Old Zip Coon."*

She continued picking her way across the deck. At one point she stumbled and almost fell, and the second pirate grabbed her from behind. He used the opportunity to put both hands on her breasts. Eugenie gritted her teeth to keep from crying out. That she had bound her paps tight to her with a linen bandage somehow made his touch less an affront.

Tintin descended another ladder, this one of wood. Eugenie summoned her courage and went after him. The second pirate came behind her. Belowdecks the passage was so narrow they had to walk in single file, Eugenie between the two men. Somehow they contrived to repeatedly bump their bodies against hers front and back. Her face burned with rage and shame, but she pretended not to notice and said nothing.

"My quarters," Tintin said, throwing open a door. The cabin into which he showed her was small and cramped, and as filthy as everything else she had seen on this wolverine from hell. She'd heard that pirates lived like kings, surrounded with gold and jewels. With this lot at least, it appeared not to be true.

"Sit down, Madame Eugenie. You may take off that ridiculous hat. Here we are quite safe."

"I will keep the hat on, thank you." She had pulled her dark hair back from her face, forcing every curl into compliance, and pinned the lot into a bun on the top of her head. If she removed the stovepipe, it might all tumble free.

"Suit yourself. You will drink something? A refreshment is called for after a journey such as brought us here. Sadly, I can offer you only rum. My stores do not run to Madeira or Malmsey."

"I wish nothing, thank you. Only my money."

"*Oui*, your money. I almost forgot."

"Rest assured, Monsieur Tintin, I did not." He had wanted her to wait until they had captured all six of the slaves for which they had papers. Perhaps even longer. If she waited until the business was well and truly concluded, he told her, her share of the profit would be greater.

"You must think me mad or a fool, monsieur," had been her answer. "This sale you speak of, where is it to take place?"

"South of here. Where I have many allies and such sales are held frequently. Where it is both protected and profitable."

"I believe you speak of Barataria Bay, Monsieur Tintin. It is south of here as you say. Many miles distant, is it not? Near New Orleans?"

"I do not speak of it, madame. You do. It is unwise to be so forthcoming. On occasion, even the walls have ears."

They had been in Eugenie's boudoir at the time. "I do not fear my walls," she'd told him. "But I very much fear this distant sale you are suggesting. I will not under any circumstances give you the other papers the magistrate has signed, those for the five additional runaways, unless I am first paid for the one you say you have captured. That was our arrangement, Monsieur Tintin. It is the only one I will honor."

Eventually, he agreed, but said she must come to the ship and claim what was hers. "*Le Carcajou*, madame, that is where the money is to be found." The disguise had been Tintin's suggestion when she first objected to the excursion. In the end, Tintin having insisted that the plan was impossibly dangerous without it, Eugenie was forced to get herself up in the ridiculous outfit. Dear God, she would give anything for her own clothes. Somehow nothing of what was happening would feel so terrifying if she were not dressed as she was.

Tintin drank two shots of straight rum in quick succession. Eugenie, who had declined as well his offer of a chair, stood watching him. When his thirst was satisfied, Tintin leaned back in his chair, reached into the pocket of his green-velvet coat, and withdrew a small moneybag. "Your share, Madame Eugenie. One hundred dollars in good coin. You may count it if you wish, but I assure you it is all there."

"Oh!" She hated herself for admitting to her surprise, but she could not suppress the gasp. "You had it on your person all the time."

Tintin smiled and shrugged.

"But why did you make me come here in that case? What earthly reason was there to— It will not be in your best interests," she whispered as the only reason she could imagine for this trickery became a vivid scene in her mind. "I cannot fight you and win, I know that. But there are five more sets of documents and—"

"You fancy yourself entirely too much, Eugenie Fischer. You are a desirable woman, *oui,* but there are many others. Compose yourself, madame, I prefer to use you for things other than fucking."

The shock of the casual insult was more profound than the admission that he'd lied about the money. Her heart pounded and her palms were sweaty. "How dare you speak to—"

"I dare whatever I choose. Because"—he got up while he spoke and went to the door—"you are now as much a part of this scheme as I am. That is why I have brought you here, Madame Eugenie, to show you exactly what that means. When you understand, then I will take you home. And your cunny will be as dry and as empty as it is right now." He yanked open the door and shouted, "Bring the prisoner," then he returned to his chair. "It will not take long, but I suggest you will be more comfortable seated then standing." And when she didn't answer, but also didn't move, "*Eh bien,* suit yourself, madame. Only be aware," he said chuckling, "that if you decide to faint we may have to undress you to bring you back to yourself."

The door opened. The second pirate shoved a naked black man into the cabin ahead of him.

Eugenie turned her head away. "No," Tintin said softly. "Take a good look. I must insist."

She heard the menace in his tone. I can do this, she reminded herself. I must do this.

Not a man, a boy, ten or eleven perhaps. His entire body was bruised and welted; some of the cuts were still bleeding—others had started to scab over. One eye was swollen shut, the other open and staring at her. Eugenie pressed the back of her hand to her lips to keep from crying out.

"So," Tintin said, turning to the youth, "now, please tell me your name."

"Josh—"

The second pirate held up his hand. Eugenie saw the cat-o'-nine-tails. So did the boy. "Want more, do ye?" the man asked.

The boy shook his head.

"Then tell 'em what your name is. Your real name. It's not Joshua. That's a white name. That's not a runaway slave name. What's your name, boy?"

"Pompey," the boy whispered. "My name be Pompey."

"And you runned away from yer lawful owner, didn't ye? Went into hiding up there in Five Points where we found ye, ain't that so?"

The boy who had claimed his name was Joshua until the cat taught him otherwise nodded his head.

"Not good enough, you little bastard. Speak when yer spoken to!" The cat lashed out viciously and opened yet another wound on the boy's shoulder.

"Yes. Yes, I be a runaway slave."

Tintin nodded. "Excellent, *mon ami*. You have done well with him. Now take him away before we too much strain the sensibilities of our guest."

The pirate and the prisoner left. Tintin waited. Eugenie said nothing.

"You understand now?" Tintin asked after a long minute of more silence. "It is important that you understand."

Eugenie nodded.

"*Non, ma petite,* that is not sufficient. As with our Pompey, I wish to hear you say it."

"I understand."

"Excellent. You and I, Madame Eugenie, we do not play a game for the fainthearted. I brought you here to demonstrate that. Now, I will take you home." Tintin stood up. He still had hold of the moneybag. He crossed to where Eugenie stood, and gave it to her. "I suggest you put it down the front of your trowsers, Madame. Then you will have a bulge where it belongs." His laughter went ahead of her as he led the way to the deck.

"You cannot leave me here. It is still some distance to my house."

Tintin had rowed her across the harbor to Manhattan, to the Old Slip at the southern tip of the city. The moon had set and the blackness was relieved only by splashes of yellow light that came from the waterside bawdy houses and grog shops. It was after two. Respectable taverns had long since shuttered their windows and doors, but down here the watch ignored the regulations concerning closing times. This stretch of the waterfront was a lawless area that belonged to tars and thieves, and the ladies of the night who traveled with them.

Tintin had left Eugenie to clamber up on the dock herself, giving him the opportunity to once more put his hands on her backside and push her up from behind. Now he kept the boat into the shore by hanging on to an iron bolt set in the stone wall of the dock. "I regret, madame, I cannot accompany you further. An area such as this . . . *Mon Dieu!* How could I leave my little craft unattended in such a dangerous place?"

"You are a coward as well as a cad, monsieur. Otherwise you would not choose to exercise your power over a mere woman."

"And if you were the *garçon* you are dressed to be, I would cut off your cock and put it in your mouth. But since you have none . . . *Adieu,* Madame Eugenie. If you go quickly, I am sure you will arrive home unmolested." He picked up an oar and seemed ready to leave, but lingered a moment longer. "Ah, yes, I almost forgot . . . There is a woman in the town. She runs a gambling establishment called the Dancing Knave and goes by the name Delight Higgins. She is always very fashionably dressed. I wish to know the name of her mantua maker. I am sure it is information you can find out for me."

"Very well, but please, if you would only accompany me as far as . . ."

Tintin pushed off and Eugenie allowed the plea to trail away.

Dear God! How was she to get home? Chatham Street was at least a mile away, and she had no knowledge of this area of the city. Damn you to hell, Tintin. Damn you to everlasting fire. Oh, why bother? If the preachers were correct, that's where he was going, and probably herself as well. But she had no time just now to worry about what might await her in the afterlife, and cursing the pirate would not get her away from the waterfront and back to the civilized neighborhoods she knew. Not that they would be entirely safe at this hour. What would a watchman think if he spotted a lad walking the darkened streets of the city alone at this time of night? That he was up to no good, of course. And would her disguise bear a close look? Highly un- likely. And how, if it were discovered, would she explain a moneybag stuffed with coins? Damn you, Tintin! Damn you!

The shadows were thick at the edge of the quay. It was a place of reasonable safety, but she must cross the road and somehow get by the doors of the string of drinking establishments and head north. Wall Street was in that direction, she was fairly sure. Once she crossed it, she'd know her way.

The wretched boots were her worst enemy. They slid off her feet with every step and clattered and clicked on the cobbles. Eugenie slipped her feet out of them and out of Timothy's silken hose as well. For a moment she considered stringing the boots around her neck by the laces as she'd seen boys do in summer. No, that would only be one more burden when she must be as free as possible. She knelt down and allowed the boots and the hose to slide into the river. Then, bare- foot and trying to ignore the discomfort of the pebbles and gravel of the road, she moved out of the shadows into the light of the wanton world of the waterfront.

For a time luck was with her. Eugenie cleared Front Street without at- tracting any attention. Dock Street next, at least that's what she thought it was called. Dear heaven, it was speckled with as much light as the area closer to the wharf. The sound of raucous singing and loud laughter rolled toward her. Eugenie paused and looked around. An alley, dark as pitch. She turned into the blackness, stretching one hand to her side to guide her through the narrow passage. If she could just . . .

"Hello! What have we here?"

The door to the grog shop had been closed. She hadn't known it was there until it opened and the two men came out, allowing light and noise to tumble into the alley.

"Nice bit o' young stuff, that's what we have."

"Oh my, yes! Bit of a nob as well. Wager you bend over nicely, dearie boy." The man who spoke allowed the door to the groggery to close behind him, and they were once more in darkness. "Wager your arse is tight as a bunghole. Two coppers for both of us. What do you say?"

Eugenie pushed past them, walking as fast as she could.

"Here, that's not very friendly. What you want to run away for? Three coppers then. Can't say we're not bein' fair, dearie boy. Could just take what we want, 'stead we're offerin' to pay for it."

They were keeping pace with her, but the end of the passage was just a few steps away, and the street she could see up ahead appeared to be lit by proper city oil lamps, not the glow of illicit nightlife. She hurried toward it.

One of the men put out a hand to stop her. Eugenie pulled away and ran. Her hat fell off, and some of her hair came loose. No matter. She must get to the light.

"Hold up," she heard the second man say. "Let him go. No point in chasing him."

"Plenty o' point. I want to roll down those trousers and see if what's underneath looks as good bare as it does covered."

The footsteps behind her speeded up, but the men's disagreement had given her two or three moments' advantage. She was in the adjoining road, a short curved street with countinghouses and— Oh! She was on Hanover Street. And the sign illuminated by the nearest lamp said BLAKEMAN COACHING. Eugenie threw herself at the door and banged on it with both fists.

The door opened instantly. She was looking at the biggest man she'd ever seen, clothed entirely in black and holding a long, uncoiled bullwhip. Nonetheless, Eugenie found him less fearsome than what she'd just escaped. "Mr. Blakeman . . ." She could hardly speak for gasping. "Please . . . I must . . . Mr. Blakeman."

The whipper looked not at her but over her shoulder. The pair of creatures who had been coming after the supplicant in the doorway paused, saw what waited for them at the countinghouse, and retreated into the alley.

"Mr. Blakeman," Eugenie repeated, her words a little clearer now. "I am a friend of his. Please, you must let me in."

"The lady is indeed my friend," a voice said from the shadows. "You may let her in, Mr. Clifford."

"Gornt! I cannot tell you how happy I am to see you."

"I share the sentiment, my dear Eugenie, but . . . Dear God, let me get a look at you."

"I can explain . . . It's an extraordinary story, but—"

"Extraordinary it must surely be. Mr. Clifford, I take it there is no further disturbance outside to concern us?"

"Not now, Mr. Blakeman. 'Twas a couple o' troublemakers from Buggers' Alley as was chasing the boy—chasing your friend. They're gone."

"My friend is a lady in fancy dress, Mr. Clifford. Inadvertently separated from her party. Nothing so extraordinary in that. Come upstairs, my dear. I shall give you a glass of wine before taking you home."

"Fancy dress," Eugenie said when a few sips of Madeira had restored her. "It's an excellent explanation, Gornt. Will it satisfy you?"

"Not for one minute, my precious Eugenie. Though I must say, you look as luscious in cutaway and trousers as in any frock I've seen you wear. Your late husband's?"

"Yes."

"I thought so. And I presume you had tucked your hair under a hat, a proper stovepipe no doubt, and that somehow you lost it when you tried to get away from the buggers." He reached out and fondled one of the dark curls that now hung loose.

"Exactly," Eugenie said.

"Whatever were you thinking, my dear?" One blunt finger outlined her lips.

Eugenie flicked her tongue out and licked the exploring fingertip, so quickly Gornt almost wasn't sure it had happened. "Gornt, you have never really told me your plans . . ."

"Surely this night is not about my plans. Where have you been, my Eugenie? Do you, after all, have a taste for the louche and dangerous instead of the high society I've always thought you suited for? No, I think not. What then?"

"If I told you the story involved pirates, would you believe me?"

He laughed. "You? And pirates? Here? Of course I wouldn't believe you." Christ Almighty, some connection between Tintin and Eugenie. Now there was a circumstance that required investigation. Not, however, a task that must be performed tonight. "I think you are fibbing, my beauty, but I admit the idea excites me. As much as any time I've spent in your boudoir, trying to control the visions of your bedstead only a few steps away."

"Now it is your bedstead, Gornt. And it's no more than two steps away." The bed he'd apparently rolled out of when he heard the disturbance below was hung with heavy damask curtains. They had been pulled back because of the night's warmth, and the rumpled bedclothes were plainly evident in the light of the lamp he'd lit when they came upstairs.

"Close indeed," he agreed. "Stand up and take off that cutaway, Eugenie. Let me see how you look in a man's shirt and stock." She was sitting in the very chair Jacob Astor had occupied a few hours earlier, and Bastard Devrey had left his rooms not two hours before she appeared. Sweet Christ. What a sauce for the meal he'd eaten earlier that evening.

She still hadn't moved. "Come, dear girl, it's not much to ask. I've saved you from buggery after all."

Eugenie took another sip of her wine and considered. If she took off the coat, no doubt whatever the rest would follow. And if she did not? What then? Tintin? A position in society that grew more precarious the more she tried to claw her way out of the quicksand of debt? Timothy had not lost his taste for her after the first time they bedded. Why should Gornt Blakeman be so easily satisfied? She was young enough to have lost none of her looks, and old enough to have honed her wiles. It was not a circumstance that would last much longer. She must seize the moment.

Eugenie leaned forward and set the wineglass on the table, then stood up and allowed the coat to slip from her shoulders to the floor. The bag of coins she'd gotten from Tintin was in the breast pocket, and there was a small thud as it hit the floor. She held her breath, but Gornt appeared not to have noticed. Damn the one-eyed pirate and his money. She had not planned it so, but suddenly she was playing for higher stakes.

"Delicious," Gornt said, his eyes examining her from head to toe. "Your waist looks even tinier than usual, and your hips in those trousers . . . A sight to set a man's teeth on edge, Eugenie."

"I had to make adjustments to my undergarments to pass as a boy," she said. "You would not believe the effort it required."

"Not unless you showed me."

"Then I suppose I must." She loosed the ruffled stock and dropped it on top of the coat. Then, slowly and without haste, she opened the three buttons that held the neck of the shirt closed and pulled the garment over her head. The gesture caused the last of the pins to be dislodged from her hair, and her curls hung free. "See," she said, displaying the linen wrapping that swaddled her breasts, "I am trussed like a chicken."

"Poor Eugenie. You must be set free."

"I must. But I cannot release all this by myself. You will have to assist me, Gornt."

He stood up and she turned so her back was to him. "My maid fastened the cloth in the back so the pin wouldn't show."

"Clever maid." He undid the pin.

"Too clever by half. Look what I must do to unwrap myself."

Gornt held one end of the linen binding. She released the rest by spinning across the room, until at last she stood in the shadows beside the bed, and they each held one end of the long strip of linen. "Now," she whispered, "I must be a tidy mistress and put this all neatly away."

He said nothing. Eugenie began to wind the bandage, drawing him closer with each revolution. Her breasts were exactly the sort he liked best. Pear-shaped, the aureoles the color of a crushed rose. When he was close enough, he dropped his end of the cloth and put a finger on each taut and upward-facing nipple. "Mine," he said. "At last."

"Yours." She could not control her trembling.

Gornt ran his hands down her midriff and slipped his fingers inside the snug waistband of the trousers. He gave a sharp tug and the buttons popped. He pushed the fabric down over her hips and thighs, then stopped. "Do the rest yourself," he commanded. "Present yourself to me."

Eugenie bent over and rolled the trousers down the rest of the way, then stepped out of them. She straightened, let him look, then backed up and threw herself on the bed, spreading her legs wide and opening her arms.

Gornt lunged over her and into her. Her legs gripped his hips and she arched to meet him, and he was not sure if it was her scream of triumph he heard or his own.

Chapter Seventeen

The Federal District,
the Roof of the Executive Mansion, Sunrise

THE SPYGLASS FELT HEAVY. Dolley Madison had been pressing it to her eye since dawn, turning and looking in every direction to see if her husband was returning to take her to a place of safety. He'd promised he would. Indeed, he'd wanted her to leave the day before, when he went to see about defense preparations. She had refused then and she would refuse now. That they must flee seemed likely, but she would not go alone.

"Madame Madison . . ."

Dolley turned to the sound of the servant's soft voice. "Ah, it's you, John. I might have guessed."

"I brought you this, madame," he extended a mug. "Warm milk with a touch of brandy. To soothe the stomach."

"Thank you. Mine can use soothing."

"There's this as well."

"Oh! From the president?" She snatched at the note.

"That's what the messenger said, madam. But he left the moment he'd given it over. Said he didn't have time to wait for a reply. Not even to take some food and drink."

"Mr. Madison and those with him must be hard-pressed indeed." She set the mug down on the parapet she'd been leaning against and opened the message. It was a quick scrawl written in pencil. *The enemy is much stronger than we feared. Have a carriage prepared. Be ready to leave at a moment's notice.* Signed with only his initials. Not even a promise of his affection. Never mind. She knew quite well she had it.

French John—that they called him to set him apart from at least three other Johns among the servants—was waiting. "We are to be prepared to leave if we must," she told him.

"The carriage, madame, the one you packed with Mr. Madison's papers . . ."

"Send it off, John. At once."

The servant nodded. "Yes, madame. Right away."

"Still no sign of a wagon?" She'd sent two housemen out to look for one. So she could pack up the household goods.

"No, madame, not yet. The boys be going out again to look in another direction. Soon as they have a bite of breakfast." He nodded his head toward her spyglass. "What about out there, madame? Anything you be seeing as looks promising for defending us?"

She should probably say yes. It was, after all, her responsibility to keep them all in good spirits. But French John had belonged to Mr. Madison's family for many years, and he was trusted in a way that others were not. "Nothing, John. Groups of men who appear to be wearing one or another sort of uniform, but all simply wandering the countryside as if they are not quite sure where to go. They lack . . ." If she said they lacked leadership—which was what she thought—it would reflect badly on her husband. Lord knows he had enough criticism to bear; he needed none from her. "They lack proper intelligence, I fear. Any knowledge of where to best head off the enemy."

The sun was full up now, the day's heat beginning. "Come down now, madame. You should rest."

"Not just yet, John. You go, and send that carriage on its way. I'll be along shortly."

She spent another five minutes with the spyglass before she remembered the warm drink John had brought her. By now, of course, it had gone cold. Nonetheless, the effects of the brandy were welcome.

New York City, Wall Street, 9 A.M

The rich smell of coffee pervaded the downstairs room of the Tontine, and it made Joyful's mouth water. He'd come to listen to talk and he wanted a place at one of the long communal tables, but they were all taken. He had to be satisfied with a seat at the rear, near the stairs leading to the upper floor, straddling a stool beside a tiny table that looked as if it had been shoved in place as an afterthought. He signaled to a waiter. The man nodded in acknowledgment, then hurried off to serve others who had arrived before. Astonishing that the place was so full so early. In better times the men here would be on the docks at this hour, seeing to the unlading of their cargoes, checking on schedules and berthing slots, and arranging for voyages yet to come. They wouldn't arrive at the Tontine or the other coffeehouses of the town until close to noon, when their attention would shift to the need to bargain for future cargoes.

Not these days. The snatches of conversation he overheard all related to the havoc wreaked on business by Mr. Madison's war. The big question was whether or not the city was to be attacked, and if so by land or by sea, but he heard no one ask what that would mean to the nation. From where he sat, Joyful could all but smell their desperation. Oh, they weren't paupers, not yet. These men had enough property and cash to insulate them from the worst of the losses of war. The craftsmen and shopkeepers, Barnaby and the rest of the mechanics—they suffered most because they had the least cushion. In places like Tammany Hall the anxiety must stink like a sewer. As for the privileged men upstairs, the money men, in the usual way of things they made as much profit from bad times as they did from good.

His coffee arrived, pungent and black and served in a yellow crockery bowl. The waiter proffered a large urn of sugar. Joyful took three of the rough-cut brownish-colored lumps, then put four coppers on the tray. A penny for the coffee and a penny apiece for each portion of sugar. Not long past, the sugar had sold for two lumps a penny.

"A taste for sweetness is expensive these days, isn't it, Dr. Turner?" It was Geoffrey Colden, the trader he'd seen at the Knave the night before last, and whose place he had taken at bezique.

"So it seems. But the coffee itself sells for the same price as before the war, though it must make the same perilous journey to get here."

Colden chuckled. "All a question of what the market will bear, Dr. Turner. It seems that folk will pay more for the sweet than the bitter, so at the Tontine we set our prices accordingly. From what I hear, that will be of no concern to you. I'm told my seat proved lucky for you the other night."

"The cards fell for me and not for Blakeman. Good joss, as they say in Canton."

The trader's eyes became opaque, harder to read. "Perhaps. May I ask what brings you here, Dr. Turner? I come every day, and I don't think I've seen you before. Are you perhaps planning to join us?" He inclined his head slightly, enough to allow Joyful to see that he referred to the floor above.

"I didn't think it was simply a matter of climbing those stairs." The Tontine agreement had been fixed long since and the terms were well known. A certain number of signatories and no provision for adding more.

"Takes more than making the climb," Colden agreed. "But it's not impossible. If a member wishes to sell his portion outright, for instance."

Jesus. Joyful told himself he had to contain his excitement, not let Colden know that his heart was pounding and his hands felt clammy. "The way I heard it, the other members must all first decline to buy the share of whoever wants to sell before a new member can be brought in."

"Correct," Colden said softly. "But a number of us feel that's an unwise provision. Never any new blood, and a system that doesn't allow itself to breathe. You're a medical man, Dr. Turner. Wouldn't you say that was unhealthy?"

"Yes. It is. Very unhealthy."

"Upstairs," Colden said. "That's where the kind of business is done can make a man a real fortune, presuming he has the stomach for it. Up there we determine the prices of everything—slaves, houses, ships; you might say we make the market. The men here—" he nodded to indicate the ground floor of the coffee house—"mostly work with the essentials of one or another enterprise. Less gamble, less risk, and consequently less reward. I suspect our sort of trading would suit you, Dr. Turner. It doesn't require that a man have both hands. Rather like at the Dancing Knave," he added softly.

Joyful's expression gave nothing away. The women at the Knave talked, no way to avoid it, and Colden was a regular. But Jesus God Almighty, a member of the Tontine. "I'm considering my future," he said. "I've made no decisions."

"What are you waiting for, if I may ask?"

"To see how things play out for me."

"Ah," Colden said. "Your 'joss.'"

"Exactly."

Both men saw Bastard Devrey come in the door. The trader smiled. "And here it is, coming straight towards you. Choose wisely, my young friend. I bid you good morning, Dr. Turner." Colden bowed politely and left.

Joyful stared after him. Guessing he had an interest in the Knave was one thing. But Devrey Shipping? The only people he'd told of his arrangement with Bastard were Jacob Astor and Manon. Manon would never betray his trust, and it was against Astor's interests to do so. It had to be that simply the fact he'd shown up here had tipped his hand. A good lesson. He'd have to look sharp to join the game the men upstairs played. No point in thinking otherwise.

Bastard was making his way through the public room, speaking to no one, his gaze fixed on the stairs that led to the private sanctum above. In a black cutaway carefully brushed, and a green waistcoat straining to close over his well-fed paunch, he looked a damned sight better than he had last Thursday night. More important, his eyes weren't bleary with drink. Joyful waited until Bastard drew level, then spoke. "Good morning, Cousin."

Bastard stopped short, a look of astonishment on his face. "What are you doing here?"

Joyful shrugged. "It's a public coffeehouse. Why shouldn't I be here?"

"No reason. It's just that I've never seen you in the Tontine, and—"

"Sit down." Joyful hooked another of the stools with his boot and drew it close. "Have a coffee with me."

Bastard's glance darted toward the stairs. "I've business to attend to, I can't linger."

"You've no business that doesn't concern me," Joyful said softly. "You do remember that, don't you, Cousin? I'd hate to think it was all lost in a tipsy haze. If so, the truth will come as a mighty shock."

A few men looked their way; the family's feuding history was well known, and a confrontation of some sort would surprise no one. Might be a good thing, lend a bit of interest to the morning. You could see the anticipation in their eyes. Well, they were due to be disappointed. "Sit down, Bastard," Joyful said again. "You're attracting attention."

"I can't linger," Bastard repeated while managing to settle his broad buttocks on the small seat.

"So you said. Exactly what is it you're planning to do upstairs?"

"Business. I . . ." Leaning in close now, careful not to be overheard. Joyful could smell his breath; he had not been overindulging in what was left of his Madeira. "I'm still responsible for the day-to-day running of things. We both agreed that's how it should be."

"Day-to-day as on the docks and in the countinghouse," Joyful said, his voice pitched equally low. "Nothing to do with what goes on at the Tontine."

Bastard's eyes narrowed. "Still, I warrant you came here expecting to find me. Why else are you here?"

"As a matter of fact, I didn't think to see you here." He'd come because of what Barnaby said and Reverend Fish confirmed, that Blakeman's recruiting was intense among the ordinary people of the town, the mechanics and the laborers. Did that mean Gornt Blakeman was already assured of the support of his own class? Would they all simply fall in with him once they saw the profit to be gained from doing so? No way to know. "Let's start again, Bastard. What are you doing here?"

The other man chewed his lower lip. "Habit," he admitted. "It's how I've always spent my mornings. If I stay at home . . . Well, Celinda . . . You know how it is."

Joyful didn't entirely believe him, but they were still attracting interested glances, and he could hear a buzz of talk from upstairs. Going public with their arrangement before he was ready could ruin everything. He stood up. "Nice to see you, Cousin." Loud enough so he could be heard. Then, more softly, "Be cautious about what you do or say up there, sir. It's in your best interest to be circumspect."

There was a bustle of activity outside the coffeehouse. A horse had slipped its traces and overturned a wagon full of beer kegs. The wagoner was trying roll them back into place on an improvised slide of poles, and a crowd had gathered to watch. "This way," a voice said in Joyful's ear.

He felt a hand in the small of his back, pushing him away from the Tontine and toward Water Street. He walked at a moderate pace, not turning round, waiting for additional instructions. They came in the form of another push directing him into an alley. Narrow enough so he had to mind his step to avoid rotting rubbish. Joyful turned his head to see who was behind him. He'd been fairly certain it would be Mulligan the Irishman, and he wasn't wrong. "What are you doing here, Mully? Meant to be following me?"

"Not exactly, sir. F.X. sent me. S'posed to be waiting for Mr. Blakeman, I am, outside the Tontine. But I ain't seen 'im yet. And I seen you, so . . ."

It had been two days since he'd given Mulligan a shilling and said it was an advance on six coppers a day. Time for another infusion. "Well done, Mully." He took another coin from his pocket. "Have you a note to give Mr. Blakeman?"

"No sir, a message. But . . ."

The Irishman was staring at the coin, doubtless contrasting it with visions of the butchers and their cleavers. "The sooner you're back at your post, Mully, the less likely anyone will know you left it. What's the message?"

"I'm to tell Mr. Blakeman as F.X. says, 'Astor's with us.'"

Jesus God Almighty. "Nothing else?"

"Nothing, sir."

Joyful handed over the shilling. "Another two days in advance, Mully. You've done well. Keep your eyes open, as I said, and—" He broke off, seeing something in the Irishman's expression. "You're sure there's nothing else?"

"Not from F.X., Dr. Turner."

A small cheer went up not far away. Both men heard it. "They've got those beer kegs back in place, Mully. Things will be a bit quieter outside the Tontine. Easier to spot who comes and goes. If you've something else to tell me, better do it quickly."

"Three wee ones I've got at home, Dr. Turner. And what with this war and all . . ."

Joyful put his hand in his pocket and came up with two coppers. "What else? Quickly, and it better be useful, or I'll shop you to the leather-aprons myself."

"Last night, sir, 'bout eight it was. I was in Hanover Square 'cause the missus sent me to Devrey's Pharmacy for some o' that Elixir of Well-Being. Does her a power o' good, it does, and now that we're in a little better way, well—"

"Yes, I understand. And what did you see in Hanover Square?"

"Not there exactly, sir. I went home by way o' Hanover Street. By

Mr. Blakeman's countinghouse. I was interested like—I mean seeing as how you said I should be keeping my eyes open."

Joyful waited, knowing he had to let the man tell it his own way.

"Mr. Astor's carriage, sir. It's the grandest in the city and ain't none who doesn't recognize it, right?" Waiting for Joyful's nod of agreement. "Can't be another like it, can there?"

"Not likely."

"Well, that carriage, Dr. Turner. It was waiting right outside Mr. Blakeman's countinghouse."

Hanover Square, 10 A.M.

Jonathan Devrey blinked a few times, then opened his eyes as wide as nature allowed. The vision had not changed. He was confronted by two men, both dressed in knee-length cotton gowns with loose trousers below, one all in gray, the other in blue. They were energetically gesturing and nodding their heads as they spoke. Their foreheads were shaved, and each man had a long braid down the back. They were jabbering to each other in some tongue he could not fathom. Eventually, one turned to him and jabbered some more. It was some time before Jonathan realized that the man addressing him was speaking English. Of a sort.

"Good plan. Good plan," Ah Wong said. "Rich man. Ancestor."

Thumbless Wu saw the blank look on the apothecary's face. Ahyee! The barbarian was not allowing himself to listen well enough to hear. It was possible that he had found the one man in New York who was too stupid to profit by wonderful joss. Nonetheless, it was the man the gods had put in his path. The man who knew where the red flowers grew, who walked among them with knowledge in his eyes. And the man who concocted these little vials of brown liquid Thumbless had seen the townspeople stream into the shop to buy. Another form of white smoke. He was quite certain of it.

Ah Wong was still speaking his struggling foreign devil speech, still trying to make the *yang gui zhi* understand that they had a business proposition to offer.

There was a display of the little brown bottles on the counter between them. Thumbless Wu reached out and grabbed three in each hand, using his fingers like pincers, then bringing his hands together in rapid clapping gestures and clicking the bottles under the nose of the barbarian. He tipped his head back and mimed drinking the contents of the bottles, then began to twist and turn, lifting his feet high in a kind of manic jig. Finally, he fell on the floor and closed his eyes and opened his mouth and emulated loud, contented snores.

Jesse Edwards was standing by the front door, leaning on his broom, watching everything. He took a fit of laughing and could not stop.

Jonathan continued to stare in wide-eyed disbelief.

Ah Wong nodded his head in vigorous approval. "Good plan. Good plan." He repeated.

Wu stopped his loud snoring and jumped up. He went to the counter, put down the bottles of Devrey's Elixir of Well-Being, and made gestures that indicated emptying his pockets of money and pouring it over the apothecary. "Bizness. Bizness," he shouted. "Much money. Much money. Many taels of silver, heh?"

It was Ah Wong's turn to be surprised. This Wu Without Thumbs had not said he spoke any English. On the contrary, he had insisted that Ah Wong must come with him to be his interpreter. He said that eventually, when the white smoke business was thriving, Ah Wong would be well paid for doing what Wu Without Thumbs could not do for himself. Ahyee! Very odd. Very odd.

Thumbless Wu was aware that he had lost the advantage of letting no one know that he spoke a bit of English and understood much of it. Too bad. Too bad. Sometimes one good must be given up to gain a greater good. Making this apothecary fool understand was the most important thing of all. Without that, his plan was useless.

Jonathan leaned both elbows on the counter and stretched forward so he could see directly into the eyes of Thumbless Wu. "Business, eh? Profitable business? Concerning my Elixir?"

"Much money. Much money," Thumbless Wu said.

Jonathan nodded. "Very well. We'll go upstairs and discuss it. Jesse, stop your giggling and come over here behind the counter. You'll look after the shop while I talk a bit more with these gentlemen."

The Fly Market, Noon

Astor's with us. Jacob Astor had thrown in his lot with Gornt Blakeman. What else could it mean? Confirmed by the presence of his carriage outside Blakeman Coaching. But why? Astor's trading post Astoria, the trail through Oregon, what good would any of that be if there was a breakaway nation? A woman jostled Joyful's arm with her basket and hurried past him. Joyful thought it was Manon and hurried after her. She appeared to be heading toward Elsie Gruning's table but stopped at another produce seller's stall, and when he saw her in profile, he realized it wasn't Manon at all.

Joyful moved on to where Elsie was sitting. There were four women at her table, none of them Manon. He wanted to ask if Elsie had seen her, but a steady string of customers kept him from the opportunity. By one-thirty, convinced she wasn't coming, he left.

Maryland, the British Encampment at Upper Marlboro, 4 P.M.

The general was exhausted and the battle had not yet been fought. No, that wasn't exactly correct. One engagement had taken place and he had lost: they would attack Washington first. He accepted a leg up from his batman, a lad of twelve, and swung himself into the saddle of one of the horses they'd taken at Benedict. The admiral was already mounted. He moved his horse into place beside the general. "No last-minute arguments are necessary, sir," the general said wearily. "We shall do it as you think best."

"Glad you see the wisdom of the plan, General.. Twenty-four hours is quite long enough to discuss the matter."

The general grimaced. "Quite long enough."

The admiral realized it was best to say no more. He glanced back at the marines being left behind to hold the camp as a fallback position. That had been his idea as well. Prudent, though the possibility they'd need to retreat seemed unlikely. So far they had marched nearly forty miles and met not one American, hostile or otherwise.

The general shifted in the saddle. Everything now depended on him; having gotten his way, the admiral was once more an observer. "Company sergeant-major!"

A man trotted up beside him and snapped a salute. "Here, sir."

"Prepare to move."

"Yes, sir." The sergeant-major swung his horse around. "Column formation!" he bellowed at the long line of redcoats—all on foot—behind the mounted officers, "Prepare to advance!" He pointed to the northward road. "Forward!"

The order was picked up and passed down the line. The officers spurred their horses into the lead. "Washington," the army said.

"Washington," the navy agreed with satisfaction.

The surveyor held the spyglass to his eye and watched the column move out. "The northwest road," he muttered, relieved that his educated guess had been confirmed. "No doubt now." The marksman had scrambled back to his side only moments before, after an absence of several hours. The surveyor passed him the glass.

The marksman looked, then handed it back. "Sure is a hell of a lot of 'em. You're still certain it's to be Washington? I talked to a general says Baltimore's far more—"

"The general's a horse's ass."

"How can you know that? I didn't say which general."

"They're all horse's asses. Look down there. If it was Baltimore, they'd be going east. It's to be the Federal District, exactly as I said. You see any sign folks there were making themselves ready?"

"I spread the word far as I was able. Those I warned will tell others. Anyways, they'd already sent to Pennsylvania for a regiment, and there's talk Baltimore will be sending their entire militia. Citizens too. Everyone's coming to the District's defense." Then, seeing the other man's expression: "They will do. You'll see."

"Any sign that they've felled trees? Blocked the road? Are they throwing up earthworks around the capital? Any indication they're planning to harass the redcoats as they pass?"

"None of those things," the marksman admitted. "Not yet. I did mention it to a few of the officers. About the earthworks and such like."

"And you were told what?"

"That I wasn't to worry. That their bravery would win the day. Oh, and that they'd be glad to have any more such intelligence as we're able to provide."

The surveyor cursed softly as he collapsed his glass and put his notes in his knapsack. "Let's go. And as for intelligence, that seems to be in short supply."

New York City,
Chatham Street, 5 P.M.

Eugenie had slept all day. She did not want to wake up now. It was the maid bustling about opening the curtains and pouring buckets of steaming water into a copper bath that forced her to open her eyes. "I must rest. Go away."

Meg had been caring for Eugenie since the day she was born; first as her wet nurse, then her nanny, and finally her lady's maid. She was selective about which orders she followed, and she felt no need to mince words. "There's a stink about you. You need a bath.

No telling when one of 'em might come back. You can't be found like this."

"A stink? Really? One of whom?"

"The one-eyed pirate, or the other one as pretends to be a gentleman. Ask me, he's a pirate as well, though he doesn't look like one. And fucking makes a smell. I always told you so. You gave him what he wanted last night, didn't you?"

"Not Tintin." Eugenie allowed herself to be pulled out of the bed.

"I haven't gone foolish in the head. The other one, Mr. Blakeman. Will you have the rose salts or the lavender? How was he, then? As good at it as poor Mr. Tim, Lord rest his soul, or one o' them jackrabbit sorts?"

"Lavender. And you're impertinent. That's none of your business."

"Ain't nothin' 'bout you ain't my business. Here, get that nightdress off and get in 'fore the water's cold. Hah!" she chortled when Eugenie obediently pulled the gown over her head, "left you a souvenir, he did." Meg pointed to Eugenie's belly.

She looked down. A series of puckered red marks made a trail from her navel to her groin, losing themselves in the luxuriant brush of her sex. Dear God. He had been extraordinary. "I gave as good as I got." She climbed into the bath. "Better."

"I don't doubt it." Meg picked up the sponge and rubbed it with the bar of lavender-scented soap Devrey's sold along with the bath salts. Lovely stuff. Course, they couldn't really afford such luxuries these days, but all things considered, bath salts were an investment. That's what Miss Eugenie said and she was right. Holdin' herself up on a pedestal, that had been an investment too. Not natural for her, but sensible. Only Miss Eugenie was never sensible about such things for very long. Two years this time. A miracle. "You can't help it, you know. Come by it honestly."

"Can't help what?"

"Needin' a man between your legs."

"My mother," Eugenie said with a sigh. It was a conversation they'd had many times. "Her unique legacy."

"Can't say as it's unique. There's plenty like her, truth be told, but I ain't been in service with all of 'em. Here, raise your arms." Meg busied herself with the sponge, scrubbing while she talked, soaping her charge in all the cracks and crevices where evidence of her last night's encounter might hide. "But unique or not, she was a one, your ma was. Never could get enough. Even when she was fallen pregnant, and Lord knows she was that often enough. Good thing she kept losing 'em one after t'other, else one might o' popped out as gave the game away. Yellow hair, like the farmer came to deliver eggs, or squinty-eyed, like the fellow did your pa's accounts. Course, it were a good thing she spread her legs for him. Seein' as how your pa had no other way to pay him and— Ah, what's them tears about, missy? You can't help bein' like you are. And I think it's a marvel you sayin' no to that Blakeman fellow all this time. Course, you had to say yes sooner or later. Ain't nothin' to cry about."

Eugenie knew there to be a great deal to cry about.

If there were any chance at all that she might fall pregnant—even long enough for her belly to swell just a tiny bit, even if it might end over a chamber pot, with her pushing out a thing as was already dead, the way she'd seen her mother do many a time—that might solve everything. But there was no chance. She knew beyond question she was barren. She'd taken two lovers before she married Timothy. Youthful follies, though each time she'd thought herself in the midst of a grand passion, and thank God Meg had been able to protect her from gossip. Not to mention shoving that little bladder of pig's blood up inside her, so Timothy would believe her a virgin on their wedding night. But even Meg could do nothing about the fact that Eugenie's flow came regularly every month, whomever she'd been with and however inventive their lovemaking. So she could rest assured there would be no pregnancy this time to get her what she was sure she would not get otherwise.

She had seen it in Gornt's eyes.

He had kissed her awake just before dawn, then gathered the clothes of her disguise into a sack, wrapped her in a blanket, carried her down the stairs of his countinghouse, and snuggled her on his lap in a closed and curtained carriage—being Gornt Blakeman meant having a choice of carriages—and passed every minute of the journey to her house fondling her, and murmuring that she was enchanting and delicious, and he could not get enough of her. Meaning she was a sweetmeat, not a meal. She wished she were mistaken, but she knew she was not. "Later," he'd whispered when they came to her front door. "I'll come tonight. As early as I can. Leave instructions that I'm to be admitted." Then he'd pulled the blanket over her head, thrown her over his shoulder as if she were a sack of potatoes, tucked her bag of belongings under his other arm, and carried her around to the tradesman's entrance and deposited her in Meg's waiting arms. You'd take more delicate, more discreet, care of the reputation of a woman you intended to marry.

By acting the wanton she had forfeited the opportunity to be the wife.

There was one card left to play, but it had not been dealt her. Gornt Blakeman was a man intent on founding a dynasty. If she could promise him an heir, wait a few weeks, then tell him his son already quickened in her belly, it might be different. She could lie, of course. But her lie would be found out. Gornt was not Timothy. He would not patiently wait for a miracle to occur. And her life would become a worse hell than it was right now.

Meg had got as far as scrubbing her toes, taking her usual care of each one. The bath was cooling and it was almost time to again face the world. "Scrub every bit of me really hard once more, Meg. Scalp to toes. There must be no stink. And when we're done, you're to go and fetch the Widow Tremont."

"The mantua maker? Now?"

"Immediately."

The pirate with the eye patch was a better prospect than the one without. At least with Tintin she understood the bargain and got exactly what she expected. No more, but neither any less. The bag of coins was still in the pocket of Timothy's cutaway when her night's adventure ended; Eugenie had put it safely away in the same locked drawer that contained the additional documents concerning runaway slaves before she went to sleep. Those letters would bring her yet more money, and there would be more documents and more money in the years to come. Tintin would continue to need her aura of respectability in doing business with the magistrates. Slyly Silas Danforth would be only too happy to forge documents. And there were no end of nigras in Five Points.

The Bowery, 9 P.M.

The tavern was called the Fife and Drum. It was some distance from the Bull's Head and the cattle pens and slaughtering sheds, and it seemed to have less custom than the others in the area. This evening there were two drinkers besides Blakeman; both wore the leather aprons that marked them as butchers, but neither seemed in the least interested in anything other than the bottom of his tankard.

Blakeman nursed his beer—flat and slightly sour, like everything else in the place—and sat with his back against the wall at the rear of the room. He'd blown out the single candle that burned nearby and was pretty much invisible in the shadows. He had, however, a good view of the door. He saw Maurice Vionne come in, blink a few times to let his eyes adjust to the dimness, and stand hesitant and unsure in the doorway. Blakeman cleared his throat. The place was silent as a tomb, the sound carried, and Vionne looked in his direction. Blakeman raised his hand. Vionne blinked a few more times, then moved to join him.

"Good evening to you, goldsmith."

"And to you, Mr.—"

Blakeman raised his hand. "We've no need for names here." He pushed a second glass of the inferior beer in the direction of his guest. "I took the liberty of ordering for you. Beer is the only available tipple, I'm afraid. And not the city's best. But the place offers privacy, as I promised."

Vionne looked around. "True enough."

"Caution, goldsmith," Blakeman said softly. "It is the wiser course. At least for a time."

"As you say, sir, of course. But I must tell you that I have not yet written—"

Blakeman again cut off the other man's words with a gesture. "I understand. We agreed on tomorrow for your formal assessment. In that matter it is not my intention to hurry you."

Vionne trembled. Not about the diamond perhaps, only about his daughter. He knew that he had been summoned to this meeting so far from his home and his customary haunts to talk about Manon. Just not what he meant to say about her or Blakeman's proposal. "As for that other business . . ."

"The hand of your daughter in marriage."

"Yes."

"Well? The banns, sir. Have you arranged them? It should be quite a simple matter."

Vionne glanced around. The butchers did not appear to be paying any attention. "Mr. Blakeman, it is most certainly not a matter that can be called simple. My daughter is very much a modern young woman. She is, I must admit, headstrong. I dare not make such a decision for her without you calling—on her, mind you, not me—and asking her yourself if she will have you." Vionne lifted his beer and drank down half of it in one long swallow. It tasted foul, but his mouth was so dry he didn't care.

Blakeman waited until the smith had set the tankard back on the table, then leaned forward and spoke very quietly. "In other circumstances that might be possible. As things stand now, it is not. I rely on you to make my case for me, goldsmith. I am quite sure that however—what was your word?—however modern Miss Manon may be, she is also a dutiful daughter. As I told you, sir, it suits me that the wedding take place in a fortnight's time. See to it."

Blakeman watched the goldsmith leave. He waited a few moments, then lifted his hand and nodded. One of the butchers got up and followed Vionne into the street. A precaution, nothing more. But if by some outside chance the goldsmith were going somewhere other than straight home, best he knew about it.

So, one bit of this night's business concluded. Though he did not feel as satisfied with it as he might. Hang the banns, he should have demanded the wedding take place immediately. Otherwise it might be that Joyful Turner . . . No, not likely. If Turner were going to whisk her away without her father's permission, he'd have done so by now. He would leave things as they were.

The door opened. "The blessing of *le bon Dieu* on all here. Beer, landlord! And I am to meet a gentleman . . . Ah, I see him. There in the back. Good evening to you, my friend." Tintin headed toward Blakeman, passing the tapping bench and picking up his beer as he went by.

"You've much in common with the arse of a horse," Blakeman said, when Tintin straddled a stool across from his own. "As I suspect you've been told before."

Tintin shrugged. "Not frequently by those who wish to keep their tongues in their mouths, monsieur. But in this case I will ignore the insult. As I am ignoring your little pretense of great secrecy. If this place were not entirely safe, you would not have met me here. And I note that the one man besides ourselves who drinks at the sign of the Fife and Drum is a butcher. They tell me the butchers are entirely in your camp."

"And who might these talkative folks be?"

"The populace of the great city of New York, *mon ami*. At least those with whom I have intercourse. Ha! That would make them all women, no? I love your English language. So many meanings for each word!" Tintin lifted the tankard, took a long swallow, then spat the beer onto the sawdust-covered floor. "*Merde!* You have brought me to a tavern where they serve cow piss. If this is to be the standard of brewers in your new nation, monsieur, I must think again about our—"

Blakeman reached across and gripped the pirate's arm. "Hold your tongue, you ignorant bastard!"

"Let go of me." The words were spoken very softly.

"You try my patience, pirate."

"Let go of me." A knife had materialized in Tintin's free hand and was pressed against Blakeman's wrist. "Otherwise, *mon ami,* you will have the same disfigurement as your rival."

"I do not think so, pirate." The butcher who had not followed Vionne into the street had come to stand behind Tintin. He held a cleaver above the head of the pirate. "Not unless," Blakeman said quietly, "you believe that bandanna you wear can keep your skull from splitting in two."

The tableau held for the space of three heartbeats. Then Blakeman released his hold on Tintin's wrist, Tintin put his knife away, and the butcher faded into the shadows on the other side of the room. "Tell me about the others," Blakeman said.

"What others?"

"Lafitte and the rest. Will they do business?"

"Jean Lafitte is always prepared to do business, and the others do as he suggests. But Barataria is a long distance away, *mon ami.* As I have said before, he is there and I am here."

Exactly the concern. "I must be able to tell the others we have Lafitte's agreement."

Tintin lifted the tankard a second time, then set it down with a grimace of disapproval. "Is there nothing better than this to drink in this place?"

"Answer my question and you can go off to Rivington Street and drink Delight Higgins's fine wines and superior ale, and gamble and whore as much as you like."

"I do not require your permission to come or to go, *mon ami.*" Tintin leaned forward. "I thought we had established that."

Blakeman nodded. The time to teach the pirate manners would come. It was not now. "I need to be able to assure the others that the ships that fly our flag will be unmolested, and that those flying the Stars and Stripes will be considered fair prey."

"You and all the rest of the Americans call us pirates, monsieur. But we, Captain Lafitte and all the rest of us, we think of ourselves as honorable privateers. Give us letters of marque and . . ." Tintin spread his hands in a gesture that promised much, though he specified nothing.

Wednesday, August 24, 1814

Chapter Eighteen

New York City,
Ann Street, 9 A.M.

EVERY TIME he removed a kidney stone, Andrew thought of his ancestor, Lucas Turner, a barber-surgeon come here in 1661, when the city was Nieuw Amsterdam. Then as now, a stone was among the most painful of ailments. Those suffering with it were always the easiest to persuade to the knife. "You must stand just so, sir. On the oilcloth. Now, if you can spread your legs, and bend over and rest your elbows on this table . . . Yes, that's excellent."

The man's moans were low and continuous, but Andrew's patient did exactly as he was told. So had fierce old Peter Stuyvesant, according to Lucas's journal. If the Dutch governor had been grieving with some other disease—since he couldn't have known that Lucas Turner, Andrew's four times great-uncle, was a surgeon of genius—he might not so readily have trusted himself to a stranger just arrived in the colony. Andrew pushed a sturdy leather bucket into position between his patient's legs and reached for a scalpel. "Now, sir, take a deep breath and hold it as long as you can. If your lungs are in good shape, this will all be over by the time you must take another."

In his journals Lucas claimed to be able to cut out a stone and sew the patient back up in forty-five seconds. Andrew had bested that time on one or two occasions, at least so he thought, but not in recent years. He was slowing down, whatever Joyful said. This, however, was not the time to give in to age.

He grasped the scalpel, put one hand behind the man's hanging genitalia, spread the skin taut, and made a swift single cut from the rectum to the testes. The motion was quick enough that he'd withdrawn the knife before the patient's howl of pain and his involuntary start could cause the blade to wander. He preferred speed to the method Lucas described, putting one arm around the patient's waist to hold him in position, and cutting with the other. "You're not holding your breath, sir. Try it again. That's the worst of it over."

Not exactly true, but a fib that comforted. Made the balance of the operation easier on both of them. Andrew used a pair of pincers to spread the wound. That drew only a muffled gasp. He could see the bladder wall now. Another cut—his patient let out a high-pitched squeal, like a cat on a hot stove—this one as fast and much shorter, and made with a smaller scalpel, hewn as they all were to razor sharpness. Good knives, as much a part of successful surgery as good cutting. He adjusted the pincers. Another yelp. There were stories of stonecutters who had inadvertently taken men's cocks off when writhing patients twisted out of their grip. Or still worse, half off. He'd always preferred quickness and impeccable technique to strength, though either would get the job done.

The ammonia reek of the man's urine mingled with the slightly sweet smell of blood as they mixed in the bucket. A satisfactory ping followed. And Ho Charley! A second ping after the first. Two stones, both lodged in the bladder. Andrew's belief, formulated by the hundreds of anatomies he'd performed on cadavers that came his way when he had charge of the almshouse hospital, was that the stones appeared first in the kidneys. He'd found them there during many of those explorations when he cut to know rather than to cure. He was convinced it wasn't until the stones worked their way down to the lower regions of the waterworks that excruciating pain drove the victims to stone cutters. And this poor bastard had been suffering twice over. "Two stones, sir. You were preparing to construct a cathedral in your innards." Damned fortunate he was as well. No need to probe. Lucas's journal said how grateful he'd been not to have to probe to get at Governor Stuyvesant's stone. "Only a few pricks now, sir. I'm tidying things up and stitching the wound. If you—"

A quick knock, then the door flew open. "Excuse me, Dr. Turner, sir. There's a—"

"Not now, Bridey." He'd never been able to break her of the habit of coming in before she was invited. This poor devil wasn't the first to give Bridey a display of his bare hindquarters. "Go away. I'll come when I'm done."

The door closed. Andrew continued tying off the blood vessels. A hundred and fifty years since his ancestor did this operation, and nothing much had changed. Not likely to either. Not unless someone could solve the problem of how much pain folks could endure under the knife. Wasn't likely to happen in his lifetime. Maybe his son's, or Joyful's. He'd always thought Joyful would be the one to lead the way down the paths such a transformation would make available. Opening a chest or a belly, watching the heart pump or the intestines contract, repairing—God knew what, but something—then sewing the patient back up and having him live. Bloody marvelous that would be. Make surgeons into gods.

"Only a few seconds more, sir." He picked up another of the catgut ligatures he'd prepared in advance and began stitching the wound. Always planned to give old Lucas's journals to Joyful. But if Joyful truly wasn't to practice medicine as a livelihood, they should go to Christopher. Didn't matter how unappealing he found his flesh-and-blood heir when compared to Roisin's boy. Fair was fair. "There you are, sir. Done." Andrew glanced at his pocket watch. "Close to two minutes."

Terrible time. He'd blame Bridey's interruption rather than his increasing age.

Ten minutes later the man was dressed and Andrew had led him out to his waiting carriage. "Eat a portion of this bran twice a day." He pressed a muslin bag into the man's hands. "And drink as much as you can get down. Even water. Never mind how bad it tastes. You must not strain at the stool. And come back and see me in a week's time."

He stood a moment, watching the carriage drive away. Not as many soldiers on the streets as there had been a day or two ago. Perhaps New York was not to be invaded after all.

"Dr. Turner . . . Sir . . ."

Andrew turned to the sound of his name. "Absalom. So it was you Bridey tried to announce a bit ago." His heart sank at the thought of another trip to Five Points. As usual, he knew he would go in spite of that.

"Guess it be me, sir."

"Sorry to keep you waiting. I'd already begun that man's surgery, and there was no way I could stop it. I take it Mother Zion calls?"

Absalom shook his head. "No sir, Dr. Turner. Not like usual. I be . . ." He paused and looked around.

"Come inside." Andrew hurried his caller into the front hall and closed the door behind him. "Now, what's this about?"

"I be lookin' for Joshua, Dr. Turner. You remember him. Boy as helped us when you were by Mother Zion last time. Boy you sent to get your cousin, the doctor with one hand."

"Yes, I remember. Joshua. What about him?"

"He be missing two days now. Don't be no one knows where he's at. Reverend Fish, he be right disturbed. Joshua be a great favorite o' Reverend Fish."

"I'm sorry to hear that the boy has run off, Absalom. But why tell me?"

"He was mighty taken by all your fixing and patching, Dr. Turner. Talked a fair bit about it after you left. Reverend Fish, he be thinkin' maybe Joshua come here to you. Ask to be a 'prentice or some such."

Andrew had to tell him that he had not seen the boy. He did not speak the word "blackbirders," but he knew it was the explanation in his mind and Absalom's, and no doubt in that of Zachary Fish.

Maryland, the Woods Surrounding
the Federal District, 10 A.M.

The soldiers of the Fifth Maryland Volunteer Infantry were drawn from the finest Baltimore society, and they were a sight to see. Blue jackets faced with red, white pantaloons, black gaiters, white cross-belts, and heavy leather helmets topped with two sweeping plumes, one red and the other black. They'd left Baltimore the day before—accompanied by the many nigras the individual members of the regiment had hired to look after and cook for them—marching down streets lined with cheering citizenry. A fine adventure.

It no longer felt so. They'd spent an exhausting night marching back and forth from one position to another. All, as it turned out, responses to false alarms, but no less tiring for that.

That same night another company, the Annapolis militia, pitched camp within half a mile of the British pickets at the Upper Marlboro encampment. When they discovered that, outnumbered as they were, they had all but delivered themselves into the enemy's hands, they set about moving, and did so in such disorder that they rolled their tents too loosely to fit all of them on the wagons. Many were left behind, along with other supplies they were too much in a hurry to take. The men, mostly draftees, were told to march with a ball up their muskets. As a result one accidentally killed his closest friend, and another shot a companion in the thigh. The chaos provoked a number of desertions.

Nonetheless, one way and another six thousand American men were within thirty miles of Washington. Ready to fight and, if need be, to give their lives for their country. But as the column of just over four thousand redcoats made their final approach to the spot they'd chosen to cross the Eastern Branch of the Potomac into the Federal District—the village of Bladensburg—they faced no concentrated defending force.

"They'll cross at Bladensburg, Mr. President. It's the shallowest point. They can ford if they must."

They were at the Navy Yard in Washington. Madison, God help him, was surrounded by those who felt qualified to give advice: two generals and half a dozen members of the cabinet. But only the president seemed to be paying attention to the surveyor. He was Astor's scout, not strictly speaking theirs. That, to Madison's mind, was a recommendation; Jacob Astor always employed the best. "Yes, very well. I'm sure you're right." He turned to the general on his right. "You heard?"

"The village of Bladensburg. Yes, well it's possible. But there are two other bridges into the District before they get there. Surely they'll take the most direct—"

It occurred to the president to inquire as to why all the bridges giving access to the Federal District had not long since been blown up, but he was weary of the man's excuses. "General, this man and his companion"—Madison nodded in the direction of the marksman—"have been tracking the enemy for four days. Have you, sir, had any spies in such close contact for so long a period?"

"No sir, Mr. President, I cannot say that I have."

"Very well. Bladensburg. Give the order."

There were some thousand troops nearby. Minutes later they were on the march. President Madison himself led the charge, his horse loping out ahead of all the others, the diminutive president looking slightly silly astride the mighty beast but gallantly spurring him on.

New York City, Broadway at Barclay Street, 10:30 A.M.

"*Chi le fan meiyou?*" Joyful asked. Have you eaten rice today? He gave Ah Wong a wide smile.

"*Chi le. Chi le.* Prease forrow me." The butler turned abruptly from the door.

Joyful thought they had established a degree of alliance and mutual respect after the butler gave him rice for Thumbless Wu. Now it did not seem so. Maybe because this time he arrived at the front door, and he came at Astor's summons, which Wong probably knew. He shouldn't read too much into it. No Westerner, not even he, would ever fully comprehend the Chinese idea of face, or how you lost or saved it.

He followed Ah Wong across the vast entryway, but this time they didn't go into Astor's study. He was led down a long corridor into a small dining room. It faced the gardens and sun streamed through open French windows. The warm air carried the scent of the tall lilies growing close by the house, pale purple with yellow throats and the scent of heaven. The fragrance immediately transported Joyful to his mother's garden in Canton. The lilies must have come from China as well; he'd never seen them growing in New York. "Good morning, Mr. Astor. I came as soon as I got your note."

"*Ja,* I knew you would. Even if I did not send it with one of the China people. Not sensible to have them too much on the streets while the city jumps at her shadow. Anything a little bit strange and *Pow!*" Astor mimed holding a musket to his shoulder and firing it.

Jacob Astor playing the clown; this was something new. "I'm sure you're right."

"About such things, Dr. Turner, always I am right. Though I'm sure it was disappointing to you not to have another opportunity to talk China talk. You have their language, *nicht wahr?*"

So Astor knew about his visit to the servants' quarters to speak with Ah Wong. Who told him? The butler himself? One of the other servants? It didn't matter. Joyful had assumed it would be so. Hell, he'd meant it to be so. "I speak Mandarin, yes sir. And Cantonese. A few of the other dialects as well."

"So you will be a formidable trader, Dr. Turner. A rival to be reckoned with."

"That's one way to look at it, Mr. Astor. The other is that I'll be a formidable ally."

Astor smiled and nodded. "*Ja,* to me also that interpretation occurred. Please to sit down, Dr. Turner. And tell me something, since you know China talk. What is that word they use to mean what we speak about? Common cause, as you say in English."

"*Guanxi.* Common cause is close, but . . ." The day's heat was mounting swiftly even as they sat in this shaded spot. Sweat already poured down Joyful's back. But the heat was not entirely to blame; he had a sense that something momentous was about to happen, some invisible line to be crossed. "There is no exact translation."

"*Guanxi. Ja.*" And when he saw Joyful's expression: "I bungle the pronunciation, no? It is enough what I do to English. I should not try China talk. But however funny my speech comes out, Dr. Turner, I do not mistake men's minds."

"I'm sure you do not, Mr. Astor."

"*Ja.* So I recognize when even a potential rival is more use to me strong than weak. Some things are more important than profit."

"A few," Joyful admitted. "Though that's easier to say from your position than mine."

Astor chuckled. "I take your meaning, Joyful. I may call you that since we are to be allies?"

His heart thumped and there was a wild singing in his head. Just like that and Gornt Blakeman was finished, a line on yesterday's broadside. With Devrey Shipping literally in his pocket (Joyful could think of no safer place for the papers than on his person) and Jacob Astor beside him, he was unstoppable. Except what about F.X.'s message? *Astor's with us.* The thought was enough to rein in his elation. "Allies, Mr. Astor. I'm delighted to hear it. And I'd be honored if you called me by my given name."

"Good. And I will be Jacob. Now, Joyful, try some of this coffee." He picked up a silver pot with a long spout and a gracefully turned handle. "It is the finest to be had. Even better, I think, than at the Tontine."

Who had told Astor about Joyful's visit to the coffeehouse? Geoffrey Colden probably, but any one of the traders might be thick with Astor, part of the consortium he'd formed to help finance the war. Jesus, another reason F.X.'s message made no sense. Why then give thousands to Madison? And if Jacob Astor were meeting with Gornt Blakeman to talk treason against the United States, would he leave his distinctive carriage parked in front of Blakeman's premises?

Astor poured coffee into a delicate porcelain cup and offered the sugar bowl. Joyful took three lumps, stirred the coffee, then sipped it. "Finest I've ever tasted, sir. Without doubt."

"So, I am glad, Joyful. But to praise my coffee is not why I asked you to come. That I did so I can tell you to your face. Exactly right you told it. Everything. Two nights ago I met with Gornt Blakeman in his countinghouse."

Focus on the carom you're trying to make, Joyful, and stop worrying about the shot your opponent may contemplate. "That meeting, sir. Might I ask how it came about?"

"*Ja*, of course. A note Blakeman sent me. I was to go to Hanover Street on a matter of great importance. Nonetheless, without you had come and told me what you thought would happen, I would not have gone, Joyful. Jacob Astor does not appear because someone says so. But I remembered your story and so I went to Blakeman's countinghouse."

Joyful waited. Astor sat back in his chair, sipped his coffee slowly, and watched the younger man over the rim of the cup. "He is very full of himself, our Mr. Blakeman. He fancies himself a king. To get upstairs to his private quarters I had to walk by a big man with a whip." Another chuckle. "I think I was meant to feel afraid."

"And did you?"

"*Nein*, Joyful. I was not afraid. Under my tongue I had a whistle. Look, I will show you." Astor reached into his pocket and withdrew a round wooden object about an inch across and put it in his mouth. "So, still I can talk if not too many words." The obstruction caused him only a slight lisp. "Now, listen."

Joyful heard a single shrill note. Almost at the same instant a man appeared in the open French window. He had a rifle to his shoulder and he was peering down the sight and aiming straight at Joyful. Astor spit out the whistle and laughed. "*Ja, ja.*" He waved the man away. "Go back to your post. I was making only a demonstration." He watched while the man disappeared, then turned back to Joyful. "Outside Blakeman's countinghouse, three of them. They know how to hide themselves as well as shoot, my marksmen. The best one, he is not here just now, but the three who came with me last night . . . Good enough they are. The whipper would have been dead before his arm came down."

"A private militia, Mr. Astor?" His voice sounded cooler than it might, considering that moments before he'd been looking down the barrel of a rifle.

"Jacob, you must call me. And yes, of course a private militia. It is what I need. But we waste time, Joyful." Astor leaned forward, fixing the younger man in his gaze and speaking very quietly. "Gornt Blakeman has asked me to write to Vienna, to the Holy Roman emperor, Francis II. I am to say he should recognize New York and Massachusetts and Connecticut and probably Rhode Island as a separate country. They are to leave the United States and become a united something else. The name I do not know. But that Gornt Blakeman wishes to rule this something else, of that I am quite sure."

"And in return for the recognition of the Holy Roman emperor?" He had not been sure which royal house would be chosen, only that Blakeman planned to use the stone to secure European recognition for his breakaway country. Not, as Manon feared, to cut the Great Mogul into smaller stones that could be sold in America. "He would present the world's largest diamond as a token of the new country's esteem?"

"*Ja.* Exactly as you said." Then, after a pause, "You have seen this diamond, Joyful?"

"Never, Jacob."

"Better not to see it. Blakeman showed me. So I would be impressed."

"And were you?"

"*Ja*. I tell you the truth. Blakeman," Astor snapped his fingers. "Him I think like nothing. But his diamond . . . *Ja*, it impressed me here." He pointed to his groin. "Like a beautiful woman. One you see and know you must have. Many men would be prepared to do anything for such a jewel. A Lorelei it is. A siren that sings a song no sailor can resist."

"Until he is lured onto the rocks."

"Exactly."

"So do you now plan to have the Great Mogul for yourself?"

"At the expense my country should be broken up into little pieces that are not strong enough to survive? You disappoint me, Joyful."

"But you, Jacob, do not disappoint *me*."

Astor smiled. So did Joyful. Then the older man half stood and stretched his hand out to the younger. "Now, in my language, we are *Genossen*. Allies, I think you say. For the sake of the United States. Later, in business, *Teilhaber*, partners? We will see. Now we make *guanxi*."

"Allies," Joyful said, grasping the other man's hand. Then, knowing if he didn't ask now he'd never have an opportunity, "Jacob, why would F. X. Gallagher send a message to Gornt Blakeman saying Astor's with us?"

Astor's eyes narrowed. "Of this you are sure, Joyful?"

"Yes, I believe I can safely say I am."

"And you think Mr. Gallagher, he means me?"

Joyful nodded.

"F. X. Gallagher is a butcher, *oder nicht?*"

"Yes, many things, but a butcher as well . . ."

"So. Think, Joyful."

It was so obvious it was extraordinary he hadn't seen it before. "Your brother," Joyful said. "Henry's a butcher."

"My brother, *ja*. So, thank you for telling me this, Joyful. I do not like to hear it, but I would rather know than not know. And now I will tell you something that you will not want to hear, but it is better you should know. Your cousin Bastard is deceiving you. In this business of Devrey Shipping he makes the double cross." Astor sketched a large X-shaped sign in the air.

"That's not possible. I have the signed papers."

"I know. Already you have told me this. You have now forty-nine percent of Devrey Shipping. That is indeed true. Blakeman has only forty percent. And eleven percent remains with Bastard Devrey." Joyful nodded. "So if Bastard chooses to make *guanxi* with Gornt Blakeman, they have together fifty-one percent, *nicht wahr?* Together they outvote you."

Jesus. Twice in five minutes he saw himself as a fool. "How do you know this? Are you sure?"

"Entirely sure. One of the marksmen I left on Hanover Street to watch. Bastard Devrey departed the countinghouse an hour after me. I think all the time he was there while Blakeman and I spoke. I cannot be sure: the room was dark, only one lamp." Joyful nodded, remembering the clutter and the dimness of Gornt Blakeman's private quarters. "Easy it would have been for Bastard to hide in the shadows and hear everything we said."

He thought for a moment. "Why would Blakeman want Bastard there? What advantage would that give him?"

"That Bastard knows he has made a right decision. Probably at first he only hinted. Then he sees that Gornt Blakeman can summon Jacob Astor to his countinghouse and show him a *wunderschön* jewel and get him to do what Blakeman wants him to do. A man like Bastard Devrey, he is prepared to believe such a thing."

"It appears that Gornt Blakeman also believes it."

"He hopes it," Astor corrected. "I told him I needed a few days to give him my decision. Time I was negotiating for, Joyful."

"Time for what?"

"To know whether our country—our whole country—can survive," Astor said frankly. "I expect word shortly."

❧

Bladensburg, Maryland, 11:30 A.M.

It was not so much that the men in command of the American forces did not agree as that they did not confer. The result was the same. The various companies and assorted militia meant to confront the enemy at Bladensburg were spread out in three lines that had no contact with one another. They were deployed across the face of a gentle slope that led directly to Washington along a road locals referred to as the Pike.

The cannon of the Baltimore artillery, which should have been able to lay down a line of fire from one end of the bridge to the other, were positioned in such fashion they could only shoot across it. By the time that was discovered, the Americans could already hear the tramp of the redcoats' boots, and the officer in charge decided there was no time to reposition the guns. Five companies of riflemen were stationed to the left of the artillery. They would be the first to face the enemy. The rest of the force was five hundred yards behind, out of sight of what was happening on the riverbank.

The Annapolis militia that had made such a cock-up of its billet the night before arrived minutes ahead of the enemy, jogging through the lines of the men from Baltimore in something meant to be quick time, but so out of step it looked more like a hen stomp at a barn raising. They took up a position near the top of the hill.

The British, meanwhile, were an eighth of a mile from the bridge, their internal formation perfect, their boots hitting the beaten-dirt road in a rhythm so precise it created a kind of low-pitched roar. Wave after wave of them arrived, and only one glimmer of hope for the Americans. A distance of about a mile had opened between the brigades.

The English general called a halt within sight of the bridge. The company sergeant-major trotted to his side, waiting for orders. For once, the admiral offered no opinion. The general considered. His men were exhausted, they could do with a rest while the others caught up. But the prize was close enough so he could almost see it. He lifted his sword arm and pointed straight ahead. "Charge!"

The first salvo from the Baltimore artillery met the advance. Seconds later the riflemen began firing.

In moments the redcoats in the van had formed a double red line that returned fire in perfect unison and with no pause. It was a devastating response, and the few Maryland riflemen that survived it fled into the woods.

Madison and the men with him were approaching Bladensburg from the south, those on horseback galloping full speed up the Pike, the foot soldiers trotting behind them in quick march. The president heard the shots, spurred his horse still faster, and opened up a lead that looked to make him the first of the Washington reinforcements to take the field.

It was Astor's marksman who saw what was happening and put his head down and whipped his borrowed horse into a frenzy of speed. "Mr. President! Please, sir . . ." He drew level with Madison. "Mr. President! You must fall back, sir. You cannot be part of the fight. If you were injured, sir . . . think of the country."

"What?" It was like waking from a dream. Madison and his horse, an old cavalry charger as it happened, the pair of them lusting for the fight. "No . . . you are quite right. Of course I cannot." The president reined in, and he and the marksman sidled to the edge of the road. The District militia raced ahead, taking the field alongside the men from Annapolis, while five hundred sailors and marines took up a position across the Pike. Their five big naval guns would be the city's ultimate defense.

The surveyor, also on horseback now, had taken up a position at the top of the hill. "Too far apart," he muttered. "The bloody idiots are too damned far apart." No one heard him. It was too late to make any difference if they had.

On the other side of the river the British admiral had also withdrawn to the role of observer. At this point the battle was the army's affair. He lifted his glass and looked up to the ridge ahead. He had gotten his way. Washington first, then Baltimore. And both probably a lot easier than either he or the general expected. What was it they'd said

back in Bermuda? Dolley Madison sets a fine table at the Executive
Mansion.

"What is that, John?"

"That be gunfire, Mrs. Madison."

"Yes, I supposed it is." Dolley ran to the north parapet, leaning as
far forward as she dared, pressing the glass to her eye. "I can see some
flashes, John, by the eastern branch of the river. In the direction of
Bladensburg, I think. The enemy appears to be north of us." She
turned to French John, her chest heaving, dabbing her face with a
handkerchief already soaked with perspiration. "Perhaps they are passing us by. The redcoats may be headed for Baltimore, or even New
York."

"Could be, madam. But—" A sound from below stopped his
speech. John bent over the edge of the roof. "Two wagons, Mrs. Madison. The boys be finding two wagons!"

"Yes, I see they have." Dear God. Forty-six years old and already
once a widow, wasn't that to be enough? Why did James not this very
minute come riding toward her, take her to safety. He was the president of the United States and she was his wife. Why wasn't he here?
She snapped the glass shut. "Come, John. We must go downstairs and
see how much of the house's furnishings we can pack on that blessed
pair of wagons."

New York City, Maiden Lane, Noon

Adele Tremont was a long, thin reed of a woman, fine for displaying
the latest fashions, Manon had always thought. Advertising her trade
as it were. But Manon could never see her in Mama's place, and Papa
had given no indication he wanted her there. He had carefully avoided
the Widow Tremont ever since Mama died. Now, because of Manon,
the viper had been invited into the nest.

"I can peel those potatoes for you, if you like," Manon said.

"Thank you, I can manage."

"Yes, I know you can." She made a great effort to keep the exasperation from her voice. "But there's no need. You must allow me to help."

"Monsieur Vionne has asked me to take over all the cooking for the household. All the marketing as well," she added.

"I know, but I am only too happy to take on some of those chores." Papa had left a few minutes before, and said he would probably not return until the dinner hour. She would not have a better opportunity. "If I were to go to the market for you, for instance, you could take the time to make your treacle tart. Papa loves your treacle tart, Madame Tremont. He told me so after the Independence Day church supper."

"You are kind to mention it, mademoiselle. But I do not think Monsieur Vionne would approve my letting you go to the market in my stead. He feels you have been seen too much about the town of late. And now that the nephew of Monsieur DeFane is coming—"

"A visit that may not occur for some time, given that the redcoats are all over our roads. Here, do let me at least scrape the carrots."

"There are not quite enough, I fear. I hope Elsie Gruning has more for us today."

The Widow Tremont bent her long body over the soup simmering in a heavy pot hanging over the kitchen fire. Her nose was long as well, and needle-thin. Mama had been all roundness and softness. Not so good for wearing *la dernière mode,* perhaps, but surely Papa was more interested in hugging a pillow than a stick. "Not so much salt," Manon said as the Widow Tremont added three large pinches to the pot. "Papa does not like his soup so liberally seasoned."

"My *petite marmite* has never been criticized, mademoiselle. The late Monsieur Tremont was very fond of it."

"Yes, well—"

"I am sure Monsieur Vionne will find it equally satisfactory. Now I will go and see about those carrots. I can trust you not to allow the fire to go out, mademoiselle?"

"I shall do my best. But Madame Tremont, only you know exactly how much heat you wish the marmite to have, when is the right time to stir up the coals and when to damp them down. And think what a nice surprise your treacle tart would be. If you—"

"I have already made the treacle tart, mademoiselle. It is even now cooling in the pantry." Madame Tremont tied a straw gypsy bonnet in place as she spoke. A tight tie, Manon saw, meant to stay exactly where she put it. And of course, a perfect bow. "I shall be gone no more than thirty minutes. And when I return, mademoiselle, perhaps you would like me to measure you for a new frock. For when the nephew of Monsieur DeFane arrives. I got a lovely piece of green silk at Monsieur Blakeman's sale the other day. I am to make a new gown of it for Eugenie Fischer, and she is a lady of great style. But you are both slender. There is enough for two."

"*Merci, madame,* a new frock would be lovely. You are too kind." I hope you slip on the way to the market and break both those skinny legs. Then you will not be able to interfere in my life this way, and Papa will not so quickly find a replacement for my skills. And if I hear one more word about this wretched nephew of Monsieur DeFane, I will cut out the tongue of whoever speaks it.

Adele Tremont paused with her hand on the kitchen door. "The fire, mademoiselle. Do not forget. The *marmite* will not be as good if it is allowed to cool in the middle of the cooking."

"I shall guard it with my life, madame." Manon waited until the mantua-maker had gone, then took a large handful of salt from the cannister beside the hearth and dumped it into the soup. My petite marmite has never been criticized, mademoiselle. *Alors,* madame, we shall see about that.

It was not usual for Papa to close the shop during normal business hours. Manon never remembered such a thing. But he'd looked distracted, truly distraught, when he left on whatever errand had taken him away. He had not even thought to ask her to remain behind the counter to answer customers' inquiries. Surely they were not going to cut the Great Mogul. No, she could not believe Papa would do such a thing. As for minding the shop, he had made his wishes quite clear on Sunday. She was to remain in her room and bring no more shame upon his name.

Papa, however, was not here, and for the moment neither was the Widow Tremont. Manon went into the shop and raised the blind that Papa had lowered over the front window to signal that the shop was closed. Plenty of passersby on the street outside, but no sign of Joyful. There was no reason to expect him. At this hour, if he were not detained by urgent business, he would be looking for her at the market.

What if he had managed to get to the market Monday and Tuesday and again today, and not found her come to meet him even once? Would he think that she had tired of waiting for his fortunes to change and planned to accept Monsieur DeFane's nephew? Joyful might be at the market this very minute. Dare she go and try and find him? Impossible. The Widow Tremont had the eyes of an eagle, and another quarrel with Papa might bring still more harrowing results. He would send her away, perhaps. There was said to be a great aunt in Providence . . . She could not slip out once Adele Tremont returned. She had here a golden opportunity and she was wasting it.

The boy who worked at Devrey's Pharmacy! Joyful had said she could trust him with messages at any time. It was not far to Hanover Square; she could be there and back in ten minutes. And if the boy wasn't there? Well, she'd be no worse off than she was right now.

Manon ran behind Papa's counter and found the little stub of pencil he had been guarding for weeks now—imported from England, pencils, like so many other things, were in short supply since the war and the blockade—and one of the scraps of paper on which he recorded customer orders. She would write the note on the way.

Chapter Nineteen

New York City,
Mill Street, 1 P.M.

JOYFUL HAD NO real reason to try the dovecote. Manon had said, *This week I will be at the Fly Market every day at noon. Come when you can.* But he'd gone to the Fly every day since and there was no sign of her. He'd managed to speak to Elsie Gruning today, and according to her some other woman was shopping for the Vionne household. Had she gone off with that widower from Virginia? Impossible. Even if the man had managed to get here, even if Manon accepted him, nothing would be arranged so quickly. Perhaps he'd somehow misunderstood, or Manon had somehow misremembered. The dovecote was the second most likely rendezvous.

It was going on one o'clock; he'd been here half an hour and still no sign of her. Joyful was about to leave when he saw three men coming up the hill from Peck's Slip. They were sufficiently deep in conversation not yet to have spied him, but he recognized the man in the center as Maurice Vionne.

There was one narrow house between the garden with the dovecote and the entrance to the Jews' synagogue. He ducked into its shadowy doorway and waited. The three men walked right by him without turning their heads, close enough so he caught a snatch of conversation: " . . . circumstances, it seemed this was the safest place." He knew the man speaking. Samson Simson, the lawyer. And the third? He couldn't be sure, but he'd wager it was Mordecai Frank, the Hebrew goldsmith. So—the trio Manon described as meeting in her father's shop and poring over the book that described the Great Mogul diamond.

The men had paused just outside the entrance to the synagogue a few feet from where Joyful had hidden. "I will wait out here," he heard Vionne say. "You two go."

Frank and Simson climbed the steps and disappeared inside. Vionne looked up and down the street. Once or twice he took out his watch and examined it. He walked to the corner and peered down the hill toward the waterfront. He did not, thank God, look in any doorways.

Joyful thought of approaching him. *I love your daughter. I want to marry her. What have you done with her? Is she well?* And what would Vionne say? Well, for a start he might ask how Joyful intended to support a wife.

Mordecai Frank came out of the synagogue and rejoined Vionne five minutes later.

"You have it?"

"Right here." Frank passed over what appeared to be a sheaf of documents.

"And the other set?"

"Inside, in a place no one would think to look. You can rely on that."

"I'm sure." Vionne did not examine the papers, only tucked them in the inside pocket of his cutaway. Then: "Mr. Frank, you're sure we're doing the right thing?"

"I'm . . . Yes, Mr. Vionne, I'm sure."

The hesitation made it sound doubtful, but Vionne accepted the statement. "Very well. I am also sure."

Frank put his hand on Vionne's arm. "You are rising to the challenge, sir. Magnificently."

"I pray God that is so." Another glance at his watch. "We must go. We are to meet Blakeman at half two."

The men set off together. Joyful watched until they turned the corner and were out of sight. Easy enough to follow them, but what point? He knew they were to meet with Gornt Blakeman. He knew that they were bringing him an authentification of the diamond: the statement of two highly respected New York jewelers that the gem was indeed the legendary Great Mogul and that it would be a remarkable addition to the crown jewels of the Holy Roman emperor, Francis II, king of Bohemia and Hungary, emperor of Austria. The role of Manon's father and the other smith in Blakeman's scheme was one reason he'd been so anxious to see her today. At least he could relieve her mind of the worry that the two men meant to try cutting the stone.

The question then was whether following Maurice Vionne and Mordecai Frank would take him to Manon. Unlikely in the extreme. As far as Vionne knew, his daughter had no part in this business. For Joyful, Maurice Vionne and Mordecai Frank were known quantities. So was Blakeman, for that matter. The person whose role in all this was not clear was Samson Simson.

Joyful waited until the pair of goldsmiths were out of sight, then he left the doorway and headed for the synagogue. Halfway up the steps he started to remove his hat, then remembered and kept it on.

"This is a house of worship, sir. If you wish to speak to me on a matter of law, I suggest—"

"I assure you, I mean no disrespect to your beliefs or your synagogue." Joyful had found Simson in the sanctuary, sitting on a red velvet bench beside a pair of tall white wooden doors above which a lantern

flickered. Sun poured through windows made of yellow glass, the dia-
mond-shaped panes separated by delicate leading. The whole room was
flushed gold. "Mr. Simson, you do not know me, but I am—"

"Your reputation precedes you, Dr. Turner."

"Very well. Then you know I am one-quarter Jew, along with whatever else."

"We do not claim you, sir." Simson rose.

He sounded tired, Joyful thought. "My grandfather—"

"The notorious Solomon DaSilva," Simson interrupted. "Yes, I
know. But according to *halacha*, our law, you are a Jew only if your
mother was. Now please, we must step outside."

He led the way past a raised central platform draped in red damask
with silver fringe, surrounded by a burnished mahogany railing with
exquisitely turned spindles painted gleaming white. The dais was
flanked by unlit candles in tall brass candlesticks.

Simson paused with his hand on the door to the vestibule and
looked back as if admiring the setting, as if he'd never seen the place
before. "That tablet above the *hehal*." The lawyer nodded toward the
pair of doors.

"*Hehal?*"

"The Ark of the Covenant, Doctor. It contains our holy scrolls. The
tablet above it was carved in 1730."

"And it says?"

"Words much older. The ten commandments. You see the brass
urns either side? Beautiful, aren't they?"

They were placed too high for Joyful to appreciate more than their
shape. "Very graceful."

"Yes, I think so too. They were made in the thirteenth century.
Taken from Iberia by our people when, after over a thousand years, the
Inquisition turned them first out of Spain, then Portugal. Your ancestors among them, no doubt, Dr. Turner. Mine, on the other hand,
came from Frankfurt and from Holland. But no matter, we Jews have
been wandering almost since the Holy One put us on this earth."

"Do you wander still, Mr. Simson? Do you not feel rooted here, in

New York, in these United States? This synagogue seems to me to be unmolested. 'Congress shall make no law concerning religion—"

"—or prohibit the free exercise of it.' I assure you I applaud the sentiments of the Constitution, doctor. But we were talking about the urns. Pity you can't see the etching from here. Almond blossoms. The Book of Numbers says, 'The rod of Aaron for the house of Levi was budded, and put forth buds, and bloomed blossoms and bore ripe almonds.' Hence the learned rabbis tell us only a freshly budded almond branch might be placed beside the *hehal*. Not something easy to come by in New York. So the urns are empty. As you see them."

"Beautiful and unmolested," Joyful repeated. "Here in the United States."

"For now. Thanks be to the Holy One."

Simson opened the door and Joyful followed him out of the sanctuary. "Mr. Simson," he began.

"Yes, Dr. Turner?"

"I was told that something that belonged to my father"—he hesitated—"something he'd hidden for me to find . . ." No way to say it except directly. "I was told the Jews had it."

"I see. May I ask by whom?"

"You may ask, Mr. Simson, but I may not answer. Anyway, it has no bearing on the issue."

The lawyer shrugged. "Perhaps not. People say all kinds of things about us, after all. Look around, Dr. Turner. Do you see whatever it is that belonged to your father? Or any little Christian children for that matter? So we may ritually slaughter them and drink their blood."

"I didn't mean—"

"No, I know you didn't."

"I thought you might have heard the story, and could shed some light on the mystery."

"I'm afraid I know nothing of your father, Dr. Turner, other than that he was a great patriot. Like yourself."

"And you, Mr. Simson? Are you also a patriot?"

"I hope so, Doctor. In my fashion."

He had expected one goldsmith, not two, but Blakeman received them both in the small office to the rear of the countinghouse. "A matter of such weight," Vionne murmured. "I felt I must have another opinion."

"Perfectly understandable. Please, gentlemen, sit down. It's a warm afternoon; a glass of ale might be welcome."

Blakeman lifted the pitcher, realized there were only two glasses on the table, and served his guests. He rang a small handbell that summoned Vinegar Clifford and sent him for a third. As far as Vionne could see, the three of them plus the whipper were the only people in the place.

"I sent the clerks home early. So much discontent on the street, all this talk of invasion . . . Naturally, they were concerned for their families."

"Very kind of you," Vionne said. "Very thoughtful."

"Besides, our business is no one's affair but our own, gentlemen. At least not yet."

The whipper delivered the extra glass. Blakeman filled and lifted it. "A toast, gentlemen." He looked from one to the other. "I give you the jewel of the ages."

Vionne's hand trembled when he lifted his glass. This was an entirely different man from the one he'd met on two previous occasions.

"Now"—Blakeman refilled their glasses as he spoke, emptying the pitcher and ringing his bell to summon another—"you have something for me."

Vionne waited until the whipper had come and gone, carrying away the pitcher to be refilled, then withdrew the sheaf of papers from the pocket inside his cutaway and passed them over. Blakeman took them eagerly. His hand was trembling as well, Vionne noted. "Unsealed, as you requested," he murmured.

"Exactly. I will affix a seal before . . ." Blakeman was running his eye down the page as he spoke. Most of what was written was highly specialized. Just so. You go to experts and invariably they spoke in gibberish only other experts understood. *The stone is 189.62 metric carats and measures 47.6 mm in height, 31.75 mm in width, and 34.92 mm in length . . . outstanding clarity . . . a slight bluish-green tint . . . half a pigeon's egg . . . concentrated rows of triangular facets . . . corresponding four-sided facets on the lower surface. A slight indentation one side.* He turned the last page. "Gentlemen, unless I am mistaken, there is no mention of the diamond's name."

Mordecai Frank spoke for the first time. "One cannot be entirely sure of—"

"I do not care if Vionne seeks your opinion, sir. But if I thought you had authority to countermand his, I'd have gone to you in the first place."

"No, no, Mr. Blakeman." Vionne leaned forward, tapping the papers that Blakeman had laid down. "I take full responsibility—"

"Six days ago you showed me the description of the Great Mogul and said the stone in my possession was that diamond. Now you quibble."

Vionne damned himself as a fool. He should never have given so much away. "No sir, I do not quibble. I merely tell you that based upon a description in a very old book, and one brief opportunity to examine a stone, which I grant you is truly remarkable, I cannot say with certainty that they are the same."

"You were certain enough before." Blakeman spoke to Vionne, but he looked at Mordecai Frank. "So, are the Jews better at judging the world's riches then a Huguenot? More practice perhaps?"

"I do not think it is a matter of religious belief," Frank said quietly.

"Is it not?" Blakeman stood up. Part of him wanted to march the Jew upstairs and show him the stone. Though he knew that was both unwise and unnecessary. It was Vionne's word he'd promised Astor. "Well, my religion tells me I've spent enough time breathing Hebrew . . ." He almost said "stink," but stopped himself. There weren't that many Jews in the town, but he would rather have those there were on his side than against him. "I have private business to discuss with Vionne, here," he said instead. "You'll excuse us, Mr. Frank."

The smiths exchanged a quick glance. Vionne nodded. Frank stood up and followed Blakeman to the door. "One of our guests is leaving, Mr. Clifford. See him out."

The flagrant rudeness was as revealing as the brazen character of the meeting. Something had changed since their first encounter. Vionne waited to see what it was.

Blakeman turned back to him. "The matter of your daughter," he said.

Ah, yes, Manon. Vionne's expression gave nothing away but he could not prevent the perspiration from beading on his forehead. "It is warm today, as you said." He fished a handkerchief from his pocket and mopped his face.

"Your daughter," Blakeman repeated. "Have you spoken to her?"

"Not yet. I do not think . . . To be honest with you, sir, I do not believe my daughter will agree." Vionne tried hard not to look to the closed door, beyond which, he knew, waited the man with the bullwhip.

Blakeman chuckled. "Mr. Clifford unnerves you, does he? Good, that's what he's meant to do. Here, have another ale. And stop sweating. I do not mean to have you flogged into compliance. I have asked for your daughter's hand, sir. I deserve an answer."

"I told you, Mr. Blakeman, my Manon is very strong-minded, and it was her mother's dying wish that I not force her into a marriage against her will." Forgive me, dearest. *Marry her off the minute I'm gone, Maurice, as soon as is decent. She'll rule you otherwise.* You would not have approved this match either.

"Come, Mr. Vionne. We are men of the world." The goldsmith's glass was still full, but Blakeman poured himself more ale. "We know that women, like children, need a firm hand. And all things considered . . ." He drank, watching Vionne over the rim of the glass, then put it down and wiped his mouth. "All things considered, surely your daughter could do a great deal worse."

The papers lay on the table between them. Vionne nodded in their direction. "I will try to persuade Manon. Meanwhile, perhaps you would like me to take those back and see if they can be made more satisfactory for your purposes."

Blakeman's big hand settled on the documents before Vionne could touch them. "Not required, Mr. Vionne. A diamond the size of half a pigeon's egg. And . . . what do you say here . . . just under 190 carats. Not too many of those knocking about, I expect. What you've written will do."

Vionne was sweating again. He swiped at his face a second time. "I'm delighted to hear it." He hadn't really expected to be allowed to stall longer. And what difference could it make when he didn't know how long was enough?

Blakeman leaned forward. "I'm sure you would prefer to have your daughter the wife of the most powerful man in a new . . . in New York." No point in saying too much. The meeting was set for Hartford in October. Far too distant from his point of view, but the others were more cautious. New Hampshire had argued for the delay; time to bring the citizenry along. "I'm sure you would prefer that. And so would your lovely daughter."

"Prefer it to what?" Vionne asked. "Do I detect a threat in your words?"

"Why should I threaten you, Mr. Vionne? I wish you to be my father-in-law." Blakeman stood up.

So I am dismissed, the goldsmith thought. And he has now papers which say that in his possession is a true diamond that, whatever else it may be, is the largest anyone has ever seen. Dear God, why wasn't I courageous enough to take Simson's advice? The lawyer had suggested they raise doubts about the genuineness of the stone, as well as refuse to certify its provenance, but Vionne said that might be too dangerous. *You have not looked into his eyes. He is a man who will stop at nothing, gentlemen.* Frank had come up with the compromise. One set of papers written for posterity that said what they truly thought: that Maurice Vionne had been privileged to look at the most mysterious diamond in the world, the Great Mogul, and another that said only that it was a very large jewel.

And what had they accomplished? Nothing from the look of it. After his initial dissatisfaction Blakeman seemed content. He carefully tucked the documents into the inside pocket of his coat, picked up the handbell, and rang it impatiently. "Mr. Clifford will see you out, Mr. Vionne. And I shall call in a day or two to bring that other matter to final agreement."

Walking helped Joyful think. Two hours since he left the synagogue, and he'd gone straight up the East River shore, past one dock after another, pacing the spine of New York's outreach to the world. At least that's what the riverfront had been when there was no blockade. Not now, and no way to say how much longer the war would go on. So what in Hades did he think he was doing?

Getting Jacob Astor on his side was not a small thing. Yes, but what about the offer he thought Geoffrey Colden made? Had he done so, or was Joyful imagining it? If there was a place for him in the tontine, could he become one of the money men?

What an opportunity. Not to be simply a Canton trader, bringing goods to New York and selling them for whatever the market would consent to pay, but to be one of the men who made the market, set the bedrock values of everything that was important to the economy. He remembered the commodities Colden had ticked off: houses, ships, slaves . . . Being in any way responsible for people being bought and sold like cattle made his gorge rise.

Still . . . Jefferson, Franklin, and a few of the others had strong abolitionist leanings when they were involved with writing both the Declaration and the Constitution. But they knew they didn't have the votes, so they compromised—took three-quarters of the loaf rather than give up the whole thing. He wouldn't have to go even that far. Ninety percent of what the Tontine did was perfectly fine. Good for the country, in fact, creating economic stability rather than the chaos of the old system.

Fair enough, but first there had to be a country. His country, the United States, not some amputation such as Gornt Blakeman and his cohorts had in mind. Trouble was, they were picking up converts daily.

Astor is with us. It was an idea bound to appeal to butchers. Cut the heart out and think it could survive on its own. He knew better. The whole body had to be intact for it to be healthy.

But Blakeman was only part of the problem. If this present crisis were averted, and if Colden really had been offering him a place in the upstairs room, he still needed Devrey Shipping out of debt and turning a profit. The company had to be glorious again, queen of the seven seas the way it was when his Devrey ancestor ruled an empire from his Wall Street house. The money men wouldn't let Joyful Turner into the Tontine because he was clever at bezique. It would cost a king's ransom to deal himself into their game. Hell, he needed a thriving Devrey Shipping and whatever his father's treasure might yield. Providing he could find it.

That's what had brought him to the slip at the foot of Rutgers Street. The sloop *Lisbetta* lay at anchor just beyond the dock of Parker's Shipyard. Parker's was where Devrey ships usually went for a refit, but *Lisbetta* was not here because she needed work. Bastard had her sailed upriver and moored where she was as surety against debts for past work. And a fine warrant she was. Even with all sails furled, the sloop was beautiful. Her hull was sleek and black and narrow, extended by a rapierlike bowsprit that nearly doubled her length. That and a tall single mast would allow her to spread a formidable array of canvas. Under sail, with a fair wind, *Lisbetta* would be as fast as a schooner or a brigantine, and twice as nimble. Little wonder sloops were the preferred craft of pirates.

It was because of a chance meeting with Danny Parker a few weeks before that Joyful had known to ask Bastard Devrey for the *Lisbetta*. Danny had inherited the shipyard from his father two years earlier, but shortly before Joyful first went to sea, he had been well served by Joyful's skills. A carbuncle on his left foot was giving him no end of gyp, nearly crippling him, before Joyful sawed it off. Not many had the stomach to endure the lengthy agony of having a carbuncle removed, and fewer survived without the wound festering, causing the whole foot and eventually the entire leg to turn black. Most suffered only to be killed by the cure, but not Danny Parker, because he was as tough as any man alive and because Joyful was the town's most skilled surgeon. Always, of course, after Andrew.

Danny was in the small shed that served as his countinghouse, standing at a tall desk, bent over his ledgers. "Not much comfort to be had from the accounts these days," Joyful said. "Leastwise, I don't imagine so, given what the war is doing to business."

"True enough." Parker neither lifted his head nor turned around. "But I'm not prepared to give up on the country yet, and I wouldn't have expected you to be, Dr. Turner, seeing as how you fought with Commodore Perry."

"Who said anything about giving up on the country?"

Parker turned and faced his visitor. "Isn't that what you're here about? They tell me you're taking your leisure at the Tontine these days. There's even a rumor going round that you've made peace with your cousin, that you and Bastard are to be partners, so . . . You take my meaning."

"Sorry, but I don't take it." Joyful held up his stuffed glove. "I gave the British my left hand, Danny. I do not intend to give them my country as well. Who told you I did?"

Parker shrugged. "Can't say anyone told me. Not exactly. I just assumed that to be the case."

"Listen, you're walking around on your two good feet thanks to me. I think you owe me an explanation before accusing me of treachery, if not treason."

The shipwright turned and looked out the window. As near as Joyful could see, they were entirely alone, but Parker spoke in a whisper. "There's talk of a showdown to come, an army being formed to take the town, and sooner rather than later. Most of us mechanics have been approached to throw our lot in with them as well. Leastwise that's the word in Tammany and in the taverns. We're either with Mr. Madison and his pointless war as is taking the food out of our mouths, they say, or we're with them."

"Have they convinced you, Danny? Are you for breaking up the Union?"

"I never claimed to be clever about anything except seafaring and ships"—Parker nodded toward his ledgers—"but some as ask can't easily be refused."

"A good many things aren't easy. Doesn't mean they're not worth doing. You said you'd been approached. By whom, and—"

Parker was looking over Joyful's shoulder to the path beyond the shed. "Turn around and you can ask 'em yourself."

Joyful swung around to face the door. Bastard was heading toward them, along with an old tar limping along on a wooden leg. Joyful lusted to confront his cousin, but there was a quiet voice telling him now was not the time. "It's not a conversation I choose to have at the moment, Danny. Might there be somewhere . . ."

Parker hesitated, looking hard at the man he'd once trusted with his life. Finally, he nodded toward a long and narrow cupboard door. "There's mostly brooms and the like. You can wedge yourself alongside. I'll head 'em over to another part of the yard."

Joyful hid himself. He heard Danny leave, then waited a while. Finally he crept out of the cupboard and peered cautiously out the window. The shipwright stood with Bastard and his underling across the yard. They were too far away for Joyful to hear what they were saying, but it occurred to him that, given the wooden leg of the man with Bastard, he might be Finbar's Peggety Jack, the man he met up at Henry Astor's Bull's Head Tavern.

He waited until the men were looking at something Danny was pointing out on a half-finished keel that looked as if it hadn't been worked on in months, then slipped outside and took up a well hidden position near the gate. From there it would be a simple matter to follow Bastard and the tar when they left.

The Federal District, 3:30 P.M.

"You must leave now, Mrs. Madison. The president requests it."

"You've seen my husband? Where is he?"

The marksman's buckskins were covered in dust, and the hat he held under his arm had two bullet holes through the crown. "We saw him not more'n a quarter hour past, ma'am." He jerked his head in the direction of the surveyor, who stood off to the side, saying nothing. The marksman knew why; the gall of it was a bitterness on both their tongues. The first two lines of the American defense had collapsed in minutes and having no instructions as to where to re-form, they scattered into the woods. Only the third line was holding. They could still hear the boom of the big guns the American sailors had dragged into position across the approach road to the District. "He's with our forces, ma'am. Gives 'em a good deal of courage seeing the president there." But not enough to stop them from cutting and running in the face of that relentless red tide.

"He is well?"

"Well and unhurt, Mrs. Madison. But very worried for you. That's why he sent us, to say you must leave at once."

"Thank you both for coming. I shall do so as soon as I— Oh, John, is it done?"

"It all be done, madame. The drawing room curtains be packed and on the last wagon. What with the silver and the dishes and such, that be all what can fit. I sent them on their way. Everybody else be gone too. Just you and me be left. I got the little trap all hitched up and waiting."

"Excellent. These gentleman have come to say that Mr. Madison is also well, praise the Lord, and that he bids us leave. Which of course we must do as soon as—"

"Mrs. Madison"—John looked straight at her, ignoring the two strangers—"s'cuse me, but . . . You be quite sure? There's still time to—"

"Quite sure. We will speak no more of it." French John wanted to lay a concealed train of powder to the front door, and rig a trap devised to blow up the British as soon as they tried to enter the house. "It is out of the question. Even in war, there are things civilized people do not do." She recognized his disappointment, but there was no time to deal with it. Dolley turned to face the two callers. "There is one more thing before we can go, gentlemen. We must take President Washington's portrait from the wall."

The surveyor took a step forward and put his hand on the frame. "It's screwed in place, madam. I'm afraid there isn't enough time to—"

"I refuse to leave General Washington here to be abused by the enemy. The painting is by Mr. Gilbert Stuart. It is my husband's favorite, though he says that in life the president was considerably taller, and I believe I remember him so as well. John, go and find a tool to loose the screws."

The surveyor glanced at the picture—Washington in black-velvet coat and breeches, standing beside a table laden with books meant to be the Declaration and the Constitution—then strode to the front door and threw it open. "I respectfully bid you to listen, madam."

They all listened. The navy's guns had gone quiet.

"Silence, madam. The battle has ended."

"Perhaps our troops have—"

"As God is my witness, madam. There is no such likelihood."

The marksman looked at the cannon down by the gate. "Those guns, ma'am. Might be a good idea to—"

"I be spiking those guns half an hour past," John said. "Soon as them guards meant to shoot 'em left."

"Well done. Now, ma'am, you have no choice but to leave at once. I'm sure if Mr. Madison were here, he'd insist."

"In one moment, sir. I promise. John, please break the frame and remove President Washington's portrait. Perhaps you two gentleman can help with that."

French John swung the hammer. The marksman cut the canvas free and rolled it tight. He offered it to the president's wife, but she shook her head. "You gentleman said you are from New York?"

"Yes, ma'am."

"And are you returning there?"

"We are, ma'am. Just as soon as we see you and your man here on your way."

"Then I bid you take it with you for safekeeping. I have always heard that New Yorkers were among the bravest and most loyal of our citizens."

Bladensburg, Maryland, 4 P.M.

The first two lines of defense had been short work for the redcoats. Without proper training or skilled officers, the troops—mostly civilian militia—scattered and ran before the advance. The third was different. The naval guns tore up the British lines while the D.C. militia poured in effective fire. Then, for some unfathomable reason, an American officer gave the order to retire. The troops weren't well enough drilled to do it properly, and the retreat turned into a rout. There was cavalry in reserve, but not experienced enough to gallop headlong into enemy fire.

It was over. The Pike was open and Washington was a handful of miles away.

The general gave his men two hours' rest, then he and the admiral led the third brigade forward in the evening dusk. That brigade had reached the battlefield too late to fire a shot; they smelled blood and craved a fight. For a time it appeared they might get one.

Three hundred patriots had gathered at the house belonging to the secretary of the treasury. They fired as soon as they saw the braid and plumes of the officers' hats. The admiral's horse was shot out from under him, but he was unhurt and another mount was soon made available. The redcoats formed up and returned fire. Within minutes the Americans scattered. The general gave the order to put the house to the torch. "And when you're done here, burn all the public buildings."

"The mansion as well, sir?" There was enough light left to see the white house sitting proudly on a slight rise, the heart of the carefully laid-out town.

"No, not the mansion. I shall deal with it personally." Then, to the admiral, "Shall we go, sir?"

"Lead the way, General."

Those residents of the town who had not fled, mostly servants and laborers, stood on the streets watching the progress of the conquerors. They were not molested, but the admiral made a point of inquiring as to where he might find the president of this little country. "Might he be at home, up there in that house on the hill? We wish to present our compliments."

Meanwhile a series of loud explosions announced that the retreating Americans had blown something up lest it fall into enemy hands. "I believe there's a navy yard a few miles up the east branch of the river. With two ships under construction." the general said. "That'll be it."

The burning Navy Yard and the burning city formed a point-counterpoint of flames shooting into the sky, holding off the encroaching dark. "Better than a fireworks display," the admiral chortled. Then, to the silent onlookers: "Rather like a party, isn't it? Perhaps we may have a ball a bit later on."

The door to the Executive Mansion was unlocked. The soldiers entered with fixed bayonets, in case some defenders remained behind for the purpose of engaging them in hand-to-hand combat. The place was empty. Someone commented that it was a bit of a mess. "No reflection on Mrs. Madison's housekeeping," the general said. "She had to leave in rather a hurry."

"Took a few things with her." The admiral had made a quick inspection of the ground floor. "The plate all seems to be gone, and there are no curtains in the drawing room. But there's a cold supper laid in the dining room, General. Fancy something to eat?"

French John had continued to lay the table every mealtime. There was a dish of ham and another of chicken, and a third with a mix of niblets of corn and shelled broad beans, both fresh from the garden behind the house. "Not bad," the admiral said, sniffing the contents of a decanter of wine. "A toast, General. I give you success."

They drank and ate, not from hunger but for the principle of the thing. When they rose, the admiral tipped over the table and all its contents and summoned a young soldier to set the first of many fires within the house.

The Federal District burned with such ferocity that the surveyor and the marksman could see the glow in the night sky, though by then they were many miles north, riding hard, on their way to report to Mr. Astor.

Chapter Twenty

New York City,
Holy Hannah's Shack in the Woods, 9 P.M.

"HE SAID THAT THE Jews had a treasure belonging to his father," Samson Simson whispered. "Where would he get such an idea, if not from you?"

"Don't hardly know him," Hannah said. "Likes o' him don't discuss his private business with the likes o' me."

The likes of what she'd become at any rate, Simson thought, though she'd once claimed a social station as high or higher than that of Joyful Turner.

No candle burned inside the shack, much less an oil lamp, but what remained of the evening light came in through the chinks in the walls. It was enough for him to see the utter poverty of the hovel. "Holy heaven, how can you live like . . ." He glanced over to where a boy lay on a pile of rags, propped up on his elbow, listening to every word. "Come outside," he told her. "Now."

Hannah got to her feet, conscious that Will was watching her. "Not to worry," she told him. "This gentleman's kin."

"He know anything about Jesse?" Will asked. The other boy had not returned from his day's work in the town, though Devrey's was long since locked and shuttered.

"Not likely," Hannah admitted. "But never you mind, he's a tough one, our little one-winged pigeon. He'll be back. You'll see. Go to sleep, boy. This be Hannah's business."

Cousin Samson was waiting for her by the cistern. She'd known he wouldn't simply go away. Stubborn as mules, all the Simsons, herself included.

"Come away from there," she said. "Mosquitoes will eat you alive." Hannah had lived with the cistern long enough to know that every few days waves of the tiny insects rose from the standing water and set about feeding on any human they could find. She'd have done away with the thing if it were possible.

Simson joined her near the chestnut tree, where Hannah had arranged stones and a plank to form a bench. "Good things, chestnut trees," she said. "Food, shade, shelter. Can't ask for more."

"You could have all that, and in much better form than you have it here, Cousin Hannah. In the Lord's name, why don't you come home?"

"This is my home. Don't got no other."

"You have. You could live with me. I've never married, you know, and I could use a housekeeper, and since we're blood kin—" He broke off, looking at her in the light of a rising moon: the wild hair, the eyes that glittered that strange, piercing blue. Cousins or not, it was an insane idea. They said she was mad. It might well be true.

"No home," she repeated. "Never again since they turned me out. You should know."

He did. The story still made him shiver. "They're dead and gone, Hannah. It's time to forget and forgive. You quote the holy books. 'Ye are my brethren . . . Ye are my bone and my flesh.' You know."

"Book o' Samuel," she said. "I know. But why didn't they forgive?"

She turned and spat on the ground. "They made *shiva* for me. They tore their clothes and ate *seudat havra'ah*—"

"A meal of consolation," Simson whispered, "but they could not be consoled." Lentils and eggs, round things to indicate that life was a circle, that it went on, even after loss. Traditionally prepared by friends for those who mourned their dead; in this case, for a living daughter whom her parents had declared dead to them. No wonder her mother died less than two years later and her father soon after that.

"For seven days they sat close to the ground." Hannah spoke the words in a low singsong, a litany of grievance she had nurtured for almost thirty years. "Seven days they did not wash their faces and my mother did not comb her hair, or use her Number Seven Cologne from Devrey's Pharmacy, and they burned my *shiva* candle, and—"

"Your parents were particularly observant, Hannah. Others in the family have married out and still been accepted."

"Never got a chance to marry," she said. "They saw to that."

He'd been seven, maybe eight, when the scandal broke. But he remembered all the talk, the conversations that ended when any of the children came into a room. "He was lost at sea, wasn't he? Your captain."

"Harmonious Grant, his name was, and I was s'posed to be with him on that last voyage. We were going to sea together, to faraway lands and places more beautiful than ever I could imagine. That's what he said. More beautiful than I could dream. Only thing he ever saw as beautiful was me. That's what he said." Her voice was pitched so low Simson had to bend close to hear her. "We were going to find someone to marry us." She turned to him, her tone remorseful rather than bitter. "'Twas my idea Harmonious give the money to Rabbi Seixas. Do a *mitzvah*, I said, so we will be blessed. He didn't have the actual money left o' course. But he could find the same amount. Made him a rich man, the thrice-back treasure did. I told him giving *tzedaka*, charity, is a *mitzvah* and it calls down a blessing."

Not as it turned out. The elders of the Shearith Israel Synagogue had called her parents to account. "The stewards said it was blood money. That the family must make reparation for causing it to be brought into the synagogue." That was how Hannah's parents had discovered their seventeen-year-old daughter planned to elope with a man twenty years her senior, a sea captain, and not a Jew.

"Papa sent the constables to take me off the boat—the morning just 'fore she sailed, it was. We had one night together. Then Papa claimed me."

The story was too powerful a lesson of what happened to disobedient children to be suppressed. Hannah's parents had taken her as far as their front door, then locked it against her and entered into mourning for a daughter who was dead. A year later they put up a headstone for her in the synagogue's cemetery in Chatham Square. HANNAH SIMSON, DIED 1791. And all the while she was alive, begging for bread on street corners and doing Lord knew what to survive. But according to family legend, Hannah's father had given her the money Captain Grant had tried to give Rabbi Seixas. A fortune, even today. "Twenty thousand pounds," Samson said. "That's what they said your father gave you. Hannah, was it true?" How could it be true? Would she today be living like this? "Is that what Turner's talking about? Is that money his?"

Hannah shrugged. "Folks say all sorts o' things. Mostly lies. Our blood kin, they're no different from the rest. As for Joyful Patrick Turner, he's s'posed to find what's coming to him over the water. I told him so. The Holy One, blessed be His Name, gave me the message. Find what's coming over the water."

Greenwich Street, 10 P.M.

Joyful had shadowed Bastard and Peggety Jack from the moment they left Parker's Yard. At half nine the tar had peeled off and gone into a grog shop, and Bastard returned to his Wall Street house, took a bottle into his study, and looked set to remain there. It was not a particularly enlightening few hours. Joyful never got close enough to actually overhear a conversation, so he could not say for certain what his cousin and the flunky with him were doing as they went from shipyard to shipyard. He had a grim suspicion they were seeking recruits for Gornt Blakeman's cause, but he couldn't prove it. However, there was one thing sure: Bastard and Peggety Jack had apparently eaten their dinners before Joyful began following them. There was no pause for a meal while they made their rounds. Now he was bone-tired and hungry to boot.

He had no hope of getting something to eat at Ma Allard's. She served dinner at half three to those of her lodgers who were at home, and had the kitchen cleaned up and bolted by half four. Supper, always cold—biscuits and beer most often—was at nine, and no point looking for a crumb after quarter past. But there was usually a pie cart around the corner on Rector Street. The pieman sometimes stayed late, hoping for custom from two nearby taverns that served drink but no food.

Joyful found the pieman packing up and getting ready to push his cart home. "Am I too late then?"

"Too late for choice, Dr. Turner, sir. But if beef and turnip suits ye, I can oblige with the two I have left."

"I'm the one who's obliged. Thank you." He found a couple of coppers and handed them over, then ate the first pie in three quick bites, while he watched the man trundle his cart north, the wooden wheels clattering on the cobbles. Most probably, the fellow lived up in Five Points, but like so many of the laborers the town would be infinitely poorer without, he appeared when it was time to do his job and disappeared thereafter, and no one—including Joyful—worried about where he laid his head in the hours between.

He was considering stepping into the nearest tavern for a glass of beer to wash down the second pie when he heard his name called.

"Dr. Turner. It's me, Jesse Edwards."

"Hello. What are you doing out and about at this hour?"

"Got a message for you. The lady with the yellow hair gave it to me hours ago and said I mustn't give it to anyone but you yourself. I been everywhere lookin' for you since. In between doin' Mr. Jonathan's work, o' course."

Joyful snatched the note eagerly. "You saw her then? Miss Manon? Was she well?"

"The pretty one with the yellow hair as sent me the first time. Yes sir. Came to Devrey's lookin' for me. Midday it was, and near as I could tell, she was fine."

Joyful was nearly giddy with relief. The note seemed warm in his hand, a connection to her. He almost didn't want to read it. That she'd sent a message was a sweet truth; reading what she wrote might not be. Might be she had agreed to marry the widower from Virginia, and that's why he hadn't seen her for four days. "Good lad, Jesse. I'm obliged to you. Miss Manon will be as well." He tucked the pie under his arm, reached into his pocket, and found an English sixpence and two coppers. "Here you go."

Jesse looked down at the coins in his palm, grinned widely, then thought of the Bible stories Hannah told him and shook his head. "The lady said she'd no money with her, and I was to ask you for three coppers and you'd give them to me. I'd have come anyways, Dr. Turner. Be dead, I would, if it weren't for you. Here, have the sixpence back."

"Not a chance, Jesse. You've earned it." He retrieved the pie. It was squashed, and bits of turnip and beef and coagulated gravy squeezed out the edge. No matter, Jesse was eyeing the thing as if it were manna in the desert. "Have a bite of this as well." Joyful extended the pie in the boy's direction. "We can split it down the middle since we've two good hands between us. A bit of cooperation's all that's required."

Joyful was careful to see the boy got the bigger portion, and they ate in companionable silence until Jesse said, "Better'n ship's grub, ain't it, Dr. Turner?"

"Better than most ships' grub." The sort served to the crew as didn't eat in the officers' mess, certainly. "How are things at Hannah's? You folks getting enough to eat?"

"We manage right well. There's my wages and Will's, o' course. And sometimes I find somethin' and bring it home, and sometimes Will does. And Hannah forages in the town most days. That's what she calls it. Foragin'. Does it powerful fine."

"Not likely to bring back any rice, I suspect." He had intended to return with some before this, but trying to find out about Manon had delayed him. "How's Thumbless Wu faring?"

"Well enough, seems like. And he's been coming to talk to Mr. Jonathan every day since he left Hannah's."

"Whoa, Jesse. Are you saying Wu's not staying with you at Hannah's? Is he staying at Devrey's then?"

"No sir. Leastwise, I don't think so. Wu comes to the pharmacy every day, and he and Mr. Jonathan go upstairs and talk."

"But Jonathan doesn't speak Chinese."

"I know. I wondered 'bout that as well. The first day the other China man as came with Wu did most o' the talking. But since then Wu's come by himself."

"I see." Ah Wong. It could be no one else. "An interesting development, Jesse. I'm obliged to you for the information." How had Thumbless found Ah Wong?

Jesse hesitated, then spoke. "I know I wasn't much o' a powder monkey, Dr. Turner. Back on the *Lawrence,* I mean. But I don't think I'm as much a scaredy-cat these days."

"It's not cowardice to be afraid in wartime," Joyful put his hand on the boy's shoulder. "It's natural."

"Maybe. But I'm not afraid now. Next time Thumbless comes, I'll go upstairs after 'em, and listen to—"

"Absolutely not!" He thought of what Hannah had told him about Wu's knife. "I'd have thought Jonathan harmless enough, but Thumbless Wu . . . You're to do no such thing, Jesse. I forbid it."

Come after eleven. Safe then. Look for a basket beneath the window on the horse passage side. The note was scrawled in pencil in a shaky hand and signed only with her initials. Terse enough so if by chance it had gone astray it might intrigue, but not give them away.

Maiden Lane was dark except for two public lamps at opposite ends of the road. A third, meant to light the middle section, had gone out. The oil lamps were unreliable, as well as smoky. There had been talk a couple of years back of opening a gasworks and brightening the city streets with gas lamps, but war had set the project aside. Tonight Joyful was grateful for the delay.

The horse passage, a common amenity beside many of the city's closely built houses, was a narrow walkway leading to a small stable in the rear. Well beyond any light from the street, the alley was black as pitch. He'd have to run his good hand along the wall if he was to find the basket she'd mentioned.

The bricks were still warm from the day's heat and were covered in the moss that thrived here where so little sun shone. Joyful began slowly, afraid he might miss whatever it was she meant him to find, moving his good hand up and down as well as forward, taking small steps lest he stumble over some obstruction he could not see. Once a scuffling sound by his feet told him he'd disturbed some creatures who thought they owned the night. Rats probably. Eight years aboard ships, where they grew to the size of cats, had not made Joyful indifferent to rats. He shuddered. If all his plans succeeded, he would build Manon a house with enough room either side to discourage rats' nests. His fingers grazed something that could have been a rope. He pulled back, then told himself he was being a fool as well as a coward and grasped whatever it was.

Manon felt the tug, pushed aside the curtain, and jumped up, raising the lantern she'd lit earlier. She had spent the past hour sitting on the floor beneath her bedroom window, after she'd cracked it just enough to allow the cord attached to the small basket to hang free.

Joyful saw her framed in the window, illuminated by the lantern's flickering light. She shook her head to signal silence, but he knew better than to call her name. Manon jerked the cord up and down to direct his attention. He looked into the basket. There was enough light from the window to see a folded note. He took it and she hauled up the basket at once, then set down the lantern, and the alley was again dark. Moments later the glow of the lantern was restored, and Manon was leaning out above him. Tall as he was, their faces were only a few feet apart.

"Careful," Joyful whispered. "You'll fall."

"I won't. Besides, if I did, you would catch me."

"Without doubt," he said. "I will always catch you."

"I know."

"Manon, I've been so worried. Why didn't you come to—"

"It's all in my letter. Papa has confined me to the house because I wouldn't tell him where I was on Sunday. And he and Mr. Frank—"

"That's one of the things I wanted to tell you. They've no plans to cut the stone."

"You're sure?"

"Entirely. Listen," he pressed himself to the brick wall, taking off his hat and tipping his head back so he could see her better. "I've aligned myself with Jacob Astor. It's for the sake of the country, but it also means he won't oppose me as a trader, and the other morning, at the Tontine—"

His words were interrupted by the sound of a watchman's shrill whistle. Seventy-two men under the orders of a high constable named Jacob Hays silently prowled the town at night from 9 P.M. until sunrise. They traveled in pairs, and the whistle was sounded only if they caught a criminal in the act and required help from other watchmen nearby.

There was another blast of the whistle, followed by the sound of running feet. "They're close," Joyful said. "Quick, put out the lantern."

She did and they were plunged into darkness. They heard shouts, the sound of a scuffle, and soon silence. Whatever miscreant the watch had surprised had been taken into custody and would be marched off to the New Gaol to face justice in the morning. The incident would have the watchmen who remained in the area particularly alert. "You must go," Manon whispered.

"Yes, I know. When—"

"In my letter," she whispered. "Everything. Please, Joyful, go."

"You are always my love," he said, feeling her presence just above him in the black dark. "Always."

"And you are mine. Always mine."

Nonetheless, he called next at the Knave.

Thursday, August 25, 1814

Chapter Twenty-one

·

New York City,
the Dancing Knave, 1 A.M.

FROM THE FIRST it had been their custom to settle their accounts midweek. Delight had everything ready for him. "Mostly coin," she said as she handed over the moneybag with Joyful's four percent share of the Knave's earnings. "But I had to take some paper this past week. It was that or nothing at all."

"Paper's definitely better than nothing at all," Joyful said. He'd not asked for a formal accounting since the first few months of their arrangement, and he was convinced she had never cheated him. He didn't expect she ever would, despite how much else might change. "Listen," he said, "I might not be able to come myself for the next few weeks. I'll send someone to collect for me."

They were in the little ground-floor office. Delight was seated behind the small writing table; he stood in front of it. She'd turned up the oil lamp and looked especially lovely in the glow. Diamonds sparkled in her ears tonight, and she wore a blue gown the color of the sea. "Delight . . ."

"Yes?" She would not let him see her longing.

"I . . ." There was no way he could find the words to say it was over between them, not without wounding her. Best just let it lie, and die a natural death. "Nothing," he said. "I was thinking I'd send a lad next week. Has only one arm, so you'll have no difficulty knowing he's the one."

"None at all." She stood up. "Might I ask what's to keep you so engaged?"

"Business. The things I've been sorting these past few months are coming to a head."

Delight leaned over to shorten the lamp's wick and dim the light. The exquisite curve of her breasts was accented by the movement. She remained one of the most beautiful women Joyful had ever seen, and with him, one of the most giving. But he didn't love her, at least not the way he loved Manon. If he knew why, he'd go down in history as one of the great sages. *I am confined to my room, dearest, presumably until I am given to Gornt Blakeman or Monsieur DeFane's nephew.* He'd read the letter before he came. Now it was lodged next to his heart, in the same pocket with the papers giving him forty-nine percent ownership of Devrey Shipping.

Delight moved toward the door, careful not to brush against him. "I hope your business goes well, Joyful. Now, I must see to mine."

"Delight . . ."

"Yes?"

"Thank you. For everything."

She shrugged. "It has always been a mutually satisfactory arrangement, hasn't it, Joyful?"

"Indeed. But more than merely satisfactory."

"I'm glad to hear it. I always try to give full value for money. Now, you must excuse me."

"I didn't mean . . ."

He watched her go, her back rigid, her head high. Guilt was a foul taste in his mouth, and he slammed the office door behind him and strode through the hall looking neither to the right nor to the left. Preservation Shay saw him coming and pulled open the front door. Joyful went through it without a pause or a nod, not even for Bearded Agnes, who was hovering nearby looking as if she wanted to speak with him. The mare Mary Jane was tethered at the foot of the steps. He loosed her, then leapt onto her back and headed south, bent forward, giving the old horse her head and wishing mightily that she were a younger, more powerful animal, one that would give him a ride to cool his fires in a rush of wind.

Papa is determined I must marry, Manon had written. *And I expect one suitor is as good as another, as long as he appears in a timely fashion.*

Time he talked to the goldsmith. Hell, it was past time.

The New Gaol, 7:30 A.M.

It was not the usual way of things for the high constable himself to pass judgment on those caught in flagrante delicto during the previous night. For one thing, it was the job of a police justice, a new layer of officialdom in the system of controlling crime in the city, while the high constable was meant to sit at the pinnacle of that ever growing organization. For another, despite his reputation as a crime fighter, Jacob Hays disliked rising early. He was there that morning because there was no one else. Fear of a British invasion was intense. The mayor had ordered as many able-bodied men as were on the city's payroll to fell trees and build barricades in the upper reaches of Manhattan.

Hays sat at the table on the dais behind the wooden bar that divided judge from accused in the room they called the Police Office. He tried not to let his heavy eyes close. The gaoler marched a man forward, the fourth prisoner and the last of the morning. "This here's Patrick Aloysius Burney, High Constable. Or so he says."

Irish. Hays wasn't surprised. Two of the first three miscreants had been as well. Might be the city would be a Garden of Eden where the lamb would lie down with the lion if only the Irish had stayed in their own country. "What's he done then?"

"Caught loitering near Maiden Lane. Close to midnight, it was."

"And what's he say he was doin' there?"

"Won't say." The watchman who had made the arrest the night before jumped up from one of the benches in the rear of the room. Hays thought it odd that the fellow was hanging about the Police Office at this hour. Would have supposed he wanted his bed by now. "Would't say last night, High Constable," the man shouted, "and won't say now."

"I see. Thank ye for the information."

"It's not true." Burney spoke in his own defense, since there was no one else to do it. "'Twas after taking a walk, I was. And—"

Hays struck the desk with the gavel. "Speak when you're spoken to. Otherwise, I'll have no doubt you're guilty as charged."

Burney shut his mouth, gritting his teeth to keep it shut. Holy Mother o' God, wasn't it just his luck to draw the man was said to be harder on crime than any other in the city. Looked like some sort o' scrawny little bird sitting up there on his high perch. Hooked beak and all.

Some said Jacob Hays was a Protestant and others that he was a Hebrew, but didn't matter whether he was a heretic or a Christ killer, he had the power o' life and death over Patrick Aloysius Burney this day. Never mind that he'd done nothin' except try to keep an eye on Joyful Turner the way he was paid to. And while it was true enough that New York had given up public whipping a few years before, and that nowadays they mostly only executed you for murder or theft from a church, treason was still a hanging crime. All Five Points was bubbling with talk. Were you with Mr. Madison and the Union or with Gornt Blakeman? Any mention o' Blakeman might lead to a hangman's noose, and Brigid Clare would be twice an orphan. Not that a prison sentence was much better. Who would look after his little girl if they sent him up the river to Newgate Prison in the village of Greenwich to do hard labor for a year or maybe two?

"The prisoner had this on his person as well, High Constable." The watchman held up a small moneybag marked with a green cross.

"I never did! You're a lyin'—" The denial burst out of Burney at the same time that there was a disturbance of some sort at the door in the rear of the room. Hays banged the gavel and shouted at the bailiff to maintain order, demanding to know what the trouble was.

"Some fellows want to come in, High Constable. I told 'em we was already in session, but—"

"This is a free country and it's a public hearing," Hays said. "Let 'em in."

The watchman glanced back at the bailiff, then up front to the high constable's raised perch. "Beggin' your pardon, sir, don't you want to have done with this prisoner afore you—"

Jacob Hays had been doing police business twenty years. He knew there was no way to keep a force of nearly two hundred men entirely free of one sort of influence or another, but when the conniving was going on right under his nose, bloody cheek that was. Besides, he didn't like seeing a man as was maybe innocent made the butt o' the scheming to get a few pennies more than was in a copper's regular pay packet. Even if the man was Irish. False witness was an offense against the Holy One, blessed be His Name. "Let 'em in," he repeated.

"But—"

The gavel cracked again and the door was opened.

F. X. Gallagher didn't make any effort to hide his profession. A vicious-looking cleaver hung from his belt, his trousers and his cutaway were both stained with blood, and the three men with him wore the leather aprons of their trade. But all four respectfully removed their hats and stood quietly in the back of the room.

Hays spent a few moments looking at them, trying to determine the connection between F.X. and Patrick Burney, but none came to mind in regard to this particular incident. The high constable turned his attention back to the prisoner. "As I recall, you was saying that the watchman here had made a mistake. That the moneybag with the green cross wasn't yours?"

Patrick Burney saw danger in the front and possibly worse danger behind. Jesus Christ as his witness, he wasn't afraid o' any man alive, but he had the sense he'd become a cat's-paw in something he didn't understand, and that it involved men with a great deal more power than he had. And the real victim was likely to be his little girl, the saints have mercy on her. "I didn't have that moneybag, Mr. Hays, sir." His mouth was too dry to let words come easily. "Didn't have any money at all. And that's the truth."

"No, it's not," the watchman insisted. "Three coppers I found inside." He jiggled the bag so the coins clattered. "You can see for yourself, sir."

"Mr. High Constable," Gallagher called out, "I have vital information concerning the prisoner. May I speak?"

"Ah, Mr. F. X. Gallagher. I might have known you'd not have disturbed yourself so early in the morning if you didn't have something to tell us. Speak, sir. We're paying close attention."

"The bag belongs to one of my associates, here. In a manner of speaking. He had found it not long before, and knowing that the green cross was sometimes associated with criminal activity, he intended to give it to the first watchman he saw. Then this poor fellow was apprehended and to tell the truth, my associate was frightened—at least four of your bravest and biggest watchmen were involved, Mr. High Constable—so this wretch dropped the bag and ran." F.X. had his hand on the shoulder of one of the leather-aprons during this speech, and the man kept nodding his head in agreement with what was said.

"Dropped it, did he, Mr. F. X. Gallagher? With the three coppers still inside?"

The leather-apron nodded again. "Absolutely," F.X. said. "He's a churchgoing man. Wouldn't want no truck with money as might be stained with one sort o' crime or another."

Hays was leaning on his elbow and appeared to be trying hard to suppress a repeated series of yawns. "And Mr. Patrick Aloysius Burney, he's nothing to do with the moneybag or anything else not entirely honest?"

"Nothing at all, Mr. Hays. In fact, if you wish, sir, I'd be pleased to have Mr. Burney bound over to me. I can use more help in my butcher shop, and I'm sure he'd be happy to learn a trade as would let him earn an honest living."

Hays didn't move his head, but the watchman and the bailiff were well within his view. Do 'em good to be smacked down a time or two, so's whatever scheme they were using to earn a bit on the side didn't get to be more important than the work they were supposed to be doing for Jacob Hays. He banged down the gavel. "Done, Mr. F. X. Gallagher. And you're commended for being such a high-minded citizen o' the city."

"Don't look so worried, friend Patrick. You weren't relishing a stretch up the river on Amos Street, were you? The country air in the Village o' Greenwich agrees with some, they tell me, but I don't fancy it seems as pure when you're bustin' rocks in Newgate yard."

"Air in Five Points is good enough for me. I have to get home, Mr. Gallagher, sir. Me little girl is—"

"I know, Patrick. Me and the boys here, we know all about your little Brigid Clare. Keep a close eye on her, we do. And far as I'm concerned, you could go back to her this very minute. Except there's someone as wants to see you first."

One of the leather-aprons had a tight hold on Burney's arm and he steered him to the closed carriage parked a short distance away from the gaol's door. Another opened the carriage door, and the pair of them shoved Burney inside. F. X. Gallagher climbed in behind him.

"Good morning, Mr. Burney."

"Mr. Blakeman . . . Good morning to you, sir. I didn't know you and—" Burney broke off, looking from Gallagher to Blakeman.

"Of course you didn't know. Knowing is not what you're about, Mr. Burney. You are about doing as you are told. Watching and reporting what you see back to me. Is that not so?"

"Yes sir, Mr. Blakeman. And sure it's exactly what I've been doing."

"No, Mr. Burney, not exactly. I, for instance, had to learn from one of the other watchmen about last night's scuffle in Maiden Lane. Fortunately, he was among those who observed it. Otherwise, I might not have had that information in time to send Mr. Gallagher here to see that you were spared a spell in Newgate, leaving your poor little daughter completely alone. Unlikely she'd have been alive by the time you got out of prison, isn't it, Mr. Burney? Or if she were, that you'd ever have seen her again."

"That was me biggest fear, sir. Not for meself, the Blessed Mother bear witness. For me little girl."

"Indeed. So you'd have been forced to tell them what you knew, wouldn't you, Mr. Burney. Rather than be sent to prison, I mean."

"Sure there's nothing I *could* tell 'em, sir."

"You'd have tried though, wouldn't you, Mr. Burney? I was on Maiden Lane because Mr. Gornt Blakeman sent me there, and that's what drew your watchman to within spitting distance of the very lady I'm supposed to be helping Mr. Blakeman to protect. Something like that, Mr. Burney? If you thought it might have kept you from spending long months at hard labor in the Village of Greenwich?"

"No, sir, I never—" Burney couldn't stop himself from starting to shake, and his voice became hoarse with terror. "Mr. Blakeman, I swear it. I never told 'em nothing and I wouldn't have done. Never! I swear."

"We're going to see to it that you remember that vow, Mr. Burney. Nothing too drastic, mind. You're more use to me with both your arms and legs than you would be without. But you don't particularly need the little finger of your left hand. Do your job, Mr. Gallagher."

Gallagher took hold of Burney's hand, yanked it up, and pressed it to the wooden wall of the carriage. He swung his cleaver before Burney had expelled the breath of his first scream.

The light wasn't particularly good. Later F.X. told the others that was why he'd taken both the little finger and the one next to it. Turned them out of his pocket and threw them on the table to make the point.

The East River Docks, 10 A.M.

Whatever mischief Bastard and Peggety Jack had got up to yesterday had to be undone. Joyful retraced their route, but in reverse. The last yard they'd visited had been Walton's just above Peck's Slip; it was his first call.

Hiram Walton was a small man, long-nosed and narrow-jawed and with a squint in one eye. Looked like a ferret, but most said he was the finest shipwright in New York, though young Danny Parker was coming up close behind. "In the Revolution, weren't you?" Joyful and Walton stood at the end of Rose's Wharf, in full view of row upon row of naked masts, thrusting up from the ships the blockade had made prisoners.

"Aye. One o' the few as is still alive and in one piece."

"You were young when you served."

"Turned ten the day after I marched off. A fifer, I was, with the General himself."

"Washington believed in the Union," Joyful said. "I've no doubt about that, have you?"

The shipwright turned wary. "The Union as it was when he was alive, aye."

"Are you a married man, Mr. Walton?"

"I was. A widower these past thirteen years."

"But while your wife was alive, was it always a peaceful union? One in which you both agreed on everything?"

"Mrs. Walton did as she was told. Not like the young women nowadays."

The wrong tack apparently. "But do you not think—"

"Course, Mrs. Walton spoke her mind sometimes. Wouldn't be natural otherwise. And we had a palaver or two in our years. I'll tell you something." The little man leaned in close and grinned, showing three teeth stained bright yellow from constantly sucking on a pipe, and stabbed at Joyful's chest with a dirty finger. "Just between us menfolk, as it were. A woman who won't tell you what she thinks ain't worth havin'. Besides, ain't never a time when bed's better'n after a quarrel." Walton stepped back, cocked his head, and fixed his caller with his one good eye. "And none o' that's what you came here to talk about, Joyful Turner. It's Bastard Devrey's on your mind."

"In part," Joyful admitted. "I'm not denying, I've a personal stake in all this."

"Way I heard it, you're going about saying you're the owner o' Devrey's now."

"In a manner of speaking."

"But not Bastard's manner o' speaking. He says him and Gornt Blakeman together got scrip enough to squeeze you out."

"That's true."

"Well, you're honest. I'll say that for you."

"And if I prevail, Mr. Walton, what do you reckon I'll have won?"

The ferret turned and spat on the bleached boards of the wharf. "Have yourself a parcel o' debts. Till the British blockade's lifted and *China Princess* gets here from Canton, and them ships out there is all under sail"—he nodded toward the roads—"Devrey's ain't worth spit."

"I mean to have Devrey Shipping all the same," Joyful said. "And I'll wait out this war until we have an honorable peace, and everything you and the General and all the others fought for is safe. That's not what Gornt Blakeman intends. I expect you've heard that as well."

"A separate country," Walton said quietly. "Us and the New Englanders. Good for business that would be. Pull down the Stars 'n' Stripes, run a different flag up those masts and you can sail where you like." He looked at his yard. Only one half-built hull in the ways and one carpenter working on her. "Make a damn sight's difference to me, that would."

"To all of us," Joyful admitted.

Walton swung round and tipped back his head so he could meet Joyful's gaze straight on, despite the difference in their heights. "Truth is, I been thinking all night on what Bastard and Peggety Jack said when they came round here yesterday. Made up me mind 'fore you got here."

"To what, Mr. Walton?"

"'Tain't worth it. Not after all the blood as has been spilled. I'm with Mr. Madison and the Union. And I suppose, Joyful Turner, that means I'm with you."

It was a little after 1 P.M. when Joyful left Walton's, and nearly 4 when he returned to Danny Parker's yard up north by Rutgers Slip. "Been making the rounds, I hear," Danny said.

"How in the name of Hades can you know that?"

The other man laughed. "News follows the tide"—he nodded toward the river—"and she's running this way at the moment."

"And which way are you running, Danny Parker?"

"Same way I was yesterday. I'd have told you then if you'd asked me straight out. I don't hold with cut and run and every man for himself. Say we form this new country. What's going to happen if we fall out with Connecticut, or maybe Massachusetts? We going to splinter a second time and a third? I say argue out our differences and stay together. It's the only way."

"We hang together or we hang separately," Joyful said. "That's what Franklin said in '76."

"I expect he also said something about not blubbering every thought in your head soon as it arrived there."

"No doubt. I take it you're trying to tell me you didn't send Bastard packing."

"I'm not that stupid. I said I'd think about it. Same as all the rest."

The Astor Mansion, 5 P.M.

Gott in Himmel, why would a man want these strange, yellow-skinned creatures to wait on him? Henry Astor thought the same thing every time he came to the kitchen door of his brother's elaborate home, but he had yet to find the answer. Little Johann, they had called Jacob when he was a child; so small and ordinary on the outside, with such big ideas on the inside. While he—Heinrich he'd been then—was a big boy and later a big man, physically imposing, but content to work beside Papa in the butchering business in Waldorf, near Heidelberg. So when it came time for Papa to pick one of his sons to go to America as victualer to the Hessians hired to fight with the British in '76, Heinrich was the natural choice. Johann didn't come to New York until the war was over, but look how it was now. Heinrich lived in rooms above his Bowery tavern, while little Johann had become the great Jacob Astor, living in a palace with strange yellow servants.

The girl's feet were no bigger than his hand, tied into little silk shoes as might fit an infant. She saw him looking at them, and tottered off before he could tell her he wanted to see his brother. *Wie eigenartig das Leben,* life was strange.

He waited a few moments. The servant called Ah Wong came. Astor pointed to the large bundle of meat he had deposited on the big wooden kitchen table. "Good chops," he told the butler. "*Sehr gut.* Mutton. The best. And rump steak." The Chinese nodded his head and bowed repeatedly and kept smiling. "Don't be cutting it up into little pieces," Astor warned. "Not like last time."

"No little pieces," Ah Wong said. "No pieces. No pieces."

"*Ach du lieber Gott* . . . Everything twice you say. And I am never sure you understand. Now get my brother. Tell him I want him." And when the man didn't move, "My brother, China man. Your boss. My brother." Heinrich pointed to the floor at his feet. "Here you bring him."

Wong went to the door that led to the rest of the house and opened it, then bowed in Astor's direction. "Honorable brother come. Come. Come." He waved his hand in the direction of the hallway beyond the kitchen. "Ah Wong take honorable visitor to his honorable brother."

Heinrich shook his head, hooked a stool with one booted foot, drew it close to the table, and sat down. "I'll see him here. Go get him."

There was a cleaver tucked into the leather belt that held his old-fashioned jerkin in place and he reached for it. "Go on, you yellow devil!" Ah Wong ran from the room.

Soon enough Johann—he could no longer call him little Johann—came into the kitchen. "*Guten Tag*, Heinrich. A surprise you are. Ah Wong tells me you bring meat. *Danke*." He pulled another stool close to the table and sat down. "Cold beer, Ah Wong. At once."

Ah Wong brought the beer in large steins, the way it would have been served at home. They were so cold the outside was frosted, and the beer in them was *sehr gut*. The best. Like everything else in Johann's palace. Except, to Heinrich's way of thinking, the China people. "About Gornt Blakeman I come," Heinrich said. He would never be more clever than his younger brother; there was no point in being subtle. "And that young man, the doctor with one hand only. About him, too."

"Joyful Turner. What's he to do with you?"

"You told me to watch him."

"I told you to watch Blakeman, not Turner."

"*Ja*, but Blakeman's men are watching Turner. So everything comes together."

"I see. Where?"

"Last night in Maiden Lane. Blakeman's man was arrested. He was there because the doctor was. A meeting of some sort at the home of the goldsmith, though not exactly—"

"Maurice Vionne. *Ja*, about this I know." It was Vionne who had signed the certificate of authenticity that Blakeman had brought him, and Vionne had a beautiful unmarried daughter. It was not difficult to conclude that she was the lady who had told Joyful about the stone, the lady whose name he had so gallantly protected when he first told Astor the story.

"I have a man in the Watch," Heinrich said.

Jacob smiled. "You are getting wiser in the world's ways as you get older, Heinrich."

"A few coppers I pay him. Some meat occasionally. So he is my man and he tells me things. But Blakeman, he has at least two men in the Watch. Maybe more."

Jacob shrugged. "I am not surprised. So last night, a lovers' tryst and an Irishman is taken by the Watch. This brings you and your fine mutton and your equally fine rump steak to my kitchen today, Heinrich?"

His brother did not answer immediately. Jacob took a long swallow of the cold beer. Ah Wong and the other servants had discreetly withdrawn from the kitchen. A large basket of fresh-picked corn had been left half shucked in the middle of the table. Jacob set down the stein and drew the corn closer. He began peeling the husks back from a large ear, fastidiously picking each strand of silk from between the kernels. "You like corn, Heinrich?"

"Well enough."

"When we were children, never we had such a thing at Mama's table."

"Corn is American."

"*Ja,* American. And you and I, Heinrich? What are we now? Are we American because we are here?"

His elder brother's stein was empty. Heinrich pushed it across the table, but when Jacob turned as if to summon Ah Wong for more beer, Heinrich held up a forestalling hand. "No. Leave the yellow people wherever they are. Something I wish to say."

"It doesn't matter. A little English they speak, but no German. But it will be as you say. Now, tell me what you have come to tell me."

"I do not take Blakeman's side."

"I have it on good authority that a Mr. F. X. Gallagher believes you do."

Heinrich moved a thick finger through the ring of moisture the stein of beer had left on the table. "F. X. Gallagher is not a man to cross, Johann. It is easier to tell him *ja* than *nein.* That does not mean *ja* is what is true."

"I am glad to hear it, Heinrich. Anyway, on my side I thought you were."

"*Ja,* but the same thing I am thinking it is. You are a rich man. Blakeman is a rich man. In all the city the rich men agree to be another country with Connecticut and Massachusetts and Rhode Island. They say that is a better thing than to be the United States and every day lose more and more money."

"Not all the rich men, Heinrich." Jacob's tone was mild. He began shucking a second ear of corn.

"I am not clever like you, Jacob. I need things said plain. You are not for this new country?"

"I am not, Heinrich."

Heinrich grinned. "So! So! Ach, it is a contagion in this palace of yours. To say everything twice like the yellow people. So where is he, this China man with the beer which for little Johann is cold even in August?"

"A miracle it is not, Heinrich; I have an ice house near the river. Ah Wong! Send Hai for more beer!"

It was the job of Ah Wong's son to regularly bring kegs of beer from the ice house to the kitchen. The cold beer appeared instantly, as if Ah Wong had been hovering near the door waiting until it was wanted. No German? Perhaps the Chinese butler was more clever than Jacob realized.

The brothers raised their steins. "America," Heinrich said.

"America."

"Another thing you should know, Johann." Heinrich leaned in close and whispered. "F. X. Gallagher and his boys and the rest of the butchers. They are all with Blakeman. And when they say yes, they mean it."

Greenwich Street, 9 P.M.

The tap on the door was very soft. Joyful was not sure he had heard it. A second tap came, this one a little more forceful. Joyful went and opened the door.

A man, almost as tall as he was stood in the door frame, wearing a broad-brimmed hat and buckskins. The man swept off the hat and his queue swung free. He bowed. *"Chi le fan meiyou?"*

"I'll be . . . *Chi le. Chi le.* Wong Hai?"

Ah Wong's son gave him a grin as broad as his shoulders. "Wong Hai," he agreed, motioning with the hat to the room behind Joyful.

Joyful let him in and closed the door. He was extraordinarily conscious of the fact that he wasn't wearing the harness or the leather glove. *"Ni de yifu tong nali lai de?"* Where did you get those clothes?

"There is everything a man can ever want in Mr. Astor's mansion," Hai said, his English clear despite an odd accent Joyful couldn't place.

"Holy God Almighty. You're word-perfect, aren't you?"

"I make an effort, Lord. But my English is not as good as the lord's Mandarin," Hai said, accompanying the words with another bow. "I was twelve when I came to New York."

Translation: I know all about you, including how young you were when you first went to China. Information imparted subtly, in true Chinese fashion. Joyful motioned to the room's only chair and sat himself on the bed. "I take it no one knows you're here."

"No one, Lord."

"Look, if we're going to speak English, call me Joyful. Or Dr. Turner if you prefer. There's no direct translation for the honorific, and there's no royalty here. You haven't had much opportunity to practice speaking, have you?"

"No, Lord . . . Dr. Turner. When we first came, there was an old woman, the cook of honorable Mr. Astor, Mrs. McBride—she gave me lessons."

That explained the accent, a mix of Irish brogue and German. "Where is this Mrs. McBride now?"

"With her ancestors."

"I see. And Astor doesn't know about your language skills." The young man grinned and shook his head. "What about your father?"

"Honorable father knows." Hai did not meet Joyful's glance.

"But not that you're here, right?"

"Honorable father does not know that I am here."

"And that's why you came dressed like a woodsman?"

"Honorable Mr. Astor says it is not safe these days for people of the Middle Kingdom to be seen on the streets."

"Probably correct." Joyful was still trying to assimilate all the remarkable things about this visit. "But how did you know where to find me? And how did you get past Ma Allard?"

"I read and write as well as speak, Lo— honorable Dr. Turner. The note you gave honorable Mr. Astor, saying you would come the first time to his home . . . It is my job to clean my honorable employer's study."

Joyful had given Astor his address in that note. "And what about Ma Allard?"

Hai grinned. "Easy," he said, making no attempt to disguise his pride. "I do not ever see the honorable Ma Allard. I wait with patience until one who lives here comes and opens the door and I enter behind him. Hai is very quiet. Very quiet. And honorable Dr. Turner's name is written on wall by front door. Beside name is number of the room."

On the board where they all hung their keys when they went out. "You're a clever one, Hai. I'm impressed. Now, tell me why you're here, since your father did not send you."

Hai looked down at the woodsman's hat he held in his hands and did not immediately answer.

"Let me help you," Joyful said. "It's something to do with a Cantonese *tset-ha tset-ha* called Thumbless Wu." Hai nodded. "Thumbless Wu and your father," Joyful said softly, "and Jonathan Devrey, the apothecary—who is my nephew, as it happens."

Hai looked startled, then miserable. He stood up. "Your honorable nephew. I did not know. Honorable Dr. Turner will please excuse me, I must go."

"Sit down. You're not going anywhere until you tell me what you came here to say. You stole"—the young man made an anguished sound—"all right, borrowed, clothes from your employer's house and risked whatever was involved in getting here. I don't plan to let you leave until I hear it." Hai still didn't speak. "If it makes you feel any better, I don't particularly like Jonathan Devrey, despite the fact that I'm his uncle, I don't like any of my Devrey relations if it comes to that. But you can't know—"

"Bastard Devrey," Hai said, and sketched a double cross in the air.

"Son of a bitch! You are far too clever to be running loose, Wong Hai. Now, what about Thumbless?"

"White smoke," Hai said.

"White . . . opium?"

Hai nodded. "Jonathan Devrey's Elixir of Well-Being. White smoke. Same thing. Almost."

"Near enough," Joyful agreed. "So that's why Thumbless Wu went to so much trouble to get here. He's looking for an American source of opium to compete with the stuff the British bring in from India. It's madness, you realize that? All of the laudanum in America comes nowhere near the quantities of the stuff they grow in India. And that's an established trade. Besides, bringing opium into China's illegal."

"I believe Honorable Dr. Turner speaks the truth. But honorable father . . ."

"Yes?"

"He and Wu Thumbless . . . *guanxi* . . . Because of me."

"How so?"

"Honorable father wishes his son to return to the Middle Kingdom and be a man of wealth and property. Make a fine marriage. Become an ancestor."

"In English we say 'to found a dynasty.' Not bad as ambitions go, but what do you want, Wong Hai?"

"To be an ancestor, make a dynasty as you say, yes. But not white smoke."

Joyful thought for a moment, then he stood up. "Go home, Hai. You can get there safely?" Hai grinned and flexed the muscles of his two arms. "Well, yes," Joyful said. "Doesn't seem like you need a one-handed escort. Go back to Astor's, and don't do or say anything. I will be in touch. Agreed?"

"Agreed. Agreed," Hai said.

He bowed and started to back out of the room. Joyful stuck out his left arm, forgetting for the moment that he wasn't wearing his glove, and placed the stump on Hai's shoulder. He offered his right hand. Ah Wong's son took it and pumped it mightily. *"Guanxi,"* he said softly.

"Guanxi," Joyful agreed.

Friday, August 26, 1814

Chapter Twenty-two

New York City,
the Dancing Knave, 11 A.M.

O'TOOLE WAS UNSURE how long he had slept. "What time is it?" he demanded of Bearded Agnes.

"Middle of the morning. Brought you some breakfast. Time you had something solid in your stomach." She put the tray on the table beside the bed and started to go.

The Irishman looked around him. The small bedroom was done up a bit, not like those in most bordellos. God knew he'd been in a few o' those in his day. Not usually alone, however. "Where's the woman?"

"Cecily," Agnes supplied. "She's gone about her business. This place ain't a hotel, you know—for all Miss Delight put you up here in this nice little room as is beside her own private parlor. You'd o' been turned out yesterday or the day before, weren't that Miss Delight has a kind heart."

"Kind heart? That one? She's—" The bearded lady's look silenced him. "Yesterday or the day before you said. How long have I been here then?"

"Since Monday night."

"And what day is it now?"

"Friday."

"Christ Almighty Savior. Four days. At the tables, was I?"

"Some o' the time."

"And the rest?"

"Up here with Miss Cecily. Though she says you weren't worth the bother most o' the time."

"That will do, Agnes." Delight stood at the open door. "At the Dancing Knave the ladies do not tattle. Good morning, Captain. I trust you slept well."

His head was thumping like a longboat drummer beating stroke for the oarsmen. "Well enough." He reached for the mug of spiced ale Agnes had brought and downed it in a couple of quick swallows. It helped some.

"Since you are, as you say, 'well enough,' Captain, I think it is time you got out of that bed and went on your way. Do you not agree?"

"I might do. But not until you and her get yourselves gone." He was stark naked beneath the thin summer coverlet.

"I assure you, Captain O'Toole, you have nothing to display we have not seen before. But I will leave, as I'm expecting my mantua maker, and Agnes will wait outside. When you're dressed, you will, I'm sure, wish to settle your account. You owe Miss Cecily three dollars for four full nights' companionship. I will take that out of the golden guinea you left with me. And for your gaming . . ." Delight consulted a slip of paper she carried in the pocket of her morning gown. "There is a balance due of one thousand seventeen dollars and twenty coppers. Your luck was not the best this visit, I'm afraid. The seventeen dollars are covered by what's left of your golden guinea, and . . ." She paused, frowned, then smiled. "We have enjoyed your company, Captain. I will forgive the twenty coppers."

Where in Christ's name was he to get a thousand dollars? He remembered it all now. Taking the cat to that careless bastard Tammy Tompkins, and the tar telling Blakeman about Thumbless Wu. Blakeman turning him off the *Star* so he got blind drunk, and that wretch as called himself Peggety Jack stealing the six thousand he'd made for running the blockade. Joyful thought he was lying about what Jack said about the Jews having his treasure, and that Finbar O'Toole wouldn't sail *Lisbetta* to the Caribbean for fear o' the poxed British navy. Holy Mother o' God. What a mess.

O'Toole got up, yanked the coverlet off the bed, wrapped it around his hips, and threw open the door. Agnes was still there, standing with her arms folded, waiting for him. "Get me a proper drink," O'Toole said. "Rum. I'll not manage to get my trousers on else-ways."

Agnes took a moment to consider. The ladies were all asleep on the floor below, getting their beauty rest now that their night's work was done. Except for Preservation Shay, standing guard a feet away outside Miss Delight's door, even the chuckers-out were abed. As for Miss Delight herself, her mantua maker had arrived with an assistant to carry some extra bolts of silk. The three women would likely be in Miss Delight's private parlor for some time. All the same . . .

Preservation nodded in Agnes's direction. "It's all right, Miss Agnes. Go get the captain what he wants. I'll keep an eye out."

Why not? Irish the captain might be, but not a bad sort as men went. That's why it had been in her mind to say he was there when Dr. Turner came t'other night. Never got the chance what with him and Miss Delight quarreling the way they was mostly doing these days.

"Rum, woman. For the love o' Holy Mary and all the saints."

She didn't hold with Catholic idolatry, but the poor man surely to God looked in need of that tot of rum. "I'll be back before you can blink," she promised, heading for the stairs.

Something was wrong with the mantua maker this morning. She had pricked Delight with her pins three times. Now, as she gathered a length of turquoise-colored silk tight below Delight's breasts to show how the fabric would drape when the dress was made up, there was a fourth offense. "Ouch! You must be more careful, madame. Please."

"I'm so sorry. I can't seem to . . ." The woman glanced at the caped and hooded figure who had accompained her to the fitting. So slight of . . . that it was easy enough to take him for a girl. Her assistant, she'd said. Newly hired. God forgive her, what else could she say? She was a widow with three small children and the one-eyed pirate had threatened to kill them all if she didn't cooperate. But Delight Higgins was her best customer, and sometimes the young women as worked in the place had frocks made as well. How would she survive and feed her family if she lost the custom of the Dancing Knave?

The mantua maker gathered all her courage. "I thought to see your other chucker-out today, Miss Higgins. Mr. Clifford. And his whip." It was the only thing she could think to say. Perhaps if this so-called assistant who had been wished upon her understood how well guarded these premises were, he would call off the pirate's plan. "I believe his wife was asking about having a gown made."

"His wife? I no longer employ Vinegar Clifford, but I never heard he had—" Delight broke off. The mantua maker was jerking her head in the direction of the assistant. Over and over. It was extraordinary. The girl, meanwhile, was ignoring the bolts of cloth and peering out the window. After a moment she started to open it. "Here, you! Stop. I do not wish to—"

The figure in the cape spun around, throwing back the hood of the cape and revealing himself to be not a girl but a man holding a pistol. "Don't matter much what you wish. Not just now."

Delight turned to the door. Preservation was just outside. If she yelled—

"You call out and I'll shoot," the man with the pistol said. Tammy Tompkins had never before held a pistol, much less shot one, and he had no idea if his aim would be true enough to kill the mulatto woman. But like Tintin had said, that didn't matter none long as she thought otherwise. "Come over here. Beside the window. Come on. Move."

Delight looked once more at the door, then at the pistol in the hands of the stranger that beckoned her forward. She moved toward him, the half-pinned turquoise-colored silk trailing after her.

"You," Tompkins jerked his head at the mantua maker, "get that stuff off her."

The seamstress's hands were shaking too badly to do as he asked. She fumbled with the pins, sobbing under her breath. "It's all right," Delight said, softly. "Do as he says." If she were to have any opportunity to fight the birders for her freedom—and Delight was quite sure that was what this was; a robbery would proceed in a quite different fashion—she would much prefer to be in her corset and pantaloons than tangled in a bolt of silk.

Tompkins glanced out the window. "Now," he called softly to the man below. Tintin tossed up the rope ladder. Tompkins expertly grabbed one end while maintaining his hold on the pistol, still pointing it at Delight.

"I'm a free woman. I have papers that say so," she said. "The magistrates have to approve the taking. They won't approve me."

"No concern of mine." Tompkins had fixed one end of the ladder to the leg of a heavy chest. "Either you climb down so's you get to the bottom with both arms and legs in one piece, or I toss you out and you take your chances. Choice is yours."

"Miss Higgins." The mantua maker stretched out her arms, and words bubbled out of her, a stream of remorse: "I'm so sorry, Miss Higgins. They were going to kill my babies. I couldn't say no. I—"

"It's all right. I understand." Delight was at the window. She saw Tintin standing below, grinning up at her. "You. I might have guessed."

The pirate simply bowed. Delight looked once more at the door of the parlor, then at the pistol, then at the rope ladder. It was frayed and covered in barnacles, but it was a far sight safer than being thrown to the ground by the man with the pistol. She sat on the window ledge and swung her legs over the edge.

The screams brought the women who had been sleeping on the floor below racing up the stairs in their nightdresses. The other chuckers-out as well. Finbar O'Toole, dressed only in trousers and boots, came out of the little bedroom in time to see them all converging on the doorway a few paces from his. "What's happening? What's the matter? Damn, if you ladies would stop yelling and make some sense, might be we could—"

Actually, it was only one woman doing most of the howling. "I couldn't help it! I swear to Almighty God! They were pirates and they were going to kill my babies. I couldn't help it!"

The others were clustered around her, offering comfort and questions in equal measure. O'Toole pushed his way into the heart of the melee. "Holy Mary and all the saints, couldn't help what?"

"She's the one as let 'em in," Agnes said.

"Let who in?"

"Them as got Miss Delight, from the sound o' it."

"Blackbirders?" It was the first explanation that came to O'Toole, and he had little doubt it was the correct one.

"Has to be," Agnes confirmed. Amid all the tumult her voice was strangely calm. "She lived in deadly fear of 'em, and now they got her."

Preservation Shay had been into Delight's private parlor and come out again. "A rope ladder," Preservation said. "That's how they got her out o' there and down to the ground without me knowin' a thing 'bout it."

"Pirates they were. And the one in there had a pistol," the mantua maker said between her sobs. "There was nothing I could do."

Nothing more rotten than blackbirders. Delight Higgins didn't deserve that. Same time, it weren't nothing to do with him. O'Toole slid along the wall to the door of the room he'd been in for the past three days and finished dressing, then came out, went down the stairs, and exited by the front door. In the tumult no one thought to ask him to settle his bill before he left.

❧

Aboard Le Carcajou, *Noon*

Delight told herself it was no different from the first time, behind the necessary out back in Hanover Square when she was ten. Or the second when she was thirteen and a *coureur des bois* who was setting bear traps in the Nova Scotia woods caught her instead, and forced himself on her on a winter day so cold her thirteen-year-old screams seemed to hang visible in the frozen air, then left her to die.

She didn't die then and she would not die now.

Tintin had not waited until they were aboard his ship, using her in the dinghy while the one who had forced her out of the window at the point of his pistol rowed across the river and—God help her—whistled "Old Zip Coon."

Her hands were roped tight together, so there was little point in fighting. For now she could do nothing except plan and wait, and watch for an opportunity. She made herself go limp, saying nothing, feeling nothing.

"*Alors, mademoiselle,* is that how you pleasure the men who pay for your cunny?" Angered by her blank expression, and rag doll compliance, he slapped her face over and over, getting, it seemed, more satisfaction from that than from her body.

Do what you want, you cannot touch me.

Except for Joyful, none of them touched her. Whether she pretended passion to entertain them or lay perfectly still, she was not present when they used her. Tintin was the same. They were all the same.

"Here is another one for the caves when we are home," he said when he dropped her on the deck. "She'll bring a good price, *non?* Stand up, nigra whore. Let them get a look at you."

Hindered by her bonds, she didn't do it fast enough, and he kicked her twice, the expression in his eyes showing how much he enjoyed it. "Welcome aboard *Le Carcajou,* mademoiselle. I am sure you will enjoy our hospitality." Then, to the others, "It is warm today, *non?* Cannot one of you gallant gentlemen help the lady to be more cool?"

One of the pirates used his cutlass to cut away what was left of her corset and pantaloons. "High yellow all over," he said after walking right around her, making an exaggeratedly slow tour of inspection. "Captain Tintin is correct, she'll bring a good price on the block."

"*Bien sûr,* but for now she belongs to us." Tintin kicked aside the bits of Delight's clothing that had dropped to the deck. "Take her below. Enjoy yourselves. There are only two rules. She must remain alive and"—he paused—"more or less intact. And she must come to understand what she is, so she gives us no trouble in front of the magistrates. *Alors mes amis, laissez les bons temps roule, eh?*"

New York City,
the Astor Mansion, 12:30 P.M.

The surveyor had been speaking for ten minutes. The marksman said nothing, just looked grim. Astor had interrupted only once or twice, seeking clarification concerning the American deployment, whether both men had actually seen Madison and his cabinet leave the battlefield unharmed (they had) and whether they knew where he was headed. "I heard talk of Maryland," the surveyor said, "but I believe the final choice was Virginia."

"That's where Mrs. Madison was headed as well." The marksman's first words. "The president's man, the one they call French John, he was to drive her carriage. I heard him say he would head for Alexandria."

"A good thing. Road's likely to be clearer that way," the surveyor said.

"So?" Astor asked. "This you know for certain, Mr. Randal?"

"Not for certain, Mr. Astor. But it's an informed guess."

Astor was inclined to credit it. John Randal was the man charged by New York with surveying the entire island, and laying out the numbered streets and avenues of the city to come. In the matter of directions and roads he was unlikely to make a mistake. As for his reliability as a spy, that remained to be proven. "The prize the redcoats are after next is Baltimore," Randal said.

"Not New York?"

"I don't suppose so, sir. If New York were seriously on their list, a goodly portion of the fleet wouldn't have put itself in such danger warping up the Potomac."

"'Warping'?" Astor looked puzzled. "I do not know this word."

"They were in shallow waters, sir." The marksman took over the explanation. "The only way they could get their gunboats within range of the Federal District was to drag them upriver on ropes. It's a miserable job, dangerous, and no telling how well the ships will survive it."

"So, did they shell the District?"

"Not that we saw, sir. It was burning all right, no doubt about that. Set the sky alight. But fairly certain it was the army set the fires."

It came to the same thing. Everything they had labored so hard to construct on that drained swamp. All gone. *Du lieber Gott . . .* What could he do? And which was he trying to protect, his money or the nation? In the end, it didn't matter. He could do little about what was happening miles away in Washington and Baltimore. Here in New York he might have influence.

How would people react? That was the critical question. Mr. Randal looked—resigned. *Ja.* An educated, logical man, one accustomed to making the lines meet and the road run straight. The marksman? Quentin Hale III, younger, more emotional. Family owned a huge estate up near Albany; all the same, less learning from books, more connected to the ordinary people of the city, the mechanics and laborers. The ones Blakeman must have on his side if his scheme was to work. *Security will not be a problem, Mr. Astor. Take my word for that.* So, Mr. Blakeman, we will see.

Astor nodded toward the rolled-up canvas that had been left at the door to the study when Ah Wong showed the two men in. "What is that?"

For answer Hale strode across the room and got the painting and unfurled it. "Mrs. Madison was determined not to leave it for the enemy to deface, sir. There wasn't time to get the frame off the wall. We had to cut the portrait free."

"It was her express wish that General Washington's portrait be brought here to New York for safekeeping, Mr. Astor." The surveyor's tone was approving. "I admit I tried to talk her into leaving it behind, in the interest of getting her sooner away, but Mrs. Madison was adamant."

Astor took a few steps closer to the unrolled painting. "Ja," he said after a time. "A good idea, Mrs. Dolley. A very good idea." He walked to the bellpull and tugged on it. "Into the streets you will go, gentlemen, to tell the city what has happened. Tell them everything you saw. Be sure to tell the newspapers as well. In fact, go first to them. Ah Wong," jerking his head toward the servant who had hurried into the room, "will show you out."

The marksman started to reroll the painting. "That," Astor said, "you will leave with me. For safekeeping, like Mrs. Dolley said. Ah Wong, come back to me as soon as our callers have left."

By one o'clock the broadsides were up all over the city. Redcoats burn Federal District! Executive Mansion destroyed! By half after, at least one newspaper had managed to get an extra edition on the streets: "Your Capital is taken! In six days the same enemy may be at the Hook!"

Joyful was headed for Hanover Square to see Jonathan, who was just the sort of greedy dimwit who might think going into the opium business with Thumbless Wu was possible, but the crowds gathering everywhere forced him back. He elbowed his way into a knot of people on Beaver Street, read the notice tacked to a large oak tree, and immediately started back to Ma Allard's. In New York, always a town that lived much of its life on the streets, fear and anger were easily spread from mouth to mouth like a contagion.

Greenwich Street was a bit quieter, with only a few folks gathered on the corners and in doorways, talking in hushed whispers. Doubtless they'd be noisier before long. His landlady appeared as soon as his key turned in the lock, twisting her apron in one hand and dabbing a handkerchief to her eyes with the other. "Is it true then, Dr. Turner? They say the redcoats is already in the harbor and will have us back as a colony this very night. Is it true?"

"No, Mrs. Allard. In fact, the word is they're not coming here at all. Baltimore is their next target."

"But they've burned Washington and—"

"And the president and the first lady are safe. It's only the British rattling their sabers, Mrs. Allard. We don't need the Federal District to survive."

Joyful hurried up the stairs to his room. The landlady followed. "They say the city's a powder keg, Dr. Turner. Going to blow apart and take us all to kingdom come."

"Maybe, madam. If so, I wish you a good journey. Now, if you'll excuse me . . ." He tried to shut the door with her on the other side, but she was too quick for him, inside the room as fast as he was. Joyful turned his back on her and grabbed his medical bag. In the normal way of things he'd just take it and be gone, but what was going on now was not the normal way of things. He opened the bag and began distributing the contents about his person.

"If it's true, Dr. Turner . . . I know you said it's not, but if it is . . ."

"If what's true, madam?"

"If the redcoats come. I mean if they do . . ."

"Yes, Mrs. Allard?"

"Well, sir, you being a doctor and a famous hero and all, might be they'll arrest you, or impress you into their navy, or Lord knows what else. So I was wondering if . . . Glory be, what are you planning to do with all them vicious-looking things you're after putting in your pockets?"

"Doctoring, Mrs. Allard. Some surgery if it's required. The city, as you put it, is a powder keg, feeding on rumors such as the notion that the British are in the harbor. Started, I'm sure, by well-meaning persons such as yourself. I am at somewhat of a disadvantage, as you might have noticed. I can be more effective if my one hand isn't lumbered with a bag." He shoved a wad of catgut ligatures into his left trouser pocket, the only one not already full of knives, probes, even the smallest of his saws. "That's as much as I can carry." He looked ruefully at the larger saws, decided it wasn't possible to take them, snapped the nearly empty bag shut, threw it in a corner, and headed for the stairs.

Ma Allard followed, all but shrieking his name. "Dr. Turner, please, sir."

"Please what? Out with it, madam, what do you want?"

"My rent, sir. In case the redcoats make off with you. I know it's not due till the end of the week, but I'm a poor widow has to make her way in this world . . ."

Joyful found one of the gold reichsthalers in the watch pocket of his waistcoat—the only pocket too small for any medical supplies—and flipped it at her. "Prepare yourself, madam. I'd make up any extra beds you might have immediately. No doubt at least two British admirals and a general will be looking for accommodation before nightfall."

Chapter Twenty-three

New York City in Ferment,
close to 2 P.M.

THE CROWD WAS a tidal wave, a current that flowed up the island gathering numbers, purpose, and direction as it went.

The phalanx that came from the west met the throng from the east on Broadway, and together they turned north toward the Common. Joyful was swept along by a press of bodies so powerful he had no choice but to keep moving. A man to his left spoke almost directly in his ear. "Dr. Turner, ain't ye? As was with Commodore Perry." The man shouted at the top of his lungs, "Got us a hero here as beat the British bastards once before!"

Joyful cringed, but the man's voice was swallowed up in the noise of the tramping feet and the cacophony of competing claims and rumors.

"Two British men-o'-war there be in the harbor. Shelling the city."

"Open your ears, man! Ain't no sound o' shells. It's the poxed redcoats. Burned the Federal District and think to burn us down next."

"It's the redcoats and the navy," a third voice added. "The fleet's put in up at Kips Bay, same as at the start o' the Revolution. Got another think comin' if they're planning to occupy New York a second time."

"There are no British troops in the city!" Joyful shouted. Stupid to think you could talk sense to this throng, but he had to try. "There are no redcoats in New York. You're all—"

"Got us a hero here!" The man who had tried previously to identify him made a second attempt. "Fought the British off on Lake Erie and he'll fight 'em off again. Three cheers for Dr. Turner!" Those near enough to hear cheered, with no real idea what they were cheering for or about.

Jesus God Almighty. Reason had nothing to do with it. The crowd was a beast constructed of hundreds of otherwise ordinary people, moving to the beat of its own heart, and unstoppable unless and until it met an opposing force.

In Paradise Square the beast had grown a second head. The butchers and cattlemen had marched south from the Bowery, through Chatham Square, and eventually to Orange Street, a narrow road that funneled them into the heart of Five Points. F. X. Gallagher had thought himself at the head of the column, but somewhere between the open area around the stockyards and abattoirs and the star-shaped intersection at the center of this urban maze, his place had been taken by Gornt Blakeman.

Joyful spotted Blakeman and tried to shove toward him, knowing that at any moment Gornt would take the opportunity to turn the city's fear and fury to his advantage. The crowd seethed with its pent-up need to make something happen.

It took a few seconds for him to realize that the hand pulling at his elbow was purposeful, not simply the crush of the bodies jammed up against his. "Dr. Turner, Reverend Fish sent me. We need you!"

Joyful managed to twist just enough to see who it was shouting in his ear. "Burney . . . What are you—"

"Reverend Fish," Patrick Burney repeated, grabbing hold of Joyful's arm. "He says—" The throng behind them surged and Burney's grip was broken. For a few seconds Joyful lost sight of him, then Burney was back, tugging on Joyful's left arm this time, nearly detaching the harness and the glove. "C'mon, sir! Come with me."

"I can't! I've got to get up there. That's Gornt Blakeman. I've got to—"

"Holy Mother of God, aren't I after knowing who Blakeman is? C'mon, I tell you. I know what I'm about!"

"Look, surgery can't be the priority just now. I can't—"

"It's not cutting we want. Fish says you may be the only— Ach, just come, will you!" With a mighty heave he pulled Joyful in the direction he meant him to go, away from Blakeman and Gallagher and toward the nearest alley.

Nothing for it. Burney was determined, and Fish knew more than most about everything happening in these parts. Burney meanwhile had dragged him into the mouth of the side passage he'd been aiming for, but they were stuck there, the bodies squeezed into the narrow opening all straining in the opposite direction to the one they wanted, and creating an almost impenetrable mass. He got a look at the bloody bandage on Burney's left hand. "What happened?" The noise in the alley was worse than in the square. He had to shout to be heard.

"F.X. and his poxed cleaver," Burney shouted back.

"Soon as we get out of here I'll—" He broke off. There was no point in any kind of normal interchange. They were in hell. Joyful fought his way into a better position, one that put Burney on his right, so he could hang on to Joyful's good arm. "Here, take hold and we'll bull our way forward." They linked arms, and angled their bodies to form a wedge. "Count of three," Joyful shouted. "One, two—three!" They lunged ahead, cutting their way through the mass. "Almost there," Joyful heard Burney say, "get ready."

Before Joyful could ask what he was to prepare for, Burney had launched the pair of them against one of the alley doors. It gave at the first impact, and they half tumbled into the opening. The door slammed shut behind then and a bar slid into place. "This way," someone whispered.

"Where are we?"

"Quiet," Burney leaned in close and whispered into his ear. "That crowd out there could have the door down in a minute if it took a mind to."

Joyful was conscious of the blackness, the steamy heat, and something else, the sound of breathing. Jesus God Almighty, please don't let it be rats.

"This way. Mind how you go."

Burney was leading him forward as if he were a blind man. "Where are you taking me?"

"Reverend Fish."

The feeling of being in a closed space gave way to the sensation of crossing an open area. There was a distinctive smell as well. It took him a few seconds to put a name to it, then he knew. Rum. The nose-prickling, alcoholic bite of the product in the making. They were in the vast expanse of a sugar house, a factory where tons of Caribbean sugar were hauled up from the docks and poured loose onto the distillery floor. A feeding ground for veritable armies of rats.

Joyful couldn't help himself, he stopped moving.

"Reverend Fish is waiting. Just a little further," Burney said.

A few more steps, and Joyful saw a narrow shaft of light ahead. Probably coming through a loose roof tile. Or maybe his eyes were adjusting to the gloom. The breathing shadows were not rats but men, Zachary Fish's congregants. One, near enough so a stretched-out hand would touch him, had a patch over one eye and had armed himself with a vicious-looking stevedore's metal claw. Holy God Almighty, the sugar house was full of men with more reason than most to want things to change. How would they react to Gornt Blakeman's promise of better days once they separated from the Union?

"Over here." Burney led Joyful to the right. "We have to get to the next building. Means climbing across this narrow bit. Mind the broken glass."

Joyful felt many hands behind him, helping hoist him through a shattered window to a makeshift bridge of rope high above the square. He forced himself to look down. Nothing but bodies as far as he could see, with Gornt Blakeman in the middle, haranguing the crowd.

Going on for half two and the sun a fearsome thing, beating down from a cloudless sky, at its worst in the packed square. Being stifled like this—amid a crowd so huge it seemed each man, woman, and child had to fight for air—was enough to make the sane mad, Finbar O'Toole thought. Bound to be some bad things happen this day. He'd already seen one woman stumble and fall beneath the marchers a ways back on Broadway. The man who reached down to pull her up was beaten down as well. Like as not the pair of 'em were trampled to death, and he'd lay odds they weren't the only ones. Only one way to stay alive in a crush like this, follow where it led.

Gornt Blakeman turned his head in every direction, looking for Joyful Turner. He couldn't spot him, but he'd wager anything he was here. Man like him, he'd not stay out of a set-to like this. Consider it his duty to be present and offer medical help, or talk the benighted masses home to their beds. Christ Almighty, you'd think the red-headed bastard tall enough to be seen despite the mob. Convenient if one of the butchers could plant a well-aimed knife. Never be a better time. Be that as it may, there were other things to be concerned with just now. "Listen to me, all of you! Listen! I've something to say as will put food in your bellies and those of your wives and children. Listen!"

"Up here, Mr. Blakeman!" A few of Gallagher's trusties had managed to haul some kegs to a place in front of a grocer's doorway, stacking them so as to make a platform between a pair of signs that on one side touted soft-shell clams and, on the other, good fat hams. "This way, sir. Sure and sturdy it is."

Blakeman accepted the help of Vinegar Clifford and one of the butchers and climbed to the top of the pile. The rest of F.X.'s men formed a semicircle around the structure, so no one could get close enough to topple it.

"Listen!" Blakeman shouted again. This time his voice floated out over the heads of the crowd. At least those in the front ranks could hear him. "Do you want an end to this poxed blockade and this doubly poxed war? You want your jobs back? Enough food in the shops so these hams and clams and the like don't sell for ten times what you earn in a month? Do you? I tell you this war has been wished upon us by—"

"They can't hear you, Mr. Blakeman! Try this." Clifford passed up a bellow horn of the type the cattlemen used to imitate the sounds of a bull and bring the cows to the corral.

Blakeman grabbed it eagerly. "—wished upon us by the War Hawks," he shouted into the narrow mouth. The sound expanded in the funnel and boomed out across the square. "The men in that meeting of fools they call the Congress of the United States, the ones as voted for Mr. Madison's war, not one of 'em's from our New York. Not from the New England states either. Men from the west, from Kentucky and Ohio and Tennessee, they're the ones as brought this misery on us. What do they know of our lives here on the seaboard where shipping is what puts food in our bellies?"

A hush began among the people packed into the square itself, then spread up the side streets, silencing the noise of the slobbering beast the crowd had become. "We can't be expected to see our wives and children starve so Mr. Madison can have his war!" Blakeman shouted into the sudden quiet. "Why should we—"

"We the people of the United States, in order to form a more perfect union . . ."

It was a second voice, coming from somewhere high above the heads of the crowd. "We the people of the United States," it called out a second time. ". . . in order to form a more perfect union . . ."

Finbar O'Toole tilted his head back along with many of the others, all trying to see where the voice came from. Sweet Savior Jesus and

Holy Mary Mother of God, it was Joyful, high above them in the second-floor window of the grocer's building. Standing on a narrow ledge, he was. Leaning forward, so's he could pitch his voice above Blakeman's, bellow horn or no. " . . . establish justice"—Joyful's tone was solemn, as if reciting a prayer—"insure domestic tranquillity, provide for the common defense—"

Joyful was conscious that most in the crowd were staring at him now, for the moment ignoring bloody Gornt Blakeman. He reminded himself to look across the tops of their heads, not straight down. He'd learned long ago that helped a bit. God help him, he surely hated heights. "Provide for the common defense, and . . ." What was the rest of it? " . . . common defense, and promote the general welfare and secure . . ." There was movement to the side of where Blakeman was standing. Joyful caught it just out of the corner of his eye. " . . . and secure the blessings of—"

Vinegar Clifford found an empty space to the side of the protective cordon surrounding Blakeman and moved into it, straining his whole barrel-shaped body toward the upper window.

Joyful saw him, and knew just how much hatred was concentrated in that stance. Clifford's disease had passed to the next stage; he could piss without pain, and didn't need the laudanum any longer. He doubtless believed the wretched tansy powder had cured him, and now he was full of loathing for the man who had seen him in the weakness of his misery.

The bullwhip cut through the heavy, heated air with a whistling crack of sound. Joyful twisted, bending sideways away from the protection of the window frame, hanging out over nothing. His stomach lurched, but he ignored it. The deadly thong of Clifford's whip coiled itself around his ankle. The pain was nothing he couldn't bear. Thank Christ for the sturdy leather of his boot. He pulled back so the ledge gave him better support and dropped into a crouch, using his free hand to grab one of the scalpels he'd pocketed earlier. If he could cut the weighted tip off the thong . . . The people below were craning their necks to look at him, waiting to hear what he'd say next. " . . . and secure the blessings of liberty to ourselves and our posterity," he yelled while struggling to get into a position that allowed him to cut the leather thong wrapped around his ankle.

Just then the crowd surged forward, and Clifford was wedged in place by the press of bodies. Not enough room to lean back and yank Joyful from his perch; he flicked his wrist and the tension on the long leather thong relaxed. It fell from Joyful's ankle before the scalpel could do its work.

Blakeman had seen enough to know that whatever Clifford had tried to do had failed. And damn it to hell, the crowd was buying what bloody Joyful Turner was selling. He could see it in their faces. Blakeman's throat already felt as if a carpenter had worked it over with a rasp, but he lifted the bellow horn and summoned every scrap of breath. "Don't listen to him! That's the pap they fed you in '86 in their so-called Constitution. Are you going to be fooled by it a second time? Do you call what we have now domestic tranquillity?"

"We the people of the United States, in order to form a more perfect union, establish justice, insure domestic tranquillity, provide for the common defense"—Joyful's voice came from somewhere deep inside—"promote the general welfare, and secure the blessings of liberty to ourselves and our posterity . . ." Not his voice alone, also that of his parents Morgan and Roisin, and his cousins, Sam Devrey and Andrew Turner, and all the rest who had given their blood to make a nation: " . . . do ordain and establish this Constitution—"

"Listen to me, not him!" Blakeman's voice, magnified by the bellow horn, cut over Joyful's. "You're being asked to sacrifice your livelihoods for James Madison. Nothing else. A few men of the west and a little man as can't even stop the redcoats from burning down the roof over his wife's head."

Finbar O'Toole had been listening to the battle of words, never taking his eyes from Joyful, who was hanging out so far from that poxed window it must need the Angel Gabriel to keep him from falling. Now O'Toole felt a collective shift of attention, to the windows of the other buildings that ringed Paradise Square.

Open, every damned one of 'em, and a face in each, some black, some white. There was Danny Parker and Hiram Walton, and at least a dozen more from the same waterfront fraternity of shipwrights. Word was, the town's mechanics were all with Blakeman. Here was proof that word was wrong. Something—some*one* more likely—had won the shipwrights over to the side of preserving the Union.

" . . . do ordain and establish this Constitution for the United States of America." Joyful summoned every scrap of his energy into projecting the great promise that lay behind those words. The arm he was using to anchor him to the windowsill slipped a bit, and he had to pull back to counterbalance his weight. He thought he heard his name, and looked across the square to see Barnaby Carter in the window of the building across from his.

"Tell 'em, Joyful," Barnaby called. Never mind that he and Lucretia would never see a penny of the money Blakeman owed them if the bastard's scheme didn't materialize. "You tell 'em how it is!" He aimed his voice at the crowd below. "That's Joyful Turner up there, folks. A hero and the son of a hero. Listen to him."

"We gave our solemn word," Joyful shouted. "Are we going to withdraw it the moment there's an obstacle in the path? Are we Americans, or feral cats who can be counted on to claw each other to the death rather than work together for the common good?"

"Are we slaves to the War Hawks and Madison? Are we . . ." Blakeman's voice was the louder yet again. But just when it seemed the bellow horn was master, there was a roar of sound as Jacob Hays and seven constables came thundering up Cross Street on horseback.

The crowd that had been so powerful in its unity became an aggregation of individuals screaming in terror. Men and women who had thought there was not an inch of room in which to move realized they must find room, or be trampled beneath the pounding horses' hooves. They clawed their way over and under and around their neighbors, piling body on top of body, anything to clear a path for the horsemen. A woman handed her infant up to the hands of strangers, then was sucked into the heart of the melee and disappeared.

"Cease and desist!" Hays shouted. "In the name of the law! Go back to your homes, or you'll all be up the river in Newgate by nightfall."

"Mr. Hays," Blakeman roared into the horn as the mounted officers charged into Paradise Square. "High Constable Jacob Hays, we want you with us! We're about a new nation's business. Join us and live free of war and presidential tyranny!"

"Ain't no new nation, Mr. Blakeman. Not here in New York." Hays turned in the saddle and waved the man behind him forward. "Take that man into custody! I'm charging him with the hanging offense of high treason against these lawfully joined United States."

The power of the crowd rose in a low roar of rage and defiance that could be felt even from the height of horseback. They might not be decided on Blakeman's message, but they weren't prepared to see him handed over to the law. The constable summoned to make the arrest hesitated long enough for F. X. Gallagher to take the cleaver from his belt and brandish it overhead. The other butchers did the same. Gallagher shouted something and strode forward. The butchers followed.

There was an instant of horrified stillness, the space of a single heartbeat in which every person in Paradise Square recognized that a bloodbath was now truly upon them. Then, into that moment of stunned silence, there came the crack of a gun.

A red hole appeared in the middle of Gallagher's forehead. He opened his mouth, as if to say something, then dropped to the ground. The butchers froze, cleavers still raised above their heads. Like every person present, they tilted their heads and looked up to the buildings around the square. The men who filled the windows now had muskets on their shoulders.

Hays surveyed the extent of the display of arms. "I heard you was raising a regiment, Mr. Blakeman. But somehow I get the feeling the fellows you was counting on have taken themselves over to the other side o' this argument."

"No man here fights for Gornt Blakeman!" Zachary Fish hung out a window to Hays's right. "We be the regiment of Mother Zion and Almighty God. Pledged to these United States of America."

"Nigras," a voice from up front near Blakeman shouted. "You folks going to let nigras shoot down a white man and get away with it?"

"Nigras!"

The crowd surged forward, the combined weight of their bodies enough to overcome even the power of the horses. A scuffle broke out near the platform where Blakeman had been standing, but he had climbed down from the pile of kegs and the butchers had fallen back to surround him.

"Nigras!" It had become a chorus. "Nigras gonna kill us all!"

Joyful looked across the square to the man he'd seen fire the rifle that took down Gallagher—as white as he was, and as redheaded to boot. One of Astor's marksmen, probably. Would saying so prevent carnage below?

"Joyful! Take this. It will help, I think."

Joyful turned his head, ignoring the dizziness that threatened to overwhelm him every time he moved. "Mr. Astor."

"Jacob. Remember, *Genossen* we are. Allies. Here, take this." Astor thrust a rolled canvas into Joyful's good hand.

"What is it?"

"Quick, open it. You'll see."

Joyful shook the canvas open, looked down, and laughed out loud. It took another sick-making maneuver for him to twist again and hang the unrolled canvas above the heads of the crowd so it could be seen. "Look up here folks! Look what we've got!"

"Tell them Dolley Madison saved it from the British." Astor's said quietly. "Tell them Mrs. Dolley sent it to New York to be safe."

"Look up here," Joyful shouted. "It's a painting of General Washington. Sent to us by the first lady of the land. She's safe. So's President Madison. And we are to keep this picture for when we build a new Federal District and a new Executive Mansion."

The roar was one of approval this time. "General Washington!" someone called out. "Hip, hip!"

The hoorays were deafening. The crowd fell back from the mounted men in the middle of the square. "Go to your homes," Hays called out. "Long as you're peaceable there'll be no trouble and no arrests." He looked toward the place where the one man he really had wanted to take into custody had been standing. Blakeman was gone; his butchers and their cleavers as well. "Peaceable," he said. "That's what we want, a peaceable city o' New York. Just like always."

Finbar watched the crowd disperse. As soon as he was able to move, he stood beside the door of the grocery store where Joyful had been hanging out the upper window. Grand he'd been. Would have made his da proud. Be a good thing to tell Joyful that. And might be he'd mention about what happened this morning at the Knave. Heard a few stories, he had, bout Joyful and Delight Higgins. Even some as said Joyful had a financial interest in the place. Course he'd have to say he'd been there at the Knave when Delight was snatched. Might be it would come out about his being drunk for four days and losing a thousand he didn't have.

Holy Mary and all the saints. Must be another way out of this here grocery building, because he'd seen not a lick o' Joyful Turner coming through the door, but there he was on the other side of Paradise Square, riding up behind High Constable Hays no less. The pair of 'em kicking up a storm o' dust as they galloped back downtown.

Maiden Lane, 4 P.M.

The shops of the goldsmiths and silversmiths were closed and shuttered and most folks busy with their dinners. The near riot up in Five Points, as well as the terrible story of the sack of the Federal District, provided enough table chatter to keep the residents of Maiden Lane away from their windows. A carriage—large, black, thickly curtained, drawn by a matched pair of black geldings—halted outside Maurice Vionne's house and four men got out.

"Wait where you are," Gornt Blakeman told the driver. "I don't imagine we will be very long."

He led the way to Vionne's front door, raised his fist, and pounded on the wood. The goldsmith came, a napkin still tucked in his shirt front. "I was not expecting you, Mr. Blakeman. This is not a convenient time to—"

"Convenient enough." Blakeman pushed his way inside. The three men with him followed; Vinegar Clifford and two leather-apron boys. "I've come to speak to your daughter, goldsmith. That's what you suggested, isn't it? Here I am."

"But now is not—"

Blakeman pushed past him and headed for the door to the private part of the house. Vionne tried to block his path, but he was half the other man's size. Blakeman shoved him out of the way and motioned his companions to follow.

The savory smell of hot food drew them at once to the dining room. Manon Vionne sat at one side of the table, an older woman across from her. Both stared in startled consternation at the new arrivals.

Vionne had rushed in behind his uninvited guests. Now he tried desperately to dispel the sense of menace with normalcy. "May I present Mr. Gornt Blakeman, ladies. He wishes—"

"I've asked for your hand, Miss Manon. Your father agreed."

"Never!" Manon and her father spoke in unison. Vionne continued, "I never agreed, Mr. Blakeman. You cannot say—"

"At the moment, Mr. Vionne, I can do and say as I wish." Not for much longer, if Jacob Hays took Joyful Turner's side of things. "I am claiming your hand, Miss Manon. You have need of a husband. Well, you have finally snared one."

She stood up, a pink flush rising from the scooped neckline of her frock to suffuse first the pale skin above her breasts, then her face. "I have no need of you, Mr. Gornt Blakeman." She took a step away from the table. "Papa, I beg leave to go to my—"

"Take her outside, Mr. Clifford."

Vionne flung himself in front of his daughter. The whip cracked once and coiled itself around his arm. His shriek of pain came from deep in his belly, and unbidden tears rolled down his cheeks.

"Papa! What are you doing, you animal!" Manon threw herself at the whipper. The nearest of the two butchers caught her with one arm. He held a raised cleaver in the other. Vionne shouted his daughter's name, but his voice was drowned out by Adele Tremont's scream.

"Quiet!" Blakeman roared. "I asked for your daughter like a gentleman, goldsmith. Had you treated my request with the respect it deserved, this wouldn't be necessary. As it has turned out . . ." He shrugged and turned away, heading back to the front door. "Bring her," he called to the butcher who still held Manon captive. "And make sure she doesn't cry out. Mr. Clifford, I trust your whip to keep these two in check until we're in the carriage, then you may join us."

All the while the men were inside, Jesse Edwards kept hoping for a chance to spook the horses. If he could get close enough without being seen, he could get them to take off and pull the carriage along with 'em. He wasn't sure exactly what that might achieve, but at least he'd be doing something. Not just hiding here in the doorway like he used to hide in the stores when he was meant to be running powder to the guns. He didn't want to be scaredy-cat Jesse anymore.

But as it was, didn't matter whether he was scared or he wasn't. Fellow sitting up there in the driver's seat didn't move even once, and he never relaxed his hold on the reins. And before Jesse could think of anything he might do instead, the men who'd gone into Miss Manon's house came out again. And, Holy God Almighty, they had Miss Manon with 'em.

Chapter Twenty-four

Aboard Le Carcajou, *5 P.M.*

UNTIE HER," Blakeman said. The whipper released the tie that had secured Manon's hands behind her back and freed the gag.

Blakeman stood and watched, as did five or six sailors. Not ordinary sailors, she was quite sure. And this was not an ordinary ship. "Pirates," she said.

Blakeman chuckled. "Your first word spoken as my fiancée, my dear. A mark of your powers of observation, perhaps, but hardly a sweet sound of love."

"You'll get none such from me, Gornt Blakeman. But I don't imagine you truly expect any different."

He took a step forward and grabbed hold of her hair, forcing her head back so she was looking up into his face. "I'll get exactly what I want from you, Manon Vionne. Never doubt that. The freedom of your body and sons from your belly." Blakeman grabbed her hand and held it to his crotch. "That's what's waiting for you, my girl. Count yourself lucky."

He let her go, so abruptly her head snapped forward, and laughed again. "Never mind," Blakeman said. "I quite like your spirit. What do you think, Tintin? A worthy bride? You're a sea captain of a sort, will you marry us once we're underway?"

"In the pirate code there is a price for such a service, *mon ami.* I get to bed her first."

"Over my dead body, pirate! This one is mine and mine alone."

Tintin laughed. "*Tant pis,* my friend. One woman is much like another, *non?*" He turned his back on them and walked to the side, peering down into the water. The cove was superbly well hidden, but the shape of the shore made for a treacherous mooring. Twice each day he watched anxiously while the schooner, forced to sit on the mud when the tide was dead low, floated as the waters rose. There was an incoming drift now. Fifteen, maybe twenty minutes, then he'd breathe easier. "If you mean to claim your treasure, *mon ami,* you must be quick about it. The tide comes our way. Soon we will be able to leave."

Belowdecks was mostly a narrow, open space with hammocks, a number apparently occupied though Blakeman paid them little attention, and filth from one end to the other. What passed for the captain's cabin was, if anything, worse. Too bad, but nothing to be done about it. Blakeman shoved Manon inside, kicking the door shut behind them. He felt for a lock or a bolt of some sort, but there was none. Never mind. Where could she go? He had been holding both her hands behind her back; now he freed them. "Not exactly what I'd expected to provide for your wedding night, my dear. But it will have to do."

It was a waste of time to trade barbs with him. Manon let her glance travel the small and fetid cabin, looking for something she could use as a weapon, some means of escape. Blakeman read her thoughts and chuckled. "We are on a ship, my dear. A pirate ship no less. There are many men, many cutlasses, many guns, and ashore— presuming by some miracle you got there—a deserted cove, steep cliffs, and beyond them deep woods. Now tell me, what makes more sense, a foolish, fruitless struggle that will exhaust you, though I admit it might excite me, or sweet maidenly yielding to your husband?" She said nothing. "Come, it is a reasonable question, Manon. It deserves an answer."

"You are not my husband."

Blakeman shrugged. "I will be. As soon as it can be arranged. I have no desire to leave you ravished and unmarried, my dear. It is in my best interests to have you my legal wife, and so you shall be. God, look at you . . ." He took a step closer. Manon backed away, but the cabin was only a few feet wide. She ended with the backs of her calves pressing up against the wooden frame of the bunk. Her hair had long since come loose; Blakeman curled one hand in it. "I'd have had you if you looked like the arse end of a horse, my Manon, because you suit my purposes. But I admit, I'm delighted you're a beauty. What sons we shall have, eh?" His free arm circled her waist. "Now kiss me."

She watched his face come close and stood very still, kept her mouth tight shut. She could not get away, but he would know she did not yield.

The kiss, if such it could be called, lasted only a few seconds. Blakeman lifted his head and his expression and voice were cold. "Fine, if you prefer rape, you shall have it, my dear. It makes little difference to me."

He let her go long enough to get both hands on the front of her gown. Manon panicked and pulled away, hearing the cloth rip as she did so. Apart from the bunk the only furniture in the room was a table and a couple of stools. She tripped over one of them, lost her balance and fell. Blakeman howled with laughter. Manon saw him looming above her, one hand fumbling with the front of his breeches. She screamed.

Outside there was the noise of many feet tramping through the passageway and shouts, mostly in French, but the accent strange to her and the words muffled. Rescue! It must be. Blakeman apparently had the same idea. He stopped what he was doing and listened, then he smiled. The rush was to the deck above. No one was coming to disturb them.

He lunged for her. Manon screamed.

The door to the cabin was pushed open. "Go ahead, Gornt. Prove that you are stronger than a slip of a girl. History will tell tales of your prowess."

He turned his head. "Christ Almighty! What are you doing here?"

Delight Higgins was naked. Some of her cuts and bruises were starting to scab; others yet oozed blood. "I might have guessed you'd show up. I should have figured it out before. You're the one who sent for the pirates, aren't you?" And before he could answer: "Perhaps you didn't know they do an active trade in blackbirding."

"This is no affair of yours. Get out."

"Why? What difference if I watch? I can't stop you."

There were more shouts from above, in English this time. "Blake-man! Get up here." Tintin's voice. "We're aground. We need every hand on the lines to pull free. Come, *mon ami.*"

Blakeman looked from one woman to the other. Neither of them spoke. He pulled away from Manon and ran to the cabin door. "Send someone down to help me secure these two she-cats, then I'll come."

One of the pirates brought line and helped tie up both women. Blakeman insisted on gagging them as well. The other man started to leave. "Where are you going?" Blakeman demanded.

"Above."

"We can't leave them here. There's no lock on the door."

"But they're both trussed like barnyard fowls. Ain't no way—"

"Not here." No point in explaining how resourceful Delight Higgins was likely to be, or how much spirit the other one had. "Somewhere more secure."

"There's a store up ahead below the afterdeck. The door will take a padlock—one prisoner in there already."

"Excellent," Blakeman said. He hefted Manon. "Bring the other one."

❧

New York City,
Ann Street, 5:30 P.M.

"I'm coming! No need to rip the knocker off the door." Bridey was accustomed to the sick arriving at Dr. Turner's front door demanding instant attention, but she never stopped complaining about it. "Well, what's wrong with you then? Need the other arm off as well?"

Jesse shoved his remaining hand in his pocket lest the woman grab him and start sawing. "No, ma'am. It's Dr. Joyful Turner I'm looking for."

"Well, this here's the house o' his cousin, Dr. Andrew Turner."

"Yes, ma'am. I know. I been looking everywhere and not finding Dr. Joyful Turner, so I thought he might have come—"

"Aye, well he didn't, but I suppose he might have. Come in. You look a sight, you do." The boy's face was streaked with sweat and dirt. If he'd had a hat, he'd lost it, and the brown cutaway as was anyways too big for him was ripped in a number of places. "Been in that riot up in Five Points, I reckon."

"Not really in it. I was some ways away. Got pushed about nonetheless."

"Same as all o' us." Bridey had herself gotten a good distance up Anthony Street. Near enough so she'd heard Dr. Joyful shouting out all them fine words o' the Constitution. Nearly burst with pride she had. Never mind that her best apron was torn off her and lost in the crush. "I expect you could use something to eat 'fore you go on about whatever your business might be."

"Thank ye, ma'am. But I've no time right now. Please, I have to find Dr. Turner. It's as important as—"

"As what, young man?" Andrew appeared in the open door of his study.

"I thought you was taking a nap," Bridey scolded. "You know you're supposed to take a nap every day after dinner."

"No man could sleep with you nattering away in front of his door. What's the difficulty, young man?"

"I have to find Dr. Joyful Turner, sir. It's about M . . ."

"About what? Come, I'm his cousin. You may tell me."

"It's a secret, sir. I mean I think it is. Dr. Turner's never said, but he and Miss—" Jesse broke off.

"Miss Manon Vionne," Andrew said, ignoring Bridey's look of astonishment. "That's who you're talking about, is it not?"

Jesse nodded.

"So has Miss Manon sent you? What is it she's asked you to say?" Andrew remembered Joyful's concern, that the girl's father might turn her into the street, that she'd need a place to stay. "Out with it, boy. You have my word, you betray no confidence."

"She didn't tell me nothing, sir. It's what I saw as Dr. Turner has to know about. Miss Manon . . . Four men took her away from her house in a big black carriage. I could see plain as anything she didn't want to go."

"Good God. I take it you were there?"

"Cross the street, sir. In a doorway. I been carrying notes back and forth for 'em. Dr. Turner and Miss Manon. He told me I should . . . I can't explain everything now, sir. But I have to find Dr. Turner. The man as took Miss Manon, it was Gornt Blakeman."

Hays's private apartments in the New Gaol were comfortable rather than luxurious. The green-leather chairs were well worn, the seats deeply impressed by countless posteriors of various sizes, the damask at the windows faded from the sunshine of many summers.

"A good thing ye did today, Dr. Turner," Hays said. "A mighty good thing."

He had made the same statement at least half a dozen times in the nearly three hours he'd kept Joyful talking, making him repeat every detail of what he knew of Blakeman's activities, occasionally dropping a remark of his own that let the younger man know that Jacob Hays was privy to most of what went on in his city. Not everything, however. Hays appeared not to know about the Great Mogul, and Joyful did not enlighten him.

Dinner was delayed by their talk, but eventually they'd been fed a stew of beef and onions provided by the housekeeper—Mrs. Hays was away seeing to the needs of a daughter who had just presented them with a grandchild—and when it was over, Hays belched loudly and offered what appeared to be his final assessment of the situation. "Money's what Gornt Blakeman's about, not politics. He's no interest at all in what makes a country, or the rights o' the folks as live in it."

"He's not alone in that, High Constable. Most people don't have time to think of such things until they feel those rights threatened. Too busy earning their livings."

"Aye. And nothing wrong with that neither. Same for the ordinary and the higher types, come to that. Course, depends on how you earn it, don't it?"

"What depends?" Joyful's head was wreathed in the smoke of the cigar he'd accepted after the meal.

Hays's cigar was no longer lit, but he kept the stub between his teeth, moving it from one side of his mouth to the other while he spoke. "Depends whether a man's on my good side or my bad. Gambling and wenching, for instance. That's the kind o' thing as causes no end o' trouble for me and my men." He looked straight at his guest when he said it.

"I can see where they might." There was no hint of apology or excuse in Joyful's tone. "If the enterprise is not well organized and well managed."

"Aye, better that way, I admit. Still there's things as are much safer, leastwise as concerns the law. For example, Dr. Turner, I hear tell there's someone thinking o' selling his share o' the Tontine. Now that's a respectable choice for a gentleman seeking to make his way. Course, t'other members get to vote on whoever wants to buy into their private arrangement. And likely, being the sort of men they are, some of 'em think Gornt Blakeman's way."

"I've no doubt some of them did think his way. But given how well the money men generally read the wind, there are probably none so inclined after today, High Constable. Half the town heard you charge

Blakeman with high treason and threaten to hang him. Just now he's a fugitive. I doubt he'll have any allies at the Tontine."

Hays sat back and considered Joyful for a few long moments. "Clever," he said softly, speaking, it seemed, more to himself than to his guest. "Trouble with young men like you, they can be too clever by half. Figure Blakeman's done with, do you?"

"Yes, Mr. Hays, I do. Don't you think the same?"

"Maybe, maybe not. But if I were you, I'd have my eyes open for—"

The housekeeper poked her head around the door. "Gentleman to see you, sir. Says it's urgent." Hays stood up. "Not you, High Constable," the woman said. "It's your visitor is wanted. Dr. Turner."

"How did you find me here, Cousin Andrew?"

"Young Jesse and I have been looking all over for you." They were outside on the Common, on a path between the gaol and the almshouse, both buildings looming large in the slant of the late afternoon sun. Andrew's trap was parked a few feet away, and Jesse Edwards had hold of the reins. "We finally came across someone who said they saw you leave Five Points with the High Constable, so we came here."

"Hays wanted to talk to me after the riot," Joyful said. "He wanted to know what . . ." He let the words trail away and took a step closer to the rig. "What happened, Jesse? You look as if you were in a fight."

"I was up at Five Points in the riot, Dr. Turner, sir. But that's not why we came. It's Miss Manon, Gornt Blakeman's got her."

"How could I let him take her?" Maurice Vionne kept saying. "How could I?"

Joyful, Andrew, Jesse Edwards, and Adele Tremont were in the goldsmith's front room, the small space crowded not so much by their bodies as by their anxiety. "You mustn't blame yourself, Monsieur

Vionne." The Widow Tremont spoke while making a bad job of re-placing the bloody bandage on Vionne's arm. "You gentlemen must understand that. There was truly no way we could resist."

"I've seen Mr. Vinegar Clifford at work," Andrew said. "I'm quite sure there was nothing you could have done. Here, madam, allow me." He took over the business of changing the bandage.

Joyful stood by the window, staring out into the street and pay-ing little attention to what the others were saying or doing. They had gone to Hanover Street first. The countinghouse was locked up tight, and he knew for certain there was no one upstairs because he'd climbed the damned tree and broken into Blakeman's private quarters to convince himself. So where would he take her? He turned to face the others. "Jesse says Blakeman had a couple of leather-apron boys with him. Occurs to me he might go up to the Bowery and—"

"Gornt Blakeman," Adele Tremont said, as if it were the first time she'd heard the name. "I should have guessed."

"Guessed what?" Vionne demanded.

"I suppose I knew it was him," Madame Tremont admitted. "I sim-ply didn't think about it until now."

"What didn't you think about?"

It was wicked of Manon to have ruined her *petite marmite* with salt, but perhaps it did not warrant a fate such as this. "Madame Euge-nie Fischer," Adele said. "I sew all her dresses. She will have no one else."

Joyful looked directly at her for the first time since they were intro-duced. The woman had been Manon's nemesis these past few days, but it was possible she might be able, however unwillingly, to help her now. "What about Eugenie Fischer?" he demanded. "Do you think Blakeman may have taken her to Mistress Fischer's house?"

Such a handsome gentleman, and a hero as well as a healer. He must be the reason Manon was uninterested in Monsieur DeFane's nephew and refused Gornt Blakeman. Ah, if she were twenty years younger . . . However, she was not, and Maurice would be in her debt if she assisted in this matter in any way possible. "If Mr. Blakeman brought a young woman who looked like Mademoiselle Manon to the home of Eugenie Fischer, she would murder them both. It is not the sort of situation in which Madame Fischer would conspire, Dr. Turner, because she would not shine by comparison."

"And she cares what Blakeman thinks of her?"

Men did not know how much they lost by not being privy to the gossip of servants. "Forgive my indelicacy, Dr. Turner, but in this situation . . . Mr. Blakeman is everywhere rumored to be the lover of Madame Fischer." Adele shot a quick look at Maurice, in case he might think badly of her for making such a remark. He was instead hanging on her every word. "You must understand, normally I do not approve of gossip, but— The other night, Wednesday it was, Madame Fischer summoned me to her house in the evening. After seven. Very unusual, but she said she must be fitted for a new frock immediately. Well, I had some lovely green silk that I got at Mr. Blakeman's sale Thursday last, and I mentioned that. I mean because I knew she and Mr. Blakeman were—"

"Yes, yes. You've told us. We understand." Vionne could barely contain his impatience. "What is this to do with my Manon?"

Joyful put a restraining hand on Vionne's shoulder. "Go on, madam. We're listening."

"Well, you see, I am observant. It's simply my nature. While I was fitting Madame Fischer, I developed the impression she had not brought me to her house at such an hour because of a frock. Normally, Madame Fischer is interested only in herself. That night it seemed she was interested in everyone else. Even women with whom she would normally have no intercourse whatever. A . . . Forgive me, gentlemen, but I can say it no other way. A brothel keeper."

"By the name of Delight Higgins," Joyful said, his voice very quiet, his monumental anguish turning to a rage no less fierce because it was so carefully controlled. "A mulatto woman. Runs a place called the Dancing Knave."

"Yes, that's correct. I'm sure a gentleman like yourself would never frequent such an establishment. But you know how other men are, I'm sure, Dr. Turner."

"Indeed. Tell me, Madame Tremont, exactly what did Eugenie Fischer wish to know about Miss Higgins?"

"Who sewed for her. And as it happens, I was able to tell her. Of course, I would never invite such custom myself, but there are some who are not so particular, and among us mantua makers . . ." She shrugged and kept talking, but Joyful had stopped listening.

Had Blakeman put Eugenie up to the business of finding out who sewed for Delight? Somehow Blakeman was seeking to use Delight to further his ends. The night they played bezique, when Delight so openly invited Joyful to her bed and he equally openly refused, Blakeman would have known about that. He'd figure Delight would go along with whatever he wanted because she was angry. But why seek out the name of the woman who sewed her gowns? What difference . . . Christ, it didn't matter. All that mattered was that Blakeman was the spider at the center of the web and Manon was caught in it. Damn your soul, Gornt Blakeman. This time you've miscalculated. This time we fight to the death.

He'd make much better time on horseback than in Andrew's trap. Vionne lent him a horse, taking the moment they were alone together while they saddled her to say, "You're the gentleman my Manon has been meeting, aren't you? Last Sunday, when she left church . . ."

"It was to meet me, yes. I'm sorry, sir. We never meant to deceive you. I wish to marry your daughter." Said at last, and what a time for it.

"We will speak later, Dr. Turner. For now, only know that I am grateful." He gave Joyful a leg up and watched while he galloped up the road.

It was not yet half seven when Joyful got to Rivington Street, still too early for custom at the Knave. There were no carriages, and his was the only horse tethered at the hitching post. He strode up the front steps, knowing the bar would not be across the front door at this hour, and used his key to let himself in, shouting Delight's name as soon as he was inside. "I must speak with you, Delight! It's urgent."

His voice echoed in the empty hall. "Delight!" Joyful threw open the door to the gaming salon. It was deserted. Dice and cards lay abandoned on most of the tables; glasses and tankards were everywhere, many containing the dregs of a drink. The spittoons had not been emptied; neither had the large crockery bowls provided for the convenience of smokers. The whole place reeked of last night's pleasure. He'd never known the gaming salon not to be fresh and spotless and ready by this time of day. "Delight! Where in Hades are you!" He strode across the hall to the Ladies' Parlor. It was equally slovenly. Delight's normal practice was to roust all the women from their beds by two and set them to cleaning. She'd sack anyone who didn't comply. "Delight!" Still no answer. Sweet Christ, what was going on?

Manon had been taken because Blakeman wanted to get at him. But what was the connection with Delight? He heard a sound behind him and turned to see Bearded Agnes coming down the stairs.

They talked in the Ladies' Parlor, surrounded by the soiled cups and saucers and glasses of the night before, an abandoned hand of cards turned facedown on the little table between them. "Blackbirders," Joyful said. "You're sure?"

"Course I'm sure." Agnes's eyes were red with weeping. "Terrified of 'em, she was. You must o' known that, Dr. Turner."

He nodded. "Yes, I did. But how— You say she was abducted from inside the house. How could that happen? Where were the the chuckers-out? Where were all the rest of you?"

"Asleep, like I told you," Agnes said. "Only Preservation Shay and me and Miss Higgins was up and about. She was in her private rooms with the mantua maker. She was being fitted and—"

Joyful leaned across the table and gripped Agnes's wrist. "Are you saying her mantua maker was with her when she was taken?"

"That's what I'm tryin' to tell you, Dr. Turner. Only you won't let me get the story out."

He let her go. "I'm sorry. In your own words, then. I'm listening."

"The mantua maker brought a girl with her, an assistant. Least that's what we thought. Turned out to be a man, one of them pirates with cutlasses and guns the mantua maker was screaming about, and—"

Sweet Christ, the pieces were starting to come together. "Tintin," Joyful said. "The Baratarian. He put the woman up to it."

Agnes nodded. "Pirates threatened to kill her babies, she said. Besides, everyone knows pirates are the worst blackbirders there are. And that Tintin, he was always following Miss Higgins about, baiting her, since the first night he walked into the place."

It was Blakeman who staked Tintin to a substantial wager that same first time the pirate appeared at the club. "Agnes, Gornt Blakeman, the man I played bezique with a few nights past, the one who—"

"I know who he is."

There was something in the way she said it. Not looking at him, embarrassed. It would take a lot to embarrass Bearded Agnes. "Delight invited him up to the third floor, didn't she?"

"You weren't coming around anymore, Dr. Turner. Not the way you used to. She was unhappy. A woman like Miss Higgins . . ."

"Yes, I understand." Blakeman and Tintin, Delight a pawn for both of them. "Tell me how the blackbirders got her out of the house."

"I'll show you," she said, and took him up to Delight's boudoir and led him to the rope ladder still hanging from the window. A ship's ladder.

Joyful spent less than ten seconds examining it, then started for the stairs. "Don't open for business tonight, Agnes, but get this place cleaned up. Miss Higgins will have a fit if she comes home and finds it like this."

"You think she'll be coming—"

"I guarantee it." If she was alive. If Manon was . . . He wouldn't let himself think about it. "Spotless," he called over his shoulder as he went out the door, as loudly as he could so they'd all hear him. "Spotless from top to bottom. Otherwise every one of you gets the sack."

He was again whistling past the graveyard, but as always it made him feel better.

Chapter Twenty-five

"TINTIN," Joyful said. "A pirate. He showed up at the Dancing Knave a bit over a week ago. Blakeman backed him in a high-stakes wager. He's in league with them. It's some part of his scheme for breaking the Union." Andrew, Vionne, the Widow Tremont, and young Jesse Edwards—they were all still in Vionne's front room, exactly as he'd left them a bit over an hour ago. Looking at Joyful and trying to understand the utility of the information he'd brought back.

"What has any of this to do with my daughter?" Vionne asked.

"It tells us where Blakeman has taken her. Tintin has a ship—"

Andrew shook his head. "You can't know that. Perhaps this Tintin came overland."

"I do know it," Joyful said. "I saw the rope ladder he used to abduct Delight from her private quarters." Christ, look at the expression on Vionne's face. The man who wanted to marry Manon was apparently on close terms with a brothel keeper. "It was a ship's ladder, covered in barnacles and disgracefully frayed. A pirate ship's the only kind that wouldn't have tossed it into the sea ages ago."

"Then why hasn't this pirate ship been spotted?" Andrew demanded. "The harbor's chock full of seamen with nowhere to go and nothing to do but keep an eye out. A strange craft, surely—"

"I agree. Which has to mean the pirates aren't in the harbor and have hidden their ship somewhere else." He found it hard not to let his discouragement show. "How in God's name do we find a ship that's— Yes, Jesse, what is it?" The boy was tugging at his coat.

"I know someone as can find any ship anywhere near here, Dr. Turner. That's his job o'work. Been doing it every day for three years. I can take you to him if you like."

Andrew insisted on driving Joyful and Jesse to Devrey's South Street premises, flogging his horse as if the trap were a stagecoach chased by a gang of thieves, though they raced through semideserted streets. The city had spent itself in the activities of the day; now everything was hush and calm. Both the dock and the warehouse looked deserted. Joyful cursed himself for a fool, so desperate for hope he was willing to snatch at any straw. "Looks like your friend's left for the day, Jesse."

"No sir, Dr. Turner. I'm sure he's not done that. He's always here until full dark. Look up there." Jesse pointed to the tall tower. "That's where Will is. He's Bastard Devrey's lookout boy."

"No he's not," Joyful said, confidence flooding back. "He's mine. Give him a shout, Jesse. Tell him to come down."

"Workers on this here dock answer to me, gents. You'll not be shouting any of 'em down or up lest I say so." The man's wooden leg made a tapping sound on the boards as he approached them.

"Peggety Jack, isn't it?" Joyful said.

"Aye. And you're Dr. Joyful Turner, and"—he turned to face Andrew—"and the senior Dr. Turner. I knows you both by reputation, gents. But this here be Mr. Lansing Devrey's wharf, and ye won't be—"

"You work for me, Peggety, not Bastard. I own the controlling interest in Devrey Shipping"—ignoring Andrew's startled glance.

"No one's told me nothin' about that."

"I think they have, Peggety. I think you know pretty much everything that's gone on. But in any case, I've no time to argue with you. Hail down the lad in the tower. I've something I want him to do."

"I can't—"

Joyful grabbed the front of the tar's checked shirt and pulled him close. "Hail him down, old man. Now. Else I'll cut off the other leg."

"You can't—"

"Let poor old Peggety go, Cousin Joyful." Bastard Devrey came out of the warehouse and walked toward them. "He's useful, as you'll discover. Good evening to you, and to you, Cousin Andrew."

Joyful released his hold on Peggety Jack. "Good evening, Bastard."

"I've been thinking it was time we spoke again," Bastard said. "I hear you were magnificent today in Paradise Square. I'm proud to be your partner, Cousin Joyful, and I suggest we—"

Pond scum. The sight of him made Joyful's gorge rise. "Later," he said, his terseness making it apparent he knew exactly the game Bastard had tried to play. "Jesse, shout Will down from that tower."

"No need," Jesse said, pointing to the ladder. "He's seen us, I reckon. Anyways, he's on his way down."

Andrew drove the trap to the end of Front Street. Jesse got down and trotted along on foot, running into each of the taprooms and taverns. "Check closest to the waterfront first," Joyful had instructed. "Then start on the inland taverns if you must."

No need, as it turned out. Jesse saw the tall, bald man with the full bushy beard in a grog shop up by Bruce's Wharf. Playing at cards, he was, just like Dr. Turner said was the probable way of it. "Captain O'Toole?"

"Aye. Who wants 'im?" Continuing to study the cards fanned in his large grip.

"Dr. Joyful Turner. To take the sloop *Lisbetta*."

"Take her where?"

"I can't say more here, Cap'n. But it's urgent. Dr. Joyful's cousin, Dr. Andrew, he's waitin' outside. With a trap as will bring us up to Parker's where *Lisbetta* is moored."

The men sitting at the table with O'Toole said something about playing cards and not nattering. He held up a hand to silence them and looked at Jesse. "What's your name, son? And how did you lose that arm?"

"Jesse Edwards, Cap'n. Lost me arm on the *Lawrence*. Battle o' Lake Eerie."

"And I'll wager a good part o' what's here"—O'Toole nodded to the five tall stacks of coins sitting in front of him—"that it's Joyful Turner what took the arm off, and probably saved your life in the doing of it."

"Aye, sir."

"Well, you're a good and loyal friend to him, that's obvious. And so am I, lad. Which is why I'm not about to take the *Lisbetta* on any phantom voyage."

"Begging your pardon, Cap'n. Dr. Joyful said I was to tell you he was asking you to come for his pa's sake. Said to say this was the time, and he was calling for payment o' the debt."

"Bloody poxing hell," O'Toole muttered. Finally he laid down his cards and began sweeping the piles of money into his hat. Been a lucky leprechaun perched on his shoulder the past four hours. Well, seems like he'd jumped off. "Sorry to quit whilst I'm ahead, boys." He stood up and cradled the hat in his arms. "But you heard the lad. Must be it's an emergency."

It was nearly 9 P.M., and an evening wind was gathering force from the north. Excellent joss that. Pray God it would last out this adventure. "All sails ho!" O'Toole shouted, the sap rising in him as it always did at such moments. Never mind that for crew he had only three out-of-work tars who shared a shack up by Parker's yard, one who regularly bunked down behind the yard's stores, and Danny Parker himself. And a doctor far too old to go to sea, as well as an all but useless one-armed powder monkey, both of whom had refused his suggestion that they drive back to Devrey's dock and instead insisted on coming aboard.

O'Toole was himself at the wheel, holding the forty-foot sloop steady into the wind while they made ready to sail. She heeled slightly of her own volition, and strained at the aft anchor as the leeward mainsail bellied and the snap of spreading canvas joined the creaking of the ship's boards. A song it was, best song in the world, and this *Lisbetta* was an angel ship, singing her song to welcome him. "Up aft anchor!"

Danny Parker raced the length of the deck. "Up aft anchor," he repeated. "Aye aye, sir." He hauled the heavy anchor line hand over hand, dropping it in a neat coil at his feet. "Aft anchor free, Cap'n."

The forward anchor had already been hauled aboard. The sloop moved gently, testing her liberty, but O'Toole wasn't ready to free her just yet. He scanned the river, checking for shoals—none too close to avoid—and judging the wind. Following, it was, and the tide running with them as well. Joss so good made him nervous. *Holy Mary, Mother of God, pray for us sinners, now and at the hour of our death.*

"One barrel o' grapeshot, half full, sir." Jesse surfaced from belowdecks. "And another with a few nails. That's all there be for the cannon, Captain O'Toole, sir. Two mostly empty kegs o' munitions. And there's an open crate with three muskets and five musket balls rolling around loose at the bottom. Rest o' the magazine's bare as a newborn's bottom."

"Doesn't matter, lad. It's not guns as will decide this." *Lisbetta* had never been a fighting ship. She was pierced for three cannon each side, an ordinary precaution of high-seas trade, but that was no use to him this night. He had one badly maimed powder monkey and no gun crews. The pirate ship—if they found her—would probably be better armed, but Tintin was likely to be as shy of crew as he was. He'd said as much to Dr. Andrew Turner on the drive up to Parker's, after he heard the purpose o' the voyage, and why Joyful had been so almighty determined that Finbar O'Toole bring *Lisbetta* downriver. On the prowl for prizes, a pirate ship might have a crew of fifty, sixty, even seventy blackguards. Sneaking into the waters surrounding New York and planning to sneak back out again, she'd be manned by six or seven, the bare minimum needed to run her. It was seamanship that would determine the outcome of this encounter. Aye, and hand-to-hand fighting, if it came to that. And a good measure of sheer poxing luck. "Bring the muskets up on deck," he told Jesse. "And as many musket balls as you can find. And pray God your friend has spotted the pirates." Or maybe pray he has not.

O'Toole let the sloop take the wind and her freedom. She picked up speed as the tars hoisted the foresail into position on the bowsprit, and she caught still more of the wind. "Hoist the jib!" he called, full of joy at feeling a moving ship beneath his feet once again. "South by southeast. Full speed ahead."

It was dark by the time *Lisbetta* rounded the bottom edge of Manhattan Island, but Joyful had set a pair of lanterns on the wharf in front of Devrey's dock so O'Toole could easily spot it. He brought the sloop in close and his makeshift crew quickly made her fast. "Handles as comely as she looks," he called down to Joyful and the boy standing beside him. "Any sign o' her?"

One of the tars threw a rope ladder over the side; Joyful leaned forward and caught it with his right hand, then pulled himself onto the first rung and began to climb, using his left elbow to serve as his second hand. He climbed the last few rungs and swung himself onto the deck. "Wallabout Bay. An inlet on the Bushwick side." he said. "A two-masted schooner." He spoke softly, conscious how far voices traveled on the water. "Here." He pulled a piece of paper from his pocket. "The lad sketched a chart."

O'Toole studied the drawing, leaning into the glow of the single lantern he'd allowed on the swift and silent passage downriver. "Holy Mary and all the saints," he muttered.

"You know the place?"

"Aye. I do. We passed it on the way down. There's many a soldier's ghost as haunts Wallabout Bay."

"You're not afraid of ghosts, are you, Finbar?"

"No, but I'd rather have known where I was goin' before I passed it by. I don't fancy having to come about and retrace my course against the wind."

"Nothing for it," Joyful said. I can't say as how—" He spotted his cousin up by the forecastle. "Andrew, you're a surprise."

"Didn't think I'd just trot on home after all this excitement, did you? Not a chance, Joyful."

"This isn't a pleasure cruise, Cousin Andrew. If Will's right and the pirate ship is nearby, we'll have to—"

"Fight them," Andrew finished for him. "Exactly why I'm coming with you. Even a pair of hands as old as mine may be useful for something in the circumstances. Besides, I helped deliver this United States into the world. I don't plan to let Gornt Blakeman murder her while I stand by and do nothing."

Joyful shook his head. "This isn't about the Union. Jacob Hays has pulled Blakeman's teeth on that matter."

"You're positive the wretch's got nothing else up his sleeve?"

"No, but—"

"Captain O'Toole and I have been discussing the matter," Andrew interrupted. "We're agreed Blakeman has to be stopped now. So this is more than a rescue mission and I am coming with you. Those two, on the other hand . . ." Andrew inclined his head. Joyful spun around to see what he was indicating.

Will Farrell had apparently come aboard while he and Andrew were arguing. He was standing shoulder-to-shoulder with Jesse, the intention of both of them entirely obvious. "Absolutely not," Joyful said. "Neither of you. That's final." Baratarian pirates were not likely to ask quarter or offer it.

"It's our country too, Dr. Joyful." Will was holding his two-foot-long brass spyglass under his arm. "Besides, got a head for heights, I have." He nodded toward the rigging. "And I know what I'm looking at."

"Anyways," Jesse said, looking not at Joyful but at Finbar O'Toole, "It's the captain who says yea or nay aboard ship."

"The boy's right," O'Toole said.

"All the same, it's my responsibility, Finbar. They're children and—"

O'Toole turned to the youngsters. "How old are the pair of you then?"

"I'm twelve," Will said. "Least that's what Holy Hannah says."

"I'll be twelve my next birthday." Jesse stretched to his full height. "And when's that birthday to be?"

"Christmas day. 'Fore she died, my ma told me I was born same day as the Baby Jesus."

"Twelve and eleven then," O'Toole said. "Young American men. The powder monkey and the lookout can come. It's the right thing."

An Inlet off Wallabout Bay, 9:30 P.M.

It was finally dark, with a fair wind, and *Le Carcajou* at last hauled off the sands of the cove and floating free. It had been a struggle, and all of them were exhausted, even Blakeman. Tintin thought it almost worth the trouble just to see him nursing palms blistered from hauling on the lines. "Real work, eh, *mon ami?* Not the sort of rubbish that passes for it in a countinghouse."

"Stop talking and get us out of here." Blakeman spat on his left palm, rubbing the moisture in with his thumb. "That's your job. Do it."

Tintin turned away. There was a glowing half moon and a sky alight with stars. *Eh bien,* the light would help them get safely out of the tight inlets with their shoals and sandbanks and into the bay. Might be some clouds by the time they were in the river. If not, they'd count on a swift run to get them safely through the Narrows and into the harbor. Speed and the ability to strike terror in the hearts of the enemy, a pirate's best friends. "*Alors!* Whistler!"

Tammy Tompkins looked up from the bit of scrimshaw he was working on. "Aye?"

"Get the flag," Tintin said.

"The Jolly Roger?"

"*Bien sûr*, unless you've another tucked away somewhere."

"I ain't seen it nowheres. Where's it kept?"

Tintin nodded toward a locker beside the mainmast. "Make it ready, but until I say, you do not run it up."

Aboard Lisbetta, *10 P.M.*

The tide had turned at the precise moment O'Toole needed it to do so. Mother o' God but the joss o' this night was bloody perfect. . . . *now and at the hour of our death* . . . "Prepare to come about!" Counting every body aboard, his makeshift crew had expanded to eight. "All hands at the sheets. Come about!" O'Toole spun the wheel. The tars manning the foresail and jib let them swing to center. They luffed for a few seconds, then the wind obligingly shifted to the south and caught them and they bellied taut, and the sloop headed back the way she'd come. Unnatural it was. . . . *and blessed is the fruit of thy womb, Jesus* . . .

Will Farrell had climbed high up the mast, steadying himself at the top with the grip of his knees so he could keep both hands on the fully extended spyglass. He'd never tried to see long distances by night; even with the moonlight it was harder than he expected. Shapes changed and distances seemed both shorter and further away. It took him a time to locate the cove where he'd seen the dark shadow he was sure was a ship in hiding. *It's a splotch o' dark what moves up and down and side to side, Dr. Turner. Only thing that moves so is a ship. Can't be sure, but I think she's a two-masted schooner.* He'd worked out the landmarks that would help him spot the cove a second time, but no matter how carefully he followed the shoreline into the inlet with the double bend, he could not pick out the same dark smudge with its two thrusting fingers pointing at the sky.

What would the others say if he'd brought them here on a fool's errand, if there wasn't any pirate ship. and no— Good God Almighty! There she was, under sail and heading down the inlet to the bay and the river beyond. He started to call out, then thought better of it and scurried down the mast. "Dr. Turner! Cap'n!" He whispered the words he wanted to shout. "Ship ahoy! The pirate ship's left her mooring and she's heading for the bay."

"Straight toward us," Joyful said.

"Near enough as makes no difference," O'Toole agreed. Could be their joss had at last changed. No way he would chance taking *Lisbetta* up the inlet. Danny Parker said the sloop drew eight feet o' water; if the lookout was correct and the pirates had a schooner, they probably had a draft o' five. And fast as he reckoned this angel ship could go, the pirates could likely outrun her on the open sea. He had to get to the bay before the schooner did and block her exit from the inlet. It was their only chance.

Joyful knew the Irishman's plan. "Can you get there in time?"

"Don't know. And say I do, you any notion o' what you'll do once we have 'em trapped?" O'Toole nodded toward the deck and the open crate with the lonely three muskets and the five musket balls between them.

Joyful clutched his longest scalpel. There were two more in his pocket. "Cut out Gornt Blakeman's heart, he said."

The wide curve of Wallabout Bay came into sight a ways ahead to starboard. No sign of the schooner yet, but they still had a fair distance to go, and no end of trouble possible on the way. O'Toole tacked slightly to larboard to avoid the shallows, then beat upriver as near to shore as he dared. He was close-hauled now, taking full advantage of the wind, and the men pulled the sheets as taut as their strength would allow, then tauter still. O'Toole felt every muscle afire as he leaned into the wheel, willing the ship to move faster. She raced up the reach. Nearly there. He let her fall off the wind a bit so she slowed some. Not much, but enough. "North by northeast, three degrees," O'Toole murmured. *Lisbetta* slipped into the bay.

"*Un moment*, whistler," Tintin called softly. They were nearing the end of the inlet; Wallabout Bay was dead ahead, then it was only a short run to the Inner Harbor and beyond to the open sea. They would go someplace to regroup, Blakeman said. Hartford, or perhaps Providence. But they must get out of the harbor first. Then nothing to worry about but the small annoyance of the patrols of the *diabolique* British navy. "Soon now, whistler. Make ready to hoist the flag."

Tompkins took hold of the line that would send the black flag to the top of the mast, and felt a cold hand in the pit o' his stomach. Twenty years being feared to death o' the sight o' the Jolly Roger, it was hard to imagine he was sailing under the skull and crossbones now. He looked toward the mouth of the inlet. Jesus God Almighty! There was a ship blocking the way to the bay, come like a spirit out o' the night. He pursed his lips to whistle the danger away, but his mouth was so dry it wasn't possible.

At the wheel Tintin saw the sloop racing to block his exit from the inlet. He held his course, trying to force her to change tack. She didn't waiver, just kept coming.

Blakeman, spyglass in hand, had been on deck since they left the cove. He'd thought to go below as soon as they cleared the inlet. Get the girl. Have her so she'd know there was no way— Christ! "It's Finbar O'Toole," he shouted at Tintin. "And Joyful Turner. We're twice their size. Take 'em on!"

Tintin had spread only about half his available sail, waiting to hoist his jib and his top gallants until he reached the open sea. The schooner was more maneuverable this way, but considerably slower. For the moment the sloop had greater speed, and it looked as if she were prepared to enter the inlet and ram *Le Carcajou* with her extended bowsprit. The schooner, however, had to have a shallower draft, and she certainly outweighed *Lisbetta* by at least fifty tons. "Come ahead,

Irlandais!" he shouted. "We will swallow you and shit you out our arse."

For a time it seemed that was exactly what *Lisbetta* would do. Then, at the last possible second, O'Toole swung the wheel so he was scudding for the bay's far shore.

"What's he doing?" Blakeman shouted.

"He makes ready to swing back and cover the inlet's mouth and take all our wind. He is not a fool, this *Irlandais.* He does not wish to take up such a position with his nose pointed at the lee shore."

"Can you outrace him?"

"Regretfully, *mon ami, non.* The wind has shifted again. It favors him, not us."

"Then what are you going to—"

Tintin ignored him, shouting instead to his crew. "*Préparez-vous monter à bord!* Prepare to board!"

Two crewman rushed a wooden catwalk into position between the bowsprit and the forecastle. Five others armed their pistols.

The wind was still from the south, but stiffer now, heralding a summer squall. "Come about!" O'Toole shouted, no longer afraid to be heard. He swung the wheel so hard to larboard the friction tore a strip of skin from his palms. *Lisbetta* responded by catching the wind and heeling hard over. Andrew and Will Farrell, who had never been aboard a ship, both lost their footing.

Joyful stopped his cousin's slide with his foot and grabbed the lookout by the collar of his Devrey livery. "Andrew! Are you hurt?"

"No, not a bit." Andrew seized the gunwale and hauled himself to his feet. "Look! We're blocking them!"

Lisbetta, her nose pointing toward the exit from the bay to the river beyond, lay across the mouth of the inlet, taking the wind of *Le Carcajou.* The sails of the pirate schooner went limp, but the open-mouthed beast that was her figurehead was not eight feet from the sloop, and the end of her bowsprit overhung *Lisbetta*'s deck. Joyful's chest felt banded by iron and rivulets of sweat dripped down his back.

"*Maintenant, mes amis!*" At Tintin's shout the Jolly Roger was run up the mast, and a pair of men rose on the bowsprit and dropped onto the deck of the sloop. Two muskets fired. One pirate fell, his skull shattering in a spray of blood and bone.

Joyful launched himself at the second pirate. The man carried a cutlass in one hand and a pistol in the other. The cutlass dropped to the deck as Joyful's body made contact and the pistol went off over his shoulder. He felt his scalpel bite deep into the pirate's belly and heard the man's scream as it ripped upward. Joyful fell back and his foot struck something lying on the deck. He looked down and saw Jesse Edwards with a bullet through the middle of his forehead. The boy had come up behind him, obviously intending to help take down the boarders. Damn you to everlasting hell, Gornt Blakeman.

Three more pirates shimmied swiftly along *Le Carcajou*'s bowsprit and dropped to the deck. Danny Parker picked up the dropped cutlass and one of the tars fired the third musket, but the ball went astray and did no good. The other two had managed to reload with the remaining two musket balls, and one ended the life of a pirate by plowing into his chest at point-blank range. The other smashed uselessly into the side of the ship.

There was no sign of Blakeman, or Manon. Two more pirates dropped to the deck of the *Lisbetta* and raced forward. Joyful heard the sounds of fighting behind him. He climbed onto the sloop's gunwale, found his balance, then put the scalpel between his teeth. He stretched his right hand toward the bowsprit of *Le Carcajou,* and launched himself into the air, hanging on to the sturdy spar with his single hand. Praying he wouldn't lose his grip, Joyful swung his body forward and back on his right arm, willing the momentum to increase the range of movement, forcing his strained muscles to give him enough speed to reach the bowsprit with his legs. Two attempts failed, but the third time he got one leg around the wood and was able to hoist the other to meet it. At last he could get his left arm into position to do some good. The added leverage allowed him to twist onto the topside of the spar and begin inching forward on his belly.

A pirate came toward him, so intent on maintaining his balance that he didn't see Joyful at his feet. Joyful swung his heavy sand-stuffed glove at the pirate's ankles, and the man fell screaming into the water.

A catwalk at the end of the bowsprit led to the forecastle. Joyful got to his feet and took another scalpel from his pocket. The first remained gripped in his teeth. He ran onto the deck and two bodies hurtled toward him. Joyful lashed out with the scalpel and felt it slice through cloth and into flesh.

"*Merde!*" Tintin jumped back as hot blood began pumping from his shoulder wound, then sprang forward again, his cutlass slashing but cutting through nothing but air. The force of his lunge carried him across the deck, and by the time he turned around, he saw Joyful Turner and Gornt Blakeman locked in combat, outlined by the light of the moon.

Blakeman had already discharged his pistol. The shot had gone astray and he'd dropped the useless weapon. He was heavier than Joyful, and he had two hands. But he was considerably older, and the younger man had both speed and stamina on his side. Blakeman came in close, wrapping one arm around Joyful's neck, and tried to bury his dagger in the other man's gut. Joyful swung the black glove at the side of Blakeman's head, putting the full range of his height behind the move. The blow connected, and Blakeman broke his hold and staggered back, then lunged once more.

Tintin, the front of his shirt soaked in blood, ran toward the two men, swinging his cutlass. Joyful moved aside and the pirate hurtled past them, then turned and came again. The pirate opened his mouth to shout, but what came out was not a war cry but the gurgling sound of death; he dropped to the deck, the severed artery in his shoulder having starved his heart of blood. Joyful kicked the pirate's body away and lunged for Blakeman. He still had the scalpel in his teeth, and he dropped his head. He felt the blade cut into the other man's cheek, and at the same time took a glancing blow to the forearm from Blakeman's dagger. Both men ignored their wounds and grappled again, fighting to maintain footing on a deck now slick with blood.

The silence on *Le Carcajou* was broken only by the grunts of Joyful and Blakeman, but the sound of clashing blades and shouts came from the *Lisbetta*. A door opened from amidships of the schooner, and a shaft of yellow lantern light fell across the wolverine's deck. Joyful was half aware of another figure come to join the battle, and knew that whoever it was would fight on Blakeman's side, not his. He heard the crack of the whip and managed to swing his body to one side, forcing Blakeman to move in a half circle, and scream out in pain as the lash caught him full on the back.

The stinging hurt and the force of the blow caused Blakeman's head to jerk upwards, hitting Joyful full in the chin. The scalpel he'd kept clenched between his teeth dropped and skittered across the deck. He ignored the pain, knowing he had a second, maybe two, of the barest advantage, and that if he didn't use it he was a dead man. He lunged once more. This time the scalpel he held bit deep and he ripped upwards through resisting muscle and flesh, but was forced to let go of the weapon and fling himself backward to avoid the whipper's lash.

Blakeman reeled and fell against the ship's side, instinctively struggling to tear the scalpel from his side, widening the wound as he did so. Vinegar Clifford flicked his arm and the whip snaked toward Joyful. He knew he did not have the strength to keep fleeing Clifford's lash. If the whipper chased him across the deck of the schooner, the whip would eventually win. Joyful hurled himself toward the long leather thong and fell on it, rolling toward the whipper as he did so.

Clifford howled in rage as his weapon was immobilized, then used every bit of his strength to pull free. Joyful kept rolling toward him, until the full force of his body weight yanked the handle of the whip from Clifford's hand and the whipper suddenly careened backwards. Joyful was on his knees now, and he flung himself at Clifford, head-butting him directly in the belly at the same moment that the whipper's out-of-control body made contact with the ship's rail. Dried out from years of pirate neglect, it splintered and gave way, and Clifford fell overboard.

Joyful stopped his own forward motion by grabbing hold of a line stretched from a deck-mounted block and tackle to one of the sails, hanging on and gasping for air. He heard Clifford shout, his voice rising from the surface of the water fourteen feet below. Something about not being able to swim. Joyful turned his head, checking to see if either the pirate or Blakeman had gotten up and was coming for him, but both lay motionless on the deck. Bile rose in him and he could do nothing but retch for what seemed like an age. Finally, he got to his feet and staggered toward the opening that led below. "Manon! Manon! Where are you?"

He hadn't thought to detach the lantern at the top of the ladderway, and the dark of the lower deck was relieved only by thin shafts of starlight coming through the occasional porthole. "Manon!"

There was a muffled thump from somewhere straight ahead. He called again and was answered by a series of thumps. Joyful ran toward them as fast as he dared, aware that on this ship nothing could be counted on to be in good repair, including the deck below his feet. The padlock on the low door at the end of the narrow passage was an exception. He yanked at it, but it held. He pounded on the door. "Manon! Manon, are you in there?" More thumps. "Thank God! Be brave, my love. I'll be straight back. I've got to find something to smash this lock."

He had to climb back up the ladderway to the upper deck. As soon as he surfaced, he saw a man coming toward him, swinging a cutlass over his head. Joyful reached into his pocket and found only one tiny scalpel left, the one he used for the most delicate of surgical operations, with a blade no more than an inch long. He brought it out, then heard his name called. "Dr. Turner? Is that you?"

"It's me, Danny. What are you doing here?"

"Dr. Andrew sent me to look for you. Young Will said he saw you climb out on the bowsprit. Dr. Turner's tending the wounded and—"

No time to ask now who lived and who had died. "Miss Vionne's below. I need something to smash a padlock."

Parker turned to the locker beside the mizzenmast and pried it open with the cutlass he'd doubtless taken from a fallen pirate. The tools were mostly useless, rusted and rotten, except for one stone-headed hammer. Joyful seized it and raced back the way they'd come. The shipwright followed him. "Grab that lantern," Joyful shouted, and Parker did, and this time the two men made their way along the lower passage in decent light. "Manon!" Joyful called. "Manon, I'm coming."

Parker set down the lantern. He took the hammer from Joyful, gripped it with two hands, swung, and the padlock gave way. Joyful shouldered open the door and bent and went into the tiny cabin. "Manon, oh my God . . ."

She lay on the floor, bound and gagged. He dropped to his knees beside her and used the small scalpel to cut away the gag and the ropes. She was not alone. A few feet away lay Delight, and next to her a young black boy.

"I'm all right," Manon said as soon as she could speak. "I'm fine, Joyful. I knew you'd come. Help her."

Joyful knelt beside Delight and cut her free, then took off his coat and helped her into it. Neither of them said a word.

"She saved me," Manon said. "If it wasn't for her . . ."

"Thank you," he said, "for more than I can say."

Delight got shakily to her feet, and didn't answer. Joyful tossed the little scalpel to Parker, who grabbed it in midair. "Free the boy." Manon had gotten to her knees, and Joyful helped her up the rest of the way. The front of her gown was torn away, but other than that she looked unharmed. He put his good hand on one side of her face and his wretched glove—which had this night proved to be such a useful weapon—on the other, and leaned forward and kissed her.

"I knew you'd come," she said again. "Right from the first, I knew you'd come."

The boy was in much the worst shape. He'd been severely beaten with the cat; none of his wounds had been treated and some had already started to fester. "In God's name . . ." Joyful murmured. Then, "What's your name, lad?"

"They be whipping me so I say my name be Pompey and I be a

runaway slave. But I not be Pompey, and all the beatings on the earth
don't make me be a slave. I be Joshua, Dr. Turner, as came to get you
and bring you to Mother Zion."

"This time it was my turn to come and get you," Joyful said.

Joshua smiled, a wide grin despite cut lips and two missing teeth.
"Yes sir, Dr. Turner. Yes sir."

They went slowly back the way they'd come. Joyful had his arm
around Manon's waist. Delight walked ahead of them, her back
straight, her head high. Above decks he saw both women take note of
the bodies of Tintin and Gornt Blakeman.

Danny Parker led the way to the catwalk and the bowsprit that
would get them back aboard *Lisbetta,* but Manon hung back. "Wait,"
she murmured.

"Go ahead with Joshua and Miss Higgins, Danny," Joyful called.
"Miss Vionne and I will follow." He saw the others safely crossed over
to the sloop, then turned to Manon. "What is it?"

She nodded toward the body of Gornt Blakeman. "The stone. It is
on his person."

Sweet Christ! He should have thought of that. No way on earth
Blakeman would have left the city without the Great Mogul.

"Look in his breeches," Manon called softly as she watched him
cross the deck, "between his legs."

Joyful knelt beside Blakeman. The diamond was in a small black-
leather box, tied tight around his thigh and nestled in his crotch. Joyful cut it free, wondering how Manon knew it was there, then decided
he'd rather not have an answer to the question. "Here," he said when
he returned to her. "You're the one who best understands what this is.
Keep it safe."

Aboard the *Lisbetta,* Andrew tended the wounded, only one long slash
down the front of his cutaway to indicate he'd had a share in the fighting of this night. That, and his thumping heart. Nearly forty years past
he and Sam Devrey had drawn straws to see who would go to war and

who would stay in New York and spy. Andrew had drawn the short straw. He'd always had some regret about missing the action, if not the danger.

He'd been considerably luckier than his patients: two of the tars and Finbar O'Toole. One of the sailors had a wicked bone-deep cut along one thigh that might cause him to lose the leg, but the bleeding could be stopped now and a decision to amputate made later. The other had lost an ear and required that the wound be stanched and sewn. As for the Irishman, Joyful's old friend, his belly had been slit open. Andrew had done what he could, but it was just a matter of time.

Joyful came up behind his cousin. Andrew didn't look up from the wound he was closing. "You found her?"

"Yes. Unharmed, thank God. I'd not have been able to do it without you. Without all of you."

"No," Andrew said, no emotion in his voice, "you would not. Meanwhile, four pirates and three of the sailors are dead."

"Tintin and Blakeman as well," Joyful said. "I killed them both. With scalpels."

"Think of it as cutting away a cancer," Andrew said brusquely. "Young Jesse Edwards is dead as well."

Joyful looked over to where Will Farrell sat beside the body of his friend. "I know."

"And Captain O'Toole . . ." Andrew let the sentence trail away. No point in mouthing a lot of platitudes about the nature of war and the price of freedom. "Back there," he said.

Joyful went and knelt beside the Irishman, taking his hand. "I'm sorry," he said. "I knew you'd have to come if I said it was because you owed my father. I had no right."

"Every right," O'Toole said. "That was part o' your legacy as well." O'Toole's voice rasped and his breathing was shallow, but the words were clear. "Grand it was. A grand way to go. Better'n an argument over a mahjong tile or a roll o' the dice. Captain o' a fine ship and done a fine thing for the nation. A proud thing." His eyes fluttered closed, and Joyful stayed beside the Irishman, as he drew one breath, then another, and then no breath at all. Across from them, still wearing only Joyful's ripped and filthy cutaway, Delight Higgins was walking up and down the length of the sloop's deck, inspecting the faces of the dead.

She was looking for the whistler, the one who had come with the mantua maker to the Dancing Knave and forced her to climb down the ladder to where Tintin waited to take her captive. He was the only one of the pirates who had not raped her. Maybe he was dead and his body had fallen into the sea, or maybe he'd been killed aboard *Le Carcajou*. She'd probably never know. When she reached the end of the row of bodies, she turned and walked back, pausing beside each dead pirate long enough to spit into his face.

They set sail with Danny Parker at the helm and the two tars manning abbreviated sails.

When they came out of Wallabout Bay into the river, Danny headed *Lisbetta* into the wind long enough to put the bodies of the dead over the side. All except Jesse. "Hannah will want to bury him," Joyful said after he and Will conferred. "We've decided to take him home."

Finbar O'Toole was a different matter. Finbar would have wanted his last resting place to be the sea. They let him go after Andrew said the prayers for his soul, because Joyful was too choked to do so.

Delight waited until the end of the spare, brief service, then went to where Joyful stood beside the ship's railing, looking into the water that had claimed the body of his friend. "I know you didn't come for me, but thank you."

"I would have come for you. Even if Manon were not— I'll never forget you, Delight."

"Not likely," she said, keeping her voice light, pretending the ache of her heart wasn't a thousand times worse than that caused by her bruised body. "Your four percent of the Knave will serve to keep me in mind."

"It's not just that."

"I know. Joyful . . ."

"Yes."

"I'm the one who told Gornt Blakeman about you and Manon. I'd seen you with her in the Fly Market. The vegetable seller told me Manon's name and I told Blakeman. Because I was so angry."

"I'm sorry, Delight. I . . . It's just not possible to control whom you love."

"It wasn't simply because you love her and you don't love me."

"I love her differently from how I love you," he amended.

She shook her head. "You don't understand. All this time, you never recognized me. 'Dearie my soul, Miss Clare . . .'" She waited, but there was still no light of recognition in his face. "Laniah, Joyful. The little slave girl who worked for your sister and worshiped you from afar. That first night, when you appeared in Barnaby Carter's shay, it was as if you'd materialized from my dreams. But despite everything that happened between us, no matter how often you looked at me, you never saw Laniah."

He stared at her, trying to see the skinny little girl instead of the beautiful woman in front of him. "You and Molly weren't killed? You ran away?"

Manon stood across from them, watching. Delight lowered her voice so only Joyful could hear. "Dearie my soul, Mr. Joyful, that surely do be what Laniah be telling. That be exactly how it was and how it do be. Miss Molly, she be in Nova Scotia. And Laniah, she be right here."

"My God, Delight, why did you never tell me?"

She looked out at the water rippling along the sloop's hull, fading into stillness after they passed. "I wanted you to see for yourself. I wanted not to be so different from what I had been. Laniah was a person too, Joyful."

He shook his head. "I'm sorry. You changed so, it never occurred to me."

"Never mind, it's no longer important. But what is important is that Blakeman never finished what he started with your Manon."

"It doesn't matter," he said.

"Still," Delight said. "It's better."

"Yes, it is."

"Go on." Delight nodded toward Manon. "She's waiting for you."

"Delight . . ."

"Go on," she said again, and Joyful left her where she stood and went to join Manon.

They'd reached the Inner Harbor by then, heading for the river. Delight turned and looked back the way they'd come. A tune floated out across the water. At least she thought it did. *He played in time and he played in tune, but he wouldn't play nothin' but "Old Zip Coon."*

Saturday, August 27, 1814

Chapter Twenty-six

The Manhattan Woods,
Soon After Midnight

HANNAH WON'T BE SLEEPING," Will said. "Not with it so late and neither of us back from town."

He was right. When Joyful trotted his horse out of the woods and into the clearing, he could see Hannah there in the glittering blue-gray starlight, sitting on the bench beneath the chestnut tree. "I'm glad you brought him home," she said when she stood up and came to meet them. "That was the right thing."

He should have guessed. All the way from Maiden Lane he had been pondering how to tell Holy Hannah of Jesse's death. It was not, of course, necessary. She knew. "Felt it, I did," she said in a voice that had finished with grieving.

Jesse's body lay across the horse's neck, with Will sitting behind him, keeping his dead friend steady. Joyful sat behind, them, the need to keep hold of the reins giving him an excuse to have his arms around both boys. Hannah reached up and put her finger on the bullet wound in the center of Jesse's forehead. "I was sitting right here wondering where my two lads had got themselves to, and I knew the minute that danged bullet got my one-winged pigeon. He was acting truly brave, was Jesse. He'd o' wanted to go like that, acting brave."

"Enormously brave." Joyful said. "He stopped the bullet meant for me."

"He'd be right pleased with that," she said. "Give him here, Will. We can bury him out behind the cabin tomorrow, under them sycamore trees he liked. Don't seem there'd be any place he'd rest better, seein' as he had no family, and no proper religion so far as we know."

Will allowed his friend's body to slide free into Hannah's arms. He and Joyful dismounted and tried to help her, but Hannah insisted on carrying the body into the cabin by herself, and didn't let him go until she put him down on the pile of rags that had been his bed since he came to stay with them. "Only nine days since you brought him home, Will. Him and that big fat kidney from Henry Astor's private store. You did a real good deed bringing him here. A *mitzvah*. You can be happy about that."

"But I'm the one found the pirate ship." Will was crouched beside Jesse's body, keening over him, at last letting his grief show. "If I hadn't o' done that, we wouldn't have gone after 'em and Jesse would still—"

"You saved our country, lad," Joyful said. "I don't think that's putting too fine a point on it. There are still those who want to break up the Union, but Gornt Blakeman was the loudest voice among them. With him gone it's going to be a lot more difficult for them to have their way."

"Saved the country, did they? Seems to me that makes both my boys real military heroes. You stay with Jesse now, Will. You be his *shomer*. It's a *mitzvah* to watch beside the dead until they're in the earth. There's some as say it's the greatest good deed of all, 'cause they can't thank you this side of the grave."

Hannah put her hand on Joyful's arm. He followed her outside.

"End of a lot of things tonight," she said when they once again stood beneath the stars. "Beginning of lots of others. Twice around and thrice back. You figured any of it out yet?"

"Some maybe. The treasure's not where my father left it. I'm sure of that. But Shearith Israel doesn't have it."

"They had it for a day or two. Then they gave it back. Captain Harmonious Grant, man I was going to marry, he gave it to the congregation. My doing, that was. But Rabbi Seixas and the others, they said it was blood money and they wouldn't accept it."

"How did this Captain Grant get it?"

"Heard talk years back, after the war with the French and their Indians. Harmonious was only a wee lad at the time, but his father had a grog shop down by the waterfront and he heard a Dutchman as had sailed with your papa talk about twice around and thrice back, seventy-four degrees thirty minutes west of Greenwich. Don't know who else might o' heard, but they didn't do nothing about it. Harmonious did. His pa died in the Revolution, and soon as it was over, Harmonious sold the grog shop, got a ship, and that's where he sailed to, seventy-four degrees thirty minutes west of Greenwich."

She sat down on the bench beneath the chestnut tree and patted a place beside her. Joyful took it and waited. "You know where that is?" Hannah asked after a time.

"No. Somewhere in the Caribbean, but I went to sea as a surgeon, never learned to navigate."

"Island in the Bahamas called San Salvador. S'posed to be the place Columbus landed when he came first time, to this New World, like they calls it."

"And twice around and thrice back?"

"Bit of almighty clever that is. Clever o' your papa to think of it the first time, and clever o' my Harmonious to remember it all those years."

She was quiet for a while, laughing softly to herself, as if at a joke only she knew. "Bit of almighty clever."

Joyful waited, knowing it was best to be silent or he'd leave empty-handed yet again.

"Time now," she said at last. "The Holy One, Blessed Be His Name, he let me know it was time. In fact, time's what it was all about. Just south of twenty-four degrees north, that was t'other part of the coordinates. Took my Harmonious to a sweet little cove, that did, with a bit of an inlet leading away to the interior. Midday, according to the sextant, and the chronometer pointing exactly upstream."

Hannah spoke as if she were repeating a story memorized in careful detail, not one word of the telling changed from the first recitation.

"Twice around," Hannah said. "That meant two sweeps o' the chronometer's hand. Two o'clock that would be. Thirty degrees to port. Harmonious was rowing a dinghy by then. Not enough draft for a ship. Just as well, seeing how a man can row alone. He came to another cove. Just where it should be. 'Twice around and thrice back.' Hand o' the chronometer goes backwards three times, that makes it eleven o'clock. Forty-five degrees to port. Rowed himself that way, and turned out Harmonious was looking straight at a twisted tree as no man was likely to forget the shape of, and sure to the Almighty, the place to bury a treasure."

One mystery solved, but not the only one. "A treasure coming to me over the water, you said, Hannah. What did you mean by that?"

She chuckled yet again. "'Above the water' would o' been clearer, but I didn't want it to be too easy for you. Over there . . ." She nodded toward the cistern. "Built the thing so's I could have a safe place for the treasure once and for all. A place to leave all that blood money, until it was to be returned to its rightful owner. Never spent a single copper from it. Never even opened the moneybag as Rabbi Seixas gave my papa, the moneybag he throwed at me the night . . ." She stopped speaking and shuddered. "Never mind that. It's nothin' to do with you. Your treasure's behind the fourth course o' stones down from the top. Well above the level o' the water. Couldn't be otherwise, else we had a flood like made Noah build the Ark. So you might say the treasure was over the water."

Joyful stood and started for the cistern, but Hannah put out a hand and stopped him. "Been waiting for you all these years—it can wait a bit longer. Come back tomorrow morning. We'll bury Jesse in the sunshine. After that, Will can help you dig out the treasure."

Wall Street, Late Morning

Joyful walked into Blakeman's Hanover Street premises looking stern and purposeful, letting none of his elation show. The price paid had been high, but sweet God Almighty, he had done it.

There was a single clerk in the countinghouse—no sign of Bastard—standing behind one of the tall desks. The man looked at him. "Gornt Blakeman is dead," Joyful said. "That's a fact, and Jacob Hays will confirm it later today." He had himself sent word to the High Constable; where to find the pirate ship and the bodies of Blakeman and Tintin. "As for me, I'm Joyful Turner, and I wish to buy Blakeman's interest in Devrey Shipping, I've got cash money in good coin. Tell me where I'll find the attorney as handles Blakeman's affairs."

The clerk stared at him in silence for a moment, then shrugged. "You're too late. Jacob Astor was here two hours past and made the same request. I expect he's made all the arrangements by now."

"Why?" Joyful demanded. "You said we were allies. You gave your word not to—"

"Allies yes. But my word not to buy Gornt Blakeman's assets when they were available? I do not think so, Joyful."

They were in Astor's study. Astor stood by the spinning globe, turning it idly round and round. The sunlight streaming through the windows was so bright there was no need to light the globe's interior lantern. Sea and land, mountain and meadow, blended in a blur of ivory and sepia. "Tell me when I ever said any such thing."

"Not exactly, I grant you that. But naturally I assumed . . ."

"In business it is not good to assume." Astor abruptly stopped the globe from spinning and turned to face the younger man. "And that is why I bought Blakeman's interest in Devrey's. Bastard's also. That I think is a surprise."

"That means you have fifty-one percent. You're the majority holder."

"*Ja,* my intention exactly, that was. To be the senior partner. So you will make no foolish mistakes, Joyful. So Devrey Shipping can wait out the end of this miserable war and not go bankrupt before peace comes. To have too little capital, in business that is not a good thing. This way—"

"I have capital. A very great deal." As soon as he said it, Joyful knew that the coin equivalent to twenty thousand sterling, one hundred and sixty thousand American dollars, would seem considerably less to Jacob Astor than it did to him. Nonetheless.

"*Ja,* the 'thrice back' legacy. Very good, Joyful. I am happy for you. But you—"

"How did you even know the treasure exists? I never spoke a word to you about it? For that matter, how did you know Gornt Blakeman was dead?"

Astor chuckled and tapped his temple, much as he'd done the first time Joyful came to this room with his tale of a wondrous jewel and a scheme to divide the nation. "Observation, Joyful. Only observation." He would not say much about Heinrich and his men in the Watch and the Police Office. But it was right he should explain a little. "Mr. Samson Simson, the Hebrew attorney. He is a good man, a sensible man. That is why Maurice Vionne consulted him as well as Mr. Mordecai Frank when the Great Mogul came first to his attention. But Mr. Simson, he is also my friend, part of the group I told you about, the ones who with me have joined to lend money to Mr. Madison. For the country."

Ah, yes. What had Simson told him when he asked if the man were a patriot? *In my fashion, Dr. Turner.* "So the circle is linked," Joyful said.

He had brought the money to Vionne's house that very morning, coming straight from Holy Hannah's. *My guarantee of Manon's fu-*

ture, sir. If you will grant me her hand. And guard this for us until we're married. It had not been possible to give his future father-in-law such a sum without explaining where it came from. "All along I've been less clever by half than I thought myself—that's true, isn't it, Jacob?"

"No, Joyful, it is not. You are very clever, and very brave. Even *einfallsreich . . . Ach,* what is the English word? Resourceful. And now you have a choice to make, *hein?* I'm told there is to be a place in the Tontine. And that Mr. Colden, who is an influential man, has decided yours it should be. So will you be a money-man, Joyful?"

"I'm not sure, Jacob. I am considering it. But first I will be a Canton trader."

"Excellent. I am happy to hear it. Look." He spun the globe again. "This trail through the Oregon Territory, it will be a magnificent new opportunity for the whole country. My word you have. And the president and Mrs. Dolley, already I am told they are back in the Federal District. While here in New York . . . Look."

Astor tugged on a cord. A large map of Manhattan unfurled. Joyful recognized it instantly, though it was a map he had heard about but not seen. In this rendition the city he knew was a tiny thing nestled on the southern tip of the island, dwarfed by a strict grid of streets and avenues that overlay the wilderness to the north, each thoroughfare divided into uniform lots.

"My friend Mr. Randal," Astor said. "He is a remarkable surveyor. He made this for me. For the Common Council he made one as well. They have adopted the plan, but that you know, Joyful. I will tell you what you do not know. See here how Broadway makes a little turn just by what will be Seventeenth Street? Originally, it was to go straight, but I own farms just here." Astor tapped the map. "So, I talked to my friend Mr. Randal, and to the Council . . ." Astor shrugged. "They are reasonable men."

"You are a wonder," Joyful said quietly. "It's mad to oppose you."

"I do not wish to be in opposition to you, my friend. Especially not now when we are *Teilhaberen.* Partners. Now, a good look you must have," pointing to the map once more, "here is New York's future. This is the city that will be."

"Perhaps. But Devrey's is a shipping company. We look this way." Joyful tapped the harbor and the open ocean at the eastern edge of the plan.

"To be a successful man of business, Joyful Turner, you must be like the Roman god Janus. You must look both ways." Joyful started to say something, but Astor held up his hand. "Wait, I am not finished. I have another proposition for you. Bastard Devrey's Wall Street house."

"Yes?"

"You are to marry, no? You will require a home for your wife. You do not wish to bring the lovely Mademoiselle Vionne to a boarding-house. I bought Bastard Devrey's house. Along with his shares. He will use the money I paid him to finish a house near me here on Broadway. Which he cannot afford and which he will probably mortgage sooner rather than later and lose soon after that. But you and I, we do not need to concern ourselves with Bastard Devrey. Consider instead this: I propose to sell you the Devrey house on Wall Street. It is no longer as fashionable as it once was, but still a fine residence, no? A good place for you and your bride. Later you can sell it and build something more grand. Meanwhile, I will take eight thousand for Bastard's house. A fair price, no?"

"Very fair. It will be worth half again as much in a few years."

"No doubt," Astor agreed. "But do you know what I will do with the eight thousand you pay me? I will use it to buy eighty lots north of Canal Street. I will get them for a hundred dollars each, because now it is a war. And here"—he put a hand on his stomach—"here only a few people believe this map will ever be the real New York. But it will be, Joyful. I promise you, it will be. As for the war, soon it will end. And the country will not split apart, thanks to you. And when your house is worth twelve thousand, my eighty lots, bought for a grand total of eight thousand dollars, will be worth eighty thousand."

Joyful knew he was correct. "Very well, I will buy the Devrey house at eight thousand. Meanwhile"—he took a step closer to Randal's sketch of the New York to come and put his hand on what was marked as Fourteenth Street and Sixth Avenue—"how do I find out who owns these three lots here?" It was the meadow surrounded by woods where Holy Hannah had her shack.

Astor leaned forward. "Ach, that is simple. I own those lots."

"I wish to buy them. I'm going to build a proper house there for Holy Hannah. So she can look after boys who have no homes of their own."

"But the land, Joyful, that you do not give her?"

"No, Jacob, the land I do not give her. Only the house. For as long as she lives."

Astor smiled. "*Sehr gut.* For five hundred each I will sell you the lots."

"Two hundred," Joyful said. "You've just admitted you can buy eighty lots for a hundred a piece. Two hundred each for these three is more than a fair price."

"Two," Astor agreed. He put out his hand. "*Teilhaber,* Dr. Turner."

"*Guanxi,* Mr. Astor."

"So, everything then is settled."

"Not quite." Joyful strode to the door to the hall and yanked it open. As he'd expected, Hai Wong was standing inches away. He held a polishing cloth and the moment the door opened he began frantically working on the nearest table. "Don't waste your energy, Hai. I know you've been listening to every word. Now come inside." And to Astor, "Do you know, Jacob, that Ah Wong's son understands English? And speaks it? And reads it?"

"No," Astor admitted. "These things I did not know. Though I should perhaps have guessed."

"Except for borrowing some buckskins and reading the occasional note, I don't think he's used his skills to do you any harm. But he's an ambitious lad, and his knowledge of America as well as China and the Chinese will be invaluable. I propose to send him to Canton at the earliest possible opportunity to be the comprador of Devrey Shipping.

He will earn a monthly wage, and get three percent of the annual profits of the company. And if he serves us loyally and well, we agree to
employ whatever blood relative he nominates when the time comes
for him to retire. That way he'll be what the Chinese call an ancestor.
The founder of a dynasty."

Astor's face was wreathed in smiles. "Excellent. I approve."

"And what of you, Hai? You approve as well?"

"Absolutely, Lords." Hai was breathless with excitement and bowing repeatedly. "Every word I agree. And I will serve you with—"

"Wait," Joyful said. "There's one more condition. This afternoon at
four o'clock you will meet me at Devrey's Pharmacy in Hanover
Square. And you will bring Thumbless Wu."

It was a couple of years at least since he'd been to the pharmacy, but as
far as Joyful could tell, nothing had changed. In fact, nothing might
have changed since Clare and Raif opened it in 1779. Fair chance there
had been a goodly number of the brown bottles of Devrey's Elixir of
Well-Being stacked on the counter back then as there were now.
"Good afternoon, Jonathan. How are you keeping?"

"Well enough, Joyful. I trust you can say the same."

They had agreed long since that the honorifics of uncle and
nephew, reversed from the usual age order as they were, could be
dropped. "Very well, thank you. And business, Jonathan? Business is
good?"

"Fair. Good as can be expected given the war."

Joyful picked up one of the small bottles of Elixir. "Get three coppers apiece for these, don't you?"

"I do. Of course, if you want—"

"No thanks. I was simply considering how profitable an old family
recipe can be. But you're not the simpler your mother was, are you,
Jonathan? Any more than I know all Roisin's healing secrets. The
Women of Connemara pass their knowledge from mother to daughter, never to a son. What Clare knew went to Molly. Isn't that so?"

Jonathan shrugged. "It was Molly she favored. Always."

"So with Molly gone . . ." Joyful returned the brown bottles to their place on the counter and leaned forward. "Seems to me there's not much you can do for Thumbless Wu, is there? About the white smoke, I mean."

"I've no idea what you're talking about.

"Spare us both, Jonathan. Lying will only make it worse."

The large street clock in Hanover Square tolled four times. "My dinner hour," Jonathan said. "So if there's nothing else . . ."

"Your dinner will have to wait, Jonathan. We're to have visitors."

The pharmacy door opened while Joyful was speaking. There were three as it turned out. Hai and Thumbless Wu, as expected, and Ah Wong as well. The Chinese men all bowed formally. Ah Wong, Joyful noted, did not meet his gaze. Nonetheless, he was the first to speak. "We apologize to the honorable gentlemen for interrupting their day. And since I do not speak well in English, I will speak in my language and my son will translate." He turned to Joyful. "I wish to explain—"

"I am about to close," Jonathan interrupted. "I must ask you all to leave."

"*Ta bu hui zuo ren*," Joyful said to Ah Wong, referring to his nephew: He does not know how to be a human being. Then, to Jonathan, "These visitors will leave after we explain to Thumbless Wu here that you have not the least idea how to make the smoking opium he wishes to buy. That you know only how to follow to the letter your mother's instructions for making the Elixir. And that even if you did know the technique, you'd have not the least idea where to find enough poppies to make the quantities that would be required. It would take a mountain of poppies, Jonathan, and there's nothing like that anywhere here."

Hai translated, repeating what Joyful was saying in quick Cantonese, speaking directly into Wu's ear. "*Saan ma. Saan ma. Hung sik fa ma.*" A mountain of red flowers. "*Bat ni do.*" Not here.

Wu stared at Joyful, the malevolence in his gaze knife-sharp. A dagger that could thrust and kill only with good joss, or a scalpel wielded by a hand that knew where to cut? There was no way to know until it came to the test. Then it was up to joss. Joyful turned to him. *"Nei ming baak, tset-ha, tset-ha?"* Did the limp stalk entirely understand?

"Daan duk, ma," Wu said. *"Jeung loi, ma."* Some day we'll be alone. *"Ji di sin tset-ha tset-ha."* We will see whose stalk is limp.

Joyful felt Ah Wong and Hai looking at him, waiting to see how he handled the threats. He laughed and saw Wu's face darken. *"San nin,"* he said. Make it a New Year's Day. *"Ho wan joss, Wu."* So Wu's joss will be at its best and all the gambling junk Wu clan can see him fail despite that. *"Sei. Sei."* Dead. *"Bu yam jing. Bu yam jing."* Without his male stalk, limp or otherwise.

Wu let loose a string of Cantonese curses. Joyful turned away.

"One thing more, Jonathan. The opium trade's illegal in China, run by murderous gangs. So it's highly likely that even if you could figure out how to do what Thumbless here wants, and once you had gone to all the trouble and expense of setting up the production, he would be found dead and probably castrated in some Cantonese alley, murdered by the traders he plans to oppose. So this scheme ends right here. Is that entirely clear?"

Jonathan's demeanor changed. "Of course, I'm quite sure you are right, Joyful. Mr. Wu and I will have to give up our plans, won't we, Mr. Wu? We're going to do everything exactly as cousin Joyful says."

"Pitiful," Joyful said very quietly. "Jonathan, listen carefully, because I've a number of things to tell you and I shall not repeat myself. First, as soon as the war is over, Hai here is going to Canton to be comprador of Devrey's Shipping. Meaning he will be working for me. If there is even the least hint of opium coming in from America, Hai will know about it and he will tell me. And I will see to it that you will most sincerely regret getting into that trade."

"What makes you think you can—"

"I know I can, Jonathan, because, among other reasons, Molly is alive and well. He watched the blood drain from Jonathan's face and saw his white-knuckled grip on the counter. "Your sister is living in Nova Scotia practicing surgery." He would not explain the rest of the story Delight had told him as they sailed back from Wallabout Bay. The part about Molly assuming her brother's identity and living all these years as if she were a man. *Always seemed to me she was a lot more comfortable being Jonathan than she had ever been as Molly. And since she wanted to be a cutter, like you and Dr. Andrew . . . Well, a woman can't be that in Canada any more than she can here.*

"No surprise her wanting to be a surgeon, is there, Jonathan? Molly inherited the family skill and the inclination, and ran away to follow her dream. Mind you, after all these years, she might be happy to run back. Have her share of the pharmacy, live here with you . . . But I don't imagine that would be entirely to your liking, would it?" He turned to the Chinese. "This is our family history, *jia ting lishi.* Nothing to do with you. What you must do now is take Thumbless home with you. Mr. Astor has agreed to find work for him until the blockade's lifted. After that he'll return to Canton with first son Hai. Ah Wong, *ni dong ma?*" Do you understand?

"Understand. Understand. And the honorable gentleman should also understand. Ah Wong never meant any disrespect. Only to do what is right for son and family and—"

"*Mei guanxi,* Ah Wong." No harm. "And providing Hai lives up to his promise, your son will definitely be an ancestor. Mr. Astor and I agree that it is to be so." He led the three Chinese to the door as he spoke; as soon as they were on the street, he closed and turned the lock.

Jonathan looked terrified. "I never really considered . . . You mustn't think it was in my mind to—"

"I don't give a tinker's damn what you considered or what was in your mind, Jonathan. As long as you don't get into the opium trade with Thumbless Wu, you can do as you like."

"You're not going to write to Molly?"

"Absolutely not. Unless . . ."

"Unless what?"

"Unless you refuse to grant Laniah manumission."

"Laniah? What she's to do with any of this?"

"Everything, Jonathan. Her complete freedom from ever being or having been a runaway slave."

His nephew apparently didn't realize his expression was so revealing. "Of course a runaway slave is just what she is. My mother bought Laniah when she was eight years old, and she escaped three years later."

"She ran away with Molly, Jonathan. Reclaiming Laniah means Molly would have to be involved. As I said, she might like to come home and rest a bit."

"Manumission," Jonathan said, the word coming out rather like a sigh. "Very well."

Chatham Street, 5 P.M.

Eugenie had little appetite for dinner. She ate a few bites, then pushed her plate away and went to the front room, standing by the window, waiting for Meg to come back. She'd had no word from Gornt since yesterday. Since the riot. Meg had been there, and brought home the story. "Remarkable it was. Never seen the like. Mr. Blakeman rallying the crowd, and that handsome redheaded cutter hanging out a window and shouting about the Constitution. Then along came the High Constable and his men on the biggest horses you've ever seen and—"

"What about Tintin?"

"The pirate?"

"Yes, of course the pirate."

"Never saw hide nor hair of him. Why should you think he'd be there?"

"They're connected somehow. I know they are. The time I . . . When I spent the night at Hanover Street—"

"Let Blakeman between your legs, you mean." They'd been alone in Eugenie's bedroom, and Meg was eating a peach so ripe the juice dripped down her chin. "You never told me Tintin was there as well."

"Of course he wasn't there. I'm not a whore who goes with two—

Wipe your chin, Meg. You're dripping. It's disgusting. And it is disrespectful for you to eat in my presence."

"Gave you suck and changed your shitty nappies," Meg reminded her. "Don't talk to me 'bout respect. Have you got yourself into more trouble than you've told me about?"

"No," Eugenie shook her head. "You know everything, Meg. You always do."

"So with you and the pirate, it's just about the blackbirding?"

"Yes. But the night I was with Gornt, he said something about pirates, as if he knew . . ."

Eugenie was nibbling her lower lip. Meg knew that was always a sign of worry. "No way he could know. Ain't nothing to be scared of."

"There is," Eugenie said. "I feel it in my bones. Where's Gornt now?"

"No idea," Meg admitted. "One minute he was there, with all the butchers and their cleavers in a ring around him, next minute he was gone."

And no sign of him all day today. The *Evening Post* had published an early noon edition with a full description of the riot, including a number of details Meg hadn't reported, but had nothing to say about where Gornt Blakeman might be. Finally, a little after three, she'd sent Meg into the streets to see if there was news. Over two hours now and . . . Ah! Thank heaven. There she was, hurrying up the road.

Eugenie ran to the door, throwing it open before Meg had come all the way up the path. "Well? What's happened? What did you hear?"

"Just a minute. Let me get my shawl off and rest my bones." They went inside, into the front room, and Meg plopped her bulk into the nearest chair. "Might be you'd like to sit down as well," she said.

"Bad news," Eugenie whispered, sitting not because Meg told her to but because her knees felt weak.

"Depends. Gornt Blakeman's dead."

It shouldn't really matter. He was never going to marry her. She'd

known as much and made her choices. Still the thought of never seeing him again . . . "How did it happen, Meg?"

"No idea. Someone said stabbed. Someone else said he was shot.
Heard he was drowned as well. Thing is, Jacob Hays and his men
brung his body back to the city and he's dead for sure."

"Back from where?"

"A pirate ship as was hiding over near Wallabout Bay. I figure it's
the same one you was taken to."

"Of course it's the same. There aren't going to be two of them." Eugenie sprang up, starting to pace. "I knew it! I told you there was some
connection." Her mind racing, trying to figure out what, if anything,
an alliance between Gornt Blakeman and Tintin meant to her. Particularly since Blakeman was dead. "It shouldn't change anything. Even if
he was trying to get Tintin to do business with him—"

"Stop talking and listen. I told you the news was bad. You ain't
heard the worst of it yet."

Eugenie stopped pacing and put her hands on the back of a chair
to support herself. "What?"

"Tintin's dead as well. Along with all his pirates. And they're fixing
to sink the pirate ship. Talk is, it was the cutter, Joyful Turner, as
brought them all down."

Eugenie stayed where she was, not moving, her eyes closed, her
mind racing. It took her a moment to see it all.

"You want me to get you some hot tea?" Meg said gently. "Or
maybe fix a bath? I know things look black now, pet, your lovely
scheme all gone to naught and no money coming in after all. But
you'll find another man to marry. Ain't one alive can resist the way you
look, and—"

"Where's the newspaper?" Eugenie said. "The early edition of the
Evening Post. Find it."

"What you want a paper for, when—"

"Find it, Meg. It must have been taken down to the kitchen. Get it.
Go! Go!"

She couldn't stay still now. Her body needed to move, to keep up with her mind. Back and forth, back and forth, across the room, window to door. It would work. There was no reason why it shouldn't. She'd make it work.

"Here it is." Meg came back, carrying the paper that had just missed going onto the kitchen fire. "Cook was about to—"

"Give it to me. And you can leave now, Meg. Go fix that bath you promised me."

She waited until she was alone to read the story a second time. It had run over to the second page, two columns above the usual advertisements about runaway slaves and another reminding the public that Devrey's Pharmacy now offered delivery of their superior goods. "F. X. Gallagher," Eugenie read the words aloud in a soft whisper. "A butcher by trade, but also believed to have numerous dealings with the Irish blackbirding gangs of Five Points."

Gornt dead. Tintin dead. F. X. Gallagher dead. A great hole left in the ordering of the Irish blackbirding gangs. How could they function without someone to organize their activities, speak to the magistrates, obtain the proper papers . . . Her heart was thudding the same way it did when she had her legs wrapped around a man's hips and he was . . . Forget all that. Forever if need be. Forget Meg's notion that she return to the endless scheming to attract a rich husband. Another road was open. She would take it.

The Synagogue on Mill Street, 9 P.M.

The Jewish Sabbath was over, but the sanctuary was as beautiful by candlelight as it had been when the sunlight poured through the golden-colored glass of the windows. "The urns, Dr. Turner," Samson Simson said. "You may remember I went to great trouble to call your attention to them when we met here before."

The pair of urns were set high above the two doors to what Joyful remembered was called the *hehal*, the Ark of the Covenant. "Engraved with almond branches, I do remember, Mr. Simson."

"Excellent. Because you're considerably taller than I am, sir, that was why. I could see nothing amiss, but I had to be sure that for a man of greater stature, someone such as yourself, that would also be the case."

"Because you hid the real authentification in one of the urns."

"The one on the left, yes. Some might see that as sacrilege, Dr. Turner. I do not believe it to be so. I saw it as a way to protect this country, and therefore the future of my people. And that, sir, is why we meet here, not in my law office, or in a private home."

Joyful waited, knowing there was more to come.

"I told you before, Dr. Turner, I consider these United States not just my country as it is any citizen's. To me this land is a place of sanctuary for my people, a nation where we may live in peace." Then, in an abrupt change of subject, he said, "A jewel such as the Great Mogul, it is one of the world's great rarities, an extraordinary treasure. I'm sure you agree."

Joyful had been thinking almost continuously about the stone since he gave it to Manon. It had, for example, struck him as strange that Astor hadn't asked him about it when they spoke that morning, or that Vionne had said nothing about the diamond when Joyful dined with him and Manon earlier. "One of the most extraordinary treasures," he agreed. "I have considered what may be best to do with it, and I must admit, I am unsure."

"We," Simpson said, "Jacob Astor and Mordecai Frank and Maurice Vionne and myself, we are no longer unsure. We have conferred and decided to form ourselves into a society to be known as the Club of New York. We will not advertise our existence or seek any political office, but if it becomes necessary, we will attempt to be a modifying influence should the nation stray from the ideals of the Constitution."

"I see."

"No, I think you do not just yet. This republic, Dr. Turner, it is more fragile than we care to admit. These last days have proved that. The possession of something as unique as the Great Mogul could prove decisive in such circumstances. It can be a factor of great influence."

"That is exactly how Gornt Blakeman tried to use it."

"Precisely my point, Dr. Turner."

"Let us be quite clear, sir. Are you asking me to join this Club of New York?"

"I am. On behalf of the others."

"I'm honored, and I accept."

"Forgive me, Dr. Turner, but I do not think you should do so quite so quickly. Quite frankly, we are asking more of you than of ourselves. It is our collective judgment that you, sir, should be the guardian of the Great Mogul. And since it has fallen that you have the stone in your possession—"

"No, I do not. I gave it to Mademoiselle Vionne. I assumed that by now she had given it to her father and—"

Simson smiled. "Your fiancée is apparently wiser than most young women. She told her father the jewel had been recovered, but did not say that she had it rather than you. I choose to think that bodes well for the future, Dr. Turner. I am asking you, here in this holy place, to swear before the Ark of the Covenant—and I remind you that in this very place you named yourself a Jew, though our law does not recognize you as such—that you will guard the diamond with your life, and that you will never consider it a personal possession but something you hold in trust for the Club of New York."

Joyful took one deep breath, a pause long enough to remind himself that vows could be dangerous things, but that a man must have faith in his instincts about the future. "I am honored by the trust of all of you, sir. I do so swear."

Maiden Lane, Near Midnight

It was hard to believe it was more difficult for them to be together now that they were betrothed, but it was. "The horse passage," Manon had whispered, when he was leaving after dinner, in the very few seconds when they were alone. "Tonight."

Joyful knew there was no way she could get out of the house at such an hour. She had to have meant the window.

And the window, it was opened just enough so she could hear his step. He saw her behind the glass, framed in the light of the lamp she held high just long enough to be sure it was him, then extinguished.

He heard the window open. Manon leaned toward him. There was only the starlight to see by now; it was enough.

"You are so beautiful," he said.

"I will not always be so, Joyful. I will grow old."

"But with me."

"With you."

"I cannot wait," Joyful said, "to begin the journey."

A Few Words More

THE HISTORY in this book is true—except for the bit I made up. There is no evidence that New York was in any way part of the secessionist movement that played such a large role in what is generally referred to as "the crisis of 1814." Serious intent to break up the Union appears to have been confined to New England, and only to a few individuals. The Hartford Conference to consider the subject was held in October 1814, but by then talk of a separate country was petering out and the meeting became one of history's footnotes.

The discovery of the Oregon Trail, on the other hand, was unquestionably a seminal event for the nation. Jacob Astor, who financed the expedition that found the southerly route through the Rockies—one which did not require a painfully slow passage up the Missouri by keelboat, and could be traveled entirely by wagon—nonetheless had one of his rare business failures in the matter of Astoria. He could not engage a war-preoccupied Madison as thoroughly as he wished in the venture's potential, and a duplicitous partner (certainly not Joyful Turner!) resulted in the colony being bought by rivals before Astor could prevent it. The Oregon Trail, however, was the "open sesame" that filled the American West with settlers. The anti-Indian prejudice of the time was so pervasive that the fact that they were yet again displacing a native culture with a prior claim simply meant nothing.

The loss of Astoria did not prevent Astor from continuing to flower as the greatest businessman of his age and the country's first true tycoon. By the 1830s he was living in a still more grand and more remote manor in what would now be the Upper East Side, and the site of the Broadway mansion (which truly was staffed by the first Chinese in New York) where Astor and Joyful met to hatch their schemes became the city's first luxury hotel, the Park. Eventually, the Park was torn down and a new and even more grand hotel was built on the site and named the Astor House.

As for the war, the attack on Baltimore was repulsed and became the occasion for Francis Scott Key's composition of the lyrics for "The Star Spangled Banner," celebrating the glorious truth that, despite the efforts of the highly professional British military, the often bumbling Americans prevailed, and after a night's desperate fighting ". . . our flag was still there." A short time later, far from throwing in his lot with the secessionists, the pirate king Jean Lafitte (a man without a country and a smuggler and slave trader) showed himself to be nevertheless a great patriot and a true believer in the American idea. He and his Baratarians played an important part in the U.S. victory at the Battle of New Orleans, fought in December of 1814, after the peace was agreed but before the fighting men on either side knew the war was over.

Jacob Hays, the most famous policeman of his era and often called America's first detective, was born to Jewish parents living in Westchester. He was put in service as a "bound boy," a kind of cross between an apprentice and an indentured servant, to a Presbyterian family with whom he remained close throughout his life. Consequently, many resources claim he was a Protestant. However, Hays is listed on the Shearith Israel rolls as a member of the congregation, and when he died in 1850, he was buried in the Chatham Square Jewish cemetery. That evidence seems to me conclusive, so in this story he has at least an interior Jewish identity.

The tale of Dolley Madison and her heroic deeds in the hours be-fore the attack on Washington, D.C., is part of our national folklore, and most of what she says in this book—including her refusal to allow French John (another real character) to set a booby trap for the ex-pected British invaders—is taken directly from her papers and corre-spondence. The painting of George Washington, which she famously saved and gave for safekeeping to two unnamed New Yorkers, was one of a few copies the artist made from an original that was a gift to the first marquis of Landsdowne, a former British prime minister and a strong supporter of American causes in Parliament during the Revolu-tion. It now hangs in the East Room of the White House.

Madison was in his second term as president during the period of this story, and when it ended in 1816, he retired to his beloved estate of Montpelier in Virginia and died there—still a slaveholder—in 1836. Dolley Payne Todd Madison outlived him by thirteen years. For much of that time she was a popular Washington hostess, but her profligate son by her marriage to Todd all but bankrupted her. In 1842 she was forced to borrow $25,000 from Jacob Astor for what were to her "the bare necessities."

As for the Great Mogul, that is among the most extraordinary of sto-ries. Well documented by Tavernier and others, the huge and spectacu-larly brilliant but flawed diamond disappeared soon after it was taken from the Mogul Empire to Persia as part of the spoils of war that in-cluded the legendary Peacock Throne. Its present-day whereabouts re-mains a mystery. There are those who insist it is the Koh-I-Noor, but that diamond does not have the fiery sparkle associated with the Great Mogul, and the Koh-I-Noor is believed to have had a separate existence recorded earlier. The Orlov diamond, part of the Russian crown jewels, is a more likely candidate based upon the appearances of both stones, but no one is prepared to state unequivocally that the Orlov and the Great Mogul are the same. Personally, I have an entirely different idea of what happened to the diamond after Joyful Turner became its guardian.

And finally, "Old Zip Coon" was an earlier form of the tune we now know as "Turkey in the Straw."

Acknowledgments

Once more I must say that this book, like all books, stands on the shoulders of those that have been written before and owes a huge debt to authors without number, none more so than James Clavell, master of the genre. The resources for *City of Glory* were initially the same as those I used for the earlier two books about the Turner and Devrey families, *City of Dreams* and *Shadowbrook,* most particularly Edwin G. Burrows and Mike Wallace's Pulitzer Prize–winning *Gotham: A History of New York City to 1898* (Oxford University Press, 1999). That book remains the lodestar. In the matter of the geography of Five Points, however, I accepted the analysis of Tyler Anbinder, author of *Five Points: The 19th-Century New York City Neighborhood That Invented Tap Dance, Stole Elections, and Became the World's Most Notorious Slum* (Plume, 2002).

For details of the war that is the background to this story, I leaned heavily on *The War of 1812: A Forgotten Conflict* by Donald R. Hickey (University of Illinois Press, 1989), and John K. Mahon's *The War of*

1812 (University of Florida Press, 1972). The description of the uniforms of the Maryland Volunteers is in fact quoted verbatim from the latter source. Were this a work of nonfiction I would, of course, credit Mr. Mahon in a footnote. Since that is not practical, I am doing so here. Any errors made in the depiction of the battles or the outfitting or maneuvering of the opposing forces are in no way attributable to either book, but are the result of my taking a novelist's license with a few, hopefully unimportant, details.

The story of Jacob Astor's involvement with the Oregon Trail is told in *Across the Great Divide: Robert Stuart and the Discovery of the Oregon Trail* by Laton McCartney (Free Press, 2003).

I am enormously grateful for the kindness of friends and colleagues, without whom this book would be less than it is. Some deserve special mention: Tom Kirkwood, whose mastery of the writing of suspense is without parallel, is also a German speaker who was willing to consider with me the way the Astor brothers might have used the language in 1814. Janie Chang, teller of wondrous tales and keeper of many Chinese memories, supplied both the letter and the spirit of the Mandarin, and gave her imprimatur to my decision to use the Wade-Giles romanization because the Pinyin system had not been invented at the time of the story. (The Cantonese curses and slang came from English-Cantonese dictionaries downloaded from the Internet. I have no idea how accurate to the time they may be, but they certainly seemed sufficiently lusty to qualify for my purpose.) To check on the terminology appropriate to His Majesty's army of the period, I relied on the kindness of Richard G. Lyntton, in another life a captain in the Life Guards, Household Cavalry Regiment. Mel Croucher proved himself still the most brilliant setter and solver of puzzles on two continents. Henry Morrison once more gave unstintingly of his professional skill, his patience, his constant belief, and above all his friendship, and Danny Baror yet again made it possible for my work to reach beyond my nationality and my language. Sydny Miner, editor nonpareil, can be relied on as always to give me back a better book than I give her, and here in New York's "Village of Greenwich," in a house built less than a decade after Manon and Joyful married, Jane and Jay Martin made celebratory the writing of these last few pages.

The book is the best thank-you I can offer; I hope it gives pleasure to each of its readers, but most especially to all of you.

City of Glory

1. *City of Glory* opens with an act of heroic chivalry by Joyful Patrick Turner. Why do you think Beverly Swerling chose this incident as a springboard for her novel? What does it reveal about Joyful? How does the alliance he forges in the prologue affect his successes and failures later in the story?

2. "Joyful knew joss was more than luck, it was fate, something you had to accept. But in New York as in Canton, money trumped luck every time" (50). Joss, both good and bad, is a recurring theme in the novel. Note the references to it throughout the story and discuss the circumstances under which the characters mention that they either rely on or fear joss. Does the conclusion of the book prove that Joyful's theory about money and joss is correct?

3. Delight Higgins, Joyful Patrick Turner, Bastard Devrey, Vinegar Clifford—in the early nineteenth century it was common to assign names and nicknames that sound strange today. In the novel, do these names have any symbolic meanings that point to larger themes? How did they influence your opinion of the characters? Are these names accurate assessments of their personalities? Did they entertain you, or would you have preferred everyone be called the equivalent of Dick or Jane?

4. Two of the main characters in this novel are surgeons, and amputations and amputees figure prominently throughout the story. Why do you think the author chose this imagery? How does it relate to the state of the country at the time?

5. The female characters all play significant behind-the-scenes roles in the struggle for control of New York. Discuss the contributions of Delight, Manon, and the others. How would the conclusion of the story have been different if these women were not involved? How did the options available to women of the time impact the life choices they made? Compare, for example, Holy Hannah's choices with those of Eugenie.

6. Beverly Swerling depicts the influence of Cantonese trading on the budding American economy. How are the Chinese represented in the novel? Were you able to glean a sense of their culture from their roles in the story? Did these characters cause you to think ahead to what the Asian-American community was to become in New York and elsewhere?

7. The novel portrays—accurately—how early the present tight grid of streets and avenues was laid out in Manhattan. Other great cities have circular or ring patterns, and historians and sociologists tell us that each determines the interaction of the populace in a different way. How do you think the choices made in Manhattan in the early 1800s caused the city to develop as it has? Would the concept of a "New York minute" exist in a city of majestic boulevards and sweeping vistas?

8. On page 120, Manon says, "The Great Mogul is one of the world's rarest treasures. To attempt to cut it and fail, have it shatter into splinters . . . Papa would never forgive himself." What do you think the Mogul is intended to symbolize? What does its fate (as far as we know it in this story) tell us about the uses of power?

9. What role does blackbirding play in the day-to-day life of Swerling's Manhattan? What are the motivations behind the characters who partake in it? In what ways (other than the most obvious) is it used to exert power over others?

10. Throughout the novel, groups such as the butchers and the jewelers exert a certain influence over the successes and failures of the men in power. Is this different from the way business and politics are handled today? Discuss the relationship. Was this surprising to you?

11. What role does Tintin play in this novel? Do you find it surprising that there were actual pirates operating in America at the time of this story? Can you see any similarities between privateers and pirates? Would either of them be called terrorists today?

12. On page 149, Astor tells Joyful that his fortune—already magnificent—is based on "the power of seeing. Observation." What role does observation play in this novel? Particularly in terms of each character's attempts to further his or her own ambitions?

13. What did you think of the depiction of the early Jewish community in Manhattan? Were you surprised to learn of the Mill Street Synagogue, and how do you think its existence influenced—or failed to influence—contemporary Jewish life in New York?

14. *City of Glory* is a historical novel, and Swerling is noted for her historical accuracy, though she admits to bending things to suit the needs of her story. In the afterword she tells us about some of those bends. Did they surprise you? Do you think it is fair of her to do this?

15. If you have read Beverly Swerling's earlier *City of Dreams,* compare and contrast the novels. How has the landscape of Manhattan changed from the way it was in 1661, when Lucas and Sally Turner arrived in Nieuw Amsterdam?

See how Five Points developed fifty years after the close of the novel by watching Martin Scorsese's *Gangs of New York.*

Enliven your get-together by meeting at a local Irish or English pub and discussing the book over a pint or two.

For historic sites in Manhattan, visit www.greenmap.org/nyc/tour/his torytour.html.

Take a virtual tour of 2,000 years of parks in Manhattan at www.nyc govparks.org/sub_about/parks_history/historic_tour/historic_tour.ht ml. For tour information on historic sites in Manhattan, visit http:// home2.nyc.gov/portal/site/nycgov/menuitem.e7852eded1ed6107a62fa 24601c789a0.

For more information about New York City, go to http://en.wikipedia .org/wiki/New_York_City.

And for more about Beverly Swerling and her next Simon & Schuster book continuing the story of the Turners and the Devreys in old Manhattan, be sure to visit http://www.BeverlySwerling.com.

Q: Why did you choose *City of Glory* as the book's title?

A: Actually, I did not. I originally called the book *Kingdom Come,* and I really liked that title. So did Sydny Miner, my terrific editor at Simon & Schuster. It seemed to be descriptive of the future of the city and the young America that are the background subjects of the story. But when the book was finished and the manuscript started to circulate in-house, lots of people said since it was a sequel to *City of Dreams,* and since that book had so many fans, it was foolish not to give it a title that alerted readers to the connection. Since Sydny and I had known right along that we wanted a cover linking the two books, the argument made a lot of sense. So after some trial and error we came up with *City of Glory.*

Q: How did the idea for *City of Glory* originate?

A: Well, once I'd created the Turners and the Devreys in *City of Dreams,* they wouldn't leave me alone. I wrote *Shadowbrook* almost as a way to widen the scope of what I knew by then was going to be a series of books—a chance to tell about the broader world these people found themselves in, with its clash of Native American and European cultures and the way the Old World conflicts played out in the New, but the story of Manhattan and New York City kept drawing me back. That's the milieu of these two families, the great city is their backdrop, and their dreams and desires are constantly mixed up with the enormous energy of their city. No one can ignore New York, least of all the people who live there. Not now and not then. So it became absolutely necessary to do what so many fans of the first book wanted me to do, pick up the tale of the two families. Joyful Patrick Turner sails home to New York from Canton at the end of *City of Dreams. City of Glory* tells his story. At least the part that occurs when he's a young man in his thirties and captures the woman he loves, as well as helping to save not just his city but his country.

Q: Did you plot the story in advance?

A: I don't write outlines. If I did I would be bored with the idea of actually writing the book. Instead I write what I call a matrix—an overview of the history of the period and some general explanations of where the story is going. I never try to include every plot twist, because I don't know what the twists are going to be. Make no mistake, I am always in control. But the story does make its own demands. For example, there's a diamond in *City of Glory* that is critical to the plot. I didn't get that idea until I was doing some checking on the Huguenot gold- and silversmiths of old New York and how they were congregated on Maiden Lane. I was wondering if they bought and sold jewels as well as gold and silver, and if they didn't, who did? It was that line of research that caused me to run across the history of the mysterious diamond known as the Great Mogul. The largest diamond ever found to that date, it was well over two hundred carats when first seen in the seventeenth century, and it had disappeared by some time in the eighteenth. So I could do what I wanted with it without breaking my rule never to do violence to history by contradicting it. By then I was a third of the way through the book, but I saw instantly how I could use this marvelous and mysterious diamond, and I went back to the beginning and wrote in the Great Mogul. Working without a fixed outline allows me that liberty. Since I haven't already laid out every twist and turn of the plot, I don't find such a change of direction daunting.

Q: Critics always comment on how meticulous you are about getting all the details correct. How do you do your research?

A: First, I'm sure I don't get everything right, as careful as I try to be. Sometimes I deliberately change something because the story demands it; when that happens I always acknowledge the changes in an author's foreword or afterword. In other instances I probably make mistakes because I go only as far as my story requires me to go. I'm after knowledge for the sake of my characters and my book.

That's different from seeking knowledge for its own sake as an academic does. That said, I've mentioned before that, for the historical novelist, New York on New York is as good as it gets. I spend countless hours in the city's libraries and collections. Some examples are the New York Public Library's magnificent Stokes Collection—a compilation of manuscripts, books, artworks, and contemporary sources from the pre- and post-revolutionary era in New York—as well as the NYPL's Schomburg Center for Research in Black Culture, another truly remarkable resource. I also draw on the expertise of many other writers, importantly, the very unusual urban archaeologist Hope Cooke, and Professors Mike Wallace and Ted Burrows, whose Pulitzer Prize–winning history of the city, *Gotham,* was published when I was halfway through the writing of *City of Dreams.* All in all, between the research and the writing it takes me about two and a half years to complete one of these books.

Q: What has surprised you most as you researched New York?

A: Well, there are two levels. There's the chuckle I get when learning that Jacob Astor's mansion at Broadway and Barclay Street was considered to be in the farthest northern reaches of the city, and many people expected it to remain so. Or discovering that the grid, the streets and avenues laid out so precisely, was already a fully fledged idea by 1809. Or even that until 1812 flogging was an official and legal punishment meted out by the city, the way we use fines today, and there was an official whipper. (Vinegar Clifford with his bull whip, one of the characters in this book, is based on a very real man with a very real job.) Then there are the really serious revelations. The things that truly make your jaw drop. Such as learning that the entire economy of New York depended on slavery. Until I researched these books I didn't know that America's first slave uprising occurred in New York in 1712, or that Wall Street was the location of the biggest organized slave market in the North. By the time of *City of Glory,* which mostly takes place during ten days in 1814, there are

fewer slaves in the city because the uprisings made the white populace afraid, and they switched to using indentured servants from Europe—men and women who sold themselves into bonded labor for
a period, usually ten years, to pay for their passage to America—but
slavery was still entirely legal. That's what gave rise to the gangs of
what were called blackbirders, bounty hunters who would pick up
any black person on the street, drag him or her off to the magistrates, and get a reward for catching a runaway slave. It didn't matter
if the person they'd caught was really a runaway or not. Any black
person was fair game, and God alone knows how many were deprived in this way of what liberty they had. New York was a hotbed
of blackbirding. It's shocking, but it's absolutely true. In fact, fear of
the blackbirders is a driving motive for a young woman called Delight Higgins, one of the major characters in the story.

Q: If Northern slavery was the big surprise of *City of Dreams* and
Shadowbrook, what do you think will be the biggest surprise for
readers of *City of Glory*?

A: Probably the same thing that surprised me. That the Union came
so close to being split apart in 1814. Scholars call it the Crisis of
1814; the country was so polarized and so divided and distraught
about the war President Madison and his congressional allies had
declared in 1812 that New England was seriously considering sepa-
rating from the other states and becoming an independent country. If that had happened—and maybe had New York joined in, as I
have it in this book—there was no way it could have been stopped.
Unlike what happened fifty years later under Lincoln, Madison's
central government was so young and tentative it wouldn't have
been strong enough to hold the nation together, much less wage
war to do so. We would have had at least two countries right away,
and I suspect many more as the continent was explored and taken
over. Maybe eventually these small nations would have united
again, or maybe we'd have developed into something that looked

like today's Balkans, or all the independent republics around the Black Sea. I don't know, but learning how close we came to going that route was a shock. I don't remember ever being taught about that in American history in school, and I bet many readers will be as astounded as I was. Particularly when they consider that it's all true and the only thing I made up was the involvement of my characters and their motives. But . . . no, I better stop there. You'll have to read *City of Glory* to know the rest. Both the story and the real history they forgot to teach you in high school.

Q: What can you tell us about your website?

A: It's called BeverlySwerling.com and features all three books, and also a lot about me and how I work. I even post some of the matrixes I discussed above. It's very different from what I did before at cityofdreams.com. That was a site that concentrated on one particular book and had very little about me or how I work. But readers have told me it's those personal details that interest them. And of course the Internet has since moved on. It's such a new medium, and it has become such an important way for authors to communicate with readers and let them know a book is out there. Any writer would be foolish not to take major advantage of that. In my case, too, I have a wonderful webmaster, Mel Croucher, with whom I've been working for seven years. Having that kind of world-class professional to rely on makes it possible to dream large. That's what we've done on BeverlySwerling.com. The "coming attraction" trailers we've created for each of these books are an excellent example.

Q: What do you hope readers will get from this book?

A: Mostly enjoyment. I hope this is a book that makes you look forward to every chance you have to read more. But I also hope it will make those fans of historical fiction who have concentrated on wonderful stories of kings and princesses in Europe more aware of our own American history, and perhaps help them come to understand what a price was paid in blood and treasure to build our nation, and the high principles on which it rests. Particularly in these times it seems to me vitally important that we're constantly reminded of what our founding fathers sought to create, the legacy they left us, and how easy it is to lose sight of their great vision simply because our courage fails and we are so afraid of our enemies that we become like them, that we take the easy road rather than the high road.

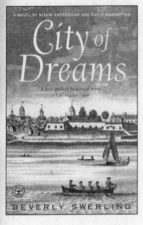
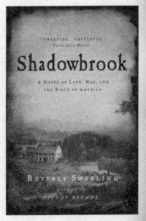